ROSE TERRY COOKE

Somebody's Neighbors

The American Short Story Series

VOLUME 41

GARRETT PRESS

95676

512-00112-X

Library of Congress Catalog Card No. 69-11883

*This volume was reprinted from the 1881 edition
published by James R. Osgood Co.*

First Garrett Press Edition published 1969

The American Short Story Series
Volume 41
©1969

Manufactured in the United States of America

GARRETT PRESS, INC.
Publishers

250 West 54th Street, New York, N.Y. 10019

I OFFER

THIS BOOK OF NEW-ENGLAND PROSE

To My Friend

JOHN GREENLEAF WHITTIER,

MASTER AND MAKER

OF NEW-ENGLAND POETRY.

PUBLISHERS' NOTE.

OF the pieces contained in this volume, Squire Paine's Conversion. Miss Beulah's Bonnet, Cal Culver and the Devil, Amandar, Poll Jennings's Hair, and Mrs. Flint's Experience, are reprinted from "Harpers' Magazine."

The remainder are reprinted from "The Atlantic Monthly," "The Galaxy," and "Putnam's Monthly."

CONTENTS.

SOMEBODY'S NEIGHBORS.

EBEN JACKSON.

"Fear no more the heat o' the sun,
Nor the furious winter's rages;
Thou thine earthly task hast done."

THE large tropical moon rose in full majesty over the
Gulf of Mexico, that beneath it rolled a weltering
surge of silver, which broke upon the level sand of the
beach with a low, sullen roar, prophetic of storms to
come. To-night a south wind was heavily blowing
over gulf and prairie, laden with salt odors of weed
and grass, now and then crossed by a strain of such
perfume as only tropic breezes know, — a breath of
heavy, passionate sweetness from orange-groves and
rose-gardens, mixed with the miasmatic sighs of rank
forests, and mile on mile of tangled cane-brake, where
jewel-tinted snakes glitter, and emit their own sickly·
sweet odor, and the deep blue bells of luxuriant vines
wave from their dusky censers steams of poisonous
incense.

I endured the influence of all this as long as I dared,
and then turned my pony's head from the beach, and,
loitering through the city's hot streets, touched him
into a gallop as the prairie opened before us, and fol-

1

lowed the preternatural, colossal shadow of horse and
man cast by the moon across the dry dull grass and
bitter yellow chamomile growth of the sand, till I
stopped at the office-door of the hospital, when, con-
signing my horse to a servant, I commenced my nightly round of the wards.

There were but few patients just now ; for the fever
had not yet made its appearance, and until within a
week the unwontedly clear and cool atmosphere had
done the work of the physician. Most of the sick
were doing well enough without me : some few needed
and received attention ; and, these disposed of, I betook myself to the last bed in one of the long wards,
quite apart from the others, which was occupied by a
sailor, — a man originally from New England, whose
hard life, and continual exposure to all climates and
weathers, had at length resulted in slow tubercular
consumption.

It was one of the rare cases of this disease not su-
pervening upon an original strumous diathesis, and,
had it been properly cared for in the beginning, might
have been cured. Now there was no hope ; but, the
case being a peculiar and interesting one, I kept a
faithful record of its symptoms and progress for publi-
cation. Besides, I liked the man. Rugged and hardy
by nature, it was curious to see what strange effects a
long, wasting, and painful disease produced upon him.
At first he could not be persuaded to be quiet. The
muscular energies were still unaffected ; and, with continual hemorrhage from the lungs, he could not understand that work or exercise could hurt him. But, as
the disease gained ground, its characteristic languor
unstrung his force ; the hard and sinewy limbs became

attenuated and relaxed; his breath labored; a hectic
fever burnt in his veins, like light flame, every afternoon, and subsided into chilly languor toward morning;
profuse night-sweats increased the weakness, and as
he grew feebler, offering of course less resistance to
the febrile symptoms, they were exacerbated, till at
times a slight delirium showed itself: and so, without
haste or delay, he "made for port," as he said.

His name was Eben Jackson, and the homely appellation was no way belied by his aspect. He never
could have been handsome: and now fifteen years of
rough-and-tumble life had left their stains and scars on
his weather-beaten visage, whose only notable features
were the deep-set eyes, retreating under shaggy brows,
that looked one through and through with the keen
glance of honest instinct; while a light tattooing of red
and blue on either cheek-bone added an element of
the grotesque to his homeliness.   He was a natural
and simple man, with whom conventionalities and the
world's scale went for nothing, — without vanity, as
without guile.   But it is best to let him speak for himself.   I found him that night very feverish, yet not
wild at all.

"Hullo, doctor!" said he, "I'm all afire!   I've
ben thinkin' about my old mother's humstead up to
Simsbury, and the great big well to the back-door;
how I used to tilt that 'are sweep up, of a hot day, till
the bucket went 'way down to the bottom, and come up
drippin' over, — such cold, clear water!   I swear I'd
give all Madagascar for a drink on't!"

I called the nurse to bring me a small basket of
oranges I had sent out in the morning expressly for
this patient: and, squeezing the juice from one of them

on a little bit of ice, I held it to his lips, and he drank eagerly.

"That's better for you than water, Jackson," said I.

"I dunno but 'tis, doctor; I dunno but 'tis; but there a'n't nothin' goes to the spot like that Simsbury water. You ha'n't never v'yaged to them parts, have ye?"

"Bless you, yes, man! I was born and brought up in Hartford, just over the mountain; and I've been to Simsbury, fishing, many a time."

"Good Lord! *You* don't never desert a feller, ef the ship *is* a-going down!" fervently ejaculated Eben, looking up, as he did sometimes in his brief delirium, when he said the Lord's Prayer, and thought his mother held his folded hands. But this was no delirious aspiration. He went on, —

"You see, doctor, I've had somethin' in the hold a good spell 't I wanted to break bulk on, but I didn't know as I ever was goin' to see a shipmet agin. And now you've jined convoy jist in time, for Davy Jones's a'n't fur off. Are you calculatin' to go North afore long?"

"Yes, I mean to go next spring," said I.

Jackson began to fumble with weak and trembling hands about his throat to undo his shirt-collar, — he would not let me help him, — and presently, flushed and panting from the effort, he drew out a length of delicate Panama chain fastened rudely together by a link of copper wire, and suspended on it a little, old-fashioned ring of reddish gold, twisted of two wires, and holding a very small dark garnet. Jackson looked at it as I have seen many a Catholic look at his reliquary in mortal sickness.

"Well," said he, "I've carried that 'are gimcrack nigh twenty long year round my old scrag; and, when I'm sunk, I want you to take it off, doctor. Keep it safe till you go to Connecticut, and then some day take a tack over to Simsbury. Don't ye go through the gap, but go 'long out on the turnpike over the mountain, and down t'other side to Avon, and so nor'ard till jist arter you git into Simsbury town you see an old red house 'longside o' the mountain, with a big ellum-tree afore the door, and a stone well to the side on't. Go 'long in, and ask for Hetty Buel, and give her that 'are thing, and tell her where you got it, and that I ha'n't never forgot to wish her well allus, though I couldn't write to her."

There was Eben Jackson's romance. It piqued my curiosity. The poor fellow was wakeful and restless: I knew he would not sleep if I left him, and I encouraged him to go on talking.

"I will, Jackson, I promise you. But wouldn't it be better for you to tell me something about where you have been all these long years? Your friends will like to know."

His eye brightened: he was, like all the rest of us, pleased with any interest taken in him and his. He turned over on his pillow, and I lifted him into a half-sitting position.

"That's ship-shape, doctor! I don't know but what I had oughter spin a yarn for you: I'm kinder on a watch to-night; and Hetty won't never know what I did do, if I don't send home the log 'long 'i' the cargo.

"Well, you see, I was born in them parts, down to Canton, where father belonged; but mother was a

Simsbury woman; and afore I was long-togged, father he moved onter the old humstead up to Simsbury, when gran'ther Peck died. Our farm was right 'long-side o' Miss Buel's. You'll see't when you go there, but there a'n't nobody there now. Mother died afore I come away, and lies safe to the leeward o' Simsbury meetin'-house. Father he got a stroke a spell back, and he couldn't farm it: so he sold out, and went West, to Parmely Larkum's, my sister's, to live. But I guess the house is there, and that old well. How etarnal hot it's growin'! Doctor, give me a drink.

"Well, as I was tellin', I lived there next to Miss Buel's; and Hetty 'n' I went to deestrict school to-gether, up to the cross-roads. We used to hev' ovens in the sand together, and roast apples an' ears of corn in 'em; and we used to build cubby-houses, and fix 'em out with broken chiny and posies. I swan 't makes me feel curus when I think what children du contrive to get pleased, and likewise riled about. One day I rec'lect Hetty'd stepped onto my biggest clam-shell and broke it, and I up and hit her a switch right across her pretty lips. Now, you'd 'a' thought she would cry and run, for she wasn't bigger than a baby, much; but she jest come up and put her little fat arms round my neck, and says, —

"'I'm so sorry, Eben!'

"And that's Hetty Buel! I declare I was beat, and I hav'n't never got over bein' beat about that. So we growed up together, always out in the woods between schools, huntin' checkerberries, and young winter-greens, and prince's-piney, and huckleberries, and saxifrax, and birch, and all them woodsy things that children hanker arter; and by-m-by we got to goin' to

the 'cademy. And when Hetty was seventeen she went
in to Hartford to her aunt Smith's for a spell, to do
chores, and get a little seminary larnin', and I went to
work on the farm; and when she come home, two year
arter, she was growed to be a young woman, and,
though I was five year older'n her, I was as sheepish
a land-lubber as ever got stuck a-goin' to the masthead, whenever I sighted her.

"She wasn't very much for looks, neither. She
had black eyes, and she was pretty behaved; but she
wasn't no gret for beauty, anyhow, only I thought the
world of her, and so did her old grandmother; for
her mother died when she wa'n't but two year old, and
she lived to old Miss Buel's 'cause her father had married agin away down to Jersey.

"Arter a spell I got over bein' so mighty sheepish
about Hetty: her ways was too kindly for me to keep
on that tack. We took to goin' to singin'-school together; then I always come home from quiltin'-parties
and conference-meetin's with her, because 'twas handy,
bein' right next door: and so it come about that I
begun to think of settlin' down for life, and that was
the start of all my troubles. I couldn't take the home
farm; for 'twas such poor land, father could only jest
make a live out on't for him and me. Most of it was
pastur', gravelly land, full of mulleins and stones:
the rest was principally woodsy, — not hickory, nor oak
neither, but hemlock and white-birches, that a'n't of
no account for timber nor firing 'longside of the other
trees. There was a little strip of a medder-lot, and
an orchard up on the mountain, where we used to make
redstreak cider that beat the Dutch; but we hadn't
pastur' land enough to keep more'n two cows, and

altogether I knew 'twasn't any use to think of bringin'
a family on to't. So I wrote to Parmely's husband,
out West, to know about government lands, and what
I could do ef I was to move out there and take an
allotment; and, gettin' an answer every way favorable,
I posted over to Miss Buel's, one night arter milkin',
to tell Hetty. She was settin' on the south door-step,
braidin' palm-leaf; and her grandmother was knittin'
in her old chair, a little back by the window. Sometimes, a-lyin' here on my back, with my head full o'
sounds, and the hot wind and the salt sea-smell
a-comin' in through the winders, and the poor fellers
groanin' overhead, I get clear away back to that night,
so cool and sweet, — the air full of treely smells, dead
leaves like, and white-blows in the ma'sh below, and
wood-robins singin' clear fine whistles in the woods,
and the big sweet-brier by the winder all a-flowered
out, and the drippin' little beads of dew on the clover-
heads, and the tinklin' sound of the mill-dam down
to Squire Turner's mill.

"I set down by Hetty; and, the old woman bein' as
deaf as a post, it was as good as if I'd been there
alone. So I mustered up my courage, that was sinkin'
down to my boots, and told Hetty my plans, and asked
her to go along. She never said nothin' for a minute.
She flushed all up as red as a rose, and I see her little
fingers was shakin', and her eye-winkers shiny and
wet; but she spoke presently, and said, —

"'I can't, Eben.'

"I was shot betwixt wind and water then, I tell you,
doctor! 'Twa'n't much to be said. But I've allers
noticed afloat that real dangersome squalls comes on
still: there's a dumb kind of a time in the air; the

storm seems to be waitin', and holdin' its breath, and then a little low whisper of wind, — a cat's-paw we call't, — and then you get it real 'arnest. I'd rather she'd have taken on, and cried, and scolded, than have said so still, ' I can't, Eben.'

" ' Why not, Hetty?' says I.

" ' I ought not to leave grandmother,' said she.

" I declare, I hadn't thought o' that! Miss Buel was a real infirm woman, without kith nor kin, exceptin' Hetty; for Jason Buel he'd died down to Jersey long before: and she hadn't means. Hetty nigh about kept 'em both since Miss Buel had grown too rheumatic to make cheese, and see to the hens and cows, as she used to. They didn't keep any men-folks now, nor but one cow: Hetty milked her, and drove her to pastur', and fed the chickens, and braided hats, and did chores. The farm was all sold off. 'Twas poor land, and didn't fetch much; but what there was went to keep 'em in vittles and firin'. I guess Hetty 'arnt most of what they lived on, arter all.

" ' Well,' says I, after a spell of thinkin', ' can't she go along too, Hetty?'

" ' Oh, no, Eben! she's too old. She never could get there, and she never could live there. She says very often she wouldn't leave Simsbury for gold untold. She was born here, and she's bound to die here. I know she wouldn't go.'

" ' Ask her, Hetty.'

" ' No, it wouldn't be any use. It would only fret her always to think I staid at home for her; and you know she can't do without me.'

" ' No more can't I,' says I. ' Do you love her the best, Hetty?'

"I was kinder sorry I'd said that; for she grew real white, and I could see by her throat she was chokin' to keep down somethin'. Finally she said, —

"'That isn't for me to say, Eben. If it was right for me to go with you, I should be glad to; but you know I can't leave grandmother.'

"Well, doctor, I couldn't say no more. I got up to go. Hetty put down her work, and walked to the big ellum by the gate with me. I was most too full to speak; but I catched her up, and kissed her soft little tremblin' lips, and her pretty eyes; and then I set off for home as if I was goin' to be hanged.

"Young folks is obstreperous, doctor. I've been a long spell away from Hetty, and I don't know as I should take on so now. That night I never slept. I lay kickin' and tumblin' all night; and before mornin' I'd resolved to quit Simsbury, and go seek my fortin' beyond seas, hopin' to come back to Hetty, arter all, with riches to take care on her right there in the old place. You'd 'a' thought I might have had some kind of feelin' for my old father, after seein' Hetty's faithful ways. But I was a man, and she was a woman; and I take it them is two different kind o' craft. Men is allers for themselves first, an' devil take the hindmost; but women lives in other folks's lives, and ache, and work, and endure all sorts of stress o' weather afore they'll quit the ship that's got crew and passengers aboard.

"I never said nothin' to father, — I couldn't 'a' stood no jawin', — but I made up my kit, an' next night slung it over my shoulder, and tramped off. I couldn't have gone without biddin' Hetty good-by: so I stopped there, and told her what I was up to, and charged her to tell father.

"She tried her best to keep me to home; but I was
sot in my way: so, when she found that out, she run
up stairs an' got a little Bible, and made me promise
I'd read it sometimes; and then she pulled that 'are
little ring off her finger and give it to me to keep.

"'Eben,' says she, 'I wish you well always, and I
sha'n't never forget you.'

"And then she put up her face to me, as innocent
as a baby, to kiss me good-by. I see she choked up
when I said the word, though, and I said, kinder
laughin', —

"'I hope you'll get a better husband than me,
Hetty.'

"I swear, she give me a look like the judgment-
day, and, stoopin' down, she pressed her lips onto that
ring, and says she, 'That is my weddin'-ring, Eben,'
and goes into the house as still and white as a ghost;
and I never see her again, nor never shall. — O doctor, give me a drink!'"

I lifted the poor fellow, fevered and gasping, to an
easier position, and wet his hot lips with fresh orange-
juice.

"Stop now, Jackson," said I: "you are tired."

"No, I a'n't, doctor; no, I a'n't. I'm bound to
finish now. But, Lord deliver us! look there! — one
of the Devil's own imps, I b'lieve!"

I looked on the little deal stand where I had set the
candle, and there stood one of the quaint, evil-look-
ing insects that infest the island, — a praying Mantis.
Raised up against the candle, with its fore-legs in the
attitude of supplication that gives it the name, its long
green body relieved on the white stearine, it was eying
Jackson, with its head turned first on one side, and

then on the other, in the most elfish and preternatural way. Presently it moved upward, stuck one of its fore-legs cautiously into the flame, burnt it of course, and drew it back, eyed it, first from one angle, then from another, with deliberate investigation, and at length conveyed the injured member to its mouth, and sucked it steadily, resuming its stare of blank scrutiny at my patient, who did not at all fancy the interest taken in him.

I could not help laughing at the strange manœuvres of the creature, familiar as I was with them.

"It is only one of our Texan bugs, Jackson," said I: "it is harmless enough."

"It's got a pesky look, though, doctor. I thought I'd seen enough curus creturs in the Marquesas, but that beats all."

Seeing the insect really irritated and annoyed him, I put it out of the window, and turned the blinds closely, to prevent its re-entrance; and he went on with his story : —

"So I tramped it to Hartford that night, got a lodgin' with a first-cousin I had there, worked my passage to Boston in a coaster, and, after hangin' about Long Wharf day in and day out for a week, I was driv' to ship myself aboard of a whaler, 'The Lowisy Miles,' Twist, cap'en; and I writ from there to Hetty, so't she could know my bearin's so fur, and tell my father

"It would take a week, doctor, to tell you what a rough-an'-tumble time I had on that 'are whaler. There's a feller's writ a book about v'yagin' afore the mast that'll give ye an idee on't. He had an eddication so't he could set it off, and I fell foul of his book down

to Valparaiso more'n a year back, and I swear I wanted
to shake hands with him. I heerd he was gone ashore
somewheres down to Boston, and he'd cast anchor for
good. But I tell you he's a brick, and what he said's
gospel truth. I thought I'd got to hell afore my time
when we see blue water. I didn't have no peace, exceptin' times when I was to the top, lookin' out for
spouters ; then I'd get nigh about into the clouds that
was allers a-hangin' down close to the sea mornin' and
night, all kinds of colors, — red an' purple an' white ;
and, 'stead of thinkin' o' whales, I'd get my head full
o' Simsbury, and get a precious knock with the butt-
end of a handspike when I come down, 'cause I'd
never sighted a whale till arter they see'd it on deck.

"We was bound to the South Seas after sperm
whales ; but we was eight months gettin' there, and we
took sech as we could find on the way. The cap'en
he scooted round into one port an' another arter his
own business, — down to Caraccas, into Rio ; and
when we'd rounded the Horn, and was nigh about dead
of cold an' short rations, and hadn't killed but three
whales, we put into Valparaiso to get vittled, and there
I laid hold o' this little trinket of a chain, and spliced
Hetty's ring on to't, lest I should be stranded somewheres, and get rid of it onawares.

"We cruised about in them seas a good year or
more, with poor luck, and the cap'en growin' more and
more outrageous continually. Them waters aren't
like the Gulf, doctor, nor like the Northern Ocea;
nohow. There a'n't no choppin' seas there, but a great,
long, everlastin', lazy swell, that goes rollin' and fallin'
away, like the toll of a big bell, in endless blue rollers.
And the trades blow through the sails like singin', as

warm and soft as if they blowed right out o' sunshiny
gardens; and the sky's as blue as summer all the time,
only jest round the dip on't there's allers a hull fleet o'
hazy, round-topped clouds, so thin you can see the
moon rise through 'em; and the waves go ripplin' off
the cut-water as peaceful as a mill-pond, day and
night. Squalls is sca'ce some times o' the year; but,
when there is one, I tell you a feller hears thunder.
The clouds settle right down onto the masthead, black
and thick, like the settlin's of an ink-bottle; the lightnin' hisses, an' cuts fore and aft; and corposants come
flightin' down onto the boom or the top, gret balls o'
light; and the wind roars louder than the seas; and
the rain comes down in spouts (it don't fall fur
enough to drop), you'd think heaven and earth was
come together, with hell betwixt 'em: and then it'll
all clear up as quiet and calm as a Simsbury Sunday,
and you wouldn't know it could be squally, if 'twan't
for the sail that you hadn't had a chance to furl was
drove to ribbons, and here an' there a stout spar
snapped like a cornstalk, or the bulwarks stove by a
heavy sea. There's queer things to be heerd, too, in
them parts, — cries to wind'ard like a drowndin' man,
and you can't never find him; noises right under the
keel; bells ringin' off the land, like, when you a'n't
within five hundred miles of shore; and curus hails out
o' ghost-ships that sails agin' wind an' tide. Strange,
strange, I declare for't! seems as though I heerd my
old mother a-singin' Mear now."

I saw Jackson was getting excited: so I gave him a
little soothing draught, and walked away to give the
nurse some orders. But he made me promise to return,
and hear the story out: so, after half an hour's inves-

tigation of the wards, I came back, and found him composed enough to permit his resuming where he had left off.

"Howsomever, doctor, there wa'n't no smooth sailin' nor fair weather with the cap'en: 'twas always squally in his latitude, and I begun to get mutinous, and think of desartin'. About eighteen months arter we sot sail from Valparaiso, I hadn't done somethin' I'd been ordered, or I'd done it wrong, and Cap'en Twist come on deck, ragin' and roarin', with a hand-spike in his fist, and let fly at my head. I see what was comin', and put my arm up to fend it off; and, gettin' the blow on my fore-arm, it got broke acrost as quick as a wink, and I dropped. So they picked me up, and, havin' a mate aboard who knew some doctorin', I was spliced and bound up, and put under hatches, on the sick-list. I tell you I was dog-tired them days, lyin' in my berth hearin' the rats and mice scuttle round the bulkheads, and skitter over the floor. I couldn't do nothin'; and finally I bethought myself of Hetty's Bible, and contrived to get it out o' my chist, and when I could get a bit of a glim I'd read it. I'm a master-hand to remember things; and what I read over and over in that 'are dog-hole of a cabin never got clean out of my head, no, nor never will; and, when the Lord above calls all hands on deck to pass muster, ef I'm ship-shape afore him, it'll be because I follered his signals, and l'arn't 'em out of that 'are log. But I didn't foller 'em then, nor not for a plaguy long cruise yet.

"One day, as I laid there, readin' by the light of a bit of tallow-dip the mate gave me, who should stick his head into the hole he called a cabin, but old Twist '

He'd got an idee I was shammin'; and, when he saw me with a book, he cussed and swore and raved, and finally hauled it out o' my hand, and flung it up through the hatchway clean and clear overboard.

"I tell ye, doctor, if I'd 'a' had a sound arm, he'd 'a' gone after it; but I had to take it out in ratin' at him, and that night my mind was made up: I was bound to desart at the first land. And it come about that a fortnight after my arm had jined, and I could haul shrouds agin, we sighted the Marquesas; and, bein' near about out o' water, the cap'en laid his course for the nearest land, and by daybreak of the second day we lay to in a small harbor on the south side of an island where ships wa'n't very prompt to go commonly. But old Twist didn't care for cannibals nor wild beasts when they stood in his way; and there wasn't but half a cask of water aboard, and that a hog wouldn't 'a' drank, only for the name on't. So we pulled ashore after some, and, findin' a spring near by, was takin' it out, hand over hand, as fast as we could bale it up, when all of a sudden the mate see a bunch of feathers over a little bush near by, and yelled out to run for our lives, the savages was come.

"Now I had made up my mind to run away from the ship that very day; and, all the while I'd been baling the water up, I had been tryin' to lay my course so as to get quit of the boat's crew, and be off. But natur' is stronger than a man thinks. When I heerd the mate sing out, and see the men begin to run, I turned and run too, full speed, down to the shore; but my foot caught in some root or hole, I fell flat down, and, hittin' my head ag'inst a stone near by, I lay as good as dead; and, when I come to, the boat was gone, and

the ship makin' all sail out of harbor, and a crew of
wild Indian women were a-lookin' at me as I've seen
a set of Simsbury women-folks look at a baboon in a
caravan ; but they treated me better.

"Findin' I was helpless, — for I'd sprained my
ankle in the fall, — four of 'em picked me up, and carried me away to a hut, and tended me like a baby.
And when the men, who'd come over to that side of the
island 'long with 'em, and gone a-fishin', come back,
I was safe enough ; for women are women all the world
over, — soft-hearted, kindly creturs, that like any thing
that's in trouble, 'specially if they can give it a lift
out on't. So I was nursed and fed, and finally taken
over the ridge of rocks that run acrost the island, to
their town of bamboo huts ; and now begun to look
about me, for here I was, stranded, as one may say,
out o' sight o' land.

"Ships didn't never touch there, I knew by their
ways, — their wonderin', and takin' sights at me. As
for Cap'en Twist, he wouldn't come back for his own
father, unless he was short o' hands for whalin'. I
was in for life, no doubt on't ; and I'd better look at
the fairweather side of the thing. The island was as
pretty a bit of land as ever lay betwixt sea and sky ;
full of tall cocoanut-palms, with broad feathery tops,
and bunches of brown nuts ; bananas hung in yellow
clumps, ready to drop off at a touch ; and big bread-
fruit trees stood about everywhere, lookin' as though a
punkin-vine had climbed up into 'em, and hung half-
ripe punkins off of every bough ; beside lots of other
trees that the natives set great store by, and live on
the fruit of 'em ; and, flyin' through all, such pretty
birds as you never see except in them parts ; but one

brown thrasher'd beat the whole on 'em singing'. Fact
is, they run to feathers : they don't sing none.

" It was as sightly a country as ever Adam and Eve
had to themselves, but it wa'n't home. Howsomever,
after a while the savages took to me mightily. I was
allers handy with tools, and by good luck I'd come off
with two jack-knives and a loose awl in my jacket-
pocket : so I could beat 'em all at whittlin'. And I
made figgers, on their bows an' pipe-stems, of things
they never see, — roosters and horses, Miss Buel's old
sleigh, and the Albany stage, driver'n' all, and our
yoke of oxen a-ploughin', — till nothin' would serve
them but I should have a house o' my own, and be
married to their king's daughter. So I did.

" Well, doctor, you kinder wonder I forgot Hetty
Buel. I didn't forget her, but I knew she wa'n't to
be had anyhow. I thought I was in for life ; and
Wailua was the prettiest little craft that ever you set
eyes on, — as straight as a spar, and as kindly as a
Christian. And, besides, I had to, or I'd have been
killed, and broiled, and eaten, whether or no. And
then in that 'are latitude it a'n't just the way 'tis here :
you don't work ; you get easy and lazy and sleepy ;
somethin' in the air kind of hushes you up ; it makes
you sweat to think, and you're too hazy to if it didn't ;
and you don't care for nothing much but food and
drink. I hadn't no spunk left : so I married her after
their fashion, and I liked her well enough ; and she was
my wife, after all.

" I tell ye, doctor, it goes a gret way with men-
folks to think any thing's their'n, and nobody else's.
But, when I married her, I took the chain with Hetty
Buel's ring off my neck, and put 'em in a shell, and

buried the shell under my doorway. I couldn't have Wailua touch that.

" So there I lived fifteen long year, as it might be, in a kind of a curus dream, doin' nothin' much, only that when I got to know the tongue them savages spoke, little by little I got pretty much the steerin' o' the hull crew, till by-'n'-by some of 'em got jealous, and plotted and planned to kill me, because the king, Wailua's father, was gettin' old, and they thought I wanted to be king when he died, and they couldn't stan' that noway.

" Somehow or other Wailua got word of what was goin' on ; and one night she woke me out of sleep, an' told me I must run for't, and she would hide me safe till things took a turn. So I scratched up the shell with Hetty's ring in't ; and afore morning I was over t'other side of the island, in a kind of a cave overlookin' the sea, near by to a grove of bananas and mammee-apples, and not fur from the harbor where I'd landed, and safe enough, for nobody but Wailua knew the way to't.

" Well, the sixth day I sot in the porthole of that cave I see a sail in the offing. I declare I thought I should 'a' choked. I catched off my tappa-cloth, and h'isted it on a pole ; but the ship kep' on stiddy out to sea. My heart beat up to my eyes ; but I held on ag'inst hope, and I declare I prayed. Words come to me that I hadn't said since I was a boy to Simsbury, and the Lord he heerd ; for, as true as the compass, that ship lay to, tacked, put in for the island, and afore night I was aboard of ' The Lysander,' a Salem whaler, with my mouth full of grog and ship-biscuit, and my body in civilized toggery. I own I felt queer to go away so, and leave Wailua; but I knew 'twas gettin' her out of danger, for the old king was just a-goin' to die, and, if ever I'd have gone back, we should both have been murdered. Besides, we didn't always agree: she had to walk straighter than her wild natur' agreed with, because she was my wife; and we hadn't no children to hold us together; and I couldn't a' taken her aboard of the whaler if she'd wanted to go. I guess it was best: anyhow, so it was.

"But this wasn't to be the end of my v'yagin'. 'The Lysander' foundered just off Valparaiso; and, though all hands was saved in the boats, when we got to port there wasn't no craft there bound any nearer homeward than an English merchant-ship for Liverpool by way of Madeira. So I worked a passage to Funchal; and there I got aboard of a Southampton steamer bound for Cuba, that put in for coal. But, when I come to Havana, I was nigh about tuckered out; for goin' round the Horn in 'The Lemon,'—that 'are English ship,—I'd ben on duty in all sorts o' weather; and I'd lived lazy and warm so long I expect it was too tough for me, and I was pestered with a hard cough, and spit blood, so't I was laid up a long spell in the hospital at Havana. And there I kep' a-thinkin' over Hetty's Bible; and I b'lieve I studied that 'are chart till I found out the way to port, and made up my log all square for the owner; for I knowed well enough where I was bound, but I did hanker to get home to Simsbury afore shovin' off.

"Well, finally there come into the harbor a Mystic ship that was a-goin' down the Gulf for a New-York owner. I'd known Seth Crane, the cap'en of her, away back in old Simsbury times. He was an Avon boy,

and when I sighted that vessel's name, as I was crawlin' along the quay one day, and, seein' she was Con-
necticut-built, boarded her, and see Seth, I was old fool
enough to cry right out, I was so shaky. And Seth —
he was about as scart as ef he'd seen the dead, havin'
heerd up to Avon, fifteen year ago nearly, that " The
Lowisy Miles " had been run down off the Sandwich
Islands by a British man-of-war, and all hands lost
exceptin' one o' the boys. However, he come to his
bearin's after a while, and told me about our folks, and
how't Hetty Buel wasn't married, but keepin' deestrict
school, and her old grandmother alive yet.

" Well, I kinder heartened up, and agreed to take
passage with Seth. — Good Lord, doctor ! what's
that ? "

A peculiar and oppressive stillness had settled down
on every thing in and out of the hospital while Jackson
was going on with his story. I noticed it only as the
hush of a tropic midnight ; but as he spoke I heard,
apparently out on the prairie, a heavy jarring sound,
like repeated blows, drawing nearer and nearer the
building.

Jackson sprung upright on his pillows. The hectic
passed from either gaunt and sallow cheek, leaving the
red-and-blue tattoo marks visible in most ghastly dis-
tinctness ; while the sweat poured in drops down his
hollow temples.

The noise drew still nearer. All the patients in the
ward awoke, and quitted their beds hastily. The noise
was at hand. Blows of great violence and power,
and a certain malign rapidity, shook the walls from one
end of the hospital to the other, — blow upon blow,—
like the fierce attacks of a catapult, only with no like

result.   The nurse, a German Catholic, fell on his knees, and told his beads, glancing over his shoulder in undisguised horror; the patients cowered together, groaning and praying; and I could hear the stir and confusion in the ward below. In less than a minute's space the singular sound passed through the house, and in hollow, jarring echoes died out toward the bay.

I looked at Eben. His jaw had fallen; his hands were rigid, and locked together; his eyes were rolled upward, fixed and glassy. A stream of scarlet blood trickled over his gray beard from the corner of his mouth. He was dead. As I laid him back on the pillow, and turned to restore some quiet to the ward, a Norther came sweeping down the Gulf like a rush of mad spirits, tore up the white crests of the sea and flung them on the beach in thundering surf, burst through the heavy fog that had trailed upon the moon's track and smothered the island in its soft, pestilent brooding, and in one mighty pouring-out of cold, pure ether changed earth and sky from torrid to temperate zone.

Vainly did I endeavor to calm the terror of my patients, excited still more by the elemental uproar without; vainly did I harangue them, in the plainest terms to which science is reducible, on atmospheric vibrations, acoustics, reverberations, and volcanic agencies: they insisted on some supernatural power having produced the recent fearful sounds. Neither common nor uncommon sense could prevail with them: and when they discovered, by the appearance of the extra nurse I had sent for to perform the last offices for Jackson, that he was dead, a renewed and irrepressible horror attacked them; and it was broad day before composure or stillness was regained in any part of the building except my own rooms, to which I betook myself as soon as possible, and slept till sunrise, too soundly for any mystical visitation whatever to have disturbed my rest.

The next day, in spite of the brief influence of the Norther, the first case of yellow-fever showed itself in the hospital: before night seven had sickened, and one, already reduced by chronic disease, died.

I had hoped to bury Jackson decently, in the cemetery of the city, where his vexed mortality might rest in peace under the oleanders and china-trees, shut in by the hedge of Cherokee roses that guards the enclosure from the prairie, a living wall of glassy green, strewn with ivory-white buds and blossoms, fair and pure; but, on applying for a burial-spot, the city authorities, panic-stricken cowards that they were, denied me the privilege even of a prairie grave outside the cemetery hedge for the poor fellow. In vain did I represent that he had died of lingering disease, and that nowise contagious: nothing moved them. It was enough that there was yellow-fever in the ward where he died. I was forthwith strictly ordered to have all the dead from the hospital buried on the sand-flats at the east end of the island.

What a place that is it is scarcely possible to describe, — wide and dreary levels of sand some four or five feet lower than the town, and flooded by high tides, the only vegetation a scanty, dingy gray, brittle, crackling growth, — bitter sandworts, and the like, over and through which the abominable tawny sand-crabs are constantly executing diabolic waltzes on the tips of their eight legs, vanishing into the ground like

imps as you approach. Curlews start from behind the
loose drifts of sand, and float away with heart-broken
cries seaward; little sandpipers twitter plaintively,
running through the weeds; and great, sulky gray
cranes droop their motionless heads over the still salt
pools along the shore.

To this blank desolation I was forced to carry poor
Jackson's body, with that of the fever-patient, just at
sunset. As the Dutchman who officiated as hearse,
sexton, bearer, and procession stuck his spade into
the ground, and withdrew it full of crumbling shells
and fine sand, the hole it left filled with bitter black
ooze. There, sunk in the ooze, covered with the shifting sand, bewailed by the wild cries of sea-birds, note-
less and alone, I left Eben Jackson, and returned to
the mass of pestilence and wretchedness within the
hospital walls.

In the spring I reached home safely. None but the
resident on a Southern sandbank can fully appreciate
the verdure and bloom of the North. The great elms
of my native town were full of tender buds, like a
clinging mist in their graceful branches; earlier trees
were decked with little leaves, deep-creased, and silvery with down; the wide river in a fluent track of
metallic lustre weltered through green meadows that
on either hand stretched far and wide; the rolling land
beyond was spread out in pastures, where the cattle
luxuriated after the winter's stalling; and on many a
slope and plain the patient farmer turned up his heavy
sods and clay to moulder in sun and air for seedtime
and harvest; and the beautiful valley that met the
horizon on the north and south rolled away eastward
and westward to a low blue range of hills that guard

ıt with granite walls, and bristling spears of hemlock
and pine.

This is not my story; and, if it were, I do not know
that I should detail my home-coming. It is enough to
say, that I came, after a five-years' absence, and found
all that I had left nearly as I had left it. How few
can say as much!

Various duties and some business arrangements kept
me at work for six or seven weeks, and it was June
before I could fulfil my promise to Eben Jackson. I
took the venerable old horse and chaise that had carried my father on his rounds for years. and made the
best of my way out toward Simsbury. I was alone,
of course : even cousin Lizzy, charming as five years
had made the little girl of thirteen whom I had left
behind on quitting home, was not invited to share my
drive : there was something too serious in the errand
to endure the presence of a gay young lady. But I
was not lonely. The drive up Talcott Mountain, under
the rude portcullis of the toll-gate, through fragrant
woods, by trickling brooks, past huge bowlders that
scarce a wild vine dare cling to with its feeble, delicate tendrils, is all exquisite, and full of living repose ;
and turning to descend the mountain, just where a
brook drops headlong with clattering leap into a steep
black ravine, and comes out over a tiny green meadow,
sliding past great granite rocks, and bending the grass-
blades to a shining track, you see suddenly at your feet
the beautiful mountain valley of the Farmington River,
trending away in hill after hill, rough granite ledges
crowned with cedar and pine, deep ravines full of
neaped rocks, and here and there the formal white
rows of a manufacturing village, where Kühleborn is

captured, and forced to turn water-wheels, and Undine picks cotton, or grinds hardware, dammed into utility.

Into this valley I plunged; and, inquiring my way of many a prim farmer's wife and white-headed school-boy, I edged my way northward under the mountain side, and just before noon found myself beneath the "great ellum," where, nearly twenty years ago, Eben Jackson and Hetty Buel had said "good-by."

I tied my horse to the fence, and walked up the worn footpath to the door. Apparently no one was at home. Under this impression I knocked vehemently, by way of making sure; and a weak, cracked voice at length answered, "Come in!" There, by the window, — perhaps the same where she sat so long before, — crouched in an old chair covered with calico, her bent fingers striving with mechanical motion to knit a coarse stocking, sat old Mrs. Buel. Age had worn to the extreme of attenuation a face that must always have been hard-featured; and a few locks of snow-white hair straying from under the bandanna handkerchief of bright red and orange that was tied over her cap and under her chin, added to the old-world expression of her whole figure. She was very deaf: scarcely could I make her comprehend that I wanted to see her grand-daughter; at last she understood, and asked me to sit down till Hetty should come from school; and before long, a tall, thin figure opened the gate, and came slowly up the path.

I had a good opportunity to observe the constant, dutiful, self-denying Yankee girl, — girl no longer, now that twenty years of unrewarded patience had lined her face with unmistakable graving. But I could not agree with Eben's statement that she was not pretty.

She must have been so in her youth: even now there was beauty in her deep-set and heavily fringed dark eyes, soft, tender, and serious, and in the noble and pensive Greek outline of the brow and nose. Her upper lip and chin were too long to agree well with her little classic head; but they gave a certain just and pure expression to the whole face, and to the large, thin-lipped mouth, flexible yet firm in its lines. It is true her hair was neither abundant, nor wanting in gleaming threads of gray; her skin was freckled, sallow, and devoid of varying tint or freshness; her figure angular and spare; her hands red with hard work; and her air at once sad and shy: still Hetty Buel was a very lovely woman in my eyes, though I doubt if Lizzy would have thought so.

I hardly knew how to approach the painful errand I had come on; and, with true masculine awkwardness, I cut the matter short by drawing out from my pocket-book the Panama chain and ring, and placing them in her hands. Well as I thought I knew the New-England character, I was not prepared for so quiet a reception of this token as she gave it. With a steady hand she untwisted the wire fastening of the chain, slipped the ring off, and, bending her head, placed it reverently on the ring-finger of her left hand, — brief but potent ceremony, and over without preface or comment, but over for all time.

Still holding the chain, she offered me a chair, and sat down herself, a little paler, a little more grave, than on entering.

"Will you tell me how and where he died, sir?" said she, evidently having long considered the fact in her heart as a fact; probably having heard Seth Crane's story of the loss of "The Louisa Miles."

1 detailed my patient's tale as briefly and sympathet-
ically as I knew how. The episode of Wailua caused
a little flushing of lip and cheek, a little twisting of the
ring, as if it were not to be worn after all; but as I
told of his sacred care of the trinket for its giver's
sake, and the not unwilling forsaking of that island
wife, the restless motion passed away, and she listened
quietly to the end, only once lifting her left hand to
her lips, and resting her head on it for a moment, as I
detailed the circumstances of his death, after supply-
ing what was wanting in his own story, from the time
of his taking passage in Crane's ship to their touching at the island expressly to leave him in the hospital
when a violent hemorrhage had disabled him from
further voyaging.

I was about to tell her I had seen him decently
buried, of course omitting descriptions of the how and
where, when the grandmother, who had been watching
us with the impatient querulousness of age, hobbled
across the room to ask "what that 'are man was
a-talkin' about."

Briefly and calmly, in the key long use had suited to
her infirmity, Hetty detailed the chief points of my
story.

"Dew tell!" exclaimed the old woman. "Eben
Jackson a'n't dead on dry land, is he? Left means,
eh?"

I walked away to the door, biting my lip. Hetty,
for once, reddened to the brow, but replaced her
charge in the chair, and followed me to the gate.

"Good-day, sir," said she, offering me her hand,
and then, slightly hesitating, "Grandmother is very
old. I thank you, sir. I thank you kindly."

As she turned, and went toward the house, I saw the glitter of the Panama chain about her thin and sallow throat, and, by the motion of her hands, that she was retwisting the same wire fastening that Eben Jackson had manufactured for it.

Five years after, last June, I went to Simsbury with a gay picnic party. This time Lizzy was with me: indeed, she generally is now.

I detached myself from the rest, after we were fairly arranged for the day, and wandered away alone to "Miss Buel's."

The house was closed, the path grassy, a sweetbrier-bush had blown across the door, and was gay with blossoms : all was still, dusty, desolate. I could not be satisfied with this. The meeting-house was as near as any neighbor's, and the graveyard would ask me no curious questions. I entered it doubting ; but there, "on the leeward side," near to the grave of "Bethia Jackson, wife of John Eben Jackson," were two new stones, one dated but a year later than the other, recording the deaths of "Temperance Buel aged 96," and "Hester Buel aged 44."

MISS LUCINDA.

BUT that Solomon is out of fashion, I should quote him here and now, to the effect that there is a time for all things; but Solomon is obsolete, and never — no, never — will I dare to quote a dead language, "for raisons I have," as the exiles of Erin say. Yet, in spite of Solomon and Horace, I may express my own less concise opinion, that even in hard times, and dull times, and war times, there is yet a little time to laugh, a brief hour to smile and love and pity; just as through this dreary easterly storm, bringing clouds and rain, sobbing against casement and door with the inarticulate wail of tempests, there comes now and then the soft shine of a sun behind it all, a fleeting glitter, an evanescent aspect of what has been.

But if I apologize for a story that is nowise tragic, nor fitted to "the fashion of these times," possibly somebody will say at its end that I should also have apologized for its subject, since it is as easy for an author to treat his readers to high themes as vulgar ones, and velvet can be thrown into a portrait as cheaply as calico; but of this apology I wash my hands. I believe nothing in place or circumstance makes romance. I have the same quick sympathy for Biddy's sorrows with Patrick that I have for the Empress of France and her august but rather grim lord and master. I think words are often no harder to bear than " a blue bating ; " and I have a reverence for poor old maids as great as for the nine Muses. Commonplace people are only commonplace from character, and no position affects that. So forgive me once more, patient reader, if I offer to you no tragedy in high life, no sentimental history of fashion and wealth, but only a little story about a woman who could not be a heroine.

Miss Lucinda Jane Ann Manners was a lady of unknown age, who lived in a place I call Dalton, in a State of these Disuniting States, which I do not mention for good cause. I have already had so many unconscious personalities visited on my devoted head, that, but for lucidity, I should never mention persons or places, inconvenient as it would be. However, Miss Lucinda did live, and lived by the aid of "means," which in the vernacular is money. Not a great deal, it is true, — five thousand dollars at lawful interest, and a little wooden house, do not imply many luxuries even to a single woman ; and it is also true that a little fine sewing taken in helped Miss Manners to provide herself with a few small indulgences otherwise beyond her reach. She had one or two idiosyncrasies, as they are politely called, that were her delight. Plenty of dish-towels were necessary to her peace of mind ; without five pair of scissors she could not be happy ; and Tricopherous was essential to her well-being : indeed, she often said she would'rather give up coffee than Tricopherous, for her hair was black and wiry and curly, and caps she abhorred ; so that, of a winter's day, her head presented the most irrelevant and volatile aspect, each particular hair taking a twist

on its own responsibility, and improvising a wild halo
about her unsaintly face, unless subdued into propriety
by the aforesaid fluid.

I said Miss Lucinda's face was unsaintly; I mean
unlike ancient saints as depicted by contemporary art-
ists: modern and private saints are after another fashion. I met one yesterday, whose green eyes, great
nose, thick lips, and sallow wrinkles, under a bonne
of fifteen years' standing, further clothed upon by
scant merino cloak and cat-skin tippet, would have cut
a sorry figure in the gallery of the Vatican or the
Louvre, and put the tranquil Madonna of San Sisto
into a state of stunning antithesis. But if St. Agnes
or St. Catharine was half as good as my saint, I am
glad of it.

No, there was nothing sublime and dolorous about
Miss Manners. Her face was round, cheery, and
slightly puckered, with two little black eyes sparkling
and shining under dark brows, a nose she unblushingly
called pug, and a big mouth, with eminently white and
regular teeth, which she said were such a comfort, for
they never ached, and never would to the end of time.
Add to this physiognomy a small and rather spare
figure, dressed in the cleanest of calicoes, always made
in one style, and rigidly scorning hoops, without a
symptom of a collar, in whose place (or it may be over
which) she wore a white cambric handkerchief knotted
about her throat, and the two ends brought into subjection by means of a little angular-headed gold pin,
her sole ornament, and a relic of her old father's days
of widowhood, when buttons were precarious tenures.
So much for her aspect. Her character was even more
quaint.

She was the daughter of a clergyman, one of the
old school, the last whose breeches and knee-buckles
adorned the profession, who never "outlived his usefulness," nor lost his godly simplicity.   Parson Manners held rule over an obscure and quiet village in the
wilds of Vermont, where hard-handed farmers wrestled with rocks and forests for their daily bread, and
looked forward to heaven as a land of green pastures
and still waters, where agriculture should be a pastime,
and winter impossible.   Heavy freshets from the mountains, that swelled their rushing brooks into annual
torrents, and snow-drifts that covered five-rail fences
a foot above the posts, and blocked up the turnpike-
road for weeks, caused this congregation fully to appreciate Parson Manners's favorite hymns, —

> "There is a land of pure delight,"

and

> "On Jordan's stormy banks I stand."

Indeed, one irreverent but "pretty smart feller," who
lived on the top of a hill known as Drift Hill, where
certain adventurous farmers dwelt for the sake of its
smooth sheep-pastures, was heard to say, after a
mighty sermon by Parson Manners about the seven-
times heated furnaces of judgment reserved for the
wicked, that "parson hadn't better try to skeer Drift-
Hillers with a hot place: 'twouldn't more 'n jest warm
'em through down there, arter a real snappin' winter."

In this out-of-the-way nook was Lucinda Jane Ann
born and bred. Her mother was like her in many
things, — just such a cheery, round-faced little body,
but with no more mind than found ample scope for
itself in superintending the affairs of house and farm,

and vigorously "seeing to" her husband and child.
So, while Mrs. Manners baked, and washed and
ironed, and sewed and knit, and set the sweetest
example of quiet goodness and industry to all her
flock, without knowing she *could* set an example, or
be followed as one, the parson amused himself, between sermons of powerful doctrine and parochial
duties of a more human interest, with educating Lucinda, whose intellect was more like his own than her
mother's. A strange training it was for a young girl,
— mathematics, metaphysics, Latin, theology of the
dryest sort; and after an utter failure at Greek and
Hebrew, though she had toiled patiently through seven
books of the "Æneid," Parson Manners mildly sniffed
at the inferiority of the female mind, and betook himself to teaching her French, which she learned rapidly,
and spoke with a pure American accent, perhaps as
pleasing to a Parisian ear as the hiss of Piedmont or
the gutturals of Switzerland. Moreover, the minister
had been brought up himself in the most scrupulous
refinement of manner: his mother was a widow, the
last of an "old family;" and her dainty, delicate
observances were inbred, as it were, in her only son.
This sort of elegance is perhaps the most delicate test
of training and descent, and all these things Lucinda
was taught from the grateful recollection of a son who
never forgot his mother through all the solitary labors
and studies of a long life. So it came to pass, that,
after her mother died, Lucinda grew more and more
like her father; and, as she became a woman, these
rare refinements separated her more and more from
those about her, and made her necessarily solitary.
As for marriage, the possibility of such a thing never

crossed her mind : there was not a man in the parish
who did not offend her sense of propriety, and shock
her taste, whenever she met one ; and though her
warm, kind heart made her a blessing to the poor and
sick, her mother was yet bitterly regretted at quiltings
and tea-drinkings, where she had been so " sociable-
like "

It is rather unfortunate for such a position as Lucinda's, that, as deacon Stowell one day remarked to
her father, " Natur' will be natur' as much on Drift
Hill as down to Bosting ; " and when she began to feel
that " strong necessity of loving," that sooner or later
assails every woman's heart, there was nothing for it
to overflow on when her father had taken his share.
Now, Lucinda loved the parson most devoutly. Ever
since the time when she could just remember watching
through the dusk his white stockings as they glim-
mered across the road to evening meeting, and looked
like a supernatural pair of legs taking a walk on
their own responsibility, twilight concealing the black
breeches and coat from mortal view, Lucinda had
regarded her father with a certain pleasing awe. His
long abstractions, his profound knowledge, his grave,
benign manners, and the thousand daily refinements
of speech and act that seemed to put him far above
the sphere of his pastorate, — all these things inspired
as much reverence as affection ; and when she wished
with all her heart and soul she had a sister or a brother
to tend and kiss and pet, it never once occurred to her
that any of those tender familiarities could be expended
on her father. She would as soon have thought of
caressing any of the goodly angels, whose stout legs,
flowing curls, and impossible draperies, sprawled among

the pictures in the big Bible, and who excited her wonder as much by their garments as their turkey-wings and brandishing arms. So she betook herself to pets, and growing up to the old maidenhood of thirty-five before her father fell asleep, was by that time the centre of a little world of her own, — hens, chickens, squirrels, cats, dogs, lambs, and sundry transient guests of stranger kind; so that when she left her old home, and removed to the little house in Dalton that had been left her by her mother's aunt, and had found her small property safely invested by means of an old friend of her father's, Miss Manners made one more journey to Vermont to bring in safety to their future dwelling a cat and three kittens, an old blind crow, a yellow dog of the true cur breed, and a rooster with three hens, "real creepers," as she often said, "none of your long-legged, screaming creatures."

Lucinda missed her father, and mourned him as constantly and faithfully as ever a daughter could. But her temperament was more cheerful and buoyant than his; and when once she was quietly settled in her little house, her garden and her pets gave her such full occupation that she sometimes blamed herself for not feeling more lonely and unhappy. A little longer life, or a little more experience, would have taught her better: power to be happy is the last thing to regret. Besides, it would have been hard to be cheerless in that sunny little house, with its queer old furniture of three-legged tables, high-backed chairs, and chintz curtains, where red mandarins winked at blue pagodas on a deep yellow ground, and birds of insane ornithology pecked at insects that never could have been hatched, or perched themselves on blossoms totally

unknown to any mortal flora.   Old engravings of
Bartolozzi, from the stiff elegances of Angelica Kauf-
man and the mythologies of Reynolds, adorned the
shelf; and the carpet in the parlor was of veritable
English make, older than Lucinda herself, but as
bright in its fading, and as firm in its usefulness, as
she.   Up stairs the tiny chambers were decked with
spotless white dimity, and rush-bottomed chairs stood
in each window, with a strip of the same old carpet
by either bedside; and in the kitchen the blue settle
that had stood by the Vermont fireside now defended
this lesser hearth from the draught of the door, and
held under the seat thereof sundry ironing-sheets, the
blanket belonging to them, and good store of ticking
and worsted holders.   A half-gone set of egg-shell
china stood in the parlor-closet, — cups and teapot
rimmed with brown and gold in a square pattern, and a
shield without blazon on the side; the quaint tea-caddy
with its stopper stood over against the pursy little cream-
pot; and the three-legged sugar-bowl held amid its
lumps of sparkling sugar the oddest sugar-tongs, also
a family relic; beside this, six small spoons, three
large ones, and a little silver porringer comprised all
the "plate" belonging to Miss Manners, so that no
fear of burglars haunted her, and, but for her pets,
she would have led a life of profound and monotonous
tranquillity.   But this was a vast exception: in her
life her pets were the great item now; her cat had
its own chair in the parlor and kitchen; her dog, a
rug and a basket never to be meddled with by man or
beast; her old crow, its special nest of flannel and
cotton, where it feebly croaked as soon as Miss Lucinda began to spread the little table for her meals;

and the three kittens had their own playthings and
their own saucer as punctiliously as if they had been
children.   In fact, Miss Manners had a greater share
of kindness for beasts than for mankind.   A strange
compound of learning and unworldliness, of queer simplicity, native penetration, and common sense, she had
read enough books to despise human nature as it
develops itself in history and theology, and she had not
known enough people to love it in its personal development.   She had a general idea that all men were
liars, and that she must be on her guard against their
propensity to cheat and annoy a lonely and helpless
woman ; for, to tell the truth, in her good father's
over-anxiety to defend her from the snares of evil men
after his death, his teachings had given her opinion this
bias, and he had forgotten to tell her how kindly and
how true he had found many of his own parishioners,
how few inclined to harm or pain him.   So Miss Lucinda made her entrance into life at Dalton, distrust-
ful, but not suspicious ; and, after a few attempts on
the part of the women who were her neighbors to be
friendly or intimate, they gave her up as impracticable :
not because she was impolite or unkind ; they did not
themselves know why they failed, though she could
have told them ; for old maid as she was, poor and
plain and queer, she could not bring herself to asso-
ciate familiarly with people who put their teaspoons
into the sugar-bowl, helped themselves with their own
knives and forks, gathered up bits of uneaten butter
and returned them to the plate for next time, or replaced on the dish pieces of cake half eaten, or cut with
the knives they had just introduced into their mouths.
Miss Lucinda's code of minor morals would have for-

bidden her to drink from the same cup with a queen,
and have considered a pitchfork as suitable as a knife
to eat with ; nor would she have offered to a servant
the least thing she had touched with her own lips or
her own implements of eating ; and she was too delicately bred to look on in comfort where such things
were practised.   Of course these women were not
ladies ; and, though many of them had kind hearts
and warm impulses of goodness, yet that did not make
up to her for their social misdemeanors ; and she drew
herself more into her own little shell, and cared more
for her garden and her chickens, her cats and her dog,
than for all the humanity of Dalton put together.

Miss Manners held her flowers next dearest to her
pets, and treated them accordingly.   Her garden was
the most brilliant bit of ground possible.   It was big
enough to hold one flourishing peach-tree, one Siberian
crab, and a solitary egg-plum ; while under these fruit-
ful boughs bloomed moss-roses in profusion, of the
dear old-fashioned kind, every deep pink bud, with its
clinging garment of green, breathing out the richest
odor.   Close by, the real white rose, which fashion has
banished to country towns, unfolded its cups of pearl,
flushed with yellow sunrise, to the heart ; and by its
side its damask sister waved long sprays of bloom and
perfume.   Tulips, dark-purple and cream-color, burning scarlet and deep maroon, held their gay chalices
up to catch the dew ; hyacinths, blue, white, and pink,
hung heavy bells beneath them ; spiced carnations of
rose and garnet crowded their bed in July and August ;
heart's-ease fringed the walks ; May honeysuckles clambered over the board-fence ; and monthly honeysuckles
overgrew the porch at the back-door, making perpetual

fragrance from their moth-like horns of crimson and
ivory. Nothing inhabited those beds that was not
sweet and fair and old-fashioned. Gray-lavender-
bushes sent up purple spikes in the middle of the garden, and were duly housed in winter; but these were
the sole tender plants admitted, and they pleaded their
own cause in the breath of the linen-press and the
bureau-drawers that held Miss Lucinda's clothes. Beyond the flowers, utility blossomed in a row of bean-
poles, a hedge of currant-bushes against the farther
fence, carefully tended cauliflowers, and onions enough
to tell of their use as sparing as their number. A few
deep-red beets and golden carrots were all the vege-
tables beside. Miss Lucinda never ate potatoes or
pork.

Her housekeeping, but for her pets, would have been
the proper housewifery for a fairy. Out of her fruit
she annually conserved miracles of flavor and trans-
parence, — great plums like those in Aladdin's garden,
of shining topaz; peaches tinged with the odorous
bitter of their pits, and clear as amber; crimson crabs
floating in their own ruby sirup, or transmuted into
jelly crystal clear, yet breaking with a grain; and
jelly from the acid currants to garnish her dinner-
table, or refresh the fevered lips of a sick neighbor.
It was a study to visit her tiny pantry, where all these
"lucent sirops" stood in tempting array, where spices
and sugar and tea in their small jars flanked the sweetmeats, and a jar of glass showed its store of whitest
honey, and another stood filled with crisp cakes. Here
always a loaf or two of home-made bread lay rolled in
a snowy cloth, and another was spread over a dish of
butter. Pies were not in favor here, nor milk, — save

for the cats. Salt fish Miss Manners never could abide :
her savory taste allowed only a bit of rich old
cheese, or thin scraps of hung beef, with her bread
and butter. Sauces and spices were few in her reper-
tory ; but she cooked as only a lady can cook, and
might have asked Soyer himself to dinner. For verily,
after much meditation and experience, I have divined
that it takes as much sense and refinement and talent
to cook a dinner, wash and wipe a dish, make a bed as
it should be made, and dust a room as it should be
dusted, as goes to the writing of a novel, or shining in
high society.

But because Miss Lucinda Manners was reserved
and "unsociable," as the neighbors pronounced her,
I did not, therefore, mean to imply that she was inhu-
man. No neighbor of hers, local or scriptural, fell ill,
without an immediate offer of aid from her. She made
the best gruel known to Dalton invalids, sent the ripest
fruit and the sweetest flowers ; and if she could not
watch with the sick because it interfered with her duties
at home in an unpleasant and inconvenient way, she
would sit with them hour after hour in the day-time,
and wait on all their caprices with the patient tenderness of a mother. Children she always eyed with
strange wistfulness, as if she longed to kiss them, but
didn't know how ; yet no child was ever invited across
her threshold, for the yellow cur hated to be played
with, and children always torment kittens.

So Miss Lucinda wore on happily toward the farther
side of the middle ages. One after another of her
pets passed away, and was replaced ; the yellow cur
barked his last currish signal ; the cat died, and her
kittens came to various ends of time or casualty ; the

crow fell away to dust, and was too old to stuff; and
the garden bloomed and faded ten times over, before
Miss Manners found herself to be forty-six years old,
which she heroically acknowledged one fine day to the
census-taker. But it was not this consciousness, nor
its confession, that drew the dark brows so low over
Miss Lucinda's eyes that day: it was quite another
trouble, and one that wore heavily on her mind, as we
shall proceed to explain. For Miss Manners, being,
like all the rest of her sex, quite unable to do without
some masculine help, had employed for some seven
years an old man by the name of Israel Slater to do
her "chores," as the vernacular hath it. It is a mor-
tifying thing, and one that strikes at the roots of
women's rights terribly sharp blows, but I must even
own it, that one might as well try to live without one's
bread and butter as without the aid of the dominant
sex. When I see women split wood, unload coal-carts,
move wash-tubs, and roll barrels of flour and apples
handily down cellar-ways or up into carts, then I shall
believe in the sublime theories of the strong-minded
sisters; but as long as I see before me my own forlorn
little hands, and sit down on the top stair to recover
breath, and try in vain to lift the water-pitcher at table,
just so long I shall be glad and thankful that there are
men in the world, and that half a dozen of them are
my kindest and best friends. It was rather an affliction to Miss Lucinda to feel this innate dependence;
and at first she resolved to employ only small boys,
and never any one of them more than a week or two.
She had an unshaped theory that an old maid was a
match for a small boy, but that a man would cheat and
domineer over her. Experience sadly put to flight

these notions ; for a succession of boys in this cabinet
ministry for the first three years of her stay in Dalton
would have driven her into a Presbyterian convent,
had there been one at hand.   Boy Number One caught
the yellow cur out of bounds one day, and shaved his
plumy tail to a bare stick, and Miss Lucinda fairly
shed tears of grief and rage when Pink appeared at
the door with the denuded appendage tucked between
his little legs, and his funny yellow eyes casting side-
long looks of apprehension at his mistress.   Boy Number One was despatched directly.   Number Two did
pretty well for a month ; but his integrity and his appetite conflicted, and Miss Lucinda found him one moonlight night perched in her plum-tree devouring the
half-ripe fruit.   She shook him down with as little
ceremony as if he had been an apple ; and, though he
lay at death's door for a week with resulting cholera-
morbus, she relented not.   So the experiment went on,
till a list of casualties that numbered in it fatal acci-
dents to three kittens, two hens, and a rooster, and at
last Pink himself, who was sent into a decline by repeated drenchings from the watering-pot, put an end
to her forbearance, and she instituted in her viziership
the old man who had now kept his office so long, — a
queer, withered, slow, humorous old creature, who
did " chores " for some six or seven other households,
and got a living by sundry " jobs " of wood-sawing,
hoeing corn, and other like works of labor, if not of
skill.   Israel was a great comfort to Miss Lucinda :
he was efficient counsel in the maladies of all her pets,
had a sovereign cure for the gapes in chickens, and
could stop a cat's fit with the greatest ease ; he kept
the tiny garden in perfect order, and was very honest,

and Miss Manners favored him accordingly. She compounded liniment for his rheumatism, herb-sirup for
his colds, presented him with a set of flannel shirts,
and knit him a comforter; so that Israel expressed
himself strongly in favor of "Miss Lucindy," and
she said to herself he really was "quite good for a
man."

But just now, in her forty-seventh year, Miss
Lucinda had come to grief, and all on account of
Israel, and his attempts to please her. About six
months before this census-taking era, the old man had
stepped into Miss Manners's kitchen with an unusual
radiance on his wrinkles and in his eyes, and began,
without his usual morning greeting, —

"I've got so'thin' for you naow, Miss Lucindy.
You're a master-hand for pets; but I'll bet a red cent
you ha'n't an idee what I've got for ye naow!"

"I'm sure I can't tell, Israel," said she: "you'll
have to let me see it."

"Well," said he, lifting up his coat, and looking
carefully behind him as he sat down on the settle, lest
a stray kitten or chicken should pre-occupy the bench,
"you see I was down to Orrin's abaout a week back,
and he hed a litter o' pigs, — eleven on 'em. Well, he
couldn't raise the hull on 'em, — 't a'n't good to raise
more'n nine, — an' so he said ef I'd 'a' had a place o'
my own, I could 'a' had one on 'em; but as 'twas he
guessed he'd hev to send one to market for a roaster.
I went daown to the barn to see 'em; an' there was
one, the cutest little critter I ever sot eyes on, — an'
I've seen more'n four pigs in my day, — 'twas a little
black-spotted one, as spry as an ant, and the dreffullest
knowin' look out of its eyes. I fellowshipped it right

off ; and I said, says I, ' Orrin, ef you'll let me hev that
'ere little spotted feller, I'll git a place for him, for I
do take to him consarnedly.'   So he said I could, and
I fetched him hum ; and Miss Slater and me we kinder
fed him up for a few days back, till he got sorter
wonted, and I'm a-goin' to fetch him to you."

" But, Israel, I haven't any place to put him in."

" Well, that a'n't nothin' to hender.   I'll jest fetch
out them old boards out of the wood-shed, and knock
up a little sty right off, daown by the end o' the shed,
and you ken keep your swill that I've hed before, and
it'll come handy."

" But pigs are so dirty ! "

" I don't know as they be.   They ha'n't no great
conveniences for washin' ginerally ; but I never heerd
as they was dirtier'n other critters where they run wild.
An' beside, that a'n't goin' to hender, nuther.   I cal-
culate to make it one o' the chores to take keer of
him ; 't won't cost no more to you, and I ha'n't no
great opportunities to do things for folks that's allers
a-doin' for me : so 't you needn't be afeard, Miss
Lucindy : I love to."

Miss Lucinda's heart got the better of her judgment.
A nature that could feel so tenderly for its inferiors in
the scale could not be deaf to the tiny voices of humanity when they reached her solitude ; and she thanked
Israel for the pig so heartily, that the old man's face
brightened still more, and his voice softened from its
cracked harshness, as he said, clicking up and down
the latch of the back-door, —

" Well, I'm sure you're as welcome as you are
obleeged, and I'll knock up that 'ere pen right off. He
sha'n't pester ye any, that's a fact.' '

Strange to say, yet perhaps it might have been
expected from her proclivities, Miss Lucinda took
an astonishing fancy to the pig. Very few people
know how intelligent an animal a pig is ; but, when one
is regarded merely as pork and hams, one's intellect is
apt to fall into neglect, — a moral sentiment which
applies out of pigdom. This creature would not have
passed muster at a county fair ; no Suffolk blood com-
pacted and rounded him : he belonged to the "racers,"
and skipped about his pen with the alacrity of a large
flea, wiggling his curly tail as expressively as a dog's,
and "all but speakin'," as Israel said. He was always
glad to see Miss Lucinda, and established a firm friend-
ship with her dog Fun, — a pretty, sentimental German
spaniel. Besides, he kept tolerably clean by dint of
Israel's care, and thrust his long nose between the
rails of his pen for grass or fruit, or carrot and beet
tops, with a knowing look out of his deep-set eyes,
that was never to be resisted by the soft-hearted spinster. Indeed, Miss Lucinda enjoyed the possession of
one pet who could not tyrannize over her. Pink's
place was more than filled by Fun, who was so oppress-
ively affectionate, that he never could leave his mistress alone. If she lay down on her bed, he leaped up
and unlatched the door, and stretched himself on the
white counterpane beside her with a grunt of satisfaction ; if she sat down to knit or sew, he laid his head
and shoulders across her lap, or curled himself up on
her knees ; if she was cooking, he whined and coaxed
round her till she hardly knew whether she fried or
broiled her steak ; and if she turned him out, and but-
toned the door, his cries were so pitiful, she could never
be resolute enough to keep him in exile five minutes

for it was a prominent article in her creed that animals have feelings that are easily wounded, and are of " like passions " with men, only incapable of expression. Indeed, Miss Lucinda considered it the duty of human beings to atone to animals for the Lord's injustice in making them dumb and four-legged. She would have been rather startled at such an enunciation of her practice, but she was devoted to it as a practice. She would give her own chair to the cat, and sit on the settle herself; get up at midnight if a mew or a bark called her, though the thermometer was below zero; the tenderloin of her steak, or the liver of her chicken, was saved for a pining kitten or an ancient and toothless cat; and no disease or wound daunted her faithful nursing, or disgusted her devoted tenderness. It was rather hard on humanity, and rather reversive of Providence, that all this care and pains should be lavished on cats and dogs, while little morsels of flesh and blood, ragged, hungry, and immortal, wandered up and down the streets. Perhaps that they were immortal was their defence from Miss Lucinda. One might have hoped that her " other-worldliness " accepted that fact as enough to outweigh present pangs, if she had not openly declared, to Israel Slater's immense amusement and astonishment, that *she* believed creatures had souls, — little ones perhaps, but souls, after all, and she did expect to see Pink again some time or other.

" Well, I hope he's got his tail feathered out ag'in," said Israel dryly. " I do'no' but what hair'd grow as well as feathers in a speretooal state, and I never see a pictur' of an angel out what hed consider'ble many feathers."

Miss Lucinda looked rather confounded. But hu-

manity had one little revenge on her in the shape of her
cat, — a beautiful Maltese with great yellow eyes, fur
as soft as velvet, and silvery paws as lovely to look at
as they were thistly to touch. Toby certainly pleaded
hard for Miss Lucinda's theory of a soul: but his was
no good one; some tricksy and malign little spirit had
lent him his share of intellect, and he used it to the
entire subjugation of Miss Lucinda. When he was
hungry, he was as well-mannered and as amiable as
good child; he would coax and purr, and lick her
fingers with his pretty red tongue, like a "perfect
love: " but when he had his fill, and needed no more,
then came Miss Lucinda's time of torment. If she
attempted to caress him, he bit and scratched like a
young tiger: he sprang at her from the floor, and fas-
tened on her arm with real fury. If he cried at the
window and was not directly let in, as soon as he had
achieved entrance his first manœuvre was to dash at
her ankles, and bite them if he could, as punishment
for her tardiness. This skirmishing was his favorite
mode of attack. If he was turned out of the closet, or
off the pillow up stairs, he retreated under the bed, and
made frantic sallies at her feet, till the poor woman
got actually nervous, and if he was in the room made a
flying leap as far as she could to her bed, to escape
those keen claws. Indeed, old Israel found her more
than once sitting in the middle of the kitchen-floor,
with Toby crouched for a spring, under the table, his
poor mistress afraid to move for fear of her unlucky
ankles. And this literally cat-ridden woman was
hazed about and ruled over by her feline tyrant to that
extent that he occupied the easiest chair, the softest
cushion, the middle of the bed, and the front of the

fire, not only undisturbed, but caressed. This is a
veritable history, beloved reader, and I offer it as a
warning and an example. If you will be an old maid,
or if you can't help it, take to petting children, or
donkeys, or even a respectable cow, but beware of
domestic tyranny in any shape but man's.

No wonder Miss Lucinda took kindly to the pig, who
had a house of his own, and a servant as it were, to
the avoidance of all trouble on her part, — the pig who
capered for joy when she or Fun approached, and had
so much expression in his physiognomy that one almost
expected to see him smile. Many a sympathizing
conference Miss Lucinda held with Israel over the per-
fections of piggy, as he leaned against the sty, and
looked over at his favorite after this last chore was
accomplished.

"I say for 't," exclaimed the old man one day,
"I b'lieve that cre'tur' knows enough to be professor
in a college. Why, he talks! he re'lly doos; a leetle
through his nose, maybe, but no more'n Dr. Colton
allers does, — 'n' I declare he appears to have abaout
as much sense. I never see the equal of him. I
thought he'd 'a' larfed right out yesterday when I gin
him that mess o' corn. He got up onto his forelegs
on the trough, an' he winked them knowin' eyes o'
his'n, an' waggled his tail, an' then he set off an'
capered round till he come bunt up ag'inst the boards.
I tell _you_, that sorter sobered him. He gin a growlin'
grunt, an' shook his ears, an' looked sideways at me;
and then he put to and eet up that corn as sober as a
judge. I swan! he doos beat the Dutch!"

But there was one calculation forgotten, both by Miss
Lucinda and Israel: the pig would grow, and in conse-

quence, as I said before, Miss Lucinda came to grief;
for, when the census-taker tinkled her sharp little
door-bell, it called her from a laborious occupation at
the sty, — no more and no less than trying to nail up a
board that piggy had torn down in struggling to get
out of his durance. He had grown so large, that Miss
Lucinda was afraid of him; his long legs and their
vivacious motion added to the shrewd intelligence of
his eyes; and his nose seemed as formidable to this
poor little woman as the tusk of a rhinoceros : but what
should she do with him? One might as well have proposed to her to kill and cut up Israel as to consign
piggy to the " fate of race." She could not turn him
into the street to starve, for she loved him; and the
old maid suffered from a constancy that might have
made some good man happy, but only embarrassed her
with the pig. She could not keep him forever, that
was evident. She knew enough to be aware that time
would increase his disabilities as a pet; and he was an
expensive one now, for the corn-swallowing capacities
of a pig, one of the " racer" breed, are almost incredible, and nothing about Miss Lucinda wanted for
food, even to fatness. Besides, he was getting too big
for his pen; and so " cute" an animal could not be
debarred from all out-door pleasures, and tantalized
by the sight of a green and growing garden before his
eyes continually, without making an effort to partake
of its delights. So, when Miss Lucinda endued herself
with her brown linen sack and sun-bonnet to go and
weed her carrot-patch, she was arrested on the way by
a loud grunting and scrambling in piggy's quarter, and
found, to her distress, that he had contrived to knock off
the upper board from his pen. She had no hammer at

hand: so she seized a large stone that lay near by, and pounded at the board till the twice-tinkling bell recalled her to the house; and, as soon as she had made confession to the census-taker, she went back — alas, too late! Piggy had redoubled his efforts, another board had yielded, and he was free. What a thing freedom is! — how objectionable in practice! how splendid in theory! More people than Miss Lucinda have been put to their wits' end when "hoggie" burst his bonds, and became rampant instead of couchant. But he enjoyed it. He made the tour of the garden on a delightful canter, brandishing his tail with an air of defiance that daunted his mistress at once, and regarding her with his small bright eyes as if he would before long taste her, and see if she was as crisp as she looked. She retreated forthwith to the shed, and caught up a broom, with which she courageously charged upon piggy, and was routed entirely; for, being no way alarmed by her demonstration, the creature capered directly at her, knocked her down, knocked the broom out of her hand, and capered away again to the young arrot-patch.

"Oh, dear!" said Miss Manners, gathering herself up from the ground, "if there only was a man here!"

Suddenly she betook herself to her heels; for the animal looked at her, and stopped eating: that was enough to drive Miss Lucinda off the field. And now, quite desperate, she rushed through the house, and out of the front-door, actually in search of a man. Just down the street she saw one. Had she been composed, she might have noticed the threadbare cleanliness of his dress, the odd cap that crowned his iron-gray locks, and the peculiar manner of his walk; for our little old maid had stumbled upon no less a person than Monsieur Jean Leclerc, the dancing-master of Dalton. Not that this accomplishment was much in vogue in the embryo city; but still there were a few who liked to fit themselves for firemen's balls and sleighing-party frolics, and quite a large class of children were learning betimes such graces as children in New England receive more easily than their elders. Monsieur Leclerc had just enough scholars to keep his coat threadbare, and restrict him to necessities; but he lived, and was independent. All this Miss Lucinda was ignorant of: she only saw a man; and, with the instinct of the sex in trouble or danger, she appealed to him at once.

"O sir! won't you step in and help me? My pig has got out, and I can't catch him, and he is ruining my garden!"

"Madame, I shall!" replied the Frenchman, bowing low, and assuming the first position.

So Monsieur Leclerc followed Miss Manners, and supplied himself with a mop that was hanging in the shed as his best weapon. Dire was the battle between the pig and the Frenchman. They skipped past each other and back again as if they were practising for a cotillon. Piggy had four legs, which gave him a certain advantage; but the Frenchman had most brain, and in the long-run brain gets the better of legs. A weary dance they led each other; but after a while the pet was hemmed in a corner, and Miss Lucinda had run for a rope to tie him, when, just as she returned, the beast made a desperate charge, upset his opponent, and giving a leap in the wrong direction, to his manifest astonishment landed in his own sty. Miss Lucinda's courage rose: she forgot her prostrate friend in

need, and, running to the pen, caught up hammer and
nail-box on her way, and with unusual energy nailed
up the bars stronger than ever, and then bethought
herself to thank the stranger. But there he lay quite
still and pale.

"Dear me!" said Miss Manners. "I hope you
haven't hurt yourself, sir."

"I have fear that I am hurt, madame," said he,
trying to smile. "I cannot to move but it pains me."

"Where is it? Is it your leg, or your arm? Try
and move one at a time," said Miss Lucinda promptly.

The left leg was helpless, it could not answer to the
effort; and the stranger lay back on the ground, pale
with the pain. Miss Lucinda took her lavender-bottle
out of her pocket, and softly bathed his head and face;
then she took off her sack, and folded it up under his
head, and put the lavender beside him. She was good
at an emergency, and she showed it.

"You must lie quite still," said she. "You must
not try to move till I come back with help, or your leg
will be hurt more."

With that she went away, and presently returned
with two strong men and the long shutter of a shop-
window. To this extempore litter she carefully moved
the Frenchman; and then her neighbors lifted him,
and carried him into the parlor, where Miss Lucinda's
chintz lounge was already spread with a tight-pinned
sheet to receive the poor man; and, while her helpers
put him to bed, she put on her bonnet, and ran for the
doctor.

Dr. Colton did his best for his patient, but pronounced it an impossibility to remove him till the bone
should be joined firmly, as a thorough cure was all-

essential to his professional prospects. And now, indeed, Miss Lucinda had her hands full. A nurse could
not be afforded; but Monsieur Leclerc was added to
the list of old Israel's " chores," and what other nursing he needed Miss Lucinda was glad to do; for her
kind heart was full of self-reproaches to think it was
her pig that had knocked down the poor man, and her
mop-handle that had twisted itself across and under his
leg, and aided, if not caused, its breakage. So Israel
came in four or five times a day to do what he could,
and Miss Lucinda played nurse at other times to the
best of her ability. Such flavorous gruels and por-
ridges as she concocted! such *tisanes* after her guest's
instructions! such dainty soups and sweetbreads and
cutlets, served with such neatness! After his experience of a second-rate boarding-house, Monsieur Leclerc
thought himself in a gastronomic paradise. Moreover,
these tiny meals were garnished with flowers, which his
French taste for color and decoration appreciated, —
two or three stems of lilies-of-the-valley in their folded
green leaves, cool and fragrant; a moss-rosebud and
a spire of purple-gray lavender bound together with
ribbon-grass; or three carnations set in glittering myr-
tle-sprays, the last acquisition of the garden.

Miss Lucinda enjoyed nursing thoroughly, and a
kindlier patient no woman ever had. Her bright needle
flew faster than ever through the cold linen and flaccid
cambric of the shirts and cravats she fashioned, while
he told her, in his odd idioms, stories of his life in
France, and the curious customs, both of society and
cuisinerie, with which last he showed a surprising acquaintance. Truth to tell, when Monsieur Leclerc said
he had been a member of the Duc de Montmorenci's

nousehold, he withheld the other half of this truth, —
that he had been his *valet-de-chambre;* but it was an
hereditary service, and seemed to him as different a
thing from common servitude as a peer's office in
the bed chamber differs from a lackey's. Indeed, Monsieur Leclerc was a gentleman in his own way, not of
blood, but of breeding; and while he had faithfully
served the "aristocrats," as his father had done before
him, he did not limit that service to their prosperity,
but in their greatest need descended to menial offices,
and forgot that he could dance and ride and fence
almost as well as his young master. But a bullet from
a barricade put an end to his duty there; and he hated
utterly the democratic rule that had overturned for him
both past and future: so he escaped, and came to
America, the grand resort of refugees, where he had
labored, as he best knew how, for his own support, and
kept to himself his disgust at the manners and customs
of the barbarians. Now, for the first time, he was at
home and happy. Miss Lucinda's delicate fashions
suited him exactly. He adored her taste for the beautiful, which she was unconscious of. He enjoyed her
cookery; and though he groaned within himself at the
amount of debt he was incurring, yet he took courage,
from her kindness, to believe she would not be a hard
creditor, and, being naturally cheerful, put aside his
anxieties, and amused himself, as well as her, with his
stories, his quavering songs, his recipes for *pot-au-feu,*
tisane, and *pâtés,* at once economical and savory. Never
had a leg of lamb or a piece of roast beef gone so far
in her domestic experience. A chicken seemed almost
to outlive its usefulness in its various forms of re-ap-
pearance; and the salads he devised were as wonderful

as the omelets he superintended, or the gay dances he
played on his beloved violin, as soon as he could sit up
enough to manage it.   Moreover,— I should say *most-
over*, if the word were admissible, — Monsieur Leclerc
lifted a great weight before long from Miss Lucinda's
mind.   He began by subduing Fun to his proper place
by a mild determination that completely won the dog's
heart. " Women and spaniels," the world knows, " like
kicking ; " and, though kicks were no part of the good
man's Rareyfaction of Fun, he certainly used a certain
amount of coercion, and the dog's lawful owner admired the skill of the teacher, and enjoyed the better
manners of the pupil thoroughly.   She could do twice
as much sewing now, and never were her nights disturbed by a bark ; for the dog crouched by his new
friend's bed in the parlor, and lay quiet there.   Toby
was next undertaken, and proved less amenable to discipline.   He stood in some slight awe of the man who
tried to teach him, but still continued to sally out at
Miss Lucinda's feet, to spring at her caressing hand
when he felt ill-humored, and to claw Fun's patient
nose and his approaching paws, when his misplaced
sentimentality led him to caress the cat.   But, after a
while, a few well-timed slaps, administered with vigor,
cured Toby of his worst tricks : though every blow
made Miss Lucinda wince, and almost shook her good
opinion of Monsieur Leclerc ; for in these long weeks
he had wrought out a good opinion of himself in her
mind, much to her own surprise.   She could not have
believed a man could be so polite, so gentle, so patient,
and, above all, so capable of ruling without tyranny
Miss Lucinda was puzzled.

One day, as Monsieur Leclerc was getting better

just able to go about on crutches, Israel came into the
kitchen, and Miss Manners went out to see him.   She
left the door open ; and along with the odor of a pot of
raspberry-jam scalding over the fire, sending its steams
of leaf-and-insect fragrance through the little house,
there came in also the following conversation.

"Israel," said Miss Lucinda, in a hesitating and
rather forlorn tone, "I have been thinking, — I don't
know what to do with Piggy.   He is quite too big for
me to keep.   I'm afraid of him, if he gets out; and
he eats up the garden."

"Well, that *is* a consider'ble swaller for a pig, Miss
Lucindy ; but I b'lieve you're abaout right abaout
keepin' on him.   He *is* too big, that's a fact; but
he's so like a human cre'tur', I'd jest abaout as lieves
slarter Orrin.   I declare, I don't know no more'n a
taown-house goose what to do with him ! "

"If I gave him away, I suppose he would be fatted
and killed, of course ? "

"I guess he'd be killed, likely ; but, as for fattenin'
on him, I'd jest as soon undertake to fatten a salt cod-
fish.   He's one o' the racers, an' they're as holler as
hogsheads.   You can fill 'em up to their noses, ef you're
a mind to spend your corn, and they'll caper it all off
their bones in twenty-four haours.   I b'lieve, ef they
was tied neck an' heels, an' stuffed, they'd wiggle thin
betwixt feedin-times.   Why, Orrin, he raised nine on
'em, and every darned critter's as poor as Job's turkey
to-day.   They a'n't no good.   I'd as lieves ha' had
nine chestnut-rails, an' a little lieveser' ; cause they
don't eat nothin'."

"You don't know of any poor person who'd like to
have a pig, do you ? " said Miss Lucinda wistfully.

"Well, the poorer they was, the quicker they'd eat him up, I guess, — ef they could eat such a razor-back."

"Ch, I don't like to think of his being eaten! I wish he could be got rid of some other way. Don't you think he might be killed in his sleep, Israel?"

This was a little too much for Israel. An irresistible flicker of laughter twitched his wrinkles, and bubbled in his throat.

"I think it's likely 'twould wake him up," said he demurely. "Killin's killin', and a cre'tur' can't sleep over it's though 'twas the stomach-ache. I guess he'd kick some, ef he *was* asleep — and screech some too!"

Dear me!" said Miss Lucinda, horrified at the idea. "I wish he could be sent out to run in the woods. Are there any good woods near here, Israel?"

"I don't know but what he'd as lieves be slartered to once as to starve, an' be hunted down out in the lots. Besides, there a'n't nobody as I knows of would like a hog to be a-rootin' round amongst their turnips and young wheat."

"Well, what I shall do with him I don't know!" despairingly exclaimed Miss Lucinda. "He was such a dear little thing when you brought him, Israel! Do you remember how pink his pretty little nose was, — just like a rose-bud, — and how bright his eyes looked, and his cunning legs? And now he's grown so big and fierce! But I can't help liking him, either."

"He's a cute critter, that's sartain; but he does too much rootin' to have a pink nose now, I expect: there's consider'ble on't, so I guess it looks as well to have it gray. But I don't know no more'n you do what to do abaout it."

"If I could only get rid of him without knowing what became of him!" exclaimed Miss Lucinda, squeezing her forefinger with great earnestness, and looking both puzzled and pained.

"If Mees Lucinda would pairmit?" said a voice behind her.

She turned round to see Monsieur Leclerc on his crutches, just in the parlor-door.

"I shall, mees, myself dispose of piggee, if it please. I can. I shall have no sound: he shall to go away like a silent snow, to trouble you no more, never!"

"O sir, if you could! But I don't see how."

"If mees was to see, it would not be to save her pain. I shall have him to go by *magique* to fiery land."

Fairy-land probably. But Miss Lucinda did not perceive the *équivoque*.

"Nor yet shall I trouble Meester Israyel. I shall have the aid of myself and one good friend that I have; and some night, when you rise of the morning, he shall not be there."

Miss Lucinda breathed a deep sigh of relief.

"I am greatly obliged, — I shall be, I mean," said she.

"Well, I'm glad enough to wash my hands on't," said Israel. "I shall hanker arter the critter some. but he's a-gettin' too big to be handy; 'n' it's one comfort abaout critters, you ken get rid on 'em some-haow when they're more plague than profit. But folks has got to be let alone, excep' the Lord takes 'em; an' he don't allers see fit."

What added point and weight to these final remarks

of old Israel was the well-known fact that he suffered at home from the most pecking and worrying of
wives, and had been heard to say, in some moment of
unusual frankness, that he "didn't see how 't could
be sinful to wish Miss Slater was in heaven, for she'd
be lots better off, and other folks too."

Miss Lucinda never knew what befell her pig one
fine September night: she did not even guess that a
visit paid to monsieur by one of his pupils, a farmer's
daughter just out of Dalton, had any thing to do with
this *enlèvement*. She was sound asleep in her bed up
stairs, when her guest shod his crutches with old
gloves, and limped out to the garden-gate by dawn,
where he and the farmer tolled the animal out of his
sty, and far down the street, by tempting red apples,
and then Farmer Steele took possession of him, and
he was seen no more. No, the first thing Miss Lucinda knew of her riddance was when Israel put his
head into the back-door that same morning, some four
hours afterward, and said with a significant nod, —

"He's gone!"

After all his other chores were done, Israel had a
conference with Monsieur Leclerc; and the two sallied
into the garden, and in an hour had dismantled the
low dwelling, cleared away the wreck, levelled and
smoothed its site, and monsieur, having previously
provided himself with an Isabella grape-vine, planted
it on this forsaken spot, and trained it carefully against
the end of the shed: strange to say, though it was
against all precedent to transplant a grape in September, it lived and flourished. Miss Lucinda's gratitude
to Monsieur Leclerc was altogether disproportioned
as he thought, to his slight service. He could not

understand fully her devotion to her pets; but he respected it, and aided it whenever he could, though he never surmised the motive that adorned Miss Lucinda's table with such delicate superabundance after the late departure, and laid bundles of lavender-flowers in his tiny portmanteau till the very leather seemed to gather fragrance.

Before long Monsieur Leclerc was well enough to resume his classes, and return to his boarding-house; but the latter was filled, and only offered a prospect of vacancy in some three weeks after his application: so he returned home somewhat dejected; and as he sat by the little parlor-fire after tea, he said to his hostess in a reluctant tone, —

"Mees Lucinda, you have been of the kindest to the poor alien. I have it in my mind to relieve you of this care very rapidly, but it is not in the Fates that I do. I have gone to my house of lodgings, and they cannot to give me a chamber as yet. I have fear that I must yet rely me on your goodness for some time more, if you can to entertain me so much more of time?"

"Why, I shall like to, sir," replied the kindly, simple-hearted old maid. "I'm sure you are not a mite of trouble, and I never can forget what you did for my pig."

A smile flitted across the Frenchman's thin dark face, and he watched her glittering needles a few minutes in silence before he spoke again.

"But I have other things to say of the most unpleasant to me, Mees Lucinda. I have a great debt for the goodness and care you to me have lavished. To the angels of the good God we must submit to be

debtors ; but there are also of mortal obligations. I
have lodged in your mansion for more of ten weeks,
and to you I pay yet no silver ; but it is that I have it
not at present. I must ask of your goodness to wait.''

The old maid's shining black eyes grew soft as she
looked at him.

'' Why,'' said she, '' I don't think you owe me much
of any thing, Mr. Leclerc. I never knew things last as
they have since you came. I really think you brought
a blessing. I wish you would please to think you don't
owe me any thing.''

The Frenchman's great brown eyes shone with suspicious dew.

'' I cannot to forget that I owe to you far more than
any silver of man repays ; but I should not think to
forget that I also owe to you silver, or I should not be
worthy of a man's name. No, mees ! I have two
hands and legs. I will not let a woman most solitary
spend for me her good self.''

'' Well,'' said Miss Lucinda, '' if you will be uneasy
till you pay me, I would rather have another kind of
pay than money. I should like to know how to dance.
I never did learn when I was a girl, and I think it
would be good exercise.''

Miss Lucinda supported this pious fiction through
with a simplicity that quite deceived the Frenchman.
He did not think it so incongruous as it was. He had
seen women of sixty, rouged and jewelled and furbe-
lowed, foot it deftly in the halls of the Faubourg St.
Germain in his earliest youth ; and this cheery, healthy
woman, with lingering blooms on either cheek, and
uncapped head of curly black hair but slightly strewn
with silver, seemed quite as fit a subject for the accom-

plishment. Besides, he was poor; and this offered
so easy a way of paying the debt he had so dreaded!
Well said Solomon, "The destruction of the poor is
their poverty." For whose moral sense, delicate sen-
sitiveness, generous longings, will not sometimes give
way to the stringent need of food and clothing, the gall
of indebtedness, and the sinking consciousness of an
empty purse and threatening possibilities?

Monsieur Leclerc's face brightened.

"Ah, with what grand pleasure shall I teach you the
dance!"

But it fell dark again as he proceeded, —

"Though not one, nor two, nor three, nor four
quarters shall be of value sufficient to achieve my payment."

"Then, if that troubles you, why, I should like to
take some French lessons in the evening, when you
don't have classes. I learned French when I was quite
a girl, but not to speak it very easily; and if I could
get some practice, and the right way to speak, I should
be glad."

"And I shall give you the real *Parisien* tone, Mees
Lucinda," said he proudly. "I shall be as if it were
no more an exile when I repeat my tongue to you."

And so it was settled. Why Miss Lucinda should
learn French any more than dancing was not a question
in Monsieur Leclerc's mind. It is true that Chaldaic
would, in all probability, be as useful to our friend as
French; and the flying over poles, and hanging by toes
and fingers, so eloquently described by apostles of the
body, would have been as well adapted to her style
and capacity as dancing. But his own language, and
his own profession! — what man would not have

regarded these as indispensable to improvement, particularly when they paid his board?

During the latter three weeks of Monsieur Leclerc's
stay with Miss Lucinda, he made himself surprisingly
useful. He listed the doors against approaching winter
breezes; he weeded in the garden, trimmed, tied,
trained, wherever either good office was needed, mended china with an infallible cement, and rickety chairs
with the skill of a cabinet-maker; and, whatever hard
or dirty work he did, he always presented himself at
table in a state of scrupulous neatness. His long brown
hands showed no trace of labor; his iron-gray hair was
reduced to smoothest order; his coat speckless, if
threadbare; and he ate like a gentleman, — an accomplishment not always to be found in the "best society,"
as the phrase goes: whether the best in fact ever lacks
it is another thing. Miss Lucinda appreciated these
traits; they set her at ease; and a pleasanter home-life
could scarce be painted than now enlivened the little
wooden house. But three weeks pass away rapidly;
and when the rusty portmanteau was gone from her
spare chamber, and the well-worn boots from the
kitchen-corner, and the hat from its nail, Miss Lucinda
began to find herself wonderfully lonely. She missed
the armfuls of wood in her wood-box that she had to
fill laboriously, two sticks at a time; she missed the
other plate at her tiny round table, the other chair beside her fire; she missed that dark, thin, sensitive
face, with its rare and sweet smile; she wanted her
story-teller, her yarn-winder, her protector, back again.
Good gracious! to think of an old lady of forty-seven
entertaining such sentiments for a man.

Presently the dancing-lessons commenced. It was

thought advisable that Miss Manners should enter a class, and in the fervency of her good intentions she did not demur. But gratitude and respect had to strangle with persistent hands the little serpents of the ridiculous in Monsieur Leclerc's soul when he beheld his pupil's first appearance. What reason was it, O rose of seventeen! adorning thyself with cloudy films of lace and sparks of jewelry before the mirror that reflects youth and beauty, that made Miss Lucinda array herself in a brand-new dress of yellow muslin-de laine strewed with round green spots, and displace her customary handkerchief for a huge tamboured collar, on this eventful occasion? Why, oh, why! did she tie up the roots of her black hair with an unconcealable scarlet string? And, most of all, why was her dress so short, her slipper-strings so big and broad, her thick slippers so shapeless, by reason of the corns and bunions that pertained to the feet within? The "instantaneous rush of several guardian angels" that once stood dear old Hepzibah Pynchon in good stead was wanting here; or perhaps they stood by all-invisible, their calm eyes softened with love deeper than tears, at this spectacle so ludicrous to man, beholding in the grotesque dress and adornments only the budding of life's divinest blossom, and in the strange skips and hops of her first attempts at dancing only the buoyancy of those inner wings that goodness and generosity and pure self-devotion were shaping for a future strong and stately flight upward. However, men, women, and children do not see with angelic eyes, and the titterings of her fellow-pupils were irrepressible. One bouncing girl nearly choked herself with her handkerchief, trying not to laugh; and two or three did not even try. Monsieur Leclerc could not blame them. At first he could scarce control his own facial muscles ; but a sense of remorse smote him, as he saw how unconscious and earnest the little woman was, and remembered how often those knotty hands and knobbed feet had waited on his need or his comfort. Presently he tapped on his violin for a few moments' respite, and approached Miss Lucinda as respectfully as if she had been a queen.

"You are ver' tired, Mees Lucinda?" said he.

"I am a little, sir," said she, out of breath. "I am not used to dancing : it's quite an exertion."

"It is that truly. If you are too much tired, is it better to wait? I shall finish for you the lesson till I come to-night for a French conversation?"

"I guess I will go home," said the simple little lady. "I am some afraid of getting rheumatism. But use makes perfect, and I shall stay through next time, no doubt."

"So I believe," said monsieur, with his best bow, as Miss Lucinda departed and went home, pondering all the way what special delicacy she should provide for tea.

"My dear young friends," said Monsieur Leclerc, pausing with the uplifted bow in his hand, before he recommenced his lesson, "I have observe that my new pupil does make you much to laugh. I am not so surprise ; for you do not know all, and the good God does not robe all angels in one manner. But she have taken me to her mansion with a leg broken, and have nursed me like a saint of the blessed, nor with any pay of silver, except that I teach her the dance and the French. They re pay for the meat and the drink ; but she wil

have no more for her good patience and care. I like
to teach you the dance; but she could teach you the
saints' ways, which are better. I think you will no
more to laugh."

"No, I guess we *won't!*" said the bouncing girl
with great emphasis; and the color rose over more than
one young face.

After that day Miss Lucinda received many a kind
smile and hearty welcome, and never did anybody venture even a grimace at her expense. But it must be
acknowledged that her dancing was at least peculiar.
With a sanitary view of the matter, she meant to make
it exercise; and fearful was the skipping that ensued.
She *chasséd* on tiptoe, and *balancéd* with an indescribable hopping twirl, that made one think of a chickadee
pursuing its quest of food on new-ploughed ground;
and some late-awakened feminine instinct of dress,
restrained, too, by due economy, endued her with the
oddest decorations that woman ever devised. The
French lessons went on more smoothly. If Monsieur
Leclerc's Parisian ear was tortured by the barbarous
accent of Vermont, at least he bore it with heroism,
since there was nobody else to hear; and very pleasant,
both to our little lady and her master, were these long
winter evenings, when they diligently waded through
Racine, and even got as far as the golden periods of
Chateaubriand. The pets fared badly for petting in
these days: they were fed and waited on, but not with
the old devotion. It began to dawn on Miss Lucinda's
mind that something to talk to was preferable, as a
companion, even to Fun, and that there might be a
stranger sweetness in receiving care and protection
than in giving it.

Spring came at last. Its softer skies were as blue over Dalton as in the wide fields without, and its footsteps as bloom-bringing in Miss Lucinda's garden as in mead or forest. Now Monsieur Leclerc came to her aid again at odd minutes, and set her flower-beds with mignonette-borders, and her vegetable-garden with salad-herbs of new and flourishing kinds. Yet not even the sweet season seemed to hurry the catastrophe, that we hope, dearest reader, thy tender eyes have long seen impending. No; for this quaint alliance a quainter Cupid waited: the chubby little fellow with a big head and a little arrow, who waits on youth and loveliness, was not wanted here. Lucinda's god of love wore a lank, hard-featured, grizzly shape, no less than that of Israel Slater, who marched into the garden one fine June morning, earlier than usual, to find monsieur in his blouse, hard at work weeding the cauliflower-bed.

" Good-mornin', sir, good-mornin' ! " said Israel, in answer to the Frenchman's greeting. " This is a real slick little garden-spot as ever I see, and a pootty house, and a real clever woman too. I'll be skwitched ef it a'n't a fust-rate consarn, the hull on't. Be you ever a-goin' back to France, mister?"

" No, my goot friend. I have nobody there. I stay here. I have friend here; but there, — oh, *non! je ne reviendrai pas! ah, jamais, jamais!*"

" Pa's dead, eh? or shamming? Well, I don't understand your lingo; but, ef you're a-goin' to stay here, I don't see why you don't hitch hosses with Miss Lucindy."

Monsieur Leclerc looked up astonished.

" Horses, my friend? I have no horse."

"'Thunder 'n' dry trees! I didn't say you hed, did I? But that comes o' usin' what Parson Hyde calls figgurs, I s'pose. I wish 't he'd use one kind o' figgur-in' a leetle more: he'd pay me for that wood-sawin'. I didn't mean nothin' about hosses. I sot out fur to say, Why don't ye marry Miss Lucindy?'"

"I?" gasped monsieur, — "I, the foreign, the poor? I could not to presume so!"

"Well, I don't see 's it's sech drefful presumption. Ef you're poor, she's a woman, and real lonesome too: she ha'n't got nuther chick nor child belongin' to her, and you're the only man she ever took any kind of a notion to. I guess 'twould be jest as much for her good as yourn."

"Hush, good Is-ray-el! it is good to stop there. She would not to marry after such years of goodness. She is a saint of the blessed."

"Well, I guess saints sometimes fellerships with sinners; I've heerd tell they did: and, ef I was you, I'd make trial for't. Nothin' ventur', nothin' have."

Whereupon Israel walked off, whistling.

Monsieur Leclerc's soul was perturbed within him by these suggestions. He pulled up two young cauli-flowers, and reset their places with pigweeds; he hoed the nicely sloped border of the bed flat to the path, and then flung the hoe across the walk, and went off to his daily occupation with a new idea in his head. Nor was it an unpleasant one. The idea of a transition from his squalid and pinching boarding-house to the delicate comfort of Miss Lucinda's *ménage*, the pros-pect of so kind and good a wife to care for his hitherto dreaded future, — all this was pleasant. I cannot hon-estly say he was in love with our friend: I must even confess that whatever element of that nature existed between the two was now all on Miss Lucinda's side, little as she knew it. Certain it is, that when she appeared that day at the dancing-class in a new green calico flowered with purple, and bows on her slippers big enough for a bonnet, it occurred to Monsieur Leclerc, that, if they were married, she would take no more lessons. However, let us not blame him. He was a man, and a poor one ; one must not expect too much from men or from poverty : if they are tolerably good, let us canonize them even, it is so hard for the poor creatures ! And, to do Monsieur Leclerc justice, he had a very thorough respect and admiration for Miss Lucinda. Years ago, in his stormy youth-time, there had been a pair of soft-fringed eyes that looked into his as none would ever look again. And they murdered her, those mad wild beasts of Paris, in the chapel where she knelt at her pure prayers, — murdered her because she knelt beside an aristocrat, her best friend, the Duchess of Montmorenci, who had taken the pretty peasant from her own estate to bring her up for her maid. Jean Leclerc had lifted that pale shape from the pavement, and buried it himself : what else he buried with it was invisible. But now he recalled the hour with a long, shuddering sigh, and, hiding his face in his hands, said softly, " The violet is dead : there is no spring for her. I will have now an amaranth : it is good for the tomb."

Whether Miss Lucinda's winter dress suggested this floral metaphor, let us not inquire. Sacred be sentiment, when there is even a shadow of reality about it : when it becomes a profession, and confounds itself with millinery, and shades of mourning, it is " bosh," as the Turkeys say.

So that very evening Monsieur Leclerc arrayed himself in his best to give another lesson to Miss Lucinda. But, somehow or other, the lesson was long in beginning. The little parlor looked so homelike and so pleasant, with its bright lamp and gay bunch of roses on the table, that it was irresistible temptation to lounge and linger. Miss Lucinda had the volume of Florian in her hands, and was wondering why he did not begin, when the book was drawn away, and a hand laid on both of hers.

"Lucinda," he began, "I give you no lesson to-night. I have to ask. Dear mees, will you to marry your poor slave?"

"Oh, dear!" said Miss Lucinda.

Don't laugh at her, Miss Tender-eyes. You will feel just so yourself some day, when Alexander Augustus says, "Will you be mine, loveliest of your sex?" Only you won't feel it half so strongly, for you are young, and love is nature to youth; but it is a heavenly surprise to age.

Monsieur Leclerc said nothing. He had a heart, after all, and it was touched now by the deep emotion that flushed Miss Lucinda's face, and made her tremble so violently; but presently he spoke.

"Do not," said he. "I am wrong. I presume. Forgive the stranger."

"Oh, dear!" said poor Lucinda again. "Oh! you know it isn't that; but how can you like *me?*"

There, mademoiselle, there's humility for you! *you* will never say that to Alexander Augustus.

Monsieur Leclerc soothed this frightened, happy, incredulous little woman into quiet before very long; and, if he really began to feel a true affection for her

from the moment he perceived her humble and entire
devotion to him, who shall blame him? Not I. If we
were all heroes, who would be *valet-de-chambre?* If
we were all women, who would be men? He was very
good as far as he went; and, if you expect the chival-
ries of grace out of nature, you "may expect," as
old Fuller saith. So it was peacefully settled that they
should be married, with a due amount of tears and
smiles on Lucinda's part, and a great deal of tender
sincerity on monsieur's. She missed her dancing-
lesson next day; and, when Monsieur Leclerc came in
the evening, he found a shade on her happy face.

"Oh, dear!" said she, as he entered.

"Oh, dear!" was Lucinda's favorite aspiration.
Had she thought of it as an Anglicizing of "*O Dieu!*"
perhaps she would have dropped it; but this time she
went on headlong, with a valorous despair, —

"I have thought of something. I'm afraid I can't!
Monsieur, aren't you a Romanist?"

"What is that?" said he, surprised.

"A Papist, a Catholic."

"Ah!" he returned, sighing, "once I was *bon
Catholique*, — once in my gone youth; after then I was
nothing but the poor man who bats for his life; now I
am of the religion that shelters the stranger, and binds
up the broken poor."

Monsieur was a diplomatist. This melted Miss Lucinda's orthodoxy right down: she only said, —

"Then you will go to church with me?"

"And to the skies above, I pray," said monsieur,
kissing her knotty hand like a lover.

So in the earliest autumn they were married, monsieur having previously presented Miss Lucinda with a

delicate plaided gray silk for her wedding attire, in
which she looked almost young; and old Israel was
present at the ceremony, which was briefly performed
by Parson Hyde in Miss Manners's parlor. They did
not go to Niagara, nor to Newport; but that afternoon
Monsieur Leclerc brought a hired rockaway to the
door, and took his bride a drive into the country.
They stopped beside a pair of bars, where monsieur
hitched his horse, and, taking Lucinda by the hand,
led her into Farmer Steele's orchard, to the foot of his
biggest apple-tree. There she beheld a little mound,
at the head and foot of which stood a daily rose-bush
shedding its latest wreaths of bloom, and upon the
mound itself was laid a board, on which she read, —

"Here lie the bones of poor piggy."

Mrs. Lucinda burst into tears; and monsieur, picking a bud from the bush, placed it in her hand, and led
her tenderly back to the rockaway.

That evening Mrs. Lucinda was telling the affair to
old Israel with so much feeling, that she did not perceive at all the odd commotion in his face, till, as she
repeated the epitaph to him, he burst out with, "He
didn't say what become o' the flesh, did he?" and
therewith fled through the kitchen-door. For years
afterward Israel would entertain a few favored audi-
tors with his opinion of the matter, screaming till the
tears rolled down his cheeks, —

"That was the beateree of all the weddin'-towers I
ever heerd tell on. Goodness! it's enough to make
the Wanderin' Jew die o' larfin'."

DELY'S COW.

I WENT down to the farmyard one day last month; and as I opened the gate I heard Pat Malony say, "Biddy, Biddy!" I thought at first he was calling a hen; but then I remembered the hens were all shut into the poultry-house that day, to be sorted, and numbered, and condemned. So I looked again, thinking perhaps Pat's little lame sister had strayed up from the village, and gone into the barn after Sylvy's kittens, or a pigeon-egg, or to see a new calf; but, to my surprise, I saw a red cow, of no particular beauty or breed, coming out of the stable-door, looking about her as if in search of somebody or something; and when Pat called again, "Biddy, Biddy, Biddy!" the creature walked up to him across the yard, stretched out her awkward neck, sniffed a little, and cropped from his hand the wisp of rowen hay he held, as composedly as if she were a tame kitten, and then followed him all round the yard for more, which I am sorry to say she did not get. Pat had only displayed her accomplishments to astonish me, and then shut her in her stall again. I afterward hunted out Biddy's history, and here it is.

On the Derby turnpike, just before you enter Haner-ford, everybody that ever travelled that road will remember Joseph German's bakery. It was a red brick house, with dusty windows toward the street, and jus

inside the door a little shop, where Mr. German retailed
the scalloped cookies, fluted gingerbread, long loaves
of bread, and scantily-filled pies in which he dealt, and
which were manufactured in the long shop, where in
summer you caught glimpses of flour barrels all a-row,
and men who might have come out of those barrels,
so strewed with flour were all their clothes, — paper
cap and white apron scarcely to be distinguished from
the rest of the dress as far as color and dustiness went.
Here, too, when her father drove out the cart every
afternoon, sitting in front of the counter with her sewing or her knitting, Dely German, the baker's pretty
daughter, dealt out the cakes, and rattled the pennies
in her apron-pocket, with so good a grace, that not a
young farmer came into Hanerford with grain, or
potatoes, or live-stock, who did not cast a glance in at
the shop-door going toward town, and go in on his
return, ostensibly to buy a sheet of gingerbread, or a
dozen cookies, for his refreshment on the drive homeward. It was a curious thing to see how much hungrier
they were on the way home than coming into town.
Though they might have had a good dinner in Hanerford, that never appeased their appetites entirely;
while in the morning they had driven their slow teams
all the way without so much as thinking of cakes and
cheese. So by the time Dely was seventeen, her black
eyes and bright cheeks were well known for miles
about; and many a youth, going home to the clean
kitchen where his old mother sat by the fire, knitting,
or his spinster sister scolded and scrubbed over his
muddy boot-tracks, thought how pretty it would look
to see Dely German sitting on the other side, in her
neat calico frock and white apron, her black hair

shining smooth, and her fresh, bright face looking a
welcome.

But Dely did not think about any one of them in a
reciprocal manner. She liked them all pretty well; but
she loved nobody except her father and mother, her
three cats and all their kittens, the big dog, the old
horse, and a wheezy robin that she kept in a cage,
because her favorite cat had half killed it one day, and
it never could fly any more. For all these dumb things
she had a really intense affection. As for her father
and mother, she seemed to be a part of them: it never
occurred to her that they could leave her, or she them;
and when old Joe German died one summer day, just
after Dely was seventeen, she was nearly distracted.
However, people who must work for their living have
to get over their sorrows practically much sooner than
those who can afford time to indulge them; and, as
Dely knew more about the business and the shop than
anybody but the foreman, she had to resume her place
at the counter before her father had been buried a
week. It was a great source of embarrassment to her
rural admirers to see Dely in her black frock, pale and
sober, when they went in. They did not know what to
say: they felt as if their hands and feet had grown
very big all at once, and as if the cents in their pockets
never could be got at, at which they turned red and hot,
and got choked, and went away, swearing internally
at their own blundering shyness, and deeper smitten
than ever with Dely, because they wanted to comfort
her so very much, and didn't know how.

One, however, had the sense and simplicity to know
how; and that was George Adams, a fine, healthy young
fellow from Hartland Hollow, who came in at least

once a week with a load of produce from the farm on which he was head man. The first time he went after his rations of gingerbread, and found Dely in her mourning, he held out his hand, and shook hers heartily. Dely looked up into his honest blue eyes, and saw them full of pity.

"I'm real sorry for you," said George. "My father died two years ago."

Dely burst into tears; and George couldn't help stroking her bright hair softly, and saying, "Oh, don't!" So she wiped her eyes, and sold him the cookies he wanted; but from that day theie was one of Dely's customers that she liked best, one team of white horses she always looked out for, and one voice that hurried the color into her face if it was ever so pale; and the upshot of pity and produce and ginger-bread was that George Adams and Dely German were heartily in love with each other, and Dely began to be comforted for her father's loss six months after he died. Not that she knew why, or that George had ever said any thing to her more than was kind and friendly; but she felt a sense of rest, and yet a sweet restlessness, when he was in her thoughts or presence, that beguiled her grief, and made her unintentionally happy. It was the old, old story, — the one eternal novelty that never loses its vitality, its interest, its bewitching power, nor ever will till time shall be no more.

But the year had not elapsed, devoted to double crape and triple quillings, before Dely's mother, too, began to be consoled. She was a pleasant, placid, feeble-natured woman, who liked her husband very well, and fretted at him in a mild, persistent way a

good deal. He swore, and chewed tobacco, which
annoyed her; he also kept a tight grip of his money,
which was not pleasant: but she missed him very much
when he died, and cried and rocked, and said how
afflicted she was, as much as was necessary, even in
the neighbors' opinion.   But, as time went on, she
found the business very hard to manage : even with Dely
and the foreman to help her, the ledger got all astray,
and the day-book followed its example.   So when old
Tom Kenyon, who kept the tavern half a mile farther
out, took to coming Sunday nights to see the " Widder
German," and finally proposed to share her troubles,
and carry on the bakery in a matrimonial partnership,
Mrs. German said she " guessed she would," and announced to Dely on Monday morning that she was
going to have a step-father.   Dely was astonished and
indignant, but to no purpose.   Mrs. German cried
and rocked, and rocked and cried again, rather more
saliently than when her husband died.   But for all
that she did not retract; and in due time she got into
the stage with her elderly lover, and went to Meriden,
where they got married, and came home next day to
carry on the bakery.

Joe German had been foolish enough to leave all his
property to his wife ; and Dely had no resource but to
stay at home, and endure her disagreeable position as
well as she could, for Tom Kenyon swore and chewed,
and smoked beside : moreover, he drank, — not to real
drunkenness, but enough to make him cross and in-
tractable.   Worse than all, he had a son, the only child
of his first marriage ; and it soon became unpleasantly
evident to Dely, that Steve Kenyon had a mind to
marry her, and his father had a mind he should.   Now,

it is all very well to marry a person one likes; but to go through that ceremony with one you dislike is more than anybody has a right to require, in my opinion, as well as Dely's: so when her mother urged upon her the various advantages of the match, — Steve Kenyon being the present master and prospective owner of his father's tavern, a great resort for horse-jockeys, cattle-dealers, and frequenters of state and county fairs, — Dely still objected to marry him. But, the more she objected, the more her mother talked; her step-father swore; and the swaggering lover persisted in his attentions at all times; so that the poor girl had scarce a half-hour to herself. She grew thin and pale and unhappy enough; and one day George Adams, stepping in unexpectedly, found her with her apron to her eyes, crying most bitterly. It took some persuasion, and some more daring caresses than he had yet ventured on, to get Dely's secret trouble to light. I am inclined to think George kissed her at least once before she would tell him what she was crying about. But Dely naturally came to the conclusion, that if he loved her enough to kiss her, and she loved him enough to like it, she might as well share her troubles; and the consequence was, George asked her then and there to share his. Not that either of them thought there would be troubles under that copartnership, for the day was sufficient to them; and it did not daunt Dely in the least to know that George's only possessions were a heifer calf, a suit of clothes, and twenty dollars.

About a month after this eventful day, Dely went into Hanerford on an errand, she said: so did George Adams. They stepped into the minister's together, and were married: so Dely's errand was done, and she rode out on the front-seat of George's empty wagon, stopping at the bakery to tell her mother, and get her trunk; having wisely chosen a day for her errand when her step-father had gone away after a load of flour down to Hanerford wharves. Mrs. Kenyon went at once into wild hysterics, and called Dely a jade-hopper and an ungrateful child. But not understanding the opprobrium of the one term, and not deserving the other, the poor girl only cried a little, and helped George with her trunk, which held all she could call her own in the world, — her clothes, two or three cheap trinkets, and a few books. She kissed the cats all round, hugged the dog, was glad her robin had died, and then said good-by to her mother, who refused to kiss her, and said George Adams was a snake in the grass. This was too much for Dely: she wiped her eyes, and clambered over the wagon-wheel, and took her place beside George with a smile so much like crying, that he began to whistle, and never stopped for two miles. By that time they were in a piece of thick pine-woods, when, looking both before and behind to be certain no one was coming, he put his arm round his wife and kissed her, which seemed to have a consoling effect; and, by the time they reached his mother's little house, Dely was as bright as ever.

A little bit of a house it was to bring a wife to, but it suited Dely. It stood on the edge of a pine-wood, where the fragrance of the resinous boughs kept the air sweet and pure, and their leaves thrilled responsive to every breeze. The house was very small and very red. It had two rooms below, and one above; but it was neater than many a five-story mansion, and far more cheerful. And, when Dely went in at the door, she

thought there could be no prettier sight than the exquisitely neat old woman sitting in her arm-chair on
one side of the fireplace, and her beautiful cat on the
other, purring and winking, while the tea-kettle sang
and sputtered over the bright fire of pine-cones. and
the tea-table at the other side of the room was spread
with such clean linen, and such shining crockery, that
it made one hungry even to look at the brown-bread
and butter, and pink radishes, that were Dely's wed-
ding-supper.

It is very odd how happy people can be when they
are as poor as poverty, and don't know where to look
for their living, but to the work of their own hands.
Genteel poverty is horrible. It is impossible for one to
be poor and elegant, and comfortable; but downright,
simple, unblushing poverty may be the most blessed of
states. And though it was somewhat of a descent in
the social scale for Dely to marry a farm-hand, foreman though he might be, she loved her George so
devoutly and healthily, that she was as happy as a
woman could be. George's mother, the sweetest and
tenderest mother to him, took his wife to a place beside
his in her heart; and the two women loved each other
the more for this man's sake. He was a bond between
them, not a division. Hard work left them no thought
of rankling jealousy to make their lives bitter; and
Dely was happier than ever she had thought she should
be away from her mother. Nor did the hard work hurt
her; for she took to her own share all of it that was
out of doors, and troublesome to the infirmities of the
old lady. She tended the calf in its little log-hut,
shook down the coarse hay for its bed, made its gruel
till it grew beyond gruel, then drove it daily to the

pasture where it fed, gave it extra rations of bread and
apple-parings and carrot-tops, till the creature knew
her voice, and ran to her call like a pet kitten, rubbing
its soft, wet nose against her red cheek, and showing
in a dozen blundering, calfish ways that it both knew
and loved her.

There are two sorts of people in the world, — those
who love animals, and those who do not. I have seen
them both, I have known both; and if sick or oppressed, or borne down with dreadful sympathies for a
groaning nation in mortal struggle, I should go for aid,
for pity, or the relief of kindred feeling, to those I had
seen touched with quick tenderness for the lower creation, who remember that the "whole creation travaileth
in pain together," and who learn God's own lesson of
caring for the fallen sparrow, and the ox that treadeth
out the corn. With men or women who despise animals, and treat them as mere beasts and brutes, I never
want to trust my weary heart or my aching head. But
with Dely I could have trusted both safely; and the
calf and the cat agreed with me.

So, in this happy, homely life, the sweet centre of
her own bright little world, Dely passed the first year
of her wedded life, and then the war came! Dreadful pivot of so many lives! — on it also this rude idyl
turned. George enlisted for the war.

It was not in Dely or his mother to stop him.
Though tears fell on every round of his blue socks, and
sprinkled his flannel shirts plentifully; though the old
woman's wan and wrinkled face paled and saddened,
and the young one's fair throat quivered with choking
sobs when they were alone; still, whenever George
appeared, he was greeted with smiles and cheer,

strengthened and steadied from this home armory
better than with sabre and bayonet, — " with might in
the inner man." George was a brave fellow, no doubt,
and would do good service to his free country; but it
is a question with me, whether, when the Lord calls out
his " noble army of martyrs " before the universe of
men and angels, that army will not be found officered
and led by just such women as these, who fought
silently with the flesh and the Devil by their own
hearth, quickened by no stinging excitement of battle,
no thrill of splendid strength and fury in soul and
body, no tempting delight of honor or even recognition
from their peers, upheld only by the dull, recurrent
necessities of duty and love.

At any rate, George went, and they staid. The
town made them an allowance as a volunteer's family;
they had George's bounty to begin with; and a friendly
boy from the farm near by came and sawed their wood,
took care of the garden, and, when Dely could not go
to pasture with the heifer, drove her to and fro daily.

After George had been gone three months, Dely had
a little baby. Tiny and bright as it was, it seemed
like a small star fallen down from some upper sky to
lighten their darkness. Dely was almost too happy;
and the old grandmother, fast slipping into that other
world whence baby seemed to have but newly arrived,
stayed her feeble steps a little longer to wait upon her
son's child. Yet, for all the baby, Dely never forgot
her dumb loves. The cat had still its place on the
foot of her bed; and her first walk was to the barn,
where the heifer lowed welcome to her mistress, and
rubbed her head against the hand that caressed her,
with as much feeling as a cow can show, however

much she may have. And Biddy the heifer was a
good friend to that little household all through that
long ensuing winter. It went to Dely's heart to sell
her first calf to the butcher; but they could not raise
it: and when it was taken away she threw her check
apron over her head, and buried her face deep in the
pillow, that she might not hear the cries of appeal and
grief her favorite uttered. After this, Biddy would
let no one milk her but her mistress; and many an
inarticulate confidence passed between the two while
the sharp streams of milk spun and foamed into the
pail below, as Dely's skilful hands coaxed it down.

They heard from George often. He was well, and
busy with drill and camp life, — not in active service
as yet. Incidentally, too, Dely heard of her mother.
Old Kenyon was dead of apoplexy, and Steve like to
die of drink. This was a bit of teamster's gossip, but
proved to be true. Toward the end of the winter, old
Mother Adams slept quietly in the Lord. No pain or
sickness grasped her, though she knew she was dying,
kissed and blessed Dely, sent a mother's message to
George, and took the baby for the last time into her
arms; then she laid her head on the pillow, smiled,
and drew a long breath — no more.

Poor Dely's life was very lonely. She buried her
dead out of her sight, wrote a loving, sobbing letter to
George, and began to try to live alone. Hard enough
it was. March revenged itself on the past toleration
of winter: snow fell in blinding fury; and drifts hid
the fences, and fenced the doors, all through Hartland
Hollow. Day after day Dely struggled through the
path to the barn to feed Biddy, and milk her; and a
warm mess of bread and milk often formed her only

meal in that bitter weather. It is not credible to
those who think no more of animals than of chairs and
stones, how much society and solace they afford to
those who do love them. Biddy was really Dely's
friend. Many a long day passed when no human face
but the baby's greeted her from dawn till dusk. But
the cow's beautiful purple eyes always turned to welcome her as she entered its shed-door; her wet muzzle
touched Dely's cheek with a velvet caress; and, while
her mistress drew from the downy bag its white and
rich stores, Biddy would turn her head round, and eye
her with such mild looks, and breathe such fragrance
toward her, that Dely, in her solitary and friendless
state, came to regard her as a real sentient being, capable of love and sympathy, and had an affection for her
that would seem utter nonsense to half, perhaps three-
quarters, of the people in this unsentimental world.
Many a time did the lonely little woman lay her head
on Biddy's neck, and talk to her about George, with
sobs and silences interspersed; and many a piece of
dry bread steeped in warm water, or golden carrot, or
mess of stewed turnips and bran, flavored the dry hay
that was the staple of the cow's diet. The cat was
old now, and objected to the baby so strenuously, that
Dely regarded her as partly insane from age; and
though she was kind to her of course, and fed her
faithfully, still a cat that could growl at George's baby
was not regarded with the same complacent kindness
that had always blessed her before; and, whenever the
baby was asleep at milking-time, pussy was locked into
the closet, — a proceeding she resented. Biddy, on
the contrary, seemed to admire the child, — she certainly did not object to her, — and necessarily obtained

thereby a far higher place in Dely's heart than the cat.

As I have already said, Dely had heard of her step-father's death some time before; and one stormy day, the last week in March, a team coming from Haner-ford with grain stopped at the door of the little red house, and the driver handed Dely a dirty and ill-written letter from her mother. Just such an epistle it was as might have been expected from Mrs. Kenyon, — full of weak sorrow, and entreaties to Dely to come home and live: she was old and tired; the bakery was coming to trouble for want of a good manager; the foreman was a rogue, and the business failing fast, and she wanted George and Dely there. Evidently she had not heard, when the letter began, of George's de-parture, or baby's birth; but the latter half said, "Cum anyway. I want to se the baby. Ime an old critur a-sinking into my graiv, and when george cums back from the wars he must liv hear the rest off his life."

Dely's tender heart was greatly stirred by the letter, yet she was undecided what to do. Here she was, alone and poor; there would be her mother, — and she loved her mother, though she could not respect her; there, too, was plenty for all: and, if George should ever come home, the bakery business was just the thing for him; he had energy and courage enough to redeem a sinking affair like that. But then what should she do with the cow? Puss could go home with her; but Biddy? — there was no place for Biddy. Pasture was scarce and dear about Hanerford: Dely's father had given up keeping a cow long before his death for that reason. But how could Dely leave and sell her faithful friend and companion? Her hear

sank at the thought: it almost turned the scale, for
one pitiful moment, against common sense and filial
feeling. But baby coughed, nothing more than a
slight cold; yet Dely thought, as she had often
thought before, with a quick thrill of terror, What if
baby were ever sick? Seven miles between her and
the nearest doctor; nobody to send, nobody to leave
baby with, and she herself utterly inexperienced in the
care of children. The matter was decided at once;
and, before the driver who brought her mother's letter
had come on his next journey for the answer he had
offered to carry, Dely's letter was written, sealed, and
put on the shelf, and she was busy contriving and
piecing out a warm hood and cloak for baby to ride in.

But every time she went to the barn to milk Biddy,
or feed her, the tears sprang to her eyes, and her mind
misgave her. Never before had the dainty bits of food
been so plentiful for her pet, or her neck so tenderly
stroked. Dely had written to her mother that she
would come to her as soon as her affairs were settled,
and she had spoken to Orrin Nye, who brought the
letter, to find a purchaser for her cow. Grandfather
Hollis, who bought Biddy, and in whose farmyard I
made her acquaintance, gave me the drover's account
of the matter, which will be better in his words than
mine. It seems he brought quite a herd of milch cows
down to Avondale, which is twenty miles from Hanerford, and, hearing that grandfather wanted a couple of
cows, he came to "trade with him," as he expressed
it. He had two beautiful Ayrshires in the lot, — clean
heads, shining skins, and good milkers, — that mightily
pleased the old gentleman's fancy; for he had long
brooded over his favorite scheme of a pure-blooded

herd, and the red-and-white-clouded Ayrshires showed
beautifully on his green hillside pastures, and were
good stock besides. But Aaron Stow insisted so per-
tinaciously that he should buy this red cow, that the
squire shoved his hat back, and put both his hands in
his pockets, a symptom of determination with him, and
began to question him. They fenced a while in true
Yankee fashion, till at last grandfather became exasperated.

"Look, here, Aaron Stow!" said he, "what in
thunder do you pester me so about that cow for?
She's a good enough beast, I see, for a native; but
those Ayrshires are better cows and better blood, and
you know it. What are you navigating round me for
so glib?"

"Well, now, squire," returned Aaron, whittling at
the gate with sudden vehemence, "fact is, I've set my
mind on your buyin' that critter, an' you jes' set down
on that 'ere milkin'-stool, an' I'll tell ye the rights
on't, though I feel kinder meechin' myself, to be so
soft about it as I be."

"Leave off shaving my new gate, then, and don't
think I'm going to trust a hundred and eighty-five solid
flesh to a three-legged stool. I'm too old for that.
I'll sit on the step here. Now go ahead, man."

So grandfather sat down on the step, and Aaron
turned his back against the gate, and kicked one boot
on the other. He was not used to narration.

"Well, you know we had a dreadful spell o' weather
a month ago, squire. There ha'n't never been such a
March in my day as this last; an' 'twas worse up our
way'n 'twas here; an' down to Hartland Holler was
the beat of all. Why, it snowed, an' it blowed, an' it

friz, till all natur' couldn't stan' it no more. Well,
about them days I was down to Hartland Centre
a-buyin' some fat cattle for Hanerford market; an' I
met Orrin Nye drivin' his team pretty spry, for he see
it was comin' on to snow; but, when he catched sight
o' me, he stopped the horses, an' hollered out to me:
so I stepped along, an' asked what he wanted. An' he
said there was a woman down to the Holler that had a
cow to sell, an' he knowed I was apt to buy cow-critters
along in the spring, so he'd spoke about it, for she was
kinder in a hurry to sell, for she was goin' to move.
So I said I'd see to't, an' he driv along. I thought
likely I should git it cheap, ef she was in a hurry to
sell, an' I concluded I'd go along next day: 'twa'n't
more'n seven mile from the Centre, down by a piece
o' piny woods, an' the woman was Miss Adams. I
used ter know George Adams quite a spell ago, an' he
was a likely feller. Well, it come on to snow jest as
fine an' dry as sand, an' the wind blew like needles;
an' come next day, when I started to foot it down
there, I didn't feel as though I could ha' gone ef I
hadn't been sure of a good bargain. The snow hadn't
driv much, but the weather had settled down dreadful
cold: 'twas dead still, an' the air sorter cut ye to
breathe it; but I'm naterally hardy, an' I kep' along
till I got there. I didn't feel so all-fired cold as I hev
sometimes; but when I stepped in to the door, an' she
asked me to hev a cheer by the fire, fust I knew I
didn't know nothin': I come to the floor like a felled
ox. I expect I must ha' been nigh on to dead with
clear cold, for she was the best part o' ten minutes
bringin' on me to. She rubbed my hands an' face
with camphire, an' gin me some hot tea. She hadn't

got no sperits in the house; but she did every thing a little woman could do, an' I was warmed through an' through afore long, an' we stepped out into the shed to look at the cow.

"Well, squire, I ha'n't got much natur' into me noway, an' it's well I ha'n't; but that cow beat all, I declare for't! She put her head round the minute Miss Adams come in; an', if ever you see a dumb beast pleased, that 'ere cow was tickled to pieces. She put her nose down to the woman's cheek, an' she licked her hands, an' she moved up agin' her, an' rubbed her ear on her: she all but talked. An' when I looked round, an' see them black eyes o' Miss Adams's with wet in 'em, I 'most wished I had a pocket-handker-cher myself.

"'You won't sell her to a hard master, will you?' says she. 'I want her to go where she'll be well cared for, an' I shall know where she is; for, if ever things comes right agin, I want to hev her back. She's been half my livin' an' all my company for quite a spell, an' I shall miss her dreadfully.'

"'Well,' says I, 'I'll take her down to Squire Hollis's in Avondale: he's got a cow-barn good enough for a representative to set in, an' clean water, an' chains to halter 'em up with, an' a dry yard where the water all dreens off as slick as can be; an' there a'n't such a piece o' land nowhere round for root-crops; an' the squire he sets such store by his cows an' things, I've heerd tell he turned off two Irishmen for abusin' on 'em; an' they has their bags washed, an' their tails combed, every day in the year, an' I don't know but what they ties 'em up with a blew ribbin.'"

"Get out!" growled grandfather.

"Can't, jest yet, squire, not till I've done. Anyway, I figgered it off to her, an' she was kinder consoled up to think on't; for I told her I thought likely you'd buy her cow. An' when we come to do the tradin' part, why, con-found it! she wa'n't no more fit to buy an' sell a critter than my three-year-old Hepsy. I said a piece back I ha'n't got much natur', an' a man that trades dumb beasts the biggest part o' the time hedn't oughter hev; but I swan to man! natur' was too much for me this time. I couldn't no more ha' bought that cow cheap than I could ha' sold my old gran'ther to a tin-peddler. Somehow, she was so innocent, an' she felt so to part with the critter, an' then she let me know't George was in the army; an' thinks I, I guess I'll help the gov'ment along some: I can't fight, 'cause I'm subject to rheumatiz in my back, but I can look out for them that can: so, take the hull on't, long an' broad, why, I up an' gin her seventy-five dollars for that cow, an' I'd ha' gin twenty more not to ha' seen Miss Adams's face a-lookin' arter me an' her when we went away from the door.

"So now, squire, you can take her, or leave her."

Aaron Stow knew his man. Squire Hollis pulled out his pocket-book, and paid seventy-five dollars on the spot for a native cow called Biddy.

"Now clear out with your Ayrshires!" said he irascibly. "I'm a fool, but I won't buy them too."

"Well, squire, good-day," said Aaron with a grin.

But I am credibly informed that the next week he did come back with the two Ayrshires, and sold them to grandfather, remarking to the farmer, that he "should ha' been a darned fool to take the old gentleman at his word; for he never knowed a man hanker

arter harnsome stock, but what he bought it fust oi
last.''

Now I also discovered that the regiment George enlisted in was one whose colonel I knew well: so I
wrote, and asked about Sergeant Adams. My report
was highly honorable to George, but had some bad
news in it: he had been severely wounded in the right
leg, and, though recovering, would be disabled from
further service. A fortnight after, I drove into Hanerford with Grandfather Hollis, and we stopped at the
old bakery. It looked exquisitely neat in the shop, as
well as prosperous externally, and Dely stood behind
the counter with a lovely child in her arms. Grandfather bought .about half a bushel of crackers and
cookies, while I played with the baby. As he paid for
them, he said in his kind old voice, that nobody can
hear without pleasure, —

"I believe I have a pet of yours in my barn at
Avondale, Mrs. Adams.''

Dely's eyes lighted up, and a quick flush of feeling
glowed on her pretty face.

"O sir! you did buy Biddy, then? And you are
Squire Hollis?''

"Yes, ma'am ; and Biddy is well, and well cared for,
— as fat and sleek as a mole, and still comes to her
name.''

"Thank you kindly, sir!'' said Dely, with an emphasis that gave the simple phrase most earnest meaning.

"And how is your husband, Mrs. Adams?'' said I.

A deeper glow displaced the fading blush grandfather had called out, and her beautiful eyes flashed at
me.

"Quite well, I thank you, and not so very lame. And he's coming home next week."

She took the baby from me as she spoke, and, looking in its bright little face, said, —

"Call him, baby."

"Pa-pa!" said the child.

"If ever you come to Avondale, Mrs. Adams, come and see my cows," said grandfather as he gathered up the reins. "You may be sure I won't sell Biddy to anybody but you."

Dely smiled from the steps where she stood; and we drove away.

SQUIRE PAINE'S CONVERSION.

SAMUEL PAINE was a hard-headed, "hard-fe'tured"
Yankee boy, who grew up in the old homestead with
out brothers or sisters.

Had any of those means of grace shared his joys
and sorrows, perhaps his nature would have been modi
fied; but he was sole heir of the few rugged acres,
scant pasturage for the old red cow, and the bit of
"medder-land" that reluctantly gave corn and rye
and potatoes enough for the household, and barely hay
sufficient to winter the cow and the venerable horse
that belonged to old Dibble Paine, Samuel's father.
Now, in such a case it is slave or starve in New England. Hard work is the initial lesson. Samuel's
youth of labor began early. At three years old, in
brief garments of yellow flannel, and a flaxen thatch
of hair for head-covering, he toddled in and out of the
kitchen with chips in a basket; he fed the chickens;
he rode in the hay-wagon, and was, moreover, ruled
already with a rod of iron, or rather a stout shingle,
which hung ready to hand by the chimney-piece. At
seven the Assembly's Catechism was drilled into
him, and he trudged daily a mile and back to the red
schoolhouse, doing "chores" at every odd interval;
getting up by daylight in summer, and long before in
winter, to fetch and carry for the poor, pale woman

who was wife and mother in that meagre household ;
going to meeting Sundays as faithfully as Parson
Wires himself ; and in the course of years growing up
to be a goodly youth, saving, industrious, correct, perfectly self-satisfied, and conscious of his own merits
and other people's demerits.

But the course of years takes as well as gives.
When Samuel was twenty, he was fatherless and motherless. The old farm was let on shares ; and behind
the counter of a country store in Bassett he dealt out
with strict justice — to his employer — scant yards of
calico, even measures of grass-seed, small pounds
of groceries, weakly rum, sugar not too sweet, and
many other necessities of life in the same proportion.
Old Si Jones never had so thrifty a clerk, never made
so much money in the same time, and never had so
few loungers about. In due time Samuel experienced
religion, — or said he did, — was duly examined, glibly
reeled off his inward exercises to the admiring deacons,
and at the proper season was propounded, and admitted
to the church in Bassett. He had always been a
strictly moral young man, and a sober one ; not in the
sense of temperance, but sober in habit and manner.

Samuel Paine never indulged in those youthful gaye-
ties that so many boys rejoice in. He did not waste
his hard-earned substance in riotous picnics, husking-
frolics, boat-rides, or sleighing-parties ; he never used
tobacco in any form, never drank cider, or " waited "
on any girl in Bassett, though there was the usual
feminine surplus of a New-England village in this one.
In the evening he read law diligently in Squire Larkin's office, because he thought it might be useful to
him hereafter. He sat in the singers' seat in the meet-

ing-house, his straight, long face. cold gray eyes,
sleek light hair, and immaculate linen, looking respectable enough for a whole congregation. He had
a class in Sunday school, — a class of big girls, all of
whom hated him thoroughly, but never dared own it.
Armed with "Barnes's Notes" and "Cruden's Concordance," he did his duty to his class in explaining
and expounding the doctrine of the lesson; but, while
he impressed the letter on their minds, the sweet an
living spirit never lit his cool eye, or warmed his accu-
rate speech. Whatever else those young girls learned
of Samuel Paine, they never learned to love the Lord
or his words; for he knew not how to teach them. His
soul had never yet found its level, had never had the
lesson that comes to us all some time in our lives,
whether we accept it or not; and he went on in his own
narrow way without let or hinderance.

Before Samuel was twenty-five, Si Jones retired from
business in Bassett, being persuaded by his wife to
remove into Vermont, where her friends lived. He
had made a good deal of money; and being childless,
and well under his wife's thumb, she had induced him
to sell out, and go back to her old home. Now came
the time Samuel Paine had long looked for. He had
saved, spared, pinched, to this end. He bought out
ne store and the small frame-house that contained it,
— a house with two rooms up stairs, and a kitchen in
the little wing, Part of the money he paid down in
cash, part borrowed on a mortgage: the rest he was
forced to give notes for.

"Well," said 'Bijah Jones, a far-off cousin of Si's,
and the village loafer and joker, "guess folks'll hev to
keep their eyes peeled now. I tell ye, Samwell Paine

beats the Dutch to drive a bargain. Ye won't know where ye be, fust ye know any thing. He'll sell ye a pair o' store pants in five minnits, when ye don't want 'em no more'n a toad wants a pocket."

"Dew tell!" sputtered old Grandsir Baker, who had just come over from the town-house with a hank of yarn to trade off for some molasses. "Well, well, well! Hows'ever, he can't sell me nothin', cos I hain't got no money. Ye can't get blood outen a stun, nohow. He, he, he!"

"Blessed be nothin'!" dryly put in 'Bijah.

And all this while Samuel was announcing his principles in the store to a knot of farmers and village worthies come in for their weekly supplies for the first time since S. Paine's name had been seen above the door.

"Yes, sir; yes, sir! I've cleaned up consider'ble. I hope to clear up more. I 'xpect to conduct this business on a line, gentlemen, — a straight line, so to speak, seemin'ly, as it were. There ain't no rewl better for all things than the Golden Rewl. That contains the sperrit and principle of the hull thing: do's you'd like ter be done by. That's my idee in short partikelar metre."

A dry, rattling laugh emphasized this conclusion, and a sort of unwilling "Haw, haw!" chorussed it from the audience. 'Bijah Jones had drawn near enough to the open door to hear part of the sentence, and grinned widely.

"Come along, grandsir," shouted he to the hobbling old fellow from the poor-house. "Strike while th' iron's hot. He's talking Scripter with all fury: naow's your time to swop that air yarn. Bet you'll git a hull cask o' 'lasses!"

Grandsir Baker did not quicken his halting pace for
this advice, and it is not on record that he got any
more molasses than he expected to: but, when he got
back to the poor-house, he told Mrs. Wells that molasses
had riz, and yarn hadn't; Samwell Paine told him so.

A village store — *the* store — is not a matter of
hazard, but a vital necessity.   There is no competition
to be dreaded in a place like Bassett.   Nobody else
had capital or experience to set up an opposition shop:
there was no better place to trade within twenty miles,
and it was by the very doors of Bassett people.   If they
did not quite like the way things were conducted, they
must still abide by it, for there was no help.   And in
many things the business was mightily improved since
Si Jones's time.   The shop itself was clean and orderly.
Cod-fish did not lurk in a dusty corner behind patent
ploughs, and tea-leaves did not fall into the open flour-
barrel.   If sand was suspected in the sugar, there were
certainly no chips of tobacco in its grainy mass; and
calico and candy did not live on the same shelf; or
raisins, bar soap, and blacking occupy a drawer together.
The floor was swept, washed, and sanded, the counters
scoured off, the cobwebs banished, the steps repaired,
the windows kept bright and clear, the scales shining.
If S. Paine's clerk had hard work for a lad of eighteen,
his employer could quote Scripture with tremendous
fluency and fitness when the boy's old mother remon-
strated.

"Well, Miss Bliss, I don't deny John has to work.
So do I; so do I.   It is good for a man to bear the
yoke in his youth, Scripter says.   There ain't nothin'
better for no man than work.   'By the sweat o' thy
brow,' ye know.   The sperrit an' principle of the

Golden Rewl is my sperrit an' principle : do's you'd be done by. Yes, yes, ef I was a boy agin, I'd want ter be fetched up jest as I was fetched up, — on hard work an' poor livin'. That rouses the grit, I tell ye. I'm a-doin' by John jest as I was done by ; so don't ye resent it. It's fur his best int'rest, soul an' **body**.'' With which chopped straw poor Mrs. Bliss's motherly heart was forced to content itself, for there was no other refreshment.

Perhaps, in this application of the " Golden Rewl," Samuel Paine forgot how his childish flesh had wept and cringed under the hardships of his early life, how his childish soul had flamed with rage under the torture and insult of the unjustly applied shingle, and the constant watching of stern and pitiless eyes. He may not have remembered how his growing bones ached under heavy burdens, and his spare flesh craved enough even of such diet as pork, cabbage, and rye-bread to allay the pangs of childish hunger and the demands of daily growth. But, if he did not, is that excuse? Is not the command explicit to " *remember* all the way the Lord thy God led thee "? and is forgetfulness without sin?

But the man kept on in his respectable career, buying and selling, — buying at the lowest rates, and selling at the highest ; faithful externally to all his duties ; ever present in church ; never late at his Sunday-school class ; never missing a prayer-meeting ; a zealous exhorter ; " a master-hand at prayin'," as Widow Bliss allowed ; deeply interested in the work of missions ; and a stated contributor to the Bible Society : but at home, — no, it was no home, — at his store, strict in every matter of business, merciless to his debtors, close and niggardly even to his best customers, harsh to his

clerk, and greedy of every smallest profit. Nobody
ever went to him for friendly offices. Nobody asked
him to be neighborly; no subscription-list for a poor
man with a broken leg or a burned-down barn ever
crossed the door-sill of the store. When all other
young men went to quiltings and sociables, he staid at
the desk, amusing himself with his ledger or a ponder-
ous law-book borrowed from Squire Larkin. So he
lived, or existed, till he was thirty years old; and one
fine day Squire Larkin died, and left behind him an
only daughter, a goodly sum of money, and a vacant
office of postmaster. Now was Samuel's time again.
He attended the funeral, and appeared to be deeply
affected by the loss of an old acquaintance. He called
on Miss Lucy as early as was proper, and made an
offer for the squire's law-books. They were useless to
Lucy now, and she had not thought of selling them.
The nearest city was full thirty miles away, and she had
not even a friend in its busy sphere; nobody in Bassett
wanted law-books: so Samuel Paine bought them for a
quarter of their value, and Lucy never found it out.
His next step was to petition for the post-office: here,
again, nobody interfered. It would be very convenient
to all concerned that the post-office should be in the
store: that was its natural and fit situation. When
Squire Larkin took it into his hands, his old law-office
stood close by Si Jones's place of business; but that
tiny tenement had been burned this long time, and the
mails carried to Mr. Larkin's house, and distributed in
the south parlor, where, also, his books and his few
clients found a place. Now, if S. Paine got the office,
it would be "everlastin' handy," everybody said: so
everybody signed the petition, and postmaster Paine
was sworn in.

Lucy Larkin was no longer young : she was twenty-eight at least, — a gentle, faded, pretty woman, with mild blue eyes, and thin soft hair of dull brown, and soft trembling lips. She was not forcible or energetic ; she pottered about the house a good deal, and had headaches, and went punctually to sewing-circles. Her literary tastes were not violent. She was fond of Tupper and the " Lady's Book ;" and every day she read a chapter in the Bible, and tried with all her simple heart to be good. But she had not much vitality in body or soul ; and after her father, who had always been her tender companion and guide, left her to herself, Lucy was dreadfully lonely. The squire left her money well tied up ; but she had all the income, and the principal was also well invested. Here was another opening for S. Paine.

"It really seems providential," he said to himself, as he carefully sanded the last barrel of sugar, having first filled his own jar. For, since he had taken the store, he had lived in the two rooms above it, taken care of his own wants himself, and hired Widow Bliss one day in the week to do his washing, ironing, and mending, all of which must be achieved within those twelve hours, or her dollar (according to agreement) was forfeited. " Yes, it does seem to be a leadin'. She can't sell that house, — there ain't nobody ni Bassett wants to buy a house, — an' it's real handy to the store. I can put Widder Bliss up stairs, an' then John won't lose no time a-comin' an' a-goin' to his meals : he'll be real handy to his work, an' I can stop the rent out o' his wages, so's to be sure on't. Guess I won't move them law-books yit. Things seems to be gittin' inter shape somehow. I'll fetch round there to-morrow

night, if I'm spared, an' visit with her a little.'' And,
covering up the sugar carefully, Samuel Paine took
himself off to bed.

Poor Lucy was lonely, and Mr. Paine made himself
agreeable. He condoled with her in good set terms,
quoted Scripture, and threw in verses of Dr. Watts in
an appropriate manner ; blew his nose sonorously when
Lucy cried a little, and thereby produced in her innocent mind the impression that he was crying too. And
after he had cheered her up a little with tender exhortations not to give way too much to her feelings, to
remember that man was made to mourn, that everybody must die some time or other, and that no doubt
Squire Larkin, or rather "our dear departed friend,''
enjoyed the "hallelooyers'' of heaven much better
than his daughter's society and keeping post-office,
with other appropriate remarks of the same kind, he
bade her good-night, tenderly squeezing her hand as he
left, and causing the poor little woman to feel doubly
lonely, and to wish he would come back.

Ah! why do we try to comfort those whom death
has bereft? Why do we go over these vain conven-
tionalisms which we know are futile? Can words like
these bring back the smile, the voice, the touch, for
which we hunger with maddening eagerness? Can it
help us, in our hopeless longing, to know that others
suffer the same vital anguish? that to die is the sure
fate of all we love, sooner or later? or that we must
submit to these solitudes and cryings, and strong tears,
because we cannot help ourselves? No, ten thousand
times no! There is but one consolation of real virtue,
and that is the closer clinging of the soul to Him who
cannot die. The rings that clasped these broken sup·

ports must close on higher branches, even on the Tree
of Life ; and if human love takes us in its tender arms,
and silently kisses away our tears, it may bring us still
nearer to the divine ; for, if we so love one another,
shall not God who made us love us eternally and
infinitely? But Lucy Larkin was one of the bending
sort of women, who never break under any blow. She
went her placid way about the world she knew, did all
her tranquil duties, and prayed hard to be resigned.
It made resignation easier to have Mr. Paine come in
once or twice a week ; and when, after a decent interval, he proposed to fill the vacant place in her heart,
the little smitten plant rose up meekly, and accepted
the pallid sunshine with gentle surprise and content.
She was so glad not to be lonely any more, and so
astonished that such a smart, pious man as Samuel
Paine should have thought to make her an offer, — " she
that wasn't talented, nor good-lookin', nor real young."

Unworldly little soul ! Her twenty thousand dollars
were more to this " smart " man than the beauty of
Helen, the gifts of Sappho, or the divine sparkle and
freshness of ideal girlhood ; but she never guessed it.
So they were married just a year after her father's
death. Mrs. Bliss was installed into the tenement over
the store ; and Squire Larkin's handsome old house,
being freshened up with paint, and set in thorough
order, though without any expense of new furnishings,
seemed to renew its youth. Perhaps, when Mrs. Paine
learned to know her husband better, she did not experience all that superhuman bliss which poets and ro-
mancers depict as the result of matrimony — but then
who does? Most of us learn to be content if we can
rub along easily with our life-partners, and cultivate a

judicious blindness and deafness, in the wise spirit of
good old Quaker Ellwood's well-known hymn : —

> "Oh that mine eyes might closèd be
> To what becomes me not to see;
> That deafness might possess mine ear
> To what becomes me not to hear!"

Lucy was not consciously so wise as this ; but she had
the greatest respect for her husband's piety and smartness ; and, if she could not understand certain of his
manners and customs, she still thought a man could
not err who made such long and fervent prayers at
family devotions, and who always had the Golden Rule
on his lips as a professed rule of life. She was not
naturally demonstrative : few New-England women
are. If they were as afraid of being angry, or cross,
or peevish before people, as they are of being affectionate and tender, life would be mightily sweetened to
many of us. But when our sour but sublime old Puri-
tan fathers made it a legal offence for a man to kiss
his wife on Sunday, what wonder that their descend-
ants' teeth should be set on edge?

But, if Mrs. Paine was not caressing and affectionate
in manner, Mr. Paine was still less so. If he had any
heart beside the muscular organ of that name, he had
it yet to discover : certainly Lucy had not awakened
it any more than his last investment in groceries.
Things went on very calmly with the pair for a year
or two ; the only disturbance being a sudden and unreasonable crying-fit of Lucy's, in which Mr. Paine
detected her, coming home on an errand quite unexpectedly.

"I ca-ca-can't help it!" she sobbed hysterically,
when he sternly demanded. —

" What on airth's the matter with ye, Loocy? Stop, now, right off. Stop, I tell ye, an' speak up."

" Oh, o-h, o-h, husband! Miss Nancy Tuttle's ben here: she's ben a-talkin' awful. She said she considered 'twas her dooty to come an' deal with me, becoz — becoz — oh, o-h, o-h!'"

" Stop it, now, thunderin' quick, Loocy! I can't stan' here all day."

" O-h! she said she heerd a lot of talk against you, husband; an' she thought I'd ought to know it, so's't I could use my influence with you, an' kinder persuade you to do different."

A grim smile twisted S. Paine's stiff lips. Lucy's influence with him, indeed!

" Well, well," said he, " go ahead: let's hear what I've ben a-doin'."

" O-h! oh, dear! She said you sanded the sugar down to the store, an' put water into the sperrits, an' asked folks two prices for butter. Oh, dear! I never was so beat in all my days."

" H-m," growled Mr. Paine. " I'll settle with her myself, Loocy."

" Oh, you can't! you can't noways. She's gone off in the stage to York State to live. She said she felt as though she must free her mind before she went, so she jest stepped in."

" Darn her!'"

Luckily for Lucy she was sobbing so hard she did not hear this expletive, which had all the force of a stronger oath, coming from those decorous lips, yet was not quite open profanity.

" Look a-here, Loocy,' Mr. Paine began: " jest you shut your head about that scandalous old maid's talk. Hain't I told ye time an' agin that the sperrit an' principle o' the Golden Rewl was my sperrit an' principle? What's the harm ef I sell poor folks butter a leetle mite cheeper'n I sell it to folks with means? An', ef I put a pint o' water inter Bije Jones's rum-jug, I do't out o' consideration for his fam'ly: he can't afford to buy clear sperrit. As for shoogar, it's sanded afore it comes to me, you better believe! Now don't ye go a-tellin' everybody all these lies: they grow every time they're sot out in fresh ground. There ain't nothin' so good for a fool's talk nor a liar's as a hullsome lettin' alone." With which piece of verbal wisdom Samuel Paine went his way, and Lucy subsided to her customary and domestic meekness.

But the current of their lives was mightily disturbed, some months after this conversation, by the advent into the quiet household of a big obstreperous baby. Lucy was blessed for once in her life to the very overflowing of her torpid heart. Mr. Paine would have been better pleased with a boy, to take the store and the post-office after him; but still he was pleased. An odd stir of feeling astonished him when he saw the helpless little creature; and with natural forecast he reflected that there might be a boy yet, and so forgave her for being only a girl. However, when years slipped by, and no boy came, the sturdy, bright, merry little girl made her way boldly into her father's good graces, and almost reconciled him to her sex. Miss Louise ruled her mother, of course; that was in the nature of things: but all the village looked on in wonder to see the mas-tery she achieved over Samuel Paine, or as he was now called, — partly because of the legal information he had acquired, and on a pinch dispensed, from his father-in-law's library, and partly because he had well stepped into that gentleman's shoes otherwise, — Squire Paine.

Louise was an unaccountable offshoot from the parental tree certainly. Her vivid complexion, waving dark hair, brilliant brown eyes, and well-made figure, were not more at variance with the aspects of her father and mother than her merry, honest, and fearless nature was with their dispositions. Neither of them tried to govern her, after a few futile attempts. Her mother did not see any need of it. To her the child was perfect, a gift of God, held in fear and trembling, lest he should recall it from mortal idolatry, but, being such a gift, to be entertained as an angel. Squire Paine never held any such nonsensical idea as this. But, if he undertook to scold or reprove mademoiselle, she instantly sprang into his arms, wound her fat hands in his coat-collar, and snuggled her curly head against his lips with a laugh like a bobolink's; and, utterly routed, the squire would lift her to his shoulder, and march her off to the store, to range among raisin-boxes, sugar-barrels, and candy-jars to her heart's content, feeling all the while half ashamed of the unwonted warmth in his breast, the difficulty of speech, the soft cowardice that carried him away captive, bound to the chariot of this small conqueror, who was gracious enough not to triumph, only because she conquered unconsciously.

So matters went on year after year. In spite of sweets and spoiling, Louise grew up strong and healthy, thanks to the open air in which it was her royal pleasure to live and move, and have her being. A city mother would have wept over the brown complexion,

in which living crimson burned with a warm splendor
unknown to milk and roses; and any boarding-school
phalanx would have shuddered at the well-tanned, slender hands that were so deft at nutting, fishing, picking
berries, and digging roots. But Bassett people were
not fine. They only laughed and nodded as Louise
tore down the wide street on the squire's ancient horse.
lashed to a horrid gallop by an old trunk-strap whanged
about his sides, and the thumps of stout country boots,
when he dared relax this spirited pace.

By and by Lucy, quite ashamed of herself, in all
these years of mild motherly bliss, to think she had
never given her husband a son, began to fade and fail
a little, and at last declined into her grave as gently as
a late spring snow-drift melts into the brown grasses.
Louise was fifteen now, and knew no more about housekeeping than a deer in the forest, though successive
seasons at the academy had given her a fair education
for a country girl who did not need or intend to teach
for her living. She mourned for her dear, patient little
mother far more than she missed her; for Lucy was too
inert, too characterless, to leave a wide vacancy in her
home. There are some people whose departure takes
the sunshine of our days, the salt of our food, the
flavor of our pleasures, yea, the breath of our lives,
away with them, whose loss is a wound never to be
healed, always bleeding, smarting, burning into our
very souls, till time shall be no more; and there are
others, whose death, after the first natural burst of feeling, fails to impress itself deeply, even on their nearest
and dearest. The selfish, the exacting, the tasteless,
timid natures, that were scarce more than vegetable in
their humanity, — these are lightly mourned; and of
these last was Lucy Paine.

It became necessary, it is true, to put a housekeeper in her place ; for the " hired girl " whom Squire Paine had unwillingly consented to install in the kitchen when his wife's strength began to fail, could not be trusted to manage the household : so Mr. Paine bethought himself of a second-cousin living in a small village up the country, of whom he had now and then heard incidentally, and happened to know was still unmarried, and pursuing her trade of tailoress about Hermon and the vicinity. So he wrote to Miss Roxy Keep to come down at once to Bassett and see him, as Hermon was too far for him to go, taking time from his business which he could not spare. It was made very plain in Squire Paine's letter that Miss Roxy's visit was purely a matter of business ; and her answer was as business-like as could be desired. She could not, she said, afford a journey to Bassett, unless it resulted in some purpose of good : if Squire Paine wanted to see her enough to pay her fare one way, she was willing to " resk " the other half. This curt and thrifty,note rather pleased the squire ; for, though he did not want to risk his money any more than Miss Roxy, still he thought her proposition showed her to be of his own frugal and forehanded sort, and he at once closed with those terms.

It might be a curious matter of investigation to note the influence different occupations have upon those who pursue them. Why is it that a tailoress was always incisive, practical, full of resource, acute, fearless, and even snappy? Did anybody ever see a meek woman useful with cloth and shears? Do the masculine habiliments which she fashions impart a virile vigor, and the implements of her trade a man-like strength, to the mind which plans and the hand which wields them? But we have no time for inductive science here. When Squire Paine met Roxy Keep at the door, he was at once struck by her compact aspect and entire self-possession. Her gown of dark home-made gingham, and thick plaid shawl, were simply the most useful garments that could be. Beauty did not excuse their being, much less that of the severe Leghorn bonnet, without flower or feather, tied down under her chin with a sturdy greenish ribbon that must have been her grandmother's. But over all these the sensible face, the keen, dark eyes, firm mouth, and dominant nose, forbade any idea of ridicule or contempt to be associated with Miss Roxy, whatever she chose to wear. The squire was as urbane as he knew how to be.

"Set down, cousin Roxy, set down. I'll take ye over to the house in a minnit. I've hed to put in a new clerk, ye see. John Bliss he tho't he could do better in the city: so he up an' left me sudden, — too sudden re'lly, considerin' him an' me hed ben together so long An' now 'Lisha Squires has took his place. 'Lisha's a likely young man, for what I know — well eddicated; father's a minister o' the gospel; got run down a-preachin'. His wife had means — not much, not much, but 'nough to buy a farm: so they traded with me for th' old humstead, an' he's a-farmin' on't, an' 'Lisha he's gi'n up goin' to college, an' took John Bliss's place here. He's ruther high-strung, to be sure; but he's smart, real smart, an' I don't know as I could ha' did better. He's a-onheadin' some barr'ls now. A-h! there he is."

And a handsome young fellow, grave and sad be-

yond his years, came up from the cellar with a hatchet
in his hand. Miss Roxy's keen eyes read that open
face at once. She felt the purest pity for the misplaced boy, whose education was wasted, and his nature disgusted, by the repellent character of his duties
as well as his employer. Elisha was indeed misplaced ,
but he was in his daily way a hero, and to be heroic
in the petty drudgery of a distasteful life is a thousand
times harder than to win splendid battles. He had
given up every thing to help his feeble father and his
six sisters ; so had his mother : and neither of them
looked upon their sacrifices as more than a matter of
course, which, perhaps, was the one touch superior
even to heroism.

But Miss Roxy, used to that sort of intercourse with
many, perhaps most, of the families in her neighbor-
hood, which is attributed to the proverbial *valet de
chambre*, was yet so much more perceptive than that
stupid French man-servant, that she knew a hero even
in a country store ; and she turned away with the
squire, carrying in her heart a fund of admiration and
good will that was to stand Elisha in stead at a future
time of need.

In the library of Squire Larkin's time the next hour
was spent by Samuel Paine and Roxy Keep in a passage of arms. He was determined to secure Roxy to
manage his establishment on his own terms : and she
was willing to be secured, but it must be on her terms ;
and, being a tailoress, she carried the day. In consideration of the little home she left in Hermon, and
the lucrative trade she left, she required of the squire
a written guaranty that her services should continue
for two years in any case, subject only to her own

change of mind; that her salary should be paid quarterly, under pain of her immediate departure if it failed to come to hand; and that the aforesaid salary should be a sufficient equivalent for the trade she gave up. After much conversation, the squire yielded all these points, though with no good grace.

"Well, now I've gi'n up to ye," said he, "I'd like to know how soon ye can come, Roxy. Things is a-goin' every which way here. Lowisy's a good girl — she's a good enough girl; but she ain't nothin' *but* a girl, an' she ain't no more fit to run a house'n she is to preach a sermon: so I'd like ye to come back's quick as ye can."

"I dono's I need to go," curtly and promptly answered Miss Roxy. "I reckoned I should stay when I come: so I sold out my house to deacon Treadwell's widder, an' I fetched my trunks along. They're over to Reading depot; and the stage-driver he'll take the checks to-morrer, and fetch 'em back. I don't never let no grass grow under *my* feet, Squire Paine."

"Land alive! I should think not!" ejaculated the astonished squire. So Miss Roxy staid, and the house was stirred up from beneath to meet her. Bridget gave notice just in time not to have it given to her; and brush in hand, the fiercest of bandanna handker chiefs tied over her crisp black hair, Miss Roxy began that awful "setting to rights" which is at once the privilege and the necessity of strenuous souls like hers. At first Louise was half inclined to rebel: the slipshod family rule, or misrule, had just suited her youthful carelessness. But Miss Roxy's keen humor, pleasant common sense, and comfortable efficiency, soon en- listed Louise on her side; and the girl could not help

enjoying the bright order, the speckless comfort, the
savory meals, the thrift that was not·meanness, and
the frugality that could be discreetly generous, which
followed Miss Roxy's reign: and at the end of two
years the squire was glad enough to renew the guaranty which this foreseeing woman still demanded of
him. Well for her, well for all of them, was it that
he did so sign.

In the mean time Squire Paine had gone his way,
buying and selling, and talking much about the "Golden
Rewl," and many small tiffs had ensued between him
and Miss Roxy on points of domestic economy. But
the squire knew, if he had never read, that discretion
is the better part of valor, and considering just in time
that housekeeping was not his forte, and was Miss
Roxy's, he always beat a retreat after these battles,
and not always with flying colors. But now, toward
the beginning of this third year, there began to be
trouble in the camp. Elisha Squires, in common with
various other youths of Bassett, had found out that
Louise Paine was charming above all other girls of the
vicinity; and the squire's house became a sort of be-
sieged castle, greatly to his disgust and indignation.

"I won't hev it! I won't hev it!" stormed he one
fine night, when the last of seven callers had gone from
the front-door, and Louise judiciously slipped off to
bed.

"Won't hev what?" calmly inquired Roxy, who sat
by the "keeping-room" table, toeing off a stocking.

"Why, I won't hev so many fellers a-comin' here
the hull etarnal time. There ain't no use on't, an' I
tell ye I won't hev it. I won't, as sure's ye live."

"What be you goin' to do about it?" was Roxy's
cool rejoinder.

"I'll lock the doors."

"Then they'll come into the back-winder," smiled the exasperating spinster. "Look here, Squire Paine," and she laid down her knitting, and confronted him as one who

"Drinks delight of battle with his peers,"

"you're a master-hand to talk about the Golden Rewl : how'd you ha' liked it ef Squire Larkin had locked the door to this house on you?"

"He hadn't no call to : he was dead."

"Now don't jump no fences that way. 'Spose he'd ben alive?"

"I dono's I'm called to tell ye. I'm a professor in good an' reg'lar standin', an' the Golden Rewl hes allers ben my standard o' livin' ; an' the sperrit and principle o' the Golden Rewl is to do to others as you'd wish to be done by ; an' ef I was a gal I should be glad to hev the doors locked on a passel o' fellers that come foolin' around nights."

"You're life-everlastin' sure o' that, be ye?" was the dry rejoinder.

"Well, ef she ain't, she'd orter be ; an' I'm free to conclude that Lowisy doos what she'd orter, bein' my child — and her ma's."

"I don't believe no great in hinderin' young folks's ways, Squire Paine. It's three wheels to a wagon to be young, an' hinderin' don't overset nothin' : it's more apt to set it, a long sight. Don't you never expect Lowisy to git married?"

"I dono's I do, an' I dono *as* I do. Married life is an onsartin state. Mebbe Lowisy'd be better off to stay to hum with me. Anyway, there ain't no sech

hurry : 'tain't the best goods go off the fust.   An'
I tell ye what, Roxy, I do expect she'll hark to me
about who she marries, and not go an' git tied up to
some poor Jack.''

'' Then I tell *you* what, Samwell Paine, you expect
nothin', an' you'll sup sorrow.   Girls will pick out
their own husbands to the day after never, for all you.
I always hold that there's two things a woman had
oughter pick out for herself, spite o' fate ; and them
two is her husband an' her carpets.''

'' An' I expect to pick 'em both out for Lowisy,''
answered the undaunted squire, as he marched off to
bed, holding his tallow candle askew, and dropping hot
tears — of tallow — as he went.

But as fate, or Louise, would have it, Squire Paine
was not to pick out either of these essentials for his
daughter.   She was fast drifting into that obstinate
blessedness which is reserved for youth and love,
which laughs at parents and guardians, defies time and
circumstance, and too often blinds the brightest eyes,
and brings the most fastidious hands to

    '' Wreathe thy fair large ears, my gentle joy,''

and finds out too late it is Bottom the weaver.

In Louise's case, however, there was no danger of
such waking : she had good reason for her preference.
Elisha Squires, her father's clerk, was a handsome,
well-educated, energetic young fellow, — a gentleman
by nature and breeding both.   Louise had pitied him
ten thousand times for his unfit position in her father's
employment, before he perceived that she was interested the least in him or his occupation ; and, when it
dawned on the busy and weary soul that one bright

blossom looked over the paling into his desert life, what was the natural impulse that followed? It is not a young man who "loves the wild rose, and leaves it on its stalk," literally or figuratively; and these juvenile idiots fell fathoms deep in love with each other, entirely unconscious of the melancholy fact that one was the richest girl in Bassett, and the other working for daily bread. Arcadia could not have shown more divine simplicity. But Bassett was not Arcadia; and when sundry jealous and disappointed swains discovered that "Lowisy Paine" would go home from prayer-meetings with 'Lisha Squires, had actually been seen lingering with him at her father's front-gate in the starry May darkness, even after the nine-o'clock bell had rung, and was sure to welcome him on a Sunday night, though she might snap and snarl at them, then Louise's troubles began. Prayer-meetings must be attended; but the squire went to and fro with her himself, and Elisha could not be spared from the store to attend them at all. Squire Paine hated to lose his clerk, but he would not lose his daughter: so, with the obtuse perception of the heavy father from time immemorial, he rushed into the *mêlée* like some floundering elephant into a flower-bed.

"Lowisy," said he, one Sunday night, after the row of adorers were dispersed, Elisha Squires among them, "hear to me now! I ain't a-goin' to hev you courted the hull time by these here fellers. You've got to stop it. 'Specially I won't have ye careerin' around with 'Lisha: he's poorer'n poverty, an' as stuck up as though he was mighty Cæsar. I've fetched ye up, an' gi'n ye a good eddication, an' you ain't a-goin' to throw yourself away on no sech trash."

The hot color rushed up to Louise's forehead, her red lip curled, and unspeakable disdain expressed itself, as she looked straight into her father's face ; but she did not say a word.   She left the room with perfect composure, stopping to pick a dry leaf from her pet geranium, and walked up the stairs with a slow precision that ought to have spoken volumes to her father's ear, as it did to Roxy's.

" Well, you've done it now," remarked that respectable woman.

" Yes, I guess I hev," was the squire's complacent answer, quite misapprehending the sense in which he had done it.   " I guess I've put a spoke inter that wheel, an' sideways too."

Roxy gave one of the silent chuckles which meant deep amusement, and took herself off to bed.   She was not a woman to interfere with the course of true love between Louise and Elisha, both of whom had become special favorites of hers since their first acquaintance ; but, as she said to herself, she would not " make nor meddle " in this matter, having full confidence in Louise's power of managing her own affairs, and far too much reverence and delicacy in her own nature to be a match-maker.   But the squire went on from bad to worse, and, in his blind zeal to have his own way, brought things to a swift conclusion ; for, having given Elisha notice that he should need him no longer, he was more than surprised one fine July morning to find that Louise had left him too, — that the pair had gone together.   The squire was black with rage when the fact was announced to him by Miss Roxy, and a brief and defiant note from Louise put into his hand.   He raved, raged, even swore, in his first wild fury, and paced up and down the kitchen like a wild animal.

Miss Roxy eyed him with a peculiar expression. She felt that her hour had come. As she afterward said, "I should ha' bust ef I hadn't spoke. I'd ben a-hankerin' to give it to him quite a spell, but I held my tongue for Lowisy's sake. But thinks sez I, now's your time, Roxanny Keep; pitch in an' do your dooty. An' I tell ye it whistled of itself. Seemed as though 'twa'n't me re'lly, but somethin' makin' a tin horn out o' my lips to rouse him up to judgment." And certainly Miss Roxy was roused herself : she confronted the squire like a Yankee lioness.

"Look a-here, Samwell Paine : it's time somebody took ye to do. You've ben a-buyin' an' a-sellin', an' a-rakin' an' a-scrapin', till your soul — ef you've got any — is nigh about petered out. You call yourself a Christian an' a professor, an' a follerer of the Golden Rewl, do ye? An' here you be, cussin' an' swearin' like a Hivite an' a Jeboosite, an' all the rest on 'em, because things ain't jest as you would have 'em to be. You hain't had no bowels of compassion for Lowisy no more'n ef you was her jailer, instead of her pa. What's the matter with 'Lisha Squires? He's a honest, good-disposed, reliable feller as ever was, good enough for anybody's girl; a Christian too, — not one o' the sugar-sandin', rum-waterin', light-weight kind, but a real one. He don't read the Golden Rewl t'other side up, as you do, I tell ye. You make it doin' to other folks just what you want to do, an' lettin' them go hang. I tell ye the hypocrite's hope shall perish, an' you're one on 'em as sure as the world. 'Tain't sayin' Lord, Lord, that makes folks pious : it's doin'

the will o' God, justice, an' mercy, an' lovin'-kind-
ness.''

Here Roxy paused for breath; and the astounded
squire ejaculated, '' Roxanny Keep!''

'' Yes, that's my name: I ain't afeared to own it,
nor to set it square to what I've said. I hain't lived
here goin' on three year, an' seen your ways, for nothin'.
I've had eyes to behold your pinchin' an' sparin' an'
crawlin'; grindin' poor folks's faces, an' lickin' rich
folks's platters; actin' as though your own daughter
was nothin' but a bill of expense to ye, an' a block to
show off your pride an' vanity, not a livin', lovin' soul
to show the way to heaven to. An' now she's quit.
She's got a good, lovin', true-hearted feller to help her
along where you didn't know the way, and didn't want
to, neither; an' you're ravin' mad 'cause he hain't got
no money, when you've got more'n enough for all on
ye. Samwell Paine, you ain't no Christian, not 'cordin'
to gospel truth, ef you have been a professor nigh on
to forty year. You no need to think you was converted, for you never was. Folks ain't converted to
meanness an' greediness an' self-seekin', an' wrath an'
malice. The Lord don't turn 'em into the error of their
ways: he turns 'em out on't. Ef you was a minister
in the pulpit, or a deacon handin' the plate, you ain't
no Christian 'thout you act like one; an' that's the
etarnal fact on't. You've ben a livin' lie all these
years; an' you've ended by drivin' your only daughter,
your own flesh an' blood, the best thing the Lord ever
give ye, out o' house an' home 'cause you was mad
after money. An' it'll happen unto ye accordin' to
the word o' the Lord about sech folks: you'll be
drownded in destruction an' perdition, an' pierce your·

self through with many sorrers, ef you don't flee for
your life from sech things, and foller after righteous-
ness, godliness, an' the rest on 'em. You'd oughter
go down on your poor old knees, an' pray to be converted at the 'leventh hour. There, I've freed my
mind, thank the Lord! an' there won't be none o' your
blood found on my skirts ef the last day comes in to-
morrer mornin'." With which the exhausted lecturer
heaved a long breath, and began to mop her heated
face vigorously with her inseparable bandanna handkerchief, which might have symbolized to the audience,
had there been any, a homely victorious banner.

The squire stood amazed and afraid. In all the long
course of his life nobody had ever before gainsaid him.
Outward respect and consideration had been his portion: now the ground cracked under his feet, and he
found himself in a new land. He did not go to the
store that day: he stumbled out of Roxy's sight, and
shut himself up in the unused parlor, where alternate
storms of rage, conviction, despair, and scorn, assailed
him for many hours. It was, indeed, a dreadful battle
that he fought in the musty silence of that darkened
room, pacing up and down like a caged tiger. Roxy
had spoken awful words; but they were milk and honey
compared to the echo which his late-awakened conscience gave them: still he fought with a certain savage courage against the truths that were toppling over
to crush him, and justified himself to his own accusing
soul with a persistent hardihood that had better served
a better cause. It was reserved for God's own stroke
to bring sweet waters out of this rock: Moses and the
rod had smitten it in vain. Just as his courage seemed
to aid him, and he had resolved to send Roxy back to

Hermon and her tailoring, and brave out the judgment of his fellow-men and the desertion of Louisa, nay, more, to revenge himself for that desertion by refusing her aid or comfort, or even recognition of any kind, — just then, as he had settled down into his self-complacency, and wilful disregard of God's own words, pelted at him as they had been by Roxy, he heard an outer door open, invading steps, voices of low tumult, a sort of whispering horror and stifled grief drawing nearer to his retreat, and the door opened very slowly, disclosing the stern features of Parson Peters, the village minister. Not altogether stern now was that long and meagre visage : a sort of terror mingled with pity softened its rigid lines.

"My brother," he said, lifting one hand, as he was wont to do when praying over a coffin, and facing the troubled and inflamed countenance of Squire Paine, — "my brother, the hand of the Lord is upon you this day. Your child has been taken. There has been a terrible accident to the train by which they left Reading station, and news has come that both are — gone."

Like a forest tree into which the woodman sets his last stroke, the squire tottered, paused for one instant of time, and fell forward prostrate.

Roxy was behind Parson Peters as the old man fell ; and, pushing that eminent divine out of her way like a spider, she was at once on her knees by his side, promptly administering the proper remedies. It was only a fainting-fit ; but, when the squire recovered, he was weak, humble, and gentle as a little child. He lay on the sofa in the parlor all day. The unused windows were opened, and the sweet summer air flowed in and out with scents of late roses and new hay on its delicate wings; but Squire Paine did not notice it. He took the broth Roxy brought him without a complaint, and actually thanked her for it. She herself guarded the outside door like a dragon, and even refused admittance to Parson Peters.

"No," said she: "it's good to let him be to-day. I tell ye the Lord's a-dealin' with the poor old creter, an' we hadn't ought to meddle. Human nater is everlastin' queer, an' there is some folks nobody can tune so well as Him that made 'em. He'll take up his bed an' walk as soon as the merracle works, an' we can't hurry it up any; but I've faith to believe it's a-workin'."

And it was according to Roxy's faith. As soon as the sun went down, the squire rose up, ate what was set before him, put his disordered dress to rights, and walked feebly over to the weekly prayer-meeting; for these things happened of a Thursday.

The lights in the little schoolhouse were dim and few, for the night's warm atmosphere made even the heat of the two necessary lamps oppressive; but Squire Paine took no advantage of this darkness, though the room was unusually full. He walked to the very front bench, and seated himself before the deacon who conducted the meeting; and, as soon as the opening hymn was sung, he waved the good man who was about to follow with a prayer aside with a certain rugged dignity, and rose, facing the assembly, and beginning with broken voice to speak.

"Brethring," he said, "I come here to-night to make a confession. I've lived amongst you for sixty odd year, man an' boy, an' the last forty on 'em I've ben a livin' lie. Brethring, I hev ben a professor it

this here church all that time, an' I wa'n't never converted.   I was a real stiddy-goin' hypocrite, an' I
hain't but jest found it out.   The marciful Lord has
kinder spared me for a day of repentance, an' it's
come : I tell ye it's come !   There was one that dealt
with me mightily, an' shook me some, — one, I may
say, that drilled the hole, an' put in the powder of the
Word, an' tamped it down with pretty stiff facts ; but
it didn't do no good.   I was jest like a rock bored an'
charged, but pooty rugged an' hard yet.   But, brethring, THE LORD HAS FIRED THE BLAST HIMSELF, an' the
nateral man is broken to pieces.   I give up right here.
The Lord is good.   God be merciful to me a sinner !
Brethring, can't you pray? "

There was but one answer to the pathetic agony of
that appeal.   Deacon Adkins rose, and prayed as if his
lips had been touched with a coal from the altar, and
there were sympathetic tears in the hardest eyes there
before he finished ; while Squire Paine's low sobs were
heard at intervals, as if they were the very convulsions
of a breaking heart.

" Let us sing

   " ' Praise God, from whom all blessings flow,' "

said the deacon, after his prayer was over.   And, when
the last line of that noble Doxology floated away into
the rafters, they all gathered round to shake hands,
and express their deep sympathy with the repentant
and bereaved father.   It was almost too much for
Squire Paine.   The breaking-up of the great deep within
had worn upon him exceedingly : humbled, sad, yet
wonderfully peaceful as his spirit felt, still the flesh
trembled, and was weak.   He was glad when Roxy

came up, and, taking hold of his arm, led him homeward.

Was he glad, or death-smitten, or, as he thought, suddenly in the heavenly places, when his own door opened before his hand touched the latch, and Louise, darting forward, threw her arms about his neck?

" Land o' liberty!" shrieked Roxy. " Do you want to kill your pa outright? An' how came ye here anyway? We heered you an' him was both stundead!"

Roxy's curt and curious interposition seemed to restore the equilibrium suddenly. Squire Paine did not faint, and Louise actually laughed. Here was something natural and homely to shelter in after the dreamlike agitation of the day.

" No," said Louise's clear voice: " we wa'n't hurt, not much — only stunned, and scared a bit. But there was two in the next seat who — well, *they* won't come home to their folks, Aunt Roxy. We thought maybe you would be anxious; and then somebody said right before us that we were both killed, and they'd sent the news over to Bassett: so we thought the best thing to do was to come back and show ourselves. Here's 'Lisha."

Squire Paine must have been converted; for he shook his son-in-law's hand with all good will, and kissed his daughter heartily. His voice was somewhat weak and husky; but he managed to say so as to be heard, " An' now ye've got home re'lly, you've got to stay home. I sha'n't hev no more sech risks run. And, 'Lisha, we'll open the store real early to-morrer. I dono when it's ben shut twenty-four hours before."

This was all he said; for the New-England man

saint or sinner, has few words when feeling is strongest. But the squire's action spoke for him. He never referred to the past, but strove with his might to live a new and righteous life. Not all at once the granite gave place to gold: there were were roots of bitterness, and strivings of the old Adam, many and often; but none who had once known him doubted that Squire Paine was a changed man. At his own earnest request he was allowed to make a new profession of religion; and, after relating his experiences in due form to the assembled deacons, he wound up the recital in this fashion: "It was the Lord's hand done it fin'lly, brethring; but, next to him, I owe this here real conversion to Roxanny Keep."

"Halleloojah!" exclaimed Aunt Roxy, when Mrs. Deacon Adkins betrayed her good husband's confidence far enough to tell her this. "I tell ye, Miss Adkins, I took my life in my hand that mornin'; but I felt a call to do it. Ye know David killed Goliath with a pebble, nothin' more; an' I allers could sling straight."

MISS BEULAH'S BONNET.

"I don't want to be too fine, ye know, Mary Jane,—somethin' tasty and kind of suitable. It's an old bunnit; but my! them Leghorns'll last a generation if you favor 'em. That was mother's weddin' bunnit."

"You don't say so! Well, it has kept remarkable well; but a good Leghorn will last, that's a fact, though they get real brittle after a spell: and you'll have to be awful careful of this, Miss Beulah; it's brittle now, I see."

"Yes, I expect it is; but it'll carry me through this summer, I guess. But I want you to make it real tasty, Mary Jane; for my niece Miss Smith, she that was 'Liza Barber, is coming to stay a while to our house this summer, and she lives in the city, you know."

"'Liza Barber! Do tell! Why, I haven't seen her sence she was knee-high to a hop-toad, as you may say. He ain't livin', is he?"

"No: he died two years ago, leavin' her with three children. Sarah is a grown girl; and then there's Jack, he's eight, and Janey, she's three. There was four died between Jack and Sarah. I guess she's full eighteen."

"Mercy to me! time flies, don't it? But about the bunnit: what should you say to this lavender ribbin?"

" Ain't I kind of dark for lavender? I had an idee to have brown, or mabbe dark green."

" Land! for spring? Why, that ain't the right thing. This lavender is real han'some; and I'll set it off with a little black lace, and put a bow on't in the front. It'll be real dressy and seemly for you."

" Well, you can try it, Mary Jane; but I give you fair warnin', if I think it's too dressy, you'll have to take it all off."

" I'm willin'," laughed Miss Mary Jane Beers, a good old soul, and a contemporary of her customer, Miss Beulah Larkin, who was an old maid living in Dorset on a small amount of money carefully invested, and owning the great red house which her grandfather had built for a large family on one corner of his farm. Farm and family were both gone now, save and except Miss Beulah and her niece; but the old lady and a little maid she had taken to bring up dwelt in one end of the wide house, and contrived to draw more than half their subsistence from the garden and orchard attached to it. Here they spun out an innocent exist-ence, whose chief dissipations were evening meetings, sewing-societies, funerals, and the regular Sunday ser-vices, to which all the village faithfully repaired, and any absence from which was commented on, investi-gated, and reprobated, if without good excuse, in the most unsparing manner. Miss Beulah Larkin was tall, gaunt, hard-featured, and good. Everybody respected her, some feared, and a few loved her: but she was not that sort of soul which thirsts to be loved; her whole desire and design was to do her duty and be respectable. Into this latter clause came the matter of a bonnet, over which she had held such anxious dis-

course. If she had any feminine vanity, — and she
was a woman, — it took this virtuous aspect of a desire
to be "respectit like the lave," for decency of dress
as well as demeanor. This spring she had received a
letter from her niece, the widowed Mrs. Smith, asking
if she could come to visit her; and, sending back a
pleased assent, Miss Beulah and her little handmaid
Nanny Starks bestirred themselves to sweep and garnish the house, already fresh and spotless from its recent annual cleaning. Windows were opened, beds
put out to sun, blankets aired, spreads unfolded, sheets
taken from the old chests, and long-disused dimity curtains washed, ironed, and tacked up against the small-
paned sashes, and tied back with scraps of flowered
ribbon, exhumed from hidden shelves, that might well
have trimmed that Leghorn bonnet in its first youth.

Mrs. Eliza Smith was a poor woman, but a woman
of resource. Her visit was not purely of affection, or
of family respect. Her daughter Sarah — a pretty,
slight, graceful girl, with gold-brown hair, dark straight
brows above a pair of limpid gray eyes, red lips, and
a clear pale skin — had been intended by her mother
to blossom into beauty in due season, and "marry
well," as the phrase goes; but Sarah and a certain
Fred Wilson, telegraph-operator in Dartford, had set
all the thrifty mother's plans at defiance, and fallen
head over heels in love, regardless of Mrs. Smith or
anybody else. Sarah's brows were not black and
straight, or her chin firm and cleft with a dimple, for
nothing: she meant to marry Fred Wilson as soon as
was convenient; and Mrs. Smith, having unusual common sense, as well as previous experience of Sarah's
capacity of resistance, ceased to oppose that young

lady's resolute intention. Master Wilson had already gone West, to a more lucrative situation than Dartford afforded; and Sarah was only waiting to get ready as to her outfit, and amass enough money for the cost of travelling, to follow him, since he was unable to return for her, both from lack of money and time. In this condition of things it occurred to Mrs. Smith that it would save a good deal of money if she could spend the summer with Aunt Beulah, and so be spared the expense of board and lodging for her family. Accordingly she looked about for a tenant for her little house; and, finding one ready to come in sooner than she had anticipated, she answered aunt Beulah's friendly letter of invitation with an immediate accept-ance, and followed her own epistle at once, arriving just as the last towel had been hung on the various wash-stands, and while yet the great batch of sweet home-made bread was hot from the oven, and, alas for Miss Beulah! before that Leghorn bonnet had come home from Miss Beers's front-parlor, in which she carried on her flourishing millinery business.

Miss Larkin was unfeignedly glad to see Eliza again, though her eyes grew a little dim, perceiving how time had transformed the fresh, gay girl she remembered into this sad and sallow woman; but she said nothing of these changes, and, giving the rest an equal wel-come, established them in the clean, large, cool cham-bers that were such a contrast to the hot rooms, small and dingy, of their city home.

Jack was a veritable little pickle, tall of his age, and light of foot and hand; nature had framed him in body and mind for mischief: while Sarah was a pleasant, handy young girl, as long as nothing opposed

her; and Janey a round and rosy poppet, who adored
Jack, and rebelled against her mother and Sarah
hourly. Jack was a born nuisance: Miss Beulah could
hardly endure him, he did so controvert all the orders
and manners of her neat house. He hunted the hens
to the brink of distraction, and broke up their nests
till eggs were scarce to find, — a state of things never
before known in that old barn, where the hens had
dwelt and done their duty, till that duty had consigned
them to the stew-pan, for years and years. He made
the cat's life a burden to her in a hundred ways; an
poor Nanny Starks had never any rest or peace till her
tormentor was safe in bed.

Mrs. Smith began to fear her visit would be prema-
turely shortened on Jack's account: and Sarah, who
had wisely confided her love-affair to aunt Beulah, and
stirred that hardened heart to its core by her pathetic
tale of poverty and separation, began to dread the
failure of her hopes also; for her aunt had more than
hinted that she would give something toward that travelling money which was now the girl's great object
in life, since by diligent sewing she had almost finished
her bridal outfit. As for Janey, she was already, in
spite of her naughtiness, mistress of aunt Beulah's
very soul. Round, fat, rosy, bewitching as a child and
only a child can be, the poor spinster's repressed
affection, her denied maternity, her love of beauty, —
a secret to herself, — and her protecting instinct, all
blossomed for this baby, who stormed or smiled at
her according to the caprice of the hour, but was
equally lovely in the old lady's eyes whether she
smiled or stormed. If Janey said, "Tum!" in her
imperative way, Miss Beulah came, whether her hands

were in the wash-tub or the bread-tray. Janey ran
riot over her most cherished customs ; and, while she
did not hesitate to scold or even slap Jack harshly for
his derelictions, she had an excuse always ready for
Janey's worst sins, and a kiss instead of a blow for her
wildest exploits of mischief. Jack hated the old aunty
as much as he feared her tongue and hand : and this
only made matters worse ; for he felt a certain right to
torment her that would not have been considered a
right, had he felt instead any shame for abusing her
kindness. But a soft answer from her never turned
away his wrath, or this tale of woe about her bonnet
had never been told.

There had been long delay concerning that article.
The bleacher had been slow, and the presser impracticable : it had been sent back once to be reshaped,
and then the lavender ribbon had proved of scant
measure, and had to be matched. But at last, one hot
day in May, Nanny brought the queer old bandbox
home from Miss Beers's, and aunt Beulah held up her
head-gear to be commented on. It was really a very
good-looking bonnet. The firm satin ribbon was a pleasant tint, and contrasted well with the pale color of the
Leghorn ; and a judicious use of black lace gave it an
air of sobriety and elegance combined, which pleased
Miss Beulah's eye, and even moved Mrs. Smith to
express approbation.

"Well, I'm free to own it suits me," said the old
lady, eying the glass with her head a little on one
side, as a bird eyes a worm. "It's neat, and it's
becomin', as fur as a bunnit can be said to be becomin'
to an old woman, though I ain't really to call old.
Mary Jane Beers is older than me ; and she ain't but

seventy-three, — jest as spry as a lark too. Yes, I
like the bunnit; but it doos — sort of — seem — as
though that there bow wa'n't really in the middle of
it. What do you think, 'Lizy?''

"I don't see but what it's straight, aunt Beulah."

" 'Tain't," said the spinster firmly. "Sary, you
look at it."

Sarah's eye was truer than her mother's. " 'Tis a
mite too far to the left, aunt Beulah; but I guess I
can fix it."

"You let her take it," said Mrs. Smith. "She's a
real good hand at millinery: she made her own hat,
and Janey's too. I should hate to have her put her
hand to that bunnit if she wa'n't; for it's real pretty —
'specially for a place like Dorset to get up."

"Lay it off on the table, aunt Beulah. I'm going
up stairs to make my bed, and I'll fetch my work-
basket down, and fix that bow straight in a jiffy."

"Well, I must go up too," said Mrs. Smith, and
followed Sarah out of the room; but Miss Beulah,
though duty called her too, in the imperative shape
of a batch of bread waiting to be moulded up, lingered
a little longer, poising the bonnet on her hand, holding
it off to get a distant view, turning it from side to
side, and, in short, behaving exactly as younger and
prettier women do over a new hat, even when it is a
miracle of art from Paris, instead of a revamped Leghorn from a country shop.

She laid it down with a long breath of content, for
taste and economy had done their best for her; and
then she, too, left the room, never perceiving that Jack
and Janey had been all the time deeply engaged under
the great old-fashioned breakfast-table, silently ripping

up a new doll to see what was inside it, — silently, because they had an inward consciousness that it was
mischief they were about; and Jack, at least, did not
want to be interrupted till he was through. But he
had not been too busy to hear and understand that aunt
Beulah was pleased; and, still smarting from the switch
with which she had whipped his shoulders that very
morning for putting the cat into the cistern, he saw
an opportunity for revenge before his eyes: he would
hide this precious bonnet so aunt Beulah could never
find it again. How to do this, and not be found out,
was a problem to be considered; but mischief is quick-
witted. There stood in the window a large rocking-
chair, well stuffed under its chintz cover, and holding
a plump soft feather cushion so big it fairly overflowed
the seat. Under this cushion he was sure nobody
would think of looking; and, to save himself from
consequences, he resolved to make Janey a cat's-paw:
so he led her up to the table, made her lift the precious
hat and deposit it under the cushion, which he raised
for the purpose; then, carefully dropping the frill, he
tugged Janey, unwilling but scared and silent, out
into the yard, and, impressing on her infant mind with
wild threats of bears and guns that she must never
tell where the bonnet was, he contrived to interest her
in a new play so intensely, that the bonnet went utterly
into oblivion, as far as she was concerned; and when
they were called in to dinner, and she had taken her
daily nap, Janey had become as innocent of mischief
in her own memory as the dolly who lay all disembow-
eled and forlorn under the table.

When Sarah came down and did not find the bonnet,
she concluded aunt Beulah had put it away in her own

room, for fear a sacrilegious fly or heedless speck of dust might do it harm : so she took up a bit of lace she was knitting, and went out into the porch, glad to get into a cool place, the day was so warm.

And when the bread was moulded up, aunt Beulah came back, and, not seeing her bonnet, supposed Sarah had taken it up stairs to change the bow. She was not an impatient woman, and the matter was not pressing : so she said nothing about the bonnet at dinner, but hurried over that meal in order to finish her baking. Mis. Smith had not come down again, for a morning headache had so increased upon her, she had lain down : so that no one disturbed the rocking-chair in which that bonnet lay hid till Mrs. Blake, the minister's wife, came in to make a call about four o'clock. She was a stout woman, and the walk had tired her. Aunt Beulah's hospitable instincts were roused by that red, weary face.

"You're dreadful warm, ain't you, Miss Blake?" said she. "It's an amazin' warm day for this time of year, and it's consider'ble more'n a hen-hop from your house up here. Lay your bunnit off, do, and set down in the rocker. I'll tell Nanny to fetch some shrub and water. Our ras'berry shrub is good, if I do say it; and it's kep' over as good as new."

So Mrs. Blake removed her bonnet, and sank down on that inviting cushion with all her weight, glad enough to rest, and ignorant of the momentous consequences. Her call was somewhat protracted. Had there been any pins in that flattened Leghorn beneath her, she might have shortened her stay. But Miss Mary Jane Beers was conscientiously opposed to pins ; and every lavender bow was sewed on with silk to match, and scrupulous care. After the whole village news had been discussed, the state of religion lamented, and the short-comings of certain sisters who failed in attending prayer-meetings talked over, — with the charitable admission, to be sure, that one had a young baby, and another a sprained ankle, — Mrs. Blake rose to go, tied on her bonnet, and said good-by all round, quite as ignorant as her hosts of the remediless ruin she had done.

It was tea-time now ; and, as they sat about the table, Sarah said, "I guess I'll fix your bonnet after tea, aunty : 'twon't take but a minute, and I'd rather do it while I recollect just where that bow goes."

"Why, I thought you had fixed it!" returned Miss Beulah.

"Well, I came right back to; but it wa'n't here. I thought you'd took it into your bedroom."

"I hain't touched it sence it lay right here on the table."

"I'll run up and ask ma : maybe she laid it by."

But Mrs. Smith had not been down stairs since she left aunt Beulah with the bonnet in her hands. And now the old lady turned on Jack. "Have you ben and carried off my bunnit, you little besom?"

"I hain't touched your old bonnet!" retorted Jack with grand scorn.

"I don't believe he has," said Sarah; "for, when I come down stairs and found it wa'n't here, I went out and set on the bench to the front-door, and I heard him and Janey away off the other side of the yard, playin'; and you know they wa'n't in here when the bonnet come."

"Well, of course Janey hasn't seen it, if Jack

hasn't; and, if she had, the blessed child wouldn't
have touched old aunty's bonnet for a dollar — would
she, precious lamb?'' And aunt Beulah stroked the
bright curls of her darling, who looked up into her
face, and laughed; while Jack grinned broadly between
his bites of bread and butter, master of the situation,
and full of sweet revenge. ''And Nanny hain't seen
it, I know,'' went on aunt Beulah; '' for she was along
of me the whole enduring time. She set right to a-parin'
them Roxbury russets the minnit she fetched home the
bunnit; and I kep' her on the tight jump ever sence,
because it's bakin'-day, and there was a sight to do
But I'll ask her: 'tain't lost breath to ask, my moth
used to say, and mabbe it's a gain.''

The old lady strode out into the kitchen with knit
brows, but came back without any increased knowledge. '' She hain't ben in here once sence she set
down the bandbox; and, come to think on't, I know
she hain't, for I cleared the table myself to-day, and,
besides, the bunnit wa'n't here at dinner-time. Now
let's hunt for it. Things don't gener'lly vanish away
without hands; but, if we can't find no hands, why, it's
as good as the next thing to look for the bunnit.''

So they went to work and searched the house, as
they thought, most thoroughly. No nook or corner but
was investigated, if it was large enough to hold that
bonnet; but nobody once thought of looking under the
chair-cushion. If it had been as plump and fluffy as
when Jack first had Janey put the lost structure under
it, there might have been a suspicion of its hiding-
place; but Mrs. Blake's two hundred pounds of solid
flesh had reduced bonnet and cushion alike to unusual
flatness. Or, if it had been any other day but Satur-

day, the chair might have been dusted and shaken up, and revealed its mystery; but early that very morning the house below stairs had been swept, and the furniture dusted, the cushions shaken out, the brasses polished, and all the weekly order and purity restored everywhere. The bonnet was evidently lost; and Jack, who had followed the domestic detectives up stairs and down, retired behind the wood-pile, and executed a joyful dance to relieve his suppressed feelings, snapping his fingers, and slapping his knees, and shouting scraps of all the expletives he knew, in the joy of his heart. How tragic would this mirth have seemed to a spectator aware of its cause, contrasted with the portentous gloom on aunt Beulah's forehead, and the abstracted glare of her eye! For several days this deluded spinster mused and mazed over her bonnet, going to church on Sunday in her shabby old velvet hat, which had scarcely been respectable before, but now, in the glare of a hot May sun, not only showed all its rubbed and worn places, its shiny streaks and traces of eaves-drops in the depressed and tangled nap, but also made her head so hot that she fairly went to bed at last with sick-headache, unable to attend evening service, — a most unheard-of thing for her.

Before the week was half done, she had settled into a profound belief that some tramp had passed while they were all out of the room, and, charmed by that lavender satin ribbon and black lace, stolen the bonnet, and carried it off to sell; and many a time did Miss Beulah sit rocking to and fro on top of her precious Leghorn, wondering and bemoaning at its loss. But murder will out — sometimes, and would certainly have come out in the weekly cleaning the next Saturday,

if, on the Friday morning, Miss Beulah had not set
down a pitcher of milk, just brought in by a neighbor,
on the end of the table nearest to that rocking-chair. —
set it down only for a moment, to get the neighbor a
recipe for sugar gingerbread peculiar to the Larkin
family. Janey happened to be thirsty, and reached
after the pitcher, but was just tall enough to grasp the
handle so low down, that when she pulled at it, steady-
ing herself against the chair, it tipped sideways, and
poured a copious stream of fresh milk on the cushion.
The chintz was old, and had lost its glaze, and the
feathers were light: so the rich fluid soaked in at
once; and before the two women, recalled from the
cupboard by Janey's scream, could reach the pitcher,
there was only a very soppy and wet cushion in the
chair.

"For mercy's sakes!" said the neighbor. But Miss
Beulah, with great presence of mind, snatched up the
dripping mass and flung it out of the open window,
lest her carpet should suffer. She reverted to the chair
in a second, and stood transfixed.

"What under the everlastin' canopy!" broke from
her dismayed lips; for there, flattened out almost beyond recognition, and broken wherever it was bent, its
lavender ribbons soaked with milk, the cheap lace limp
and draggled, lay the remains of the Leghorn bonnet.

"Of all things!" exclaimed the neighbor; but there
was an echo of irrepressible amusement in her tones.
Aunt Beulah glared at her, and lifted the damp bonnet
as tenderly as if it had been Janey's curls, regarding
it with an expression pen or pencil fails to depict, — a
mixture of grief, pity, indignation, and amazement,
that, together with the curious look of the bonnet, was

too much for the neighbor ; and, to use her own after-expression in describing the scene, she "snickered right out."

"Laugh, do," said aunt Beulah witheringly. -- "do laugh! I guess, if your best bunnit had ben set on and drownded, you'd laugh the other side o' your mouth, Miss Jackson. This is too much."

"Well, I be sorry," said the placable female ; "but it doos look so dreadful ridiculous like, I couldn't no-ways help myself. But how on earth did it git there, I admire to know?"

"I dono myself as I know ; but I hain't a doubt in my own mind it was that besom of a Jack. He is *the* fullest of 'riginal sin and actual transgression of any boy I ever see. He did say, now I call to mind, that he hadn't never touched it ; but I mistrust he did. He beats all for mischief that ever I see. I'm free to say I never did like boys. I suppose divine Providence ordained 'em to some good end ; but it takes a sight o' grace to believe it : and, of all the boys that ever was sent into this world for any purpose, I do believe he is the hatefulest. I'd jest got my bunnit to my mind, calc'latin' to wear it all summer ; and I am a mite per-nickity, I'll allow that, about my bunnits. Well, 'tain't no use to cry over spilt milk."

"I'll fetch ye some more to-morrow," said the lit-eral neighbor.

"You're real good, Miss Jackson ; but I'm more ex-ercised a lot about my bunnit than I be about the milk. -- Sary, look a-here!"

Sarah, just coming in at the door, did look, and, like Mrs. Jackson, felt a strong desire to smile, but with native tact controlled it.

"Why, where on earth did you find it, aunt Beulah?"

"Right under the rocker-cushion. It must have ben there when Miss Blake come in that day and set down there; for I remember thinkin' Nanny must ha' shook that cushion up more'n usual, it looked so comfortable and high."

"I don't wonder it's flat, if Miss Blake set on't," giggled Mrs. Jackson, at which aunt Beulah's face darkened so perceptibly that the good neighbor took her leave. Comedy to her was tragedy to the unhappy owner of the bonnet; and she had the sense to know she was alien to the spirit of the hour, and go home.

"But how did it get there?" asked Sarah.

"You tell," replied Miss Beulah, "for I can't. I do mistrust Jack."

"Jack said he hadn't touched it, though; and it couldn't get there without hands."

"Well, mabbe Jack don't always say the thing that is. 'Foolishness is bound up in the heart of a child,' Scriptur says; and I guess he hain't had enough of the rod o' correction to drive it out of him yet. He's the behavin'est youngster I ever see; and I'm quite along in years, if I be spry."

"I'll call him, aunty, and see what he'll say this time."

"'Twon't be no use: if he's lied once, he'll lie twice. Scriptur says the Devil was a liar from the beginnin'; and I expect that means that lyin' is ingrain. I never knowed it to be fairly knocked out of anybody yet, even when amazin' grace wrastled with it. There's Deacon Shubael Morse: why, he's as good as gold; but them Morses is a proverb, you may say, and always hes ben, time out o' mind, — born liars, so to speak. I've heerd Grandsir Larkin say, that, as fur back as he could call to mind, folks would say, —

> 'Steal a horse,
> An' b'lieve a Morse.'

But the deacon he's a hero at prayer, and gives heaps to the s'cieties ; but he ain't reely to be relied on. He's sharper'n a needle to bargain with ; and, if his word ain't writ down in black and white, why, 'tain't nowhere. He don't read no novils, nor play no cards : he'd jest as lives swear outright as do one or t'other. But I do say for't, I'd ruther myself see him real honest than any o' them things. I don't believe in no sort o' professin' that falls short in practisin' ; but I can't somehow feel so real spry to blame the deacon as though he wa'n't a Morse. But you call Jack anyhow.''

So Jack was called.

He came in, with Janey, flushed, lovely, and dirty, trotting behind him, and was confronted with the bonnet.

'' Jack, did you hide it ? ''

'' I hain't touched your old bonnet. I said so before.''

An idea struck Sarah.

'' Janey,'' she said sharply, '' did you put aunty's bonnet under the cushion ? ''

'' Janey don't 'member,'' said the child, smiling as innocently as the conventional cherub of art.

'' Well, you must remember ! '' said Sarah, picking her up from the floor, and setting her down with emphasis on the table.

Janey began to cry.

"Naughty Salah hurt Janey!" and the piteous tears coursed down her rosy, dust-smeared cheeks from those big blue eyes that looked like dew-drowned forget-me-nots.

Aunt Beulah could not stand this. "You let that baby alone, Sarah! She don't know enough to be naughty, bless her dear little soul! — There, there, don't you cry a mite more, Janey. Aunty'll give you ginger-cooky this very minute!"

And Janey was comforted with kisses and smiles and gingerbread, her face washed, and her curls softly turned on tender fingers; while Jack, longing for gingerbread with the preternatural appetite of a growing boy, was sent off in disgrace.

"I make no doubt you done it, you little rascal, and lied it out too. But I don't b'lieve you no more for your lyin': so don't look for no extries from me. Fellers like you don't get gingerbread nor turnovers, now I tell you!"

How Jack hated her! How glad he was he had spoiled her bonnet! Shall I draw a moral here to adorn my tale? No, dear reader: this is not a treatise on education. Miss Beulah was a good woman; and if she made mistakes, like the rest of us, she took the consequences as the rest of us do; and the consequences of this spoiled bonnet were not yet ended.

She felt as if she must have a new one for Sunday. She really did not know how to afford it; for she had promised to help Sarah, and in her eyes a promise was as sacred as an oath. And, as for giving up her subscriptions to home missions, that would be a wilful sin. But, without a bonnet, she could not go to meeting; and that was a sin too. So she put on her sun-bonnet; and taking the wreck of the Leghorn, carefully concealed in a paper, she set out after tea that same evening for a conference with Miss Beers, stopping at the post-office as she went along. She found one letter await-ing her, and knew by the superscription that it was from a second-cousin of hers in Dartford, who had charge of such money of hers as was not in the sav-ings bank or Dartford and Oldbay Railroad stock, — a road paying steady dividends. But, besides the three or four thousands in these safe investments that Miss Beulah owned, she had two shares in a manufacturing company, and one in Dartford Bridge stock, from which her cousin duly remitted the annual dividends : so, knowing what was in the letter, for the tool com-pany's payment was just due, she did not open it till she sat down in Miss Beers's shop, and first opened the Leghorn to view.

"Of all things!" said Miss Beers, lifting up hands and eyes during Miss Beulah's explanations. "And you can't do nothing with it — never. Why, it's flat-ter'n a pancake. Well, you couldn't expect nothing else, with Miss Blake on top on't: she'd squash a baby out as thin as a tin plate if she happened to set on't, which I do hope she won't. See! the Leghorn's all broke up. I told you 'twas dreadful brittle. And the ribbin is spoiled entire. You can't never clean laven-der, nor yet satin, it frays so. And the lace is all gum : anyway, that's gone. Might as well chuck the hull into the fire."

"So do, Mary Jane, so do. I never want to set eyes on't again. I haven't no patience with that boy now, and the bunnit riles me to look at. I do want to do right by the boy, but it goes against the grain dreadful. I mistrust I shall have to watch and pray real hard before I can anyway have patience with him. I tell you he's a cross to 'Liza as well as to me. But don't let's talk about him. What have you got that'll do for a bunnit for me?"

Then the merits of the various bonnets in Miss Beers's small stock were canvassed. A nice black chip suited aunt Beulah well; and a gray corded ribbon, with a cluster of dark pansies, seemed just the thing for trimming. In fact, she liked it, and with good reason, better than the Leghorn; but it was expensive. All the materials, though simple, were good and rich. Try as she would, Miss Beers could not get it up for less than six dollars, and that only allowed twenty-five cents for her own work. The alternative was a heavy coarse straw, which she proposed to deck with a yellow-edged black ribbon, and put some gold-eyed black daisies inside. But Miss Beulah did want the chip.

"Let's see," said she. "Mabbe this year's dividend is seven per cent: 'tis once in a while. I'll see what cousin Joseph says. If 'tain't more than usual, I must take the straw."

But cousin Joseph had to tell her, that owing to damage by flood and fire, as well as a general disturbance of business all over the country, the C. A. Company paid *no* dividend this year.

"Then I sha'n't have no bunnit," said Miss Larkin firmly.

"Why, you've got to have some kind of a bunnit," said the amazed Miss Beers.

"I hain't got to if I can't."

"But why can't ye, Beulah? All your money and all your dividends ain't in that comp'ny."

"Well, there's other uses for money this year besides bunnits."

"You can't go to meetin'."

"I can stay to home."

"Why, Beulah Larkin, I'll trust you, and wel come."

"But I won't be trusted. I never was, and I never will be. What if I should up and die?"

"I'd sue the estate," practically remarked Miss Beers.

"No: 'out of debt, out of danger,' mother always said, and I believe in't. I shall hate to stay to home Sundays, but I can go to prayer-meetin' in my slat bunnit well enough."

"Why, the church'll deal with ye, Beulah, if ye neglect stated means of grace."

"Let 'em deal," was the undaunted answer. Miss Beulah had faced the situation, arranged it logically, and accepted it. She had promised Sarah fifteen dollars in June. She had lost a dividend of twelve dollars on which she had reckoned with certainty; five dollars was due to home missions; and, with her increased family, there would be no margin for daily expenses. There were twenty dollars in the savings bank over and above the five hundred she had laid up for a rainy day, and left in her will, made and signed but last week, to little Janey. On this she would not trench, come what might, except in case of absolute distress; and the wenty dollars were sacred to Sarah and home missions. But this was her private affair: she would not make the poverty of her niece known abroad, or the

nature of her will. If the church chose to deal with
her, it might; but her lips should never open to explain, — a commonplace martyrdom enough, and less
than saintly because so much of human pride and
self-will mingled in its suffering; yet honesty and uprightness are so scarce in these days as to make even
such a sturdy witness for them respectable, and many
a woman who counts herself a model of sanctity might
shrink from a like daily ordeal. But aunt Beulah set
her face as a flint, and pursued her way in silence.
June came and went; and with it went Sarah to her
expectant bridegroom in Chicago, from whence a paper
with due notice of her marriage presently returned.
Aunt Beulah strove hard to make both ends meet
in her housekeeping, and, being a close manager,
succeeded. There was no margin, not even twenty-five
spare cents to take Janey to the circus; though she cut
aunt Beulah's heart with entreaties to be taken to see
"lions an' el'phants," and said, "P'ease take Janey,"
in a way to melt a stone. For to get food enough to
satisfy Jack was in itself a problem. Often and often
the vexed spinster declared to Nanny, her sympathizing
handmaid, —

"'Tain't no use a-tryin' to fill him. He's holler
down to his boots, I know. He eat six b'iled eggs for
breakfast, and heaps of johnny-cake, besides a pint o'
milk, and was as sharp-set for dinner as though he'd
ben a-mowin' all the forenoon. 'Lizy says he's growin'; if he grows anyways accordin' to what he eats,
he'll be as big as Goliath of Gath, as sure as you're
born. I don't begrudge the boy reasonable vittles,
but I can't buy butcher's-meat enough to satisfy him
noway. And as to garden sass, he won't eat none.

That would be real fillin' if he would.   Thanks be to
praise! he likes Indian.   Pudding and johnny-cake do
help a sight.''

But while aunt Beulah toiled and moiled, and filled
her wide measure of charity toward these widowed and
fatherless with generous hand, the church, mightily
scandalized at her absence from its services, was preparing to throw a shell into her premises.   It was all
very well to say to Miss Beers that she was not afraid
of such a visitation; but a trouble at hand is of quite
another aspect than a trouble afar off.   Her heart quailed
and fluttered, when, one July afternoon, Nanny ushered
into the dark, cool parlor Deacon Morse and Deacon
Flint, come to ask her why she had not attended
church since the middle of last May, when she was in
usual health and exercise of her faculties.   Miss Beulah, however, was equal to the occasion.   She faced
the deacons sternly, but calmly.

"It is so," she said, when they had finished their
accusation.   "I hain't ben to meetin' for good cause.
You can't say I've did any thing that's give occasion
to the enemy more'n this.   I've attended reg'lar to
prayer-meetin's and sewin'-circle.   I've give as usual to
home missions.   You can't say I've made any scandal,
or done nothin' out o' rule, save an' except stayin' at
home sabbath days; and my family has attended punc-
tooally."

But this did not satisfy the deacons: they pressed
for a reason.

"If you would free your mind, sister Larkin, it
would be for the good of the church," said Deacon
Morse.

"Mabbe 'twouldn't be altogether to your likin'

deacon, if I did free my mind. Seems as though stayin' at home from meetin' wa'n't no worse'n sandin' sugar an' waterin' rum; and I never heerd you was dealt with for them things."

Deacon Morse was dumb, but Deacon Flint took up the discourse.

"Well, sister Larkin, we didn't know but what you was troubled in your mind."

"I ain't!" snapped Miss Beulah.

"Or perhaps was gettin' a mite doubtful about doctrines, or suthin'."

"No, I ain't. I go by the 'Sembly's Catechism, and believe in every word on't, questions and all."

"Well, you seem to be a leetle contumacious, sister Larkin, so to speak: if you had a good reason, why, of course, you'd be willin' to tell it."

This little syllogism caught Miss Beulah.

"Well, if you must know, I hain't got no bunnit."

The deacons stared mutually; and Deacon Morse, forgetful of his defeat, and curious, as men naturally are, asked abruptly, "Why not?"

"Cause Miss Blake sot on it."

The two men looked at each other in blank amazement, and shook their heads. Here was a pitfall. Was it proper, dignified, possible, to investigate this truly feminine tangle? They were dying to enter into particulars, but ashamed to do so: nothing was left but retreat. Miss Beulah perceived the emergency, and chuckled grimly. This was the last straw. The deacons rose as one man, and said, "Good-day," with an accent of reprobation, going their ways in deep doubt as to what they should report to the church, which certainly would not receive with proper gravity

the announcement that Miss Beulah Larkin could not
come to church because the minister's wife had sat on
her Sunday bonnet. The strife of tongues, however,
did not spare aunt Beulah, if the deacons did ; and for
a long time Miss Beers, who had the key to the situation, did not hear any of the gossip, partly because
she had been ill of low fever, and then gone to her
sister's in Dartford for change of air, and partly, that,
during July and August, the sewing-circle was tempo-
rarily suspended. But it renewed its sessions in September ; and Miss Beers was an active member, sure
to be at the first meeting. It was then and there she
heard the scorn and jeers and unfounded stories come
on like a tidal wave to overwhelm her friend's character. She listened a few minutes in silence, growing
more and more indignant. Then, for she was a little
woman as far as stature went, she mounted into a
chair, and demanded the floor in her own fashion.

"Look a-here !" said she, her shrill voice soaring
above the busy clapper of tongues below. "It's a
burnin' shame to say a hard word about Beulah Larkin. She's as good a woman as breathes the breath
of life, and I know the hull why and wherefore she
hain't ben to meetin'. She hain't had no bunnit. I
made her as tasty a bunnit as ever you see last spring ;
and that jackanapes of a boy he chucked it under the
rocker-cushion jest to plague her, and Miss Blake she
come in and sot right down on it, not knowin', of
course, that 'twas there ; and, as if that wa'n't enough
to spile it" (an involuntary titter seemed to express
the sense of the audience that it was), "that other
sprig, she took and upsot a pitcher of milk onto the
cushion, and you'd better believe that bunnit was a
sight !"

"Why didn't she get another?" severely asked Deacon Morse's wife.

"Why? Why, becos she's a-most a saint. Her dividends some on 'em didn't come in, and she'd promised that biggest girl fifteen dollars to help her get out to her feller at Chicago, for Sary told me on't herself; and then she gives five dollars to hum missions every year, and she done it this year jest the same; and she's took that widder and them orphans home all summer, and nigh about worked her head off for 'em, and never charged a cent o' board; and therefor and thereby she hain't had no money to buy no bunnit, and goes to prayer-meetin' in her calico slat."

A rustle of wonder and respect went through the room as the women moved uneasily in their chairs, exchanged glances, and said, "My!" which inspired Miss Beers to go on.

"And here everybody's ben a-talkin' bad about her, while she's ben a real home-made kind of a saint. I know she don't look it; but she doos it, and that's a sight better. I don't b'lieve there's one woman in forty could ha' had the grit and the perseverance to do what she done, and hold her tongue about it too. I know I couldn't for one."

"She shouldn't ha' let her good be evil spoken of," said Mrs. Morse with an air of authority.

"I dono as anybody had oughter have spoken evil of her good," was Miss Beers's dry answer; and Mrs. Morse said no more.

But such a warm and generous vindication touched many a feminine heart, which could appreciate Miss Beulah's self-sacrifice better than the deacons could. There was an immediate clustering and chattering

among the good women, who, if they did love a bit of
gossip, were none the less kindly and well-meaning;
and presently a spokeswoman approached Miss Beers
with the proposition, that, if she would make Miss
Beulah a handsome bonnet, a dozen or more had
volunteered to buy the materials.

"Well," said Miss Mary Jane, wiping her spectacles, "this is real kind; and I make no doubt but what
Beulah'd think the same, though she's a master-hand
to be independent, and some folks say proud. Mabbe
she is; but I know she couldn't but take it kind of
friends and neighbors to feel for her. However, there
ain't no need on't. It seems that Sary's husband ain't
very forehanded, and she's got a dreadful taste for the
millinery business: so she's gone to work in one of the
fust shops there, and is gettin' great wages, for her;
and only yesterday there come a box by *ex*press for
Miss Beulah, with the tastiest bunnit in it I ever see in
my life, — good black velvet, with black satin kinder
puffed into the brim, and a dark-green wing to one side
of the band, and a big bow in under a jet buckle behind. I tell *you* it was everlastin' pretty. Sary she
sent a note to say she hoped aunt Beulah'd give her
the pleasure to accept it; for she'd knowed all along
how that she was the cause of her goin' without a
bunnit all summer (I expect her ma had writ to her),
and she felt real bad about it. You'd better b'lieve
Beulah was pleased."

And Miss Beulah was pleased again when the women
from the village began to call on her even more fre-
quently than before, and express cordial and friendly
interest in a way that surprised her, all unaware as she
was of Miss Beers's enthusiastic vindication of her

character before the sewing-circle.   Yet, poor, dear,
silly old woman, — only a woman, after all, — nothing
so thrilled and touched her late-awakened heart as little
Janey's soft caresses and dimpled patting hands on
that sallow old face, when she climbed into her lap the
next Sunday, and, surveying Miss Beulah's new bonnet
exclaimed, with her silvery baby voice, "Pitty, pitty
bonnet!"

Jack did not say any thing about it, nor did the congregation, though on more than one female face beamed
a furtive congratulatory smile ; and Deacon Flint looked
at Deacon Morse across the aisle.

If there is any moral to this story, as no doubt
there should be, it lies in the fact that Mrs. Blake
never again sat down in a chair without first lifting the
cushion.

CAL CULVER AND THE DEVIL.

" 'Tis true, 'tis pity:
Pity 'tis 'tis true."

"WELL," said Calvary Culver, sometimes called
Cal, and not infrequently Cal Cul, by such as believed
in the old adage that brevity is the soul of wit, —
"well, my mind's nigh about made up. Mother's
kinder feeble: it's time there was more folks to our
house. I guess I'll git married."

"Haw, haw, haw!" burst from the audience, — a
group of waiters and loungers in the country store,
where Cal stood, with his back against the counter,
whittling and spitting.

"'Tain't no larfin matter, boys," he went on.
"You may think it's suthin' smart to git married, but
mebbe you'll find 'tain't all honey-sugar pie. Look at
Deacon Flint, now! I tell ye his wife's as afeard o'
him as Parson Robbins is of the Devil; and you can't
say no more'n that, now can ye?"

"Oh, say!" began another lounger: "you hain't
heerd, hev ye, about the parson's last tussle with the
adversary?"

Nobody had. He was unanimously urged to go on.

"Well, you know it hain't ben real fust-rate sugarin'
weather: it ha'n't thew days, though it's friz consider'ble night-times. But it's kinder late for tappin',

153

anyway, 'cordin' to the year: so parson he reckoned he'd be amazin' forehanded this year, and git his holes bored, and spouts drove in, and buckets set, so's to be on hand, ye see. Now, them trees never dripped a drop a Thursday, nor a Friday, nor a Saturday: three days the buckets hung right there, and was empty; but sabba'-day it come round real warm, the sun shone powerful, and, when he went to the bush Monday mornin', the sap troughs and buckets was brimmin' over full, as sure as you're born! What does parson do but take and tip 'em all up; and Jim Beebe — he was behind him, 'cause his bush is over the fence, and he knowed sap had run by that time — Jim heerd him say, ' I know thy works, Satan, tempting me with Lord's Day sap. Get thee behind me!' And he up and tipped over every drop onter the ground, and went off."

"Jeerus'lem!" "Don't he beat!" "Gosh!" "Darnation!" and one rustic expletive after another chorussed this tale.

Cal Culver kept silence, shifting from one foot to the other; then he spoke meditatively, as if he had considered the subject before. " Parson Robbins does take consider'ble comfort out o' the Devil, don't he?"

"Comfort!" echoed the crowd.

"Well, mebbe you wouldn't call it that exackly; but the idee is, he gits somethin' to spend his grit on that way that's orthodox. You see, natur's awful strong in Parson Robbins, and by natur' he'd orter ha' ben a fightin' man: he's got it in him. I've seen him when I knowed he nigh about ached to pitch in and knock a feller down. He'd ha' fit Injuns like all possessed, ef they'd ben around sence he growed up. Now what's in a man, 'cordin' to my belief, 's got to come out o' him some way or nuther. Ef he's a good man, I s'pose it's kinder made over, sanctified like, ef it's grit, or lyin', or brag, or any sech thing."

"Kinder difficult to sanctify lyin'," dryly remarked Mr. Battle, the village store-keeper.

"Well, 'tis, that's a fact; but I s'pose ef it was b'iled over into 'cuteness, and sarcumventions of the Evil One, and sech, 'twouldn't do no great o' harm? Might come in useful in waterin' rum, and sandin' sugar."

Mr. Battle heard a noise at the back-door just then : and Cal winked deliberately at the crowd, who wanted to grin, but dare not; for most of them were chalked up on that dreadful slate behind the door with many marks, and all of them liked rum, with or without water.

"Parson doos pay quite a sight of 'tention to the Devil," sighed and squeaked a bent old man, — bent and worn with rheumatism, that rack and thumb-screw of the New-England climate. "'Pears to me sometimes as though he talked a sight more 'bout him than 'bout the Lord above."

"I expect he has to," answered Cal Culver. "He's round here in Bassett a good deal the most o' the two."

"You look out!" called the speaker who had told about the sap-troughs: "you'll git ketched up yet, as Mat Lines did t'other day. He said the south eend o' Bassett was as bad as hell; and I'm blamed if they didn't take him up for't, and fine him."

"'Twon't do to tell the truth allers," replied Culver. "But, boys, to go back to fust principles, I be ser'ously a mind to git married."

"Who ye goin' to mary, Cal?" inquired Mr. Battie.

"Well, I dono as I know myself, — some smart likely gal."

Here was a general shout, for Cal Culver was the village do-nothing. The owner of a small red house and "home lot," which his father had left him, the sole proceeds of a long life spent at a cobbler's bench, Cal acted as if work were as needless to his life as t was unpleasant; that is, hard work. He managed to raise enough potatoes and Indian corn on the two acres to keep his mother and himself in meal and the great vegetable staple. If he felt like it in the time of it, he raised bush-beans along by the fence; and in among the corn it was easy to drop a few pumpkin-seeds. The apple-trees in the door-yard produced their crops without trouble, and "garden-sass" was left to his mother's care: if she wanted it, she could raise it. Poor old woman! she had enough to do with loom, spinning-wheel, and needle, besides the simple house-wifery of her time and means; so that the garden only bloomed with such flowers as were hardy and perennial, — deep-red roses and glowing white ones; hollyhocks in stately spires; stiff sweet-williams, and ragged beds of moss-pink; little Burgundy roses no bigger than a copper cent, and trim as an old maid; and long wreaths of cinnamon roses, sweet as the luxuriant blooms of far-away Cashmere, but stinted in leaf and growth and blossom, as if they pined and half died in bitter North-ern airs and grudging sunshine. There was sage too, and summer-savory; for there was a pig always. The labor of feeding it bore hard on Cal; but who could live without pork? — pork that meant pies, doughnuts, suet-pudding, sausages in winter; cheeks smoked under

a barrel, and hung in the shed; slabs of fat, salt and
unctuous, adding savor and strength to a b'iled dinner
or a "fry" of any sort.   No, indeed' a pig was the
great necessity of life, and must be fed if they two
went hungry.

But Cal was a mighty hunter, so that food was seldom
wanting.   He could snare partridges, kill woodcock and
quail with his old shot-gun, bring home squirrels by
the dozen, and set rabbit-traps with unfailing success;
trout leaped to his hook; and, as to perch and sunfish,
they were to be had for the asking at his hands, and
the ponds in winter were full of pickerel: more than
he and Granny Culver could use found their way to the
store or the squire's, and resulted in rum, tea, or maple-
sugar, — luxuries of life.   Yet Cal was a shiftless,
thriftless fellow; shrewd, witty, keen-sighted, and —
lazy.   He loved to roam over the land with rod or gun,
to lie on the fragrant sand of a pine-wood and sleep
away sultry noons, to hang about the big stove in the
store in cold weather and take a hot "nip" of rum
toddy, while he told and heard stories and cracked
jokes; but how he hated to plough, to hoe, to chop, to
break stone, to mow, to tend mill!   Parson Robbins
and he were always at odds, and no wonder.   The
parson was a fiery, positive, set, energetic little man,
with enough executive power in him to have been presi-
dent of six railroads at a time, — a man who could not
be idle a moment, who rose early and read late, who
was by nature a belligerent, autocratic, eager, earnest
man, and was set down in a little country parish.   Cal
was right: to fight something was the necessity of the
parson's nature; his very face was aggressive.   Modern
clergymen, who preach one sermon a week, are victims

to dyspepsia, and use long words by the thousand to
express what they don't mean ; who dabble in æsthetics
and affinities, and have spiritual ups and downs like
the cradle-holes in a winter-drifted road, because they
have so little work that they have time to waste in
studying themselves and their feelings, — would have
made Parson Robbins stare. Three sermons a Sunday,
and a lecture Thursday evening ; prayer-meetings in
the ends of the town alternately twice a week ; visiting
such of his flock as needed it, and all of them occasionally, and writing sermons every week with conscientious diligence ; splitting wood, hoeing corn, and,
in short, farming his few acres by way of amusement
and relaxation ; his only reading the county weekly
paper, and the few solid volumes of theology on his
bedroom shelves, — what a life is this in comparison
with that of to-day? Five hundred dollars a year were
well earned, and hard earned too. No wonder that the
gospel was a daily reality to this prophet in the wilder-
ness, and the Devil a real and roaring personage, to be
baffled, fought, defied, and exorcised : and no wonder
that learning to endure hardness as a good soldier of
Christ Jesus, and to put on the whole armor of God,
this militant parson longed to test that hardness, and use
those weapons in lawful warfare with the enemy ; and he
did. He did not forget God, but he could trust him.
The Devil was persistent and at hand ; and he preached
about, prayed at, and wrestled with him to an extent
incredible to us who talk about an impersonal principle
of evil, and consider that awful solitude in the wilder-
ness and its agonies only a dramatization.

To Parson Robbins, as to Luther, the Enemy was a
real and active being ; and the flock whom he gathered

into the old red meeting-house accepted his belief with equal earnestness, except a few born sceptics who could not believe in any thing, and a few sturdy sinners who would not.

Even Cal Culver believed in the Devil; but he was too lazy to repent of his sins and lead a new life, — far too lazy to begin a warfare that must last as long as he did, and keep mind and body on the alert. To-day he was not so much troubled about Satan as he had been sometimes. His mind was given to another subject, — whom he should marry; for marriage was getting to be the only way out of his difficulties. His mother grew feebler and feebler; and he contemplated with terror the idea that he must do the work himself, and take care of her too, unless somebody stepped in to take the burden off his shoulders. He had announced his intention in the store, partly to fix it in his own mind beyond recall, partly in the hope of some gratuitous advice being offered; but nobody there had any to give. It did not occur to any of them that Cal was in earnest, or, if he was, that any girl in Bassett would look at him in a matrimonial light. But this was not Cal's opinion. He knew he was handsome. The straight, regular features, big blue eyes, and golden hair and beard he had seen mirrored in many a silent forest pool, told him a true story; and when a hearty laugh parted the full red lips, and showed his regular white teeth, and his eyes flashed with fun, or glittered with humor or craft, the too perfect face wore an added charm of bright expression. He was tall, too, straight, and strong, and being the only man in all the village, old or young: whose beard had been allowed its natural growth, simply because he was too lazy to shave, he was a marked figure wherever he went, and in constant request at raisings, apple-bees, and huskings, both as help in the work, which being only occasional, and followed by a feast, was not objectionable to him, and also as " fust-rate company," — a guest who could play all sorts of games, and dance all night, where any householder dared admit of dancing. But, though the girls all liked his society, none of them wanted to marry him ; and to-day, after he had waited for some expression of assent or opinion from the knot of his comrades in the store, and waited in vain, he sauntered off to find his special crony, Jim Beebe, and get him to go fishing. An hour or two after, they were both embarked in a dug-out on Long Lake, diligently waiting for something to bite, and Cal began discourse in a low tone, out of consideration for the fishes.

" Say, Jim, I'm a-goin' to git married."

" Be ye?" Jim answered meditatively, giving a gentle motion to his rod to see if the line was free.

" Yes, I be ; but, darn it all ! I dono who I'll marry yet, and I've got to hurry up. Mother's dreadful miser'ble along back."

" Kinder sure somebody'll hev ye, 'pears to me," sarcastically remarked Jim.

" Well, what ef I be? Gals is most gener'ly ready to say snip when a good-lookin' young feller says snap. I'll bet ye a cooky the fust gal I ask says yes right off."

Jim was disgusted with this conceit : he entertained no doubt that any girl in Bassett would marry him, but Cal Culver was another sort of person. Men have not radically changed within the last hundred years, and

both Calvary and Jim might find comrades to-day
However, Jim held his tongue, and Cal went on, —

"Trouble is to find jest the right one. There's lots
o' folks in the world ; but, come to marryin', you want
jest the right critter. It's a life bizness, you see ; and
what on airth kin a man do ef he gets haltered up tight
to the wrong un ? ' '

Cal was not " of the fashion of these times ; " for as
yet divorce facilities were unknown to decent Connecticut, and " till death " did not mean the " dying
daily " it seems to now.

" What sort o' head-marks be you sot on speci-
fyin' ? ' ' dryly remarked Jim, as he gave a little twitch
to his rod, and landed a round, fat little " punkin-
seed " in the bottom of the boat.

" Well, I want a smart un, — that, or nothin'.' '

" I knowed that afore ye told me : there's got to be
smartness some'eres,'' curtly put in Jim, pushing an
unhappy worm on to the end of his hook.

" Git out ! ' ' laughed Cal. " You shouldn't twit on
fac's, Jim. I'm smart enough when I'm a mind ter,
but I'd jest as lieves other folks would take a stiddy
job on't. I want a strong, healthy gal too.   Mother
she can't do a heap more : she's failin', that's the
truth on't. Somebody's got to step round lively to our
house while she lasts.   I want somebody that's got
faculty too : fact is, a woman that hain't got faculty
ain't good for nothin'.''

" Mebbe ye might try for Pollythi Bangs,'' put in
Jim, who was getting interested in the matter at last.

" Well, I declare for't, I hadn't had a thought o'
Pollythi Bangs. She is a masterpiece for smartness,
now, ain't she?''

"Steel traps ain't nothin' to her," assented Jim: "she's too smart a'most.   But she's got amazin' faculty, everybody says.   I dono, though, as I should reelly hanker to marry her, Cal: them Bangses is a dreadful queer lot."

"Well, I don't calkerlate to marry the hull on 'em, Jim.   I guess I could hold my own with Polly, ef she is reel masterful.   Come to that, I've the biggest bones anyway.   I can shake her up good."

Jim shook his head.   He did not feel sure that physical force could put down Pollythi Bangs, and proceeded, as delicately as he knew how, to urge this question.

"Well, I guess ye could, ef it come to that.   But, Lord, how be ye goin' to stop her tongue?   She'll talk ye lame and blind, ef ye stroke her the wrong way; and she'll hetchel the old woman mortally, I be afraid."

"Queer, ain't it?" Cal said, dropping his hook slowly into the water, having mated Jim's pumpkin-seed while he talked, — "queer how women-folks do ketch fire, come to git 'em together.   The best on 'em can't live in the same house two days 'thout some darned thing or 'nother sprouts up to set 'em by the ears.   It doos beat all."

"I expect Parson Robbins would say the Devil comes in thirdsman, Cal, them times."

"I guess there ain't no special call for an extry Devil.   'Riginal sin's actyve enough in 'em most times; but they're reel handy to hev around, for all that.   I shall begin square and fair.   Ef she wants to hetchel me, she kin try it on; but she'd better let the old woman alone.   'Twon't be for long anyway."

"Don't you reckon on that," put in the experienced

Jim. "Old women last for ever 'n' ever. They don't know how to die when they git started. Lordy! look at granny. She's ben prayed for more times in meetin'. She's ben dangerous forty times since I kin remember: but she hops up every time like a pa'tridge trap; and she's ninety, come July, as sure as you're born."

"Well, what do ye keep hevin' her prayed for?" coolly suggested Cal; an idea that tickled Jim till he dropped his rod over the side, worn out with suppressed laughter, — suppressed, for fear of startling the perch and pumpkin-seeds, which were now tempting their fate with commendable alacrity.

"Cal Culver, you do beat all!" he found breath to gasp at length. "Why, ef I didn't hand in no paper, Parson Robbins ud pray for her whether or no: so I might jest as well be kinder decent. But, ef you do go in for Pollythi Bangs, why, you ain't noways blinded. I expect you know her, root and branch."

"Jee-rusalem! I guess I do! Ain't her folks gin the name to Squabble Hill? Their house is jest like a flock o' blackbirds, — foreverlastin' a-cacklin' an' jawin' an' takin' to do: you can hear 'em nigh onto quarter of a mile when you're a-goin' along the turnpike. But mother's everlastin' hard o' hearin': that's a comfort, seein' things is as they is."

"I didn't know as they was yit," suggested Jim.

"Well, I guess there ain't no great doubt but what, ef I make up my mind, she'll make up her'n pretty much arter the same pattern. Polly hain't had no great luck with company-keepin', and she ain't no chicken nuther. I'll fetch round there next sabba'-day night, I guess, and kinder let fall a hint. I didn't want to rile her by bein' too suddin."

"I wouldn't," said Jim. "But look a-here, Cai. there's suthin' else to't. I forgot for to tell ye, for I only heerd it yesterday. She's hed a aunt, or suthin', die over to Har'ford, that's left her a couple o' housen there wuth quite a sum, — two or three thousan', I expect."

"Do tell! Now, Jim, that kinder clinches me. I'm bound for Pollythi, sure, now. Means is a help, that's a fact. I'd made up my mind pretty well afore : now I'm sartin."

All this time Pollythi Bangs was flying about the house at home, doing her annual spring-cleaning. Dreadful stage of human experience! Civilization has never softened its horrors, but rather added thereto. It is the crucial test before which all the amenities of life, its conveniences, its comforts, its elegancies, go down helplessly into the valley of humiliation. Furniture, *bric-à-brac*, carpets, paintings, china, only exasperate this insatiable epidemic, and give it more and more victims, till their number is legion. If Polly Bangs was cross over the lustration of a house with one carpet, two cracked looking-glasses, no sofa, blue-and-white crockery, and pewter platters, — a house where soap and water could be slopped about with absolute freedom, and the whitewash-brush smeared liberally everywhere, — what would she have been, turned loose among Sèvres, Dresden, Crown Derby, French porcelain, Japanese enamel, Bohemian glass, Venetian crystal; carpets of Persia, India, France, and England; furniture carved and upholstered as if for palaces ; priceless pictures ; paper of Eastlake and Morris ; and the ten thousand costly dusty bawbles of a modern mansion? Let lunatic-asylums answer. If we have gained much in these latter days, how much have we not lost?

Polly was cross naturally: her mother was cross; her father fairly growled.   The Bangs temper was proverbial in Bassett, and now it was in active exercise; for house-cleaning would test an angel's amiability, and tries that of common mortals to the extremest limit, even unto utter failure: why should a bad temper fail to find it exasperating?   But how much more furious would Pollythi have been, had she known of that discussion as to her future which was being held on the fair breast of Long Lake, while the budding trees shed soft shadows into the water, white clouds gently sailed along its depths, the fragrant reluctant breath of a New-England spring sighed tenderly over wave and shore, and Cal and Jim slaughtered little fishes with relentless hook and line as they discussed a deeper angling with a livelier bait.   Would she ever have risen to their hook?   Never!   But no officious telephone betrayed them: time and space kept the secret with their ancient honesty.   They are demoralized now; and that which is spoken in the bed-chamber is declared on the house-top, — even on the house-top miles away.   Who shall ever know safety of speech again?

Pollythi Bangs was all that Jim Beebe had painted her, and perhaps more, — strong of body and will both, imperious, quick-tempered, and absolutely unrestrained in speech.   She inherited all these traits from a father and mother so alike in character that they never were at peace with each other or their child.   Peace, indeed, was a state unknown in the Bangs family; and so notorious were their quarrels, so continuous their wars and fightings, that the hill halfway up which their old farm-house stood was known all through Bassington township as Squabble Hill, — a name borne by it to-day. But, if Polly Bangs was a scold, she was also smart, a great worker, and a woman who could turn her hand to any thing. She could weave any sort of fabric known to domestic looms in those days; she could out-spin any other woman in the town, having once, in a contest of wheels, spun seven run of yarn between sunrise and sunset, — an achievement that would have half-killed any other woman (two run being counted a legitimate day's work), but which seemed to have no effect on Pollythi's strength of nerve and muscle. Her bread was town-talk; her quilts elaborate beyond every thing, the seven-stars pattern and the sun-rising-over-the-Alleghany-Mountains pattern having originated in her own accomplished brain. As for knitting, and yeast, fine darning, election-cake, training-day gingerbread, and pot-pie, she was simply wonderful. Her root-beer always foamed, her nut-cakes fried just right, and her pork and beans were inimitable. These things never are the forte of amiable, gentle, "pretty-behaved" women. Energy, force, *Sturm und Drang*, make the world go round, not soft strokes: they have their own power, but it is not the power of leverage. Yet Polly had a certain rough kindliness about her when every thing went right.

> "Narcissa's nature, tolerably mild,
>   To make a wash would hardly stew a child."

She did not like children or animals; but she would fish a screaming infant out of the brook if need were, and had been known not to kick a lame dog that lay down on the door-step. It was wonderful to her mother that Polly had no lovers. People who live together get used sometimes to each other's faults. A husband will ignore a great deal in a wife, because he does not notice her short-comings as others do who do not come under their disturbance daily; and a mother will love and admire the spoiled child who is a nuisance to everybody else about her. Polly was handsome, after a fashion: she had hard black eyes, strong curling dark hair, red cheeks, strong white teeth, and a good tall figure, angular and awkward to be sure. But roundness, grace, dimples, are not the rule in New England; and Polly was better-looking than most of her compeers: yet she had attained the respectable age of thirty-five, without an offer, even from a widower, when Cal Culver took heart of grace, and asked her to marry him, after a three-weeks' courtship, following directly on his consultation with Jim Beebe.

Pollythi neither said yes nor no on that interesting occasion, nor did she go through the ordinary formulas of speech or action: she blushed not, neither sighed, nor drooped her head on Cal's shoulder. She was too far off for such tender demonstration, if she had intended it: so she sat bolt-upright in her chair, and answered audibly, " I'll think on't."

" Well, I wisht you would," manfully responded Cal.

He knew and she knew, and she knew he knew she knew (bless the English language!) that there was no particular love in the matter. Cal wanted a capable wife; and Pollythi, being a woman, fully understood that it is more creditable to an individual of the weaker sex to be anybody's wife than nobody's. She knew

very well that Calvary Culver was a shiftless, lazy,
penniless fellow, who wanted her to help him : handsome, to be sure ; but, if Polly's heart warmed the
least to his goodly presence, her head was cool enough
to chill such absurd flames immediately. Yet even
that very " level " head gave a casting vote in favor of
Cal. If she married him, she would have her own
house and her own way ; for she justly reckoned Mrs.
Culver as a cipher in the family. At home her mother
and her father both " drank delight of battle " with
her, and not infrequently got the victory, when they
were astute enough to join forces against her. But
with Cal she could hold her own, and take on her the
state and privileges of a matron ; while now she was
fast sinking into that purgatory of women, — old
maidenhood. So she " thought on't," as she promised,
and thought favorably ; and in due time brisk little
Parson Robbins published the banns of marriage between "Calvary Culver of this place, and Pollythi
Bangs of Squabble Hill," greatly to the edification, if
not the amusement, of his congregation. Some smiled,
and some shook their heads ; but the parson looked
like a small thunder-cloud, and, before the day was
over, effectually turned the thoughts of his flock from
Cal and Polly in this wise : —

It seems Jim Beebe had laid a bet with Squire Battle
that Parson Robbins couldn't preach a sermon without
mentioning the Devil — literally his *bête noire* — at
least a dozen times, and agreed with him that they both
should keep count the next Sunday, and so settle this
peculiar wager. Jim accordingly went to meeting
armed with a paper of big pins, and at each mention
of the Devil made by the parson stuck one of them

upright in the front-edge of the gallery where he sat. A fine row they made before that day was over, — thirteen for the morning sermon, fifteen for the afternoon's discourse, and positively twenty in the evening.

Jim won his bet, and triumphed. Brief exultation. The parson's keen eye had noticed his fixed attention, and a peering ray of sunshine had twinkled on the new pins. Parson Robbins was pleased. He was a man, after all, of mortal flesh and blood; and to have arrested the attention of such an incorrigible idler and "chuckle-head" as he had more than once stigmatized Jim Beebe, did the natural man a deal of good, and imparted power and fervency to his address. He could not quite explain the pins, but tried hard to believe Jim was so absorbed in the discourse he did not know what he was about. Even so have I known a modern minister speak with pathetic gratification of the effect "a few simple words" of his from the pulpit had upon a certain volatile young lady accidentally present, whom he fondly supposed to be sobbing with emotion, and who, alas! as I had the best reason to know, was merely struggling, with hidden face and abased head, to conquer a fit of mighty laughter, brought about by the machinations of a wicked companion. But Parson Robbins was more unlucky than the blessed man who gave me credit for my false-faced emotion; for, going home a little more upright and confident than ever, he heard a loud cackle of laughter from the steps of brother Battle's side-door, which was screened from the street by some shrubby lilacs, and Jim Beebe's voice uplifted with, —

"I stuck one in every time, squire; and you see your tally and mine is as like as peas in a pod. Forty

eight 'Devils' in them 'ere three discourses; 'bout as
bad as the herd o' swine. Haw, haw, haw! He
does beat all for givin' it to th' Enemy, now don't he?
But I got my bet."

"That's so," owned Squire Battle, re-echoing Jim's
irresistible chuckle.

Parson Robbins walked on in a state of mind quite
changed from the high content he had enjoyed before.
He was, in fact, furiously angry, and, thinking he did
well to be so, devoted himself to preparing in this week
three new sermons entirely free from any allusions to
the foul fiend, or his work and ways. It was a hard
piece of writing to do this, — hard as to stand with
level guns before the face of a hostile army, and not
pull a trigger; but yet it taught the parson one lesson
unconsciously. He learned more of the goodness of
God in the course of those three sermons than in many
a long year before, though the knowledge did not
immediately bear fruit, for it fell among the thorns of
kindled temper and wounded vanity. But they were
good sermons, and fell on the ears of his people like
dew on the mown grass, and showers that water the
field.   Sweet pale Margaret Robbins lifted up her face,
delicate as the cup of a wood-anemone, toward the
high pulpit, and wondered what fresh coal from the
altar had touched her father's lips; and Deacon Flint,
harder than his apt name, stirred uneasily in his square
pew, and thought many of such sermons might meddle
with his domestic discipline, and put new and revolu-
tionary ideas into his wife's head.   But at the end of
the evening sermon the parson destroyed the lovely
edifice he had so carefully laid up through the day, and
restored matters to their usual level by facing about

squarely at unlucky Jim Beebe, who sat as usual in the gallery, in the face and eyes of the congregation, and remarking in a loud voice, "There, young man! I have preached three sermons to-day, and have not mentioned the name of your father once."

Confusion twice confounded fell upon Jim and Squire Battle ; and a light rustle of choked and stifled laughter ran through the church, while the parson in a sonorous voice gave out the hymn beginning, —

"Why do the wicked boast abroad ?"

Under cover of this remarkable incident, the publishment of Cal and Polly went into obscurity ; and in due time they were married, and Pollythi was installed in the little red house. She came in as with a besom of destruction, fetching store of linen and blankets, fresh splint-bottomed chairs, a new clock, a set of blue-edged crockery, and sundry other plenishings. Granny Culver's rickety belongings were hustled into the second story, and she herself bundled out of her warm bedroom, opening out of the kitchen, into one of the two up stairs, which were under the roof, and, in this July weather, sweltering hot. But Polly announced at once that she " wa'n't a-goin' trapesin' up and down them stairs forevermore ; " and granny, being in a feeble minority, crept up the sharp ascent, and before long ceased to come down, but lay there, lonely and drowsy, day after day. Polly did not really neglect her. She had proper food, and was kept painfully clean. A little tenderness would have reconciled the old lady to fewer scrubbings and less food ; but Polly gave what she had to give. Can any of us do more? Cal was good to her in his lazy way ; but Cal was never so put

about in his own house before. No peace was left him
in those easy-going precincts where he had been used
to lie round at his leisure ; for now the floor was white
with abundant soaping and sanding in the kitchen, the
sills polished with scrubbing, the hearth immaculate,
the very jambs whitewashed, and a great corn-husk
mat lay before every door, whereon he was obliged, at
the point of the broom-handle, to rub his boots before
he could enter ; white curtains adorned every window ;
the walls glared with fresh whiteness ; the most elaborate quilt forbade him to nap on the bed, — to rest his
head on those shining linen pillow-cases would have
made it as uneasy as to wear a crown ; and the chintz
cushions in rocker and arm-chair were beautiful for
sight and situation, but their poppies and roses were
never meant to sit down on.

It is true that Cal had never before been regaled
with such food as Pollythi prepared. Her bread was
whiter than milk, light as cork, delicate as cake, she
wrought it after a secret process that Bassett maids and
matrons pined to discover, but never attained ; and the
game Cal brought in was converted into savory stews
and crisp broils that would have done credit to a French
chef. But what atones for domestic peace? How
pathetic is the declaration of Solomon ! — "It is better
to dwell in a corner of the house-top than with a brawl-
ing woman in a wide house."

There is but one parallel to this misery, — a man with
dyspepsia. And, if Solomon left him out in this speci-
fication, it is because he was a man himself ; and there
is a way made and provided for men or women to defend themselves against their own sex, which does not
hold good against the other.

If Cal Culver had taken into his house a brother whose days were spent in snapping and snarling, in sulking silently, or scolding mercilessly, he would forthwith have extended his good right arm, and knocked dyspepsia out of him summarily ; but against a woman, and that woman his wife, he was comparatively powerless, almost as powerless as the dyspeptic's wife or children would be against his afflictive manners and customs. So Pollythi pursued her triumphant career ; and Cal inhabited the barn and the woods chiefly through the summer, and became almost a fixture by the stove of Squire Battle's store in winter. Polly grew more and more furious over his defections and short-comings ; and, rather than consume with speechless wrath, she spent her time, between the occupations of housekeeping, in pouring that wrath into poor old granny's ears as she lay on her feather-bed in the loft. Granny was helpless ; for winter had now set in, and bound her hand and foot with " rheumatiz." She could not even creep up, and sit in her rocking-chair, which Cal had insisted should be carried up there ; but it was mighty convenient for Pollythi, who sat there by the hour, rocking and scolding and knitting, till granny learned to think the hiss of rushing snows, the crackle of sharp sleet, or the tireless drip of chilly rains, upon the roof so close to her head, a song of comfort in comparison with Polly's long diatribes. And when Cal came home at night, or occasionally to dinner, the tongue-tempest raged frantically, all the more that he seemed neither to hear nor fear this wordy assault, but bore himself like

> " Feather-bed 'twixt castle-wall
> And heavy brunt of cannon-ball,"

eating his dinner as placidly and deliberately as if Polly
and he were Darby and Joan.

He did feel one thing, though he diplomatically concealed it, and that was his mother's discomfort; for
the poor old woman feebly whimpered her woes to him
whenever they had a moment together, and he saw that
her life was a burden to her because of this daughter
of Heth.   But Cal could not help it; and his lazy, sunshiny nature shook off trouble as a duck flirts the rolling waters from her packed and glossy feathers.   He
said nothing to Polly, nor even let her know that he
appreciated his mother's sufferings: discretion was
eminently the better part of valor here.

The year rolled on into summer again, and again
found Cal and his crony fishing in latter May on Long
Lake.   The orchards were heaped with rosy bloom, the
woods fresh and odorous with young leaves; gold-and-
crimson columbines danced on the rocky shores, and
nodded to their vivid counterparts in the still wave
below; and the first wood-robin blew his fairy clarion,
resonant as a silver bell, sweet as a flute, yet shrill as
a violin, in the very highest boughs of the forest: but
Cal and Jim, blind and deaf as two images of wood,
neither saw nor heard the beauty and songs about
them; they were absorbed in discussing the rules and
regulations of a hunting-club to which they both belonged, and which gave prizes for certain achieve-
ments.   The subject had been introduced by the sight
of a heifer calf, apparently pure Devon, grazing peacefully in a near pasture.   It was Cal's calf, the captive
of his bow and spear in one sense; for he had won it
as last year's prize.

"Pretty critter, ain't it?" he said to Jim.

"Well, yes, middlin'. I dono but what I should think 'twas all-fired harnsome ef I'd got it as easy as you did, Cal."

"Easy! I tell ye it took some huntin' to git all them heads." And Cal's blue eyes twinkled with fun as he made this statement.

"Haw, haw, haw! You be the beateree, Cal Cul, of any critter I ever see. There ain't another feller in Bassett would ha' thought o' fetchin' in two hundred mouse-heads to the last minnit, and claimin' on 'em for game, so'st they couldn't help but give ye the prize."

"Well, they was game, — dreadful lively game too. I 'arned the prize, ef ever a man did."

"I say for't, Cal, ef you had as much grit as you've got gumption, I bet you'd be put up for guv'nor, or hog-herd, or suthin', afore ye die."

"Mebbe I should, mebbe I should; but 'tain't wuth the trouble, Jim. I'm 'flicted with a chronic overdid from my youth up'ard, as Parson Robbins might say. I don't see no payin' property in workin' yourself to death afore your time."

"It's awful lucky you've got a real smart wife, now I tell ye."

"Well, there might be two ways o' lookin' at that, now, Jim Beebe. There is sech a thing as bein' too everlastin' smart and spranxious for a feller's comfort."

"That's so," briefly assented Jim.

"Now, I don't say but what Pollythi's a smart woman, — an orful smart woman; but she's got a kind of a mighty way with her, so to speak, a kinder peppery nater, that makes things lively as a bumble-bee's nest in hayin'-time."

" She's dreadful neat, ain't she?"

" Neat! she's cleaner'n creation arter the flood.
There dursn't so much as one small fly skip round
where she is; and as for skeeters — my land! she'd
ketch 'em and soap their feet, if they durst to hum one
time to our house. I b'lieve, 'twixt you and me and
the post, she's 'most washed mother away: there ain't
but mighty little left of her."

" Why, she used to be kinder fat when I see her."

" Fat! well, she's 'bout as fat's a hen's forehead,
now, I tell ye. And her floor's sloshed over with a
mop so frequent, I believe honest, she's got the rheumatiz past helpin', or pokeberry rum."

" Do tell!"

" She has, sir. Priest Robbins he come to see her
a spell ago, and he praised up the looks o' things
amazin'. Polly she nussed him up with a mug o' flip
and a lot o' 'lection-cake, till he was as pleasant as a
young rooster. But thinks sez I, ' you're nearer to
the Devil, a-settin' right there, parson, than ever you
was afore.' By jinks! I don't want no wuss Devil
round than a foreverlastin' jawin' woman, Jim Beebe,
now I tell ye."

" Thunder!" ejaculated Jim, not knowing what else
to say to this astonishing burst of confidence on Cal's
part.

" Yes, *sir:* it's thunder and lightnin' too; and I
dono how to stand it, nor how to git red on't."

Jim had no advice to give. In those days a married
pair were helpless, however incompatible they might
be: they had to jog along the highways and by-ways
of life like an ill-mated pair of oxen, however the
yoke galled them, or however much they wanted to

gore each other. It was a relief to Cal to have freed his mind to Jim Beebe, whom he knew to be reticent of any real confidence; but it was only a temporary relief. He was as unhappy, or rather as uncomfortable, as a person of his temperament could be; and Pollythi was more unhappy still. Before two years of her married life had gone by, she had learned thoroughly to despise her husband: she knew him to be radically lazy and self-indulgent, — traits for which she had no mercy or patience. It did not occur to her that in her own way she equally indulged herself. This is a nice distinction often drawn by persons who do not seem able to see that self-indulgence can lie in yielding to evil temper and irritated nerves quite as surely, and far more painfully to others, than in giving way to an indolent and ease-loving nature. Pollythi even claimed to be a religious woman, or to have such intentions: she had assented to the "halfway" covenant of those times, which made her a sort of postulant for full membership at some future period, and she had an honest desire to be a good woman. But she was quite unaware how bitter and stinging her speech was to Calvary, how differently it sounded in his ears and hers. It was the habit of her life to scold; but it was an unpleasant novelty to him, and, for the sake of what little peace was left to his mother, he forbore conflict, but chose flight instead. Now, if Polly Culver ever had loved anybody on earth, it was her handsome, worthless husband; and, while she despised his character, she raged with frantic jealousy at his neglect. Anomalous, perhaps; but women are all anomalies. She would have forgotten all his sins, had he condescended to coaxing and caressing; but she would have gone on scolding just as usual. At the end of two years Granny Culver died, peacefully and joyfully. She was glad to go somewhere else, if her faith was not very vivid, or her hope clear. A sort of dim but helpful belief upheld her to the verge of the grave. Naturally dull of intellect, uneducated, wearing away her hard and simple life in the pursuit of daily bread, yet the relics of early teaching lingered with her, and she died with folded hands, saying " Our Father; " and the words at which she left off were, " Thy will be done."

Calvary went after Parson Robbins to attend the funeral. The parson himself answered that stout thump at the front-door.

" Say, parson, can you 'tend up to mother's funeral to-morrer? "

" Is your mother dead, Calvary? Why, why, why! "

" Ef she wa'n't, there wouldn't be no need o' a funeral," muttered Calvary under his breath; for the parson was a little deaf.

" Well, well! What was the matter? What was her complaint? What did she die of, eh? "

" Pollythi," stoutly responded Cal.

"Polypus? Dear, dear! Strange disorder. I never heard of a case in these parts."

" Pollythi, I said! " shouted the indignant son.

" Calvary Culver! " The parson's indignation rendered him speechless.

" Well, she did anyhow; and it's a wuss disease'n t'other polly, a heap. I'm like to die on't myself afore long, ef somebody don't doctor her for't."

" Your frame of mind is carnal indeed," began Parson Robbins, " if you can talk such talk about your lawful wife."

"Well, I shouldn't say nothin' about her ef she wa'n't my wife," answered the incorrigible Cal. "But ef a man dono what his wife is, who doos? I tell ye, Pollythi's the Devil and all."

"Hold your profane tongue, sir!" flamed the parson.

"'Tain't no sech. It don't say nowheres in the Bible nothin' about takin' Satan's name in vain, now, I'll bet ye. Besides, I took it to good puppus, an' I'll say it agin for a copper. I'd a darn sight ruther the Old Boy was arter me than Poll, anyway."

"Calvary Culver, I've a great mind to set the tithing-man after you for using profane and loose talk ; and I will surely, if you offend again. This is not to be borne."

"Well, it ain't to the p'int, that's a fact, parson. Let's commence to the beginnin' agin. Say, would you ruther hev the corpse fetched to the meetin'-house? and will you hev funeral services to-morrow, or a Thursday?"

"Thursday, in the Lord's house. And I say unto you, Beware, Calvary Culver, lest you be taken at your word, and the Enemy do indeed come after you to enlist you in his service, which is death."

"Amen!" ejaculated Calvary, and strode off. But why did he, a few rods down the road, stop, slap his thigh as in congratulation, and stifle a laugh outwardly that nevertheless shook him all over?

On Thursday the funeral took place in church. Parson Robbins preached a sermon with seventeen heads, calculated to make the flesh creep on the bones of his audience, and with abundant mention of the Enemy therein, as one lying in wait for perishing sinners, — a point he directed straight at the chief mourner on this occasion, who received it decorously, though he afterward was heard to remark to Jim Beebe, that he did think it was "everlastin' mean to jaw at a feller like that when he can't noway jaw back."

The choir also did their part at exalting the misery and despair of the occasion, by wailing out in the discordant manner of country choirs, "Mear," "China," and "Windham" to appropriate words; the whole ceremony, to an unbiassed observer, presenting rather the aspect of a heathen assemblage howling over the dead, than a Christian church celebrating the falling-asleep of a sister in the hope of a joyful resurrection. But, as this style of funeral service is still prevalent among us, we cannot cast any stones at Bassett, but must turn away, and follow Cal Culver — as far as we can.

Home did not become any more homelike, or Polly any lovelier, to Calvary after his mother's death, but rather more distasteful; and before long, exasperated by his wife's constant vituperation, and unrestrained by any fear of troubling the poor soul who lay safe asleep in the graveyard, he turned upon the astonished Polly, and gave her a good shaking.

This finished the last bit of kindly feeling in her heart. The "dynamic reasons of larger bones" did not appear logical to her: she raved and raged like a perfect fury, and retaliated by throwing the piggin of soft-soap at Calvary's head, — a missile he would have found sufficiently uncomfortable, if Polly could have thrown it straight enough to hit him; but, as it was, it only broke the flax-wheel in its flight, and poured its contents of unsavory jelly over the basket of fresh-

ironed clothes.   Polly fell into hysterics; and Cal
picked her up, deposited her on the bed, and strode
off.

"What's the matter o' you?" shouted Jim Beebe,
who was going by, seated in an ox-cart, whistling, and
balancing his long whip as the heavy red beasts made
deliberate progress along the road.

"Plenty," curtly responded Cal.

"Hain't seen the Enemy, hev ye?" queried Jim.

"Wisht I had.   I'd consider'ble ruther go to the
Devil than stay to hum 'long o' her," pointing over his
shoulder with expressive thumb toward the house.

"Cal Culver!   What ef Priest Robbins heerd ye?"

"Well, what ef he did?   He talk about the Devil!
He don't know nothin'.   Both his wives died pretty
near right off; and that gal o' his'n is 'most too good
to live, folks tell.   Folks ain't qualified to preach
about things, onless they know 'em so to be."

"Well, there is suthin' to that," allowed Jim, urging
on his slow team.   "Where you goin'?"

"Over to the store," gloomily answered Cal.   "I'm
a-goin' to hire out a spell this year; take it in jobs.
Ef I could git a mite o' cash, I'd go to York sure as
you're born, and git suthin' to do there.   Mebbe I'd git
onto a whaler."

"Why, hain't you got cash enough?   I thought she
had rents out o' the housen in Har'ford."

"Heavens-to-Betsy!   You don't think I ever see a
copper o' her cash, do ye?   It's trusted out to a bank
in Har'ford quick as lightnin'.   It don't never peek at
Bassett; and, ef it did, I shouldn't have none of it."

"But I b'lieve, accordin' to law, it's all your'n, to
nev an' to hold, ain't it?"

" 'Tain't accordin' to Pollythi; and that's more to the p'int, a lot.   I wouldn't hev it nuther, — not to git it by law.   She'd make it burn my fingers, and p'ison my pocket.   No, sir: I ain't got no hankerin' arter work. but I'd ruther hill corn than squabble for her money."

"Well, well, I don't say but I agree with ye so fur. But it doos seem cur'us, kinder, how she works it with ye.   Say!   Deacon Flint he wants help.   He's a-plantin' the ten-acre medder this year; and he reckons to hire, his rheumatics is so dreadful bad."

"I sha'n't get puss-proud on his pay," dryly remarked Cal; "but mebbe I'd better take up with it, seein' it's three mile off."

"Haw, haw, haw!" roared Jim; and the oxen, roused by that familiar sound, turned placidly off to the left.   And while Jim was trailing them back into position with, "Gee, Buck! gee, I tell ye, Bright! git up! gee, can't ye?" and sundry cracks of the whip, Calvary stalked off the other way, and at night an nounced to Pollythi that he had "got a job" at Deacon Flint's.

He worked here pretty steadily for a week or two, ploughing the great field for winter rye, and renewing the fence, which was old and feeble; being very little at home, and receiving Polly's wordy flights with contemptuous silence.   He took his dinner always to the field, — an abundant and wholesome provision, for Polly never stinted any one in their food, — and matters appeared to have settled down into an armed neutrality, when one noon-time a mighty knocking startled Parson Robbins from his sermon-writing; and he opened the door to behold Calvary Culver, his fair hair disturbed as if it had been standing on end, his eyes big as sau cers, and drops of sweat thick over all his face, which was disturbed by a wild look of terror and dismay.

"O Lord, parson! I've been and gone and done it now!" he exclaimed, as the parson's square dark visage glared sternly upon him over the lower half of the door.

"Set a guard on your lips, Calvary Culver," indignantly exclaimed the parson.

"O L— Oh! Well, th' occasion kinder needs cussin'. Well, I won't: so there. But I do want to tell ye suthin', parson. I'm under concern, so to speak: I want dealin' with."

The parson's face brightened.

"Bless the Lord! Walk in, my friend; walk in! This is indeed to be rejoiced in."

"I dono," said Cal ruefully: "I should say 'twas to be t'other thinged myself."

"Sit down there," said the parson, when he had piloted him to the study, pointing to a splint-bottomed chair hard and straight enough to have served as a stool of repentance, — "sit there, and let us reason together."

"Well, fust and foremost I want to tell ye suthin'; then you kin reason on't, ef you hanker to. I don't. I'm nigh about skeered to death, parson. I swan to man I be!"

"Cannot you tell your story without unseemly words, my friend?" objected the parson.

"Well, I dono's I can, and I dono *as* I can: fact is, I want suthin' to h'ist me along, as it might be, seemin'ly, and I'm used to them words you tell about. Lordy! what's words? They don't mean nothin' when you're used to 'em, no more'n a cat-bird's scoldin'; come kinder nateral."

"Well, well, go on!" ejaculated the parson, who really felt much more like swearing than Calvary; for it was late in the week, and a happy train of thought in his sermon curtly interrupted.

"Well, you see, I'm a-workin' for Deacon Flint; ben a-ploughin' and seedin' down and harrerin' that 'ere ten-acre medder o' his'n. He don't pay fust-rate, ye know: but for sartin private reasons, such as the man had that killed the goose, I wanted a job that wa'n't nigh hum; so I took up with that. Well, I was harrerin' away this mornin', 'most to the eend o' the lot, and kinder speculatin' whether or no I'd go to choppin' to-morrer, or whether I'd go up on to the mounting, and snare a mess o' pa'tridges."

"Boast not thyself of to-morrow," put in the parson solemnly.

"I wa'n't, as I knows of; but I kinder hankered arter them birds: they've ben a-fattin' up on the deacon's buckwheat this four weeks back, and they'll be plump as punkins. Well, that ain't here nor there. But, as I was sayin', I got nigh about to the road-eend o' the lot, and I see somebody a-comin' full tilt down the road. Thinks me, that's Jim Beebe: so I let the critters stop. They'd allers ruther stop, ye know, than go 'long, oxen would: they're slower'n molasses."

The parson wiped his damp face. To a man of his temper this prolixity was maddening. "Well, well, well, never mind the team. Go on, Calvary."

"Why, I was a-goin' on. Well, you see, I kinder leaned up agin the fence to wait for him; but, when he come along, I see 'twa'n't nobody I ever see afore, nor nobody't looked like anybody I ever see afore. 'Twas a dreadful dark-complected man, reel spry appearin'

— one that looked as though his name was Smart, now
I tell ye. My, how them eyes o' his'n did snap ! —
jest like Pollythi's when she throwed the piggin at my
head, only he didn't act noways mad, and I didn't
think nothin' strange o' his eyes till I come to rec'lect
them arter he'd gone. You know, parson, folks don't
allers sense things right off: they sorter call 'em to
mind, so to speak, as it might be, arter they've gone
by. Well, he come along and spoke reel civil ; sez,
' How be ye? ' or suthin' : 'tain't no great matter what
he did say ; I guess 'twas 'bout the weather. But he
went on fur to say, ' Got a job, hain't ye? ' — ' Well,'
sez I, ' I hev and I hain't. I've got through here :
there's quite a spell o' choppin' in his wood-lot I
could hev, I s'pose, ef I hankered to.' — ' Well,' sez
he, ' I want a feller of 'bout your heft to work for me
a spell. I'll give good wages.' So I sez, ' What'll
ye give? ' for I wa'n't gittin' but three-an'-sixpence
by the day, boardin' myself. Ye know Deacon Flint's
a dreadful near man : he dursn't look at a dollar outside his pocket, it scares him so. So I reckoned here
was a chance of a betterment ; and ef he didn't up and
offer me a dollar right off, and found ! ' '

" Filthy lucre," groaned the parson.

" No, he wa'n't filthy a mite : he was dressed up for
'lection, I tell ye, ef he was lookin' ; but I snapped
him up jest as a pickerel does a shiner. Sez I, ' I'm
your feller.' — ' Well,' sez he, ' you might go 'long an'
hire out to somebody't offered ye more : let's hev it in
writin'. I b'lieve in contracks.' — ' Hev it your own
way,' sez I : ' fetch on your contrack.' So he whipped
a little book out o' his pocket, an' sez he, ' I keep my
'greements writ out in here. I'm a-hirin' out a lot

o' men for this here coalin' job.' I dono's I mentioned, parson, he told me, fust go off, 'twas a coalin'
job. ' So now,' sez he, ' write your name down here.'
— 'Jeerus'lem!' sez I, ' I don't keep pen and ink in
my breeches-pocket; do you?' He larfed a little, and
then he sez, ' Well, prick your finger : there's a crow's
feather ; I'll make a pen for ye.' Sure enough he did,
and I jest scratched a place on my arm till I fetched a
leetle mite o' blood, and writ my name down in the
book with that crow-quill as sure as you're a livin'
critter.''

   '' Singular,'' muttered the parson.

   '' Sing'lar ! I guess it was. Fust I knew he wa'n't
there. I'd dropped my whip-stock while I was writin' ;
and, when I'd writ, sez I, ' Where do ye live?' — ' Well,
quite a ways off, down by the Kingdom,' sez he ; ' but
I'll come and fetch ye a Friday come two weeks, to-day
bein' Saturday.' So then I bent down to git my whip-
stock ; and, as sure as you're born, when I straightened
up, that black feller wa'n't there ; but there was the
all-firedest stink ! Thunder ! ef you'd had a bonfire
o' roll brimstone, 'twouldn't ha' ben no wuss. That
struck me all of a heap. I know'd what that meant
quicker'n punk. Sartin as you live, I'd gin a contrack
to the Enemy, and he'll be arter me immediate. Now,
what be I a-goin' to do, parson?''

   Parson Robbins paced up and down his small study,
his eye kindled, and his head erect, like one who snuffs
the battle afar off, muttering to himself, half aloud
'' He goeth about like a roaring lion, seeking whom he
may devour ; but resist him, yea, resist the Devil, and
he shall flee from thee. This kind goeth not out save
by prayer and fasting. — Calvary Culver,'' turning to

the victim, who sat watching him with a peculiar look of intelligence and craft in his half-shut eye, — Calvary Culver, this is an awful warning to you. Repent, and flee from all your evil doings. You have lived a kind of a shiftless life, not profitable to God or man, nor according to your chief end; and now Satan hath desired to have thee. But the Adversary shall be put to flight. I will appoint a day of fasting and prayer in the church. It shall be the day of your master's arrival to fetch you; but by the help of the Lord we will slay a thousand, yea, we will put ten thousand to flight."

"Well now, parson, I didn't expect to give ye no sech trouble," said Cal, looking a little uneasy. "I thought I'd oughter tell ye, so'st ef I was took away sudden, you might kinder suspect whereabouts I was, and I didn't know but what you could give me suthin', some kind of a word, ye know, like them long ones in the fust part o' the Bible, to scare him off, ef he reelly was the Old Boy."

"I will have the day of prayer appointed very shortly," went on the parson, giving little heed to Cal's remonstrances or suggestions. "To-morrow is already occupied with another subject: I am advised to pray for rain."

"Well, 'tis everlastin' dry, that's a fact. I dono's that winter wheat ever will come up anyhow," assented Calvary.

"Besides, I think it better to appoint the day the Evil One hath himself set; for I think he will scarcely venture into the house of the Lord to seize his prey."

And the parson smiled a grim smile, as who should say, "I have outgeneraled the enemy."

So Calvary left him, and went his way, finished his day's work, and told Pollythi the whole story at the tea-table.

At first that strong-minded woman was disinclined to accept the tale; but education and superstition were too much for her: she ended by believing it all, and prepared for church in the morning with a sense of personal importance, for heretofore she had not considered her husband of enough consequence for ever the Devil to come after him.

It was a splendid October day. The abundant forests burned in the soft red sunshine like crusted gems and dead gold; the air was sweet and sad with odors of dying foliage and fading flowers. A rich silence brooded over the hills and fields of Bassett, broken only by the first sounding of the bell for service, which aroused here and there, in answer to its summons, clouds of dust from the ash-dry roads, stirred by the heavy wagons and deliberate horses of the more distant farmers.

The day was so quiet, so serene, the blue heaven and the gorgeous misty hills so lovely in their calm repose, that Bassett might have passed for a bit of paradise. But, to the astonishment of everybody, Parson Robbins trotted across the green to church, carrying a great green umbrella.

"Why, parson," asked Squire Battle, who was "standing around" on the meeting-house steps, "ain't ye kind of prematoor? There ain't the first sign o' rain."

"I shall fetch her! I shall fetch her!" sharply answered the parson, as if his neighbor had been doubting Thomas; and, to be sure, before the second

service was well begun, the mists gathered depth and
then blackness; light winds sighed through the forest,
and died out in ominous quiet; thunder growled afar
off, drew nearer and nearer; and then the heavens
opened suddenly, dashing their stores of rain upon the
thirsty earth. and drowning the parson's triumphant
burst of praise and thanksgiving in the clatter it made
on the old church-roof. The people were impressed,
as well they might be; and when the parson went on to
appoint a day of fasting and prayer, the next Friday
week, for a brother in distress and danger, a feeling of
awe and interest stole through the congregation; and
after service was over many a question was asked, and
answer suggested. But the parson spoke to nobody:
he went home in silence. He had never felt nearer to
God, or more sure of victory over Satan, than now.

Cal and Jim Beebe went home together through the
rain, which had quieted down now to a cold drizzle.
Some neighbors had taken Pollythi into their wagon.

"Parson's a hero at prayer, ain't he?" suggested
Jim.

"Well, he ain't nothin' else."

"But who d'you suppose the feller is in sech trouble
they've got to hev a meetin' about him?"

Cal gave him an expressive punch with his elbow.
"Lawful sakes! it's me, Jim."

"Sho!" Jim exclaimed, standing still, and facing
round at Calvary with wide eyes and open mouth.

"'Tis, I tell ye. Now shet up that mouth o' your'n,
and come along, and I'll tell ye the hull on't."

So he poured his tale into Jim's willing ear, whether
with any additions or emendations, history has not
recorded: if there were, the reader's imagination must

supply them. It is only sure that Jim went home with
an expression of mixed amusement and astonishment
on his face, that did not do credit to the solemnity of
the story.

At last the eventful Friday arrived. Parson Robbins. after much pondering, had marshalled and ordered
his forces, and planned his battle-array. Calvary was
ushered into the gallery of the meeting-house, and
placed in the front-seat. He had on his Sunday suit:
his hair was laid as flat as those rebellious curls could be
by the aid of a tallow candle assiduously applied; and
his handsome face was shining with yellow soap, and
water; his boots had a portentous creak to them;
and his blue eyes were empty of all expression, as he
sat there, his great red hands clasping a still redder
bandanna handkerchief, and he himself supported by
the proud consciousness that he was the object of all
this bustle and attention. At the head of the stairs
leading into the gallery, Simeon Tucker, the black-
smith, holding a mighty stick, stood on guard, lest the
Old Boy should take on himself to come in person, and
nab Cal Culver before meeting was over; and at the
foot of the stairs another muscular brother, with
another stick, looked both ways with his cross-eyes, as
if he kept double watch and ward. Jim Beebe, escort-
ing Cal to the door, as became a true comrade, suggested the idea to him that the parson had picked out
Josiah on this very account, and Calvary found it hard
to repress an indecorous chuckle.

But, once in the church, chuckling was at an end.
The parson read long selections from the Bible; all
the minatory Psalms, to begin with, and then every
verse he could find under the heads relating to Satan in

the Concordance; then certain awful hymns, minor in key and minor in thought, were wailed and groaned out by the congregation; then the parson prayed, and Deacon Flint prayed, till the very gates of heaven seemed to be stormed. Then there was more reading, followed by a short discourse of twelve heads only, in which the parson gave a full account of " the young man's " experience, and a historic and biographic account of the Devil, going back to Eden. During the first part of the discourse Cal sat on thorns. He was not overly modest or shy, but to be the centre of all those eyes was abashing even to him; and, moreover, he was much bored with the whole matter. The seat was hard, the day was warm, as late October days sometimes are: he was hungry, and thirsty too; for though he had tied up a loaf of rye bread and several slices of cheese in a handkerchief that morning, and filled a flat bottle with cider, he did not fetch them to church.

After the sermon, praying began again. Every brother present " desired to jine " in the exercise, and the sun was ready to set before these zealous members gave out. Flesh and blood could not bear it longer; and at last Parson Robbins wound up the meeting with a pointed but brief exhortation to Cal, and a benediction. Then the two stalwart men, clubs and all, escorted Calvary to his own house, lest some outlying fiend should snap him up; while Pollythi lingered a little to talk it all over with Deacon Flint's wife.

The spiritual constables brought him safely to the red house, and declared afterward that he seemed much solemnized by the way, and thanked them kindly for their good offices. He shut the door upon them, with a composed countenance; but from that day to this Calvary Culver was never again seen in Bassett.

Many were the conjectures as to his fate; though most people believed, with Parson Robbins, that the Devil was as good as his word, and had taken him off, body and soul, as well as his new overalls, which were missing. Pollythi mourned him decorously; but in a couple of years married again, in spite of Jim Beebe's remonstrances, and his wild idea that Cal might turn up yet. But he never did; and to this day Bassett people tell the shuddering tale of Cal Culver and the Devil.

AMANDAR.

"What's in a name?"

" 'Tain't no use, Keery; you needn't take me to do no more. I shall hev that young un called accordin' to the counsel of my own will, as Cat'chism says. If a man hain't got a right to put a name to his own child, I don' know who hes."

" Well, well, talk, do talk, Bezy Hills. Who said you shouldn't? I jest kinder throwed in an idee, as ye may say. I think Scripter names are seemly for deacons' folks; an', ef you don't want no Scripter names round, why, I can't help it. Folks will be folksy, I s'pose, an' mother she always said 'twas rule or ruin with Bezy when you wa'n't more'n knee-high to a grasshopper; an' what's bred in the bone'll come out in the flesh, I've always heered, an' ' " —

The monologue was cut short here by the slam of the kitchen-door, as Bezaleel Hills fled into the shed from the scourge of tongues.

Widow Walker was his elder sister, a weakly, buzz·ing, fluent, but not unprincipled woman. She had a long nose, a fallen-in and yet wide mouth, a distinct chin, and a pair of weak gray eyes with red lids, all overshadowed by a severe front of false chestnut hair set in stiff puffs, making her face look like those triangular heads which the schoolboy's pencil bestows upon

193

a cat when he solaces the dull hours of his education, by means of a slate meant for far other purposes.

Bezaleel had lost his wife six months ago, exchanging her for the fat baby now lying in his sister's lap before the fire. He was a silent man in regard to his affections, though voluble enough as to his will and opinions. Sister Kerenhappuch had not the least idea how his soul was bound up in the delicate, shy creature who had been his wife only five years, or how he had labored to give her such rude comforts as a country village could afford. It had been the one joy of his life to see the dark, soft eyes shine when he entered the door, and his solitary reward to know, that, even in the delirium of death, his voice could quiet her, and her last conscious word was "Dear!"

When he banged the door to-day, Keery did not know that his cold eyes were dim with tears, thinking of Amanda and his own solitude. She gave a sigh of obtrusive length and volume, as who should say, "Such is life, and, slowly squeaking to and fro in the old rocker, began to sing to the baby, who threatened to awake when the door slammed, that excellent but unpleasant old hymn, —

"Broad is the road that leads to death,"

to the equally unpleasant, if not as excellent, tune of "Windham."

As the long-drawn, doleful whine of the cadences kept tune to the slow squeak of the rocker, the baby, like a child of sense, objected, and not only woke, but set up a scream so lively and so sharp, that the wail of his aunt's voice hushed before the fresh life of this infantine chorus. She stopped singing, reversed her charge across her knee, gave him two smart resounding slaps, and, tucking him vigorously under one arm, proceeded to warm his supper in the flat silver porringer that was an heirloom of unknown antiquity, and so appease his temper.

A week after, having relegated him to the care of a poor neighbor (paid for the office with a peck of turnips), she betook herself to sewing-society, a big silk bag on her left arm, a calash on her head, and her Sunday gown of black bombazine adorned by a vast tamboured muslin collar, while her chestnut front looked sterner than ever surmounted by a structure of black lace and hard dark purple satin ribbons.

Five old women about a quilt! Can the pen of one give a tithe of their conversation record? Let us attempt but a part of it. Mrs. Green began the tournament.

"I hain't seen ye a month o' Sundays, Miss Walker: where do ye keep yerself?"

"Why, I've ben to hum. 'Taint real handy to take to baby-tendin' when ye git along in years a spell; but there don't seem to be nobody else to take care of Bezy's babe but me. Bezy's as pernickity as a woman about the child: he won't lemme give it a speck of nothin' but red cow's milk; an' he's nigh about seven months old, an' he'd oughter set in lap 'o the table, an' take a taste o' vittles along with us. My land! my children used to set to an' grab things as quick as ever I fetched 'em where they could. Little Jemimy was the greatest hand for b'iled cabbage ye ever did see; an' pork!—how that child would holler for fried pork! There wa'n't no peace to the wicked till she got it. She'd ha' ben a splendid child ef she'd

lived. But the summer complaint was dreadful prevalent that year; an' it took her off in the wink of an
eye, as ye may say: allers doos the healthy children.
Then my Samwell, why, he was the greatest hand for
pickles that ever was: he'd git a hunk o' fried steak
into one leetle hand, an' a pickle into t'other, an' he
would crow an' squeal. Cuttin' of his stomach-teeth
was the end o' him: got 'em too early; was took with
convulsions, an' died right off. An' the twins: well,
they favored beans, — baked beans an' minute-puddin'.
They was eighteen months old when they died, an' they
eet toast an' cider like good fellers only the day they
was took sick. We'd hed buckwheats an' tree molasses
for breakfast that day; an' I expect they'd eet so
much sweet, it kinder made 'em squeamy, so't the
hard cider jest hed the right tang. Poor little creturs! Mabbe 'twas the bilious colic a-comin' on made
'em dry: anyway they was awful sick with 't, an' they
died a Sunday week, for they was took of a Sunday,
an' ' " —

Miss Polly Paine, a short, plump old maid, gently
interrupted here: she thought widow Walker had occupied the floor long enough.

"But say, what do ye give it *red* cow's milk for?
I never knowed there was any great o' virtoo in red
cows."

"Sakes alive!" Here Semanthy House, Deacon
House's wife, took up the thread of conversation. " I
want to know ef ye didn't? Why, red's the power-
fulest thing! You jest put a red flannel round your
throat, an' it won't never be sore; an' a red string in
your ears'll keep off fever, everybody knows. But
then I don't hold to fetchin' up a child on milk alto-

ςether: they won't never make old bones that way. I b'lieve in hearty vittles for everybody. Pie's real hearty, ef ye make it good, an' so's cheese, when ye can't git butcher's meat. I b'lieve I could stan' it the year round on pie an' cheese an' baked beans.''

"Well, ye see," pottered on Mrs. Walker, who seized a chance to begin again, "Bezy he won't hear to no reason: he claims he knows more about fetchin' up children than I do, spite of my hevin' hed four on 'em. He speaks about their all dyin' off, an' says he wants his'n to live, — a-flyin' in the face of Providence, as ye may say; for we all know folks die by the dispensations of Providence, an' mortal man can't say, 'Why do ye so?' to the Lord. But I don't know but what brother Bezy thinks he can. He sets dreadful loose to religion, 'specially doctrines an' sech; says he wishes 't Parson Pine wouldn't say sech a lot about 'lection, an' hell, an' decrees, an' more about mercy an' lovin'-kindness. Land! I want to know how you're goin' to fetch hardened old sinners like some ye could mention, ef ye was a-min' to — an' I guess we all know who they be without namin' of 'em — inter the kingdom, ef ye couldn't scare 'em out of their seven senses a-shakin' of 'em over the pit, as ye may say. They don't mind nothin' but a real scare, an' they don't mind that no great. I feel to wonder real often why sech folks is spared to" —

Polly Paine broke in again. She knew by experience that widow Walker would talk interminably if they waited for her easy tongue to stop of itself.

"Say, what be you a-goin' to call that child? I hain't heerd it spoke of save an' except 'baby,' sence ever 'twas born. I s'pose it's got to hev some handle to 't, ha'n't it?''

"Well, now, there!" said Kerenhappuch, heaving a long and quavering sigh — "there's Bezy agin! He's most too cur'us to live. I wanted he should give the child a real good Scripter name, sech as mine an' his'n is. It seems as though it give a child a kind of a pious start in this world to call it out o' Scripter. But he's jest as sot! I don' know's you know 'twas so, but so it was : he made a reg'lar idle out of 'Mandy. He a-most said his prayers to her, I do b'lieve. She was a good enough gal, for't I know ; but he took on real foolish about her. The washing was did for her ; an' he didn't keep but two cows, because he wouldn't let her be overdid."

"Dew tell!"   "Well, I never!"   "That doos beat all!"   "Sakes alive!" echoed round the quilt, as the old ladies glared over their spectacles, and suspended their needles, in the great shock of learning that a man could consider his wife's comfort before the fulness of his pocket. But they did not stop the flow of Keery's mild, incessant gabble. She went right on : —

"Well, she wa'n't real strong, kinder weakly from the fust ; an' when she up an' died, seemed as though Bezy couldn't stand it no way in the mortal world. He was cut down dreadful : the consolations of religion wa'n't of no account to him. He behaved around a sight worse'n Job in the Bible did. Why, I tell ye I was skeert for a spell ; an' then I up and I took him to do, I tell ye. I says, says I, 'Bezaleel Hills,' says I, ' be ye a perfesser, or not? I don't see how ye can fly inter the face o' Providence this way. Don't ye know ye made a idle of 'Mandy?' says I, 'so the Lord he took her away from ye. Ye thought a heap too

much of her.' — ' Git out ! ' says he, a-snappin' at me
so quick I screeched a little screech ; an' he banged
the door, an' you nor I nor nobody knows where under
the canopy he went to ; but he never come in till dark
night, an' his eyes was as red as a rabbit's, an' there
was hay-seed onto his head. I mistrust he'd ben into
the mow a-cryin', but " —

Miss Polly, who saw she must fetch the widow back
to her subject-matter of discourse, interposed again : —

" Well, he can't call the boy after her, seein' 'tain't
a girl ; an' her t'other name was Smith. I guess he
wouldn't never yoke Smith an' Hills up together."

A faint smile relaxed the severe wrinkles of Keery's
sallow forehead. " I don't suppose ye ever would
guess, nor nobody else neither ; but he doos act like all
possessed about it. He says — and, when he doos say
a thing, he sticks to't like shoemaker's wax — that he's
a-goin' to call that poor babe Amandar."

A chorus of exclamations again went round the
quilt. Mrs. Green, in the very act of snapping the
chalked twine that marked the quilters' pattern, lifted
her head, and forgot to let go of the string.

" For mercy's sakes what do you mean?" she said
sharply. " Call a boy-babe Amandy?"

" No, it ain't Amandy ; but it's as nigh to't as ye
can turn your tongue an' not say it, an' ' " —

" What upon the face of the yerth do ye let him do
it for?" severely inquired Mrs. Green.

Keery's eyes opened as far as the secretive narrow
lids would allow.

" Let him? Hear that! I want to know ef ye
think any mortal bein' can stop Bezy Hills from doin'
what he's got a mind to?"

"Or any other man," purred Miss Polly, who had an elderly maiden's contempt for the sex.

"They ain't all jest alike," dryly remarked Mrs. Green.

A look of intelligence passed round the table. It was well known in Hampton that Mrs. Green was the head of the family; and, instead of rejoicing in her supremacy as a tribute to her abused sex and a prophecy of hope, the women who should have sympathized sniffed at her. Such is human nature.

"But what will folks say when the child is presented for baptism?" asked the deacon's wife.

"There 'tis agin," wailed Keery. "Bezy don't 'b'lieve in infant-baptism. He says the' ain't no sech thing told about in the Bible, an' he don't b'lieve 'twas ever meant for folks to be baptized till they was converted; an' he won't never have it done to the babe no way, for he's got a conscience about it. An' I've talked an' talked an' talked to him; an' I might jest as well ha' talked to the side o' White Mounting, for" —

"I'll send the deacon over to deal with him," said Mrs. House, to whom the deacon was the end of the law; for which the rest of her sisters secretly sniffed at *her*. The happy medium of a bland indifference was "the thing" as to marital relations in Hampton.

"H'm!" said Miss Polly. "I don't b'lieve talk'll turn him. I've seen quite a few men-folks, bein' as I go out nursin' by spells; an' I've seen pretty clear that it takes science to manage of 'em. The mortal! I've seen a feller go boastin' around that he would be master in his own house, he would be minded, or things would crack; an', come to find out, he was jest twisted round his wife's finger, like a hank o' darnin'-cotton, all the time he was bustin' with boastin'. They're queer creturs. Like enough, now, if you let Bezaleel alone, an' keep a-peggin' at the boy how't he's got a girl's name tacked onto him, why, he'll git sick on't himself when he comes to years, an' drop it."

"Well, I declare for't! I never thought o' that," responded the astonished widow; and, just then being called to help roll the quilt, she had no chance to say any more on the matter; for the minister's wife came in, and the state of religion in the village became the topic of conversation in deference to her official position.

But the stubborn fact remained, that Bezy Hills would call his boy Amandar, — a name he had, indeed, invented, after much study, and a dull sort of sense that few, if any, feminine names ended in "r," and several masculine ones had that termination. Possibly Keery might have taken the counsel of the serpent from Polly Paine, but she did not live to try the force of iteration. Before Amandar was five years old, his aunt died, and her place in the family was taken by a fat and kindly woman, whose husband had run away and left her, in a drunken fit, and never been heard of since. Indeed, Sally Swett took no pains to discover him. She did not wish to marry again; and in taking care of Bezaleel's house, and bringing up little 'Mandy, she was nappy as she never had been during her married life, the only skeleton in her closet being the fear that Apollos might yet appear on the stage, and deprive her of a home.

'Mandy grew up, as most country children grow, sunburned, ragged, dirty, but by no means neglected; for the motherly heart of "Aunt Sally," never com

forted with offspring of her own, went out to the
motherless boy, for whom she delighted to make and
mend, to concoct pies, turnovers, gingerbread, and
fantastic doughnuts. She let him make endless work
for her in the kitchen, with his pans of molasses candy,
kettles of sirup to sugar off, pots of evil-smelling
ointment for his little boots, and roastings of chestnuts
that would explode, and fly in savory fragments all over
the kitchen-floor. But, for all Sally's indulgence, she
did not wean Amandar from his father: no temptation
of food or fun could keep him from the lonely man's
side. Together they went to salt the sheep, to mend
the rail fences, to sow rye, or plant corn and potatoes ;
and it was Bezy's great solace to tell " 'Mandy," as
he got to call his boy, all about his dead mother. The
squirrel-cups, lifting soft gray buds and blooms of
pink and purple from the dead leaves, reminded him
how glad she always was to find them, and how her
eyes sparkled when he brought them in first: he
planted them all about her low grave on the hillside,
and 'Mandy helped him. Not a thing was done about
the farm without some reference to the past.

" Yer ma liked them peach-blow potaters first best:
I guess we'll set 'em agin this year." Or, " Mother
she took to rye bread amazin', ef 'twas new rye: we'll
sow some onto that hill lot."

Great white-rose bushes were trained each year
higher and higher by the door, because the dear dead
wife had loved them ; and, by the time 'Mandy was
fifteen, it seemed to him that the whole farm was linked
to such tender associations of his unknown mother,
and her memory made so living to him by the iterations
of his father's love and loss, that it would scarcely

have startled him to see the delicate face waiting at the window, or hear the young fresh voice call from his door.

Perhaps he loved her all the more from the fact that he had borne her name at the expense of much tribulation; for, from the moment he began to attend the district school, that name had been the scorn and jest of all the other boys. Day after day he came home, his lips set with indignation, and his eyes red with tears; but never could his father get a word of complaint out of him, except, "Them boys plague me."

The child, young as he was, felt that his father would be even more hurt than he to find this dear memorial name had become only occasion of anger and shame to the son who bore it.

But Sally was a woman; and, finding it in vain to question or coax 'Mandy, her curiosity was fired at once, and, by various feminine arts and stratagems, she succeeded in discovering the secret from some of his playfellows; and one night, when 'Mandy was safe asleep up stairs, and his father toasting his feet by the kitchen-fire, preparatory to his own retirement, she laid down her knitting, and blandly plunged into the middle of things at once.

"I've got to the bottom of 'Mandy's red eyes now. I tell ye, Square Hills. I set a sight by that youngster; an it's took me aback to hev him come home every mortal day a-lookin' mad, and sorry too. It's them boys to the school. I say for't, I don't want to fault Providence; but I do wish the Lord hed kinder contrived some way to carry on the world 'thout boys. They're the most trouble to the least puppus of any thing that ever was created, except, mabbe, Dutchmen

an' muskeeters ; but, seein' they *be* here, the matter in
hand 'pears to be to do a body's darn'dest to sarcum-
vent 'em, as you may say. But I'm beat ef I know
what to do about these here boys. They've got hold
o' 'Mandy's name, it 'pears, — I guess 'twas writ into
his speller, — an' they're a-plaguin' of him to pieces ;
callin' of him ' Miss Hills,' an' ' lovely 'Manda,' an'
a-askin' of him ef he's a-makin' a quilt aginst his weddin', an' all sorts o' talk like that, an' wuss, if wuss
can be. The little feller can't thrash 'em, he's the
smallest of the hull lot ; an' I've figgered on't all day,
but *I* can't do nothin' as I know of : so I thought I'd
tell you about it, for I vum I'm to my wits' ends.''

A look of keen pain flitted across Bezy Hills's face
as Sally prattled on. He had not thought of this con-
tingency. He was a slow-minded man, possessed all
these years by one dominant idea, and every thing else
fell into the background. His daily duties had been
done because they must be : his sole enjoyment had
been thinking of his wife, and talking about her to his
boy. He had given him her name, as nearly as he
could, in order to make her near to the child who had
never seen her ; and the appellation was sacred to him.
He had never thought it could be made the jest and
weapon of rough boys, or a torment, instead of a pride,
to 'Mandy.

Perhaps if Amanda had lived, become the mother
of other children, grown old and sad with hard work
and the hard life of a farmer's wife, this devotion of
her husband would not have endured the wear and tear
of so many years. Probably he would have lost his
patience with her headaches and groans, and learned
the grim silence or the bitter speech that love never

knows. He might have become not only indifferent, but unkind : men do. But the sweet memory of their brief love and companionship became ideal because it was a memory, and he clung to it with a persistence reality never knows or inspires. Had she died at forty, and left him with two or three children and ten cows, he would have looked about him in a very few months to find some one who should fill her place : as it was, his days went on unsolaced in that way ; and he was as much an Amandian as he was a Christian, perhaps more so.

But as he sat by the fire to-night in silence, — for he made no answer to Sally, and she was too used to his silences, and cared too little for him, to resent them, — his startled soul was forced to own that he had not been judicious or considerate in making his boy wear his mother's name, dear and sacred as it was.

Nothing could be done about it now. The name was given, and he had sense enough to see that for him to interfere in the affair would only exasperate it : perhaps he had better not speak of it even to 'Mandy.

Rising, with a long sigh, at length he took the tallow candle, and stole up the stair into his boy's room, to take a good-night look.

The child lay with his cheek on one hand, the dark lashes, so like his mother's, fallen on to the rose-tinted cheek, and the red lips just parted with an even breath of young health : but the lashes were still wet; and while his father gazed at him fondly, thinking how like his mother he looked in that rest and position, a low sob, like the last swell of a storm, shook the boy's chest, and a look of anger swept across his placid forehead. Bezy Hills was grieved to the heart. Long and late he pondered what he should do; and even in his troubled sleep, when at last it came, he was haunted by 'Mandy's angry face and tearful eyes.

The next day was Saturday; and as it was good sap weather, — weather that "friz by night, and thew by day," as Sally said,— 'Mandy went up to the sugar-camp with his father to stay till Sunday morning. The hut was substantial; and a standing bed-place, laid thick with spruce-boughs and sheep-skins, was delightful hardship to the boy. He stirred the kettles, fetched sap in his small pail, and carried a milk-pan of snow from a hidden drift between two rocks at the north foot of Black Mountain, in which to cool his share of sirup, and harden it to wax,— delicious, deleterious compound, that sticks the organs of speech together, and forbids deglutition to the strongest jaw, but has withal, the flavor of wild honey, and the sweetness of nectar Olympus never knew.

When noon-mark was straightened out by the great gnomon of a tulip-tree on the turf-dial where the shanty stood, Bezy set some apples to roast before the fire, placed his tin pot of coffee on the ashes, and toasted some thick slices of cheese at the coals to eat with their rye bread and doughnuts, — a meal fit for any king, 'Mandy thought, its only objection being that a hearty dinner did somewhat limit the possibilities of eating maple-wax; but the keen air edged his appetite, and demanded solids as well as sweets.

While he was munching his last doughnut, the silence of the repast was suddenly broken by his father.

"'Mandy," said he, "I've heerd tell that the boys to school plague ye a heap about your given name?"

'Mandy blushed up to the roots of his yellow hair.

"They do plague some, pa," he said honestly, though choking a little, perhaps from the over-dry doughnut.

"Well, I've figgered on't some, an' I don't see but what ye'll hev to stan' it for a spell. Ye ain't big enough to thrash 'em, nor to knock 'em over: when you be, I s'pose you will."

"You bet!" exclaimed the eight-year-old hero.

"But meantime, don't ye fret about it no more'n ye can help. Ye've got mother's name as near as I could fix it; an' you an' me think a sight o' mother, don't we?"

'Mandy nodded: his mouth was still full, and pathos was not his forte.

"Ye see, ef ye'd ben a little gal, why, 'twould hev come right; but ye wa'n't, an' I don't know as I wanted for ye to be."

"_I_ didn't," shouted the indignant boy.

"But for all, I wanted ye to hev mother's name. She was the best an' the beautifulest cretur ever was, an' them boys hain't any one on 'em got no sech a mother. I expect if they hed, they'd be proper glad to hev her given name tacked to 'em."

"Hullo! there's a 'chuck!" shouted 'Mandy; and off he went, seizing a stake, and knocking over the apples, to wage war with a sober old woodchuck that had come out to inspect the savory odors in his usually quiet haunts.

Bezy sighed, but the sugar needed stirring: and when 'Mandy came back from the chase, disgusted that the froward beast would not stop to be killed, his father said no more to him about his school troubles; but what he had said dwelt long in the child's mind, and had its effect.

The old saying, that "the blood of the martyrs is the seed of the Church," is as applicable to other affections as to religion. The more the boys reviled and laughed at 'Mandy for wearing his mother's name, the more closely he became attached to it; and when time came to his aid with its slow security, and his thews and sinews were both strong and hard with his sturdy life and free growth, the boys of Hampton began to respect the "dynamic reasons of larger bones," and be careful how they roused the wrath they found latent under Amandar's kindly, handsome visage.

About the time he was seventeen years old, there came to the village a distant relative of Bezaleel Hills, of the same surname. Samuel Hills had lived hitherto by the seaside; but malaria, creeping slowly up the Connecticut coast, had laid its chilly, withering finger on him after he was fifty years old, and driven him northward into the pure mountain air which his father had left, a long time since, to settle on a fat farm near Guilford. He exchanged these green acres now for as many of mountain pasture on the outskirts of Hampton and, under the care of his wife and daughter, the old brown house put on a new aspect. Morning-glories twined over the windows, the white-rose trees were pruned and trained, and a "posy bed" by the south door made the yard gay and fragrant.

It was not strange that Samuel Hills's daughter should be named Amanda, though to her relatives it seemed a peculiar and startling coincidence. Amanda was as common in those days as Sus*ie*, All*ie*, Sall*ie*, or any other absurdity ending in *ie* is in these; and to the cultivated ear there is a far greater decency in the whole of any feminine appellative than in the nicknames that should be kept for household usage and private fondness. Amanda wore her grandmother's name, who received it from her mother. And so little did she know of her relatives, that, till she came to Hampton, she was all unaware of having a distant cousin of almost her own name. It was a passport at once to the good graces of Bezaleel and his son that this bright, pretty young girl should so recall the wife and mother they both idolized. Amandar, just budding into manhood, was carried away captive at once. And Amanda, who was his own age, rather looked down upon him in point of years, because a woman is always so much older than a man, whatever equality of age may be shared by the two.

Yet she was by no means unwilling to add another trophy to those already dangling at her belt; and she smiled, dimpled, coquetted, till the handsome, awkward boy, who took the serious side of the matter, felt like a bewitched creature, and wore his chains with a silent joy, not yet knowing that they were chains.

But, while he was falling fathoms deep in love with Amanda, other youths in Hampton discovered how pleasant it was to be welcomed in the cheery brown house by such sparkling eyes and red lips; and she had a welcome for all.

Amandar began to feel pangs of jealous fury, to lose his sleep by night, and his appetite by day. Being, however, a practical youth, instead of wasting his time in sighs and philandering, he worked harder than ever and "laid about him," as Robinson Crusoe says, to discover how he should be soonest able to marry, and so carry his idol off from all competitors.

The farm was his father's: he could not ask him to

give it up; nor would its sterile acres ever furnish more than the barest support to their family as it was. Amandar's desire was to go into some sort of business, and make money more rapidly; and to this end he at last persuaded Bezy to let him go to work in the iron-furnace at Hampton Falls, — a little offshoot of Hampton, on the Black River, — only two miles from Bezy Hills's farm.

He worked in the furnace four years; his intelligence and strength bringing gradual promotion, and his wages accumulating in the Rutland savings bank. But he had not the faith or the patience (whichever it was) of Jacob; for the time he served for his Rachel seemed interminable, and was rendered even more tantalizing by that young woman's persistent coquetry with other men. It was true she did not engage herself to any of them: there were too many delights in having a train of lovers for Amanda to sacrifice all to one. But no man likes to have his own idol set up for public worship; and 'Mandy was too young and too dreadfully in earnest to be philosophical about the matter.

It happened soon after he was twenty-one that his brooding jealousy exploded, and brought his affairs to a crisis. He had been away from home on some affair of the furnace; for he had now advanced so far as to have all the outside business in his hands, and he was mounted on top of the lumbering "stage" that for a few miles carried passengers between the railroad station and Hampton Falls. Before him, on either side of the driver (who happened to be a new man on the line, and quite ignorant of Hampton people), sat two young men of that class whom the English call "bagmen," and the Americans "drummers." Their

conversation was not peculiarly interesting at first;
but, as Hampton steeple came in sight, one said to the
other, —

"What takes *you* to this little hole, Harris?"

"I'm going to see 'Mandy Hills,'" answered the
other, with a smirk of such meaning that Amandar's
blood boiled.

"After a girl, eh? I thought you was drummin'."

Harris chuckled, and the other went on. "Pretty,
is she?"

"You bet!" replied the indiscreet youth, with still
another laugh.

"What style?"

"Why, Smith, I don't know: photographs haven't
been exchanged yet; that is" — chuckling again —
"no colored ones."

"Just like all country girls, I dare say, — hair
straight as a candle, and nose the length of your arm."

"Not a bit. Hair curly, and nose a little turned
up."

Here Harris laughed uproariously; and Amandar
clinched his fist, and straightened out his arm danger-
ously near the young man's head.

"Well, good luck to you! Hope she won't put on
airs, and mitten you, to wind up."

"Not she," laughed Harris, as if the idea was the
most exquisite of jokes. "She ain't that kind. She'll
fall into my mouth quick as ever I open it, you bet
your head."

The words had scarce left his lips when Amandar's
hand clutched his collar, and he was flung off the seat
just as the stage drew up at the Hampton tavern; and
our hero, jumping down after him, administered a

sound pommelling to the surprised drummer before interfering spectators could pull him off.

The bruised and bleeding youth was rescued, done up in vinegar and brown paper, and put to bed up stairs, and a justice of the peace brought immediately to deal with the assailant, who, having washed his hands at the pump, sat down and waited for arrest as calmly as if assault and battery were his profession.

However, the battered party could not appear against him that day, and there was no place to shut him up: so he gave bail, went to the office for an hour, and thence walked home to tea.

Hampton, of course, was all alive with the affair before morning; and early next day Amandar appeared before the justice, with his disfigured adversary, who had his temple covered with wet brown paper, and diffused a mingled odor of cider-vinegar and New-England rum through the assembly that crammed the little court-room. Amandar could not bring himself to confess the motive for his apparently unprovoked assault: so he submitted to the heavy fine imposed, and privately sought occasion to apologize to Harris, or rather to explain. The young man burst into a roar of laughter, all the more uncontrollable that Amandar's face blazed all over at this unseemly levity, till Harris at last caught breath.

"My dear fellow, I never saw Miss Hills in my life, nor ever knew there was such a person: but you and I have corresponded about that pig-iron, though of course as I only signed my letter Fowle, Norris, and Co., per H., you could not know my name; but I had seen yours, and been rather — beg pardon — rather amused at it: so when Jack began to question me (which he is mighty apt to do), I thought I'd blind him, and answered as I did. Particulars were made to order: I don't see how they came to fit. Honest, now, *did* they?''

'' Well, her hair does curl some,'' awkwardly admitted Amandar, unconscious of nightly papering and pinching, '' and I didn't know but you'd call her nose pug. I don't.''

Harris could not help another laugh; and Amandar almost said, '' Confound my name!'' but, just as his lips opened, loyalty and love for the dead mother closed them; and he only said, '' Well, I was a fool, and I own it.''

'' You can't say no fairer than that, old fellow. Shake hands on it, will you?''

And Amandar and Harris '' made up,'' as children say; but the unlucky name had not yet done its work. Somebody overheard this conversation, or '' Jack,'' sharing in the explanation, betrayed it with his easy tongue; for in twenty-four hours it had reached Amanda, and made her furious. New England, as a rule, does not take kindly to sentiment, even of the chival·ric sort; and Hampton people were only too glad to get a laugh on Amandar, who had always, as their phrase went, '' kept himself to himself.'' And Amanda well knew she would be teased and laughed at unmercifully. But her namesake, unconscious of her wrath, and feeling that the time had come when he had courage to ask her, since the blow he struck for her sake seemed to have roused his dormant manhood, and proved to himself that he had at last the daring to

'' Put it to the touch,
To gain or lose it all,''

vetook himself to the hill farm that very night.

He was too absorbed in his purpose to understand
Amanda's silence and the flash of her eyes; but the
moment they were alone, in good set terms he asked
her to marry him.

"I guess not!" she retorted bitterly. "I don'
know how you ask. Hain't you made my name a by-
word and a hissin' already down to the village? I've
heerd, sir, about your knockin' down that city feller;
and I don't think it's no great recommend to a man to
have him ready to quarrel for a breath, as you may
say."

"But, 'Mandy," gasped the astonished suitor, "I
couldn't set such store by you as I do, and hear a man
speak light of you that way."

"Then stop a-settin' store by me, 's all I've got to
say."

"I can't do it, I can't: I'd as lief root out twitch-
grass out o' a ten-acre lot. I can't no more stop likin'
of ye'n I can stop breathin'."

"Well, I don' know's that's my blame," retorted
Amanda, with genuine scorn.

It seemed to her this man was a weak fool: a Scy-
thian wooer, who would have knocked her down and
carried her away across his saddle, would have com-
manded her respect much more. Amandar was far too
much in love to perceive the trait in his charmer's character which would have made his marriage with her
emphatically "the curse of a granted prayer." He
could not yet take no for an answer: his misery and
his passion made him abject. He went on, "Maybe
I've hurried up matters too much; try and think on't,
Amandy. I'll wait; I can wait — I'd wait seven year,
like the man in the Bible, if so be you'd take me to the
end on't, as he was took."

There is a curious provision of Providence in the nature of girls who are not sophisticated by life or education, which makes a man whom they do not love, but who loves them, actually hateful and disgusting the moment he betrays his devotion. It seemed to Amanda that her lover was intolerable; she would have liked to drive him out of the house; her whole nature rose up in an instinctive revolt against him; she shuddered inwardly at the idea of his presence continually before her, and her wrath found words.

"Hain't you got eyes, Amandar Hills?" she said with cold fury. "Don't you see I mean no when I say no? Let alone that I wouldn't marry you ef you was the last created critter of the masculine sect in the hull universe, I wouldn't never marry a man that I set by like all possessed ef he hed a girl's name: so there now!"

This was brutal, but convincing. Amandar's head dropped on his breast. He picked up his hat, and loitered out of the door, feeling strangely weak and uncertain, yet withal a little indignant, from an odd consciousness that his mother's memory had not been respected. He was not given to analyzing his sensations. He could feel, but he could not "peep and botanize" in his own soul: he could only cast a wistful glance at the green flower-set mound in the graveyard as he went by, and send a tender thought to the memory that was so far the only religion he possessed, but, like all human religions, had no power to heal the hurt within him.

It happened that Sally had been at the hillside farm that evening to return some yeast borrowed in an emergency; and not finding Amanda's mother in the kitch-

en, and hearing voices in the front-room, she naturally
went to the door to see if Mrs. Hills was there, and in
the little entry her steps were arrested by the pleading
sound of her boy's voice. She loved Amandar little
less than if he had been her own child; and her faithful old heart sank as she gathered the sense of his low,
eager words. It did not occur to her to go away: she
had not been educated into that sense of honor, which
is not a native trait of women; and her blood boiled as
she heard Amanda's cruel words, so distinctly and
curtly uttered that they were like so many blows. Instinct taught her not to follow the rejected lover, and
offer him comfort: she only set down her yeast-pitcher
and left the house, feeling that she could not restrain
her tongue if she met Amanda then and there.

Poor old Sally! Amandar writhed and groaned and
tossed all night in purely self-centred misery; but she,
in the next chamber, sighed and woke also. Tears of
deep pity and grief stole from her dim eyes, and wet
her sallow, wrinkled cheeks with the most unselfish of
all suffering; yet the pathos and the picturesqueness of
the situation all lay with him, for is not a despairing
lover by far a finer figure than a sympathizing old
woman?

Yet could we but look at the pair, having our sight
purged by some diviner euphrasy than conventional
literature or romantic poetry supplies, would not Sally
appear the nobler and lovelier of the sufferers? However that may be, Amandar never knew what pure tears
were shed for him that night, or what honest pangs
tortured poor Sally for his sake. He got up the next
morning and went to his work as usual; but the spring
of his life was broken, its interest gone. Nothing from

within could help him; nothing without offered aid.
He set himself with listless quiet to endure: that alone
was left to him, — the resource of a dumb animal, the
vis inertia of the tree that lies where it falls. If help
was ever to come, it must seek him and save him without his will or wish. His father looked at him with
sad eyes, but said nothing. Sally cooked every dainty
dish she could remember, or invent from her small
resource of material; but all was alike to the weary
body that held this stricken soul. That the two who
idolized and attended him never offered tender speech,
gentle caress, loving look or touch, was not for want
of love, but from the dreadful reticence that underlies
all New-England character, and forbids it to blossom
in expression, though, like some abnormal plant, it may
bear fruit abundantly in deeds, from the most insignifi-
cant or unlovely flowers.

So the summer went on drearily enough. The routine
of seedtime and harvest, old as the world's gray ribs,
recurrent as the sad story of life, occupied Bezaleel
Hills as it had done over and over before: into many
a furrow he ploughed useless regrets and defeated
hopes; for he was hardly less disappointed than his
son, though the bitterest element of Amandar's trouble, the love that he had wasted, was not a part of his
father's pain. Yet, for all the ache of the sower, the
regardless seed absorbed dews of night and summer
showers, softened, sprouted, burst into the blade, shot
into the stalk, swelled into the heavy-freighted ear, with
the divine sequences of nature as gladly as if there
were no humanity in the atmosphere; also the fair
pink blooms of the orchards painted the knotted old
boughs, wiled the bees with their delicate bitter per

fume and drop of limpid honey, faded, fell, gave way
to small green spheres rounding daily to full-orbed
fruit that lay at last in heaps of gold and crimson on
the long, scant grass below; the forests feathered into
waving, verdant plumes, darkened, rioted in brilliance
indescribable, and whirled away their finery on the
wild autumnal winds : but there was no parallel growth
or loss in the dull sorrow that had taken hold of Amandar's strong nature.   Humanity is not the flower of an
hour or a season : it takes a lifetime for development,
a long tale of years for its growth, fruitage, and death.
Its harvests are sudden, and it sleeps long ages in the
dust before any resurrection ; but then comes another
and eternal up-springing, a bloom that knows no harvest, — a perennial spring.

It was in the bitter days of November that Sally
heard of her sister's death in a remote village of
Maine. Hepsy was her only living relative, and the
stringent separation of poverty had kept them apart
since they were children.   Occasionally a letter had
passed between them; but further than these brief,
clumsy, ill-spelled messages, Sally knew nothing of
her sister's life except its bare circumstances.   She
had married Sam Tucker, a poor, amiable, " shiftless "
creature, half farmer, half fisherman, and had the poor
man's blessing, -- ten children ; but six of these lay
buried in Fosdick Island graveyard, three had been
lost in a boat out blue-fishing. Sam had been dead
ten years ; and there was left of all the tribe only the
fifth child, Love, a girl of eighteen, who had been her
mother's sole comfort and company since the last
baby was laid beside its father.

Hepsy had known she was about to die, and with

much pain and delay penned a short good-by to Sally,
begging her to find some place for Love where she
could earn her living, and be near her aunt.

"For she's a kinder cossit, Sary; and I mistrust
she'll hanker after me sum. I want you should be
muther to her nigh as ken be, and sorter harten of her
upp when she taiks on, as mabbe she will. Poor
cretur! I hate to hev to leave her; but I hoap the Lord
and you'll take keer on her."

This letter came enclosed in one from a neighbor,
announcing Mrs. Tucker's death; and Sally, with red
eyes and mild snuffles, put it into Bezy's hand to read.

He puzzled through it, and wiped the back of his
hand across his eyes, muttering under his breath,
"Darn them cobwebs!" though he knew, and Sally
knew, that no spider that ever was laid in egg was the
author of the dimness he was ashamed to own.

"Well, Sally, the' ain't but one thing for to do; an'
that is for you to go to the island, an' fetch the poor
gal hum with ye. Fetch her here, I say, till she finds
a better place. She'll be dreadful lonesome an' scary,
to begin with: you must get her used to folks grad-
ooal. There's plenty room in this old barrack, an'
enough vittles; an' she's welcome. Nuf said."

So Sally, who had made a perfect autocrat of Bezy
of late years, meekly obeyed, drew out her small sav-
ings from the bank, and with trembling ignorance
went her way, managing to reach Fosdick Island
safely, and in a week returned with her charge to
Hampton, slipping back into her old place with a sigh
of satisfaction. Love was a great surprise to the
squire, who had thought of her as a lank, frightened,
homely down-East girl, and stared in amaze at the

quiet, sweet face that smiled up at him so modestly,
the trim, plump figure, the exquisitely neat dress, and
shining hair.

"I swan!" he said to Amandar, "she's the most
like one of them blue pidgins of any thing I ever see
in a woman."

But Amandar did not care.

As the year went on, a new sense of comfort stole
into the house. Love had that inborn power of making any place she inhabited attractive and home-like,
which is a greater gift to a woman than any artistic
faculty. She brightened up the dark kitchen with gay
patchwork cushions in the arm-chairs, set two scarlet-
flowered geraniums in the south window, which she had
fetched from her old home, and pinned up some chintz
curtains to the windows, relics of Sally's former housekeeping; then she scoured up the old pewter platters
to silvery brightness, and made the brass tops of shovel
and tongs radiant. A red shawl served for stand-
cover, and a few books always lay on it. The kitchen
looked like a place to live in, not a mere shelter
and feeding-trough; and not its least ornament was
Love's calm, sweet face, the brown eyes shining a welcome to each comer, the brown hair braided and pinned
up with that smooth glitter carefully kept hair shows,
and the white apron, cuffs, and collar spotlessly pure
against her black woollen dress. Her very face expressed the atmosphere that she seemed to dwell in,
and to spread about her a sense of peace, composure,
and rest.

She reminded Bezy of his lost wife many and many
a time. Her eyes were like Amanda's, so was her
shining hair; and though Love's health and plumpness

were as unlike Amanda's frail delicacy as could be,
Bezy did not place any stress on that: he thought it
merely the natural distinction between the girl and the
young mother. At any rate, she was like his 'Mandy,
almost as gentle and sweet; and his old young life
came back to him like a lovely, mournful dream as he
looked at Love sitting where his wife had sat in their
brief happiness, flitting in and out at little household
cares just as she did, and making the house home
again, as in all these years it had never been. And,
as the days went on, a subtle sense of comfort and
peace stole, even against his will, into Amandar's
heart. He scarce ever looked at Love, or spoke to
her; but he could not help hearing his father's voice
soften when he said "Lovey," nor could he fail to
see how the pucker was getting smoothed out of Sally's
forehead, or ignore the fact that the daily meals were
better cooked, more neatly served, more savory of
smell, in every way more appetizing, than before.
A man's heart and his stomach are said to be inter-
changeable terms. I would not so malign the sterner
sex as to indorse this fact; yet I certainly know of
more than one instance where a woman's sole tie to an
unloving, selfish, cold husband, has been her power of
ministering deftly to his chronic dyspepsia. I am
sure that I have seen this despised faculty avert
divorce, and preserve family unity, where all else failed
and love had never been. The moral of which is
young ladies, learn to cook well.

And how was it with Lovey? Dear girl-reader, how
would it have been with you, if, homeless, almost
friendless, you had been brought into the daily society
of a youth good-looking enough, well-to-do, intelligent,
and the victim of an unfortunate attachment?

Dear little Lovey! She pitied Amandar w ʌ all her sweet, gentle heart. She thought Amanda Hills a cruel, heartless coquette; which was rather unjust to 'Mandy, at her worst a mere coarse, commonplace girl, not at all the being Amandar painted her. So her beautiful pity worked itself out in gentle deeds: it was she who darned the youth's stockings with such an even lattice of yarn, so smoothly ended or begun that his foot never felt the new fabric; probably it never would have troubled him if she had put on flannel patches, but there are as many works of supererogation in love as in the Romish religion.

She, too, saw that no button ever missed its duty, no string was ever torn off or knotted on any of his clothes. She brushed his Sunday suit every Saturday, with a little of the same devotion that impelled her prayers, and stitched his collars with a tender thought to every two threads, as well as a stitch; and hemming his handkerchiefs gave her a more exquisite joy than the finest Kensington embroidery ever confers on its votaries.

Yes, Lovey was in love; in love after the genuine old fashion of Eden, when there was but one man for one woman; in love without an alloy of diamonds or settlements, trousseau, or lace and white satin; in love in that divine, almighty, absorbing, unselfish way, that counts not its own life dear unto itself in comparison with the lightest wish or want of the beloved. And Amandar, feeling the sun rise on him, did not see it; growing warm and light of heart as he went on with his back to the east, he yet wist not that it shone.

But spring at last kissed the land: the brown sad fields softened in tint, the brooks laughed, the winter

grain sprung up afresh on hill and dale, and bluebirds
ventured to call out their small encouragements from
leafless trees. Work at the forge was dull, and Amandar staid at home to help his father plough. The first
few days of May were warm even to sultriness : and
holding a plough on the hillside in the blaze of noon
proved too much for his unaccustomed head ; a sudden
ache smote him, so severe that he had to stop and
sit down to recover from the shock, which almost
amounted to sunstroke. His father was startled at
the pale face and blue lips, that told their own story,
and sent him home at once. When he reached the
house, Sally and Love were taking in the wash from
the lines in the orchard ; and Amandar went up to his
room without seeing them. The cool shade and soft
air flowing through his blinds relieved and soothed him ;
so that he fell asleep at once, and awoke some hours
afterward to the sound of voices. The two women
were sitting on the back door-steps ; and before he
was really conscious of where he was, and whose voices
he heard, Sally said to Love, —

" The meat-man told me a piece o' news to-day."

Lovey laughed like a song-sparrow, for it was the
joke of the house to call the meat-man Sally's newspaper.

" Well, he did really, this time. He says for true
that Amandy Hills is a-goin' to marry old Square
Shores down to Ludlow."

The listener felt a dull pang in his heart ; and a
thrill of sharp surprise followed, to feel the pang *was*
so dull.

" Isn't she goin to do well ? " asked Love, rather as
a matter of course than for any deep interest in the
subject.

" Well, I don' know's she is, an' I don' know *as*
she is. He's got means, — he's got a sight of means,
if that's all; an' he lives into a two-story yaller brick
house, with a big gardin, and a picket-fence all round
on't; but he's cur'us, dark-complected, an' jest as
pernickity as an old maid, and meaner — my land!
meaner'n dirt. If she's marryin' on him for money,
she won't get none on't.''

" I hope she won't,'' burst out Love in a righteous
indignation. " I think anybody that marries anybody
for money ought to get come up with every time.''

" Highty-tighty ! Why, Lovey, you ain't riled none,
be ye? Money's like fried cakes, real handy to hev in
the house, now I tell ye. 'F I was a gal agin, I'd
keep an eye out to't, you'd better believe, when folks
come a-foolin' round me. 'Tain't to be sneezed at.''

" I don't believe you would one bit, Aunt Sally. I
know you, and you wouldn't marry a man for his
money no more'n I would.''

" Well, ef you know so much, child, what on airth
would *you* marry a man for, ef I may be so bold? ''

Lovey's fair sweet face colored like a peach-blossom,
from soft round throat to shining hair, as she answered,
" For nothing only because I loved him so I couldn't
help it.''

" My land ! seems to know a heap about it. Well,
'Mandy ain't that sort : she wouldn't hev our 'Mandar
jest cos he's got a queer name.''

" Aunt Sally ! Is that what makes him so awful
sober? ''

" Jest exactly that. I heerd her tellin' of him myself, accidental like, as ye may say ; an' she done it as
though she knocked him down with a stun, and kinder

liked to. I tell ye I never heerd a woman no harder spoken than 'Mandy Hills was, in this mortal world.''

'' O Aunt Sally, how hateful! I should have thought she'd ha' liked him all the better for thinkin' so much of his dead mother. I'm sure I felt just like cryin' when you told me about the squire's namin' of him after the one he set such store by; seemed as though 'twas most worth while to die, if it made folks think so much of you.''

'' Why, how you talk, child! You ain't dreadful way-wise yet, it's plain to behold. It's a sight better to hev 'em set by ye whilst ye live. It don't do Miss Hills no good up there under the mulleins an' burdocks to hev the square allers thinkin' about her, and mournin' after her.''

'' I don't believe it! '' retorted Lovey, her soft voice thrilled with indignation. '' I don't believe but what she knows all about it, and is sort of comforted by it. *She* ain't up there in the forlorn old graveyard: she's in a better place, and I know she likes to be loved more'n ever. My gracious! do you think I shouldn't know, if I was ever so dead, that anybody I set my life by had forgot me, and taken another into my place? ''

'' Well, well, well, child, don't be so stirred up. I don't know nothin' about it, nor you don't nuther, an it's time to put the tea to draw. Fetch up the butter, will ye, and cut the bread? '' And Sally walked off to her work, unable to cope with the ardent young heart that life and grief had not yet tamed down to hard sense and practical philosophy.

But there was another heart, still young, if wounded, that heard and responded, in the chamber overhead,

where Amandar lay in the cool silence, listening —
very dishonorably no doubt — to the door-step conversation.   If he had read Shakspeare, probably he would
have quoted that well-worn passage : —

> " Oh ! it came o'er my ear like the sweet south,
>   That breathes upon a bank of violets."

As it was, he had a sense of comfort and peace enter
his very soul from the genuine and tender sympathy
Love bestowed on him.   There was a woman, then,
who not only did not despise his name, but could love
him the better for it, — a heart that knew what a beloved
memory was, and admired the respect in which the
living held it.

Yes, Amandar began to see the sun.   There is no
creature on earth so consolable as man.   A dog will
mourn his lost master to the death, and a woman
bewail her husband till she rejoins him ; but in man
there lies a sublime store of affection that must ex-
pend itself on somebody, — generally on some woman.
Amandar was no exception to this great compensatory
rule.   He had resisted it longer than usual, because of
a certain trait in his nature, — a tendency to monotony,
— which he inherited, diminished in descent, from his
father ; but now resistance fell, like the walls of Jeri-
cho, before the blast of a breath.   The queen was
dead : long live the queen !   He began from that hour
to recognize and cultivate a sort of healthy hatred of
Amanda, to wonder that he had never understood her
character before, and to draw daily the most odious of
comparisons between her and Lovey.

In short, he fell manfully in love again ; and, before
the ploughed land was well harrowed and seeded, the

new passion had sprouted so well, that he himself recognized it, and began to wonder if it would be successful. But Lovey was timid, shy, and evasive as a nestling partridge. It was, or seemed, many a long day before Amandar could detain her from her occupations long enough to tell the old story; and when one day, with masculine will, he swept the clothes off the line himself, and took possession of the small schemer who had made their ingathering an excuse to avoid him, it was a matter of hours to persuade her that he really was in deep earnest. She could not understand that the love which had shipwrecked him was a thing of the past; and a new passion, as genuine as the first, had taken true hold of him. It was only after long argument and iterated assurances, that Lovey, moved no doubt by the conviction so earnestly expressed, that she alone of all women could have availed to heal his wound, consented to believe in him, and revealed her own honest, tender heart, with a gentle shyness that became it as moss does a rosebud.

It was a day of rejoicing in that house when Amandar told his father and Sally that Love had consented to be his wife. Bezaleel already loved her as a daughter, and she only disputed Sally's heart with Amandar. And as for the lover, he was happy: in this case it was he who held the cheek out, and Lovey who kissed it. He was not now slave, but master; and the natural position set him at ease, and restored the self-respect Amanda had from the beginning trampled on, and at last outraged. Before the harvest came, they were married; and, under Love's household reign, peace and brightness came permanently to live in the old farmhouse. Amandar's mother found another wor-

shipper at her homely shrine ; and, if there was a thorn
in Lovey's roses, it was the fact that no little girl was
given her to wear the sacred appellation of its grandmother.   And, of all the fine boys who made in their
turn a temporary bedlam of the farm, not one was
permitted to be called after his father ; for Amandar
had answered for himself the old question, and found
out that there is a great deal in a name.

POLLY MARINER, TAILORESS.

TAUNTON STREET is long and high. A wide road, skirted by equally wide strips of turf, in whose shallow gutters (a single furrow of the plough, grassed over by time) grow Mayweed, yarrow, and nettle, herbs of repellant touch and vile odor, it runs on the top of Taunton Hill, from whose broad and long crest you can see more of Western Connecticut in its development of bare round hills, mullein-stalks, stones, and life-everlasting, than is good for the soul of the thrifty, or pleasant to the eyes of the discerning.

Whatever is agreeable to behold lies on either hand in the white, red, or brown farmhouses, each in its own green yard, with a garden on one hand and a lane leading to the barn and shed on the other; some more adorned than others with lilac-bushes and sticky rose-acacias; others more neatly ordered about doorstep, chip-yard, and picket-fence; but all wearing a certain patient and pathetic homeliness that must have risen 'housands of times before dying eyes, and filled them with homesick tears.

On the very top of Taunton Hill, or, rather, on the middle of its broad back, stood the old white meeting-house, and behind it, on the eastern slope, the grave-yard, — no elegant cemetery, where one can return to dust regardless of expense in rosewood and velvet,

wept over by marble angels holding cold blossoms,
but a quiet, deserted-looking place of burial, wearing
the natural loneliness of death; altogethe: separated
from life, except at the rare and silent funerals that
gathered there on business, or when, once in a decade,
some profane antiquary, fumbling after dates among
the brown stones, discovered among those gaping and
agonized cherubs a record to the effect that Mrs.
Lovina Jinkinson's "ethereal parts became a seraph
on the 15th of June," and smiled behind his silk
handkerchief.

Half a mile beyond this abode of religion and mortality was a small red house, standing in its own yard,
and having a little garden to the south, but neither
lane nor barn: a drooping elm-tree shaded it in front,
and one huge apple-tree spread its gnarled growth
over the end of the garden; cinnamon-roses grew on
either side of the flat gray door-stone; but no further
floral decorations softened the grim aspect of those
always-shut windows, behind whose green glass,
greener paper shades preserved a ghastly twilight in
the "front-room." But a little sidling path, well worn
through the turf, led round the corner to the south
door, a place of cheerier countenance, where broods
of chickens peeped and pecked; where the cat washed
her face in the sunshine; and where the opened door
gave pleasant glimpses of a clean kitchen, with 'Sire
Mariner, in a tall, list-bottomed arm-chair, sitting by
the fire doing nothing, and Polly his daughter bus-
tling about doing every thing. Desire Mariner (commonly called 'Sire) was a placid, weakly, peace-loving
old man, who had been sexton and shoemaker time
out of mind in Taunton Street. If you wanted a pair

of shoes, he could make them in three weeks, if nothing happened: if you wanted a grave dug, it took him
all day to do it. His wife had lived in a state of bustle
and aggravation while she did live; and, when she
died, her child carried on the business.

"Well, Polly, what be you a-goin' to do now?"
said Mrs. Perkins, the deacon's wife, to Polly, as she
entered the house behind her, coming home from
Marah Mariner's funeral.

"Learn a trade," said Polly, nowise resenting the
freedom of speech which interfered with her private
affairs on what should have been a solemn and sad occasion.

"The land's sake!" and up went Mrs. Perkins's
eyes. "Learn a trade! Well, I never! 'n' here you've
had a real good edication, 'n' might jest as well get a
good deestrick school as not, 'n' stay to home 'n' take
keer of him!"

"I ha'n't had no great schoolin', Miss Perkins,
though I s'pose I could make shift to knock what little
I had into childern's heads; but keep school I never
will. Firstly I hate damp boys: they're always gettin'
damp and steamin', and I'd as lieve be choked to
once. Secondly I hate boys anyway: they're nothin'
but torments. An' thirdly I hate school-keepin'. You
don't never suit. If you're strict, then folks sez you're
cruel and bad dispositioned: if you're easy, an' 'est
git along, then you're slack and lazy. I'd jest as
willin'ly be a minister's wife as a schoolma'am, an' I
can't say no more'n that. No, my mind's made up ·
mother 'n' me talked it over. Aunt Roxy's goin' to
stay here 'long of father for a year, while Samwell and
his wife goes out to Indianny to get settled, and then

she's goin' too; and by that time I'll have got my
trade learned, and come home."

"Well, well, I s'pose you'll do jest as you'd
ruther."

And so Polly did. Vain were all the remonstrances
of friends and neighbors. Off she went the next week
to Hartford; and there, by dint of hard work, "doing
chores" for her board, and grubbing through all the
mysteries of cutting, pressing, turning, and button-
holing, she became mistress of her art, and returned
to Taunton Street as accomplished a tailoress as the
times afforded. But alas! her fair plans of a busy and
vivacious life, going out day by day to the neighboring
farmers' houses with her beneficent press-board, shears,
and headless thimble, where she would be regaled with
the best of food and the freshest of gossip, all fell
through. 'Sire Mariner was hopelessly bed-ridden when
Polly came back, and aunt Roxy all packed for her
Western journey.

Nothing very serious seemed to ail the old man. He
had been rheumatic, taken cold, gone to bed, and
found it was a warm, comfortable place, and lain there
till the unused muscles and dulled circulation became
a fixed physical habit; and he had no energy of mind
or elasticity of nerves to combat the mild depression
that held him, as it were, in cobweb chains.

Still he needed constant care, and made constant
trouble. Polly could not leave him for more than an
hour; and he would spill his food, and drop his snuff,
and tip over the tallow candle, till Polly's hair crinkled
more fiercely than ever, and she scolded and bustled
like a domestic blackbird. Whatever tailoring she
could take in at home she did and did well, and

even condescended to plain sewing at odd times. She
hoed the garden after old Isr'el Grubb had dug and
planted it; she made root-beer to sell, and concocted
sirups of great power in cases of "humors" and
"spine in the back." Sometimes she made election-
cake, — a Connecticut institution that takes as much
"judgment" to its final success as a salad ; and nobody
made such hop-yeast as Polly. All these things eked
out a frugal existence for the two during the next ten
years ; and then one night 'Sire Mariner went to sleep,
and never woke up. Mrs. Deacon Perkins had on the
same black bombazine, the same figured lace veil over
a brown silk bonnet, and the same gray-centred broché
shawl that adorned her before, when she followed
Polly into the house this time after the funeral, with
the same question on her thin lips, —

"Well, Polly, what be you goin' to do now?"

"Tailorin'," says Polly undauntedly.

"I want to know! You ain't calculatin' to live here
all alone, be ye?"

"I don't expect to take boarders."

"Laws sakes! I wa'n't thinking o' that. I should
suppose now you'd go an' make it your home with
somebody. There's your aunt Sary: she hain't got nobody to help her, 'n' she's dreadful feeble this year;
and I should think 'twould be a kind of a dooty for
ye, and a good home."

"Well, now, Miss Perkins," said Polly, sitting
down deliberately, and evidently resolved to finish the
matter, "I a'n't a-goin' into nobody's house that
way. I don't b'lieve in't. Whilst I live by myself
an' take care of myself, I a'n't beholden to nobody;
and I know when my work's done, and what's to pay

for't. I kin sing, or laugh, or cry, or fix my hair into
a cocked hat, and nobody's got right or reason to say,
'Why do ye so?' Fact *is*, I've got my liberty, 'n' I'm
goin' to keep it: it'll be hard work, p'rhaps; but it's
wuth it.''

"Well, I never did see sech a contrary creetur in
all my born days," sighed Mrs. Perkins. "You'll live
to repent it, sure as I'm alive, Polly Mariner! 'n'
what's more, I don't b'lieve you'll stick to't more'n
a month!'"

Polly felt no sinkings of heart at this denunciation:
what had she to be afraid of? She shut her door, and
went to bed, no more solitary than she had been
before. Her work was lightened of its heaviest rou
tine; and when she had cleared away the traces of her
father's occupancy, and cleaned her tiny house from
top to bottom till the very tins shone, she sat down to
her needle with a stout and contented heart, with
nobody to make her afraid, though there were a few
to molest her.

Now, if Polly had been sixty instead of thirty-five,
she might have been let alone, except for the kindly
gifts of their abundance that the neighbors might send
in. But here was a strong, healthy, intelligent woman,
cast on her own resources, and without a relative near
enough to interfere with her choice of livelihood.
What a help and treasure she would be in a family! —
not as a mere servant, but one of the household, ready
to fill all gaps, fasten all loose threads, and be the
general "knitter-up of unconsidered trifles."

Aunt Sary came first, — aunt by courtesy, as the
second wife of Polly's step (not half) uncle. She was
a thin, pale, dreary, bilious-looking woman, with dark

eyes set in dismal hollows, drooping lips, emaciated temples, and a little iron-gray hair scratched up here and there on her head, and crowned with a fearful black lace cap, that, in its turn, wore patches of dull purple ribbon. Aunt Sary was an invalid and a desponding woman.

"And what more can I say? she said." Talk about Ossa on Pelion! what were Chimborazo on Popocatapetl compared to dyspepsia and liver-complaint on constitutional melancholy? To her, every wind blew from the east; all clouds were tempest, and all sunshine torrid; if snow "kilt" her, heat and verdure had as bad an effect; the grasshopper was more than a burden to her; and the mourners had gone about the streets of her soul for so many years, that everybody else had got worn out hearing their wails and howls, and fairly wished the funeral over. Yet aunt Sary had, like all the rest of us miserable sinners, her good and lovable points. She was kind-hearted when she could be brought to consider anybody else's woes: she was a dutiful wife and mother. Though her husband's mental thermometer always sank when he entered the door, and her children kept out of her way, there were few women in Taunton more conscientiously dutiful than Mrs. Sarah Platt. Her fate was hard; for nobody loved her, and every thing fretted her. Shall not one rather pity than condemn the nettle whose bloom is so trivial, and its foliage so repellant?

Polly Mariner did not feel any special compassion for nettles.

"Well, Polly," sighed aunt Sary, painfully laboring up the two steps into the kitchen, and dropping into the nearest chair, "you've been quite afflicted since I saw

ye. It's a real mysterious Providence 't you should
be left so to yourself!" (As if she was!)

"No 'tain't," snapped Polly.

Aunt Sarah groaned.

"Well, I'm glad to see you don't feel your par's
loss."

"Who said I didn't, aunt Sary? I a'n't one to go
a-wipin' my eyes on everybody's han'kercher. I hadn't
never felt a call to cry on the meetin'-house steps,
nuther; but that don't say but what I've got feelings
somewhere."

"You hadn't got a monerment ready to put up for
him, I s'pose? Husband's got a slab to spare, I
b'lieve. He got two when Malviny and Jane Maria
was both so took down with fever; but you see Malviny
got well, an' the slab's there in our back-shed, and
he's dreadful afraid it'll get scratched and sp'ilt: so
he'd let you hev it cheap."

"Well, I don't know but what I'll come over an'
dicker with him," said Polly respectfully, somewhat
softened by the prospect of a bargain.

"But that a'n't the most of what I come to say,
Polly. I know't you'll be dredful lonesome here, and
husband and I'll be real glad to have you come 'n' make
it your home with us. I have so many poor spells, —
and I don't seem to get the upper hand of 'em; they
ruther gain on me, — that I should be proper glad to
have some grown woman in the house, though I calkerlate to do the heft of the work myself. You could
have time to sew consider'ble, and I'd give ye the back-
chamber, where Hanner sleeps, and you could bring
along what beddin' an' furnitoor you've got; and I
guess the rent of this house would pay for your clothin',

and I wouldn't begrudge ye what it didn't.   And moreover it a'n't quite to my likin' for a young woman to
live to [by] herself so : 'n there ! ''

Mrs. Platt stoppèd, exhausted, wiped her face with
a printed cotton handkerchief, and began to rock.

Polly had been sitting speechless, with her eyes fixed
on her aunt, as if to hear what she would say to the
end ; and it was no pleasant thing to have those black
eyes, so keen, so apprehending, so persistent, looking
behind one's words into their thoughts.   No wonder
aunt Sary's face shone with unwonted drops of sweat !

" What did you pay Marthy Wade last year? '' said
she at length.

Aunt Sary stared, but spoke.

" Well, I gin her a dollar a week.''   (Dear reader,
this was forty years ago.)

" Well now, aunt Sary, I don't expect to go out to
doin' chores for nobody ; and, ef I did, I wouldn't do it
for nothin'.   Work's wuth pay ; 'n' when I can't I'll
go to the town-farm 'n' be took in.''

" O Polly, Polly ! ''

" And, what's more, if I a'n't old enough to take
keer of myself, 'n' live by myself, I don't know who is.
I'm five an' thirty year old last December, 'n' I'd cut
my eye-teeth quite a spell ago ; and I a'n't a-goin' to
live with nobody, much less for nothin', as I told ye
before.''

" O Polly !   I'm dredful disapp'inted, I do declare.
I'd lotted on havin' ye to my house.   But I ha'n't got
no strength to battle it out with ye : an', come to think
on't, I guess it's all for the best, as providences generally be ; for I shouldn't want your fellers round in
the keepin'-room evenin's.''

At this last little feminine fling Polly blazed; for it was a notorious fact in the village, that no young man had ever cared to face her temper and her tongue enough to "keep company" with her.

"There, now you've done it! I never knew a dreadful good, sickly woman but what could sting jest as well as a honey-bee. No, ma'am! you won't be troubled with me nor my company; but I wish you well and good-afternoon, and I hope you won't be troubled with nothin' wuss — nor your husband neither!"

Mrs. Platt began to wipe her eyes, and snuffle so violently that Polly knew she had driven her to the wall, and watched her retreat down the yard with grim satisfaction.

Next day came another afflicter of her peace in the sweet guise of cousin Rachel Green, a Quakeress of the gentlest sort; one of those "sporadic cases," as the doctors call them, of Quakerism, that now and then blossom out in remote New-England villages.

Peace on earth and good will toward men embodied Rachel's moral creed; and peace lived in her pure eyes, smoothed the fair old forehead, and almost bloomed on those sweet, faded lips. Something like a south wind in early spring sounded in Polly's ear as she sat by the window, stitching a pair of overalls, though it only said, —

"Good-day, Polly! Thee is as busy as ever, I see."

"Why, Miss Green! Do tell if it's you? Walk right in and sit down. I've been kind of expectin' ye quite a spell."

"And I should have been to see thee before, Polly but I have been down to Westerly to stay with Jona-

than's father, who was nigh death for quite a while.
I only came back yesterday, and heard thee had experienced a great loss. So I came over as quickly as I
could."

"Well, yes: father was a kind of a loss. He
hadn't been no great company for several years along
back, and it was consider'ble of a chore to keer for
him jest as one had oughter; but I expect I miss him
as much as most folks would, though I a'n't one o' the
frettin' kind."

"Thee has been a good daughter to him, and that is
a comfort; and then thee must feel also that he is
better off without the affliction of the body, and re
joiced to meet thy mother."

"Well, I don't know about that," rejoined Polly, a
refractory smile twisting the deep corners of her mouth
in spite of herself. "I expect we're all kind o' made
over in another state: ef we a'n't, I don't see much use
in goin' there."

Friend Green looked hard at the cooking-stove. She
was undeniably shocked; but her habitual and un-
bounded charity speedily put its own construction, like
the outpouring of a golden mist, on Polly's speech.

"Yes, we shall all be changed, it saith in Scripture;
and I think, with thee, it is a blessed change to lay off
our mortality, and take on us spiritual garments white
and clean."

Polly looked at her, but said no more.

"I came to see thee also, Polly, to ask about thy
plans; not in the spirit of curiosity, but that I might
help thee if I could."

"My plans is pretty much cut an' dried, Miss Green.
I guess I shall git enough tailorin' to do, now't I can

go out an' do't; 'n' Isr'el Grubb'll fix my garden foɪ
me; and I understand plantin' and weedin' pretty well.
I can raise what green sass I need to hev, an' yarbs,
'n' I guess potatoes enough, because I expect to gɔt a
good deal o' boardin', you know; 'n' that's why I'd
ruther go out than take work to home. Besides, it's
kinder refrashin' to go round and see folks. I don't
nanker no great to travil to see mountains, and sea-
sides, and what folks in the newspapers call 'natur'.'
I'd sights liveser see folks. I like to hear talk, and
talk myself, 'nd git sorter interested in what's goin' on.
I expect that's what people were meant to do, not go
pokin' around with their noses in the air after stumps
and trees, and sightly places thet can't say nor do so
much as a fannin'-mill any time o' day.''

"If those is thy feelings, Polly, don't thee think it's
a leading for thee to find a home in some family where
thee'll be one of the household, and have thy interests,
as it were, all in a place? There is many a family here
and elsewhere would be glad to have a capable person
like thee amongst them.''

"Oh, dear, Miss Green! Who'd ha' thought you
was goin' to pester me about that too? I tell you
what, I've made up my mind about it, 'n' it'll take a
sight to change it. I a'n't one o' them complyin' and
good-natered critturs that'll give up, 'n' give up, 'n' give
up, till they can't call their souls their own: them's
the kind that's good to live in other folks's families, 'n'
to go into the ministry; and they a'n't good for noth-
ɪn' else. I want to do what I'm a mind to, 'n' I can't
be yoked up to other folks's wants anyhow, leastways
no more'n just for a spell, — say a day or so. Also I
nust use my tongue, if I have to speak in meetin'. I've

got to call a spade a spade, an' a lie a lie; and you know that don't allers sound savory; but it doos appear better, a heap, in them that has house an' land o' their own, and a place to hide their sassy heads in, than in them that's allers under foot. Now, hain't I got reason to roast my eggs by?"

"I don't deny that thee has reason, Polly. Thy talk sounds well-considered; but I am fearful that by and by thee may get to hanker after those family ties that seem burdensome to thee now. Thee knows the Scripture, 'It is not good for man to be alone,' which, I think, meaneth not a man, but the whole humanity. It hath pleased the Lord to leave thee solitary in respect of relations; but 'he setteth the solitary in families.'"

"Well I don't feel to be sure that they're other people's families; 'n' if I ha'n't got no relations, 'pears to me, ef you git to talkin' about Providence, that it looks's though I was kinder intended to be left by myself."

Rachel had to smile. The inherent dry sense of humor that seems to be the calyx of a Quakeress blossom like this was tickled by Polly's ingenious defence of her own will and way.

"Well, thee must act by thy lights, Polly; and remember thee has plenty of good friends if thee changes thy mind."

"Thankey kindly, Miss Green. I guess I a'n't like to forget you amongst 'em."

This was so much more sentiment than Polly often indulged in, that she retired behind the overalls, under pretence of some omitted overcasting, and only said "Good-by," in a prim and grim way, when Friend Green departed.

Alas for the weakness of human nature! No sooner had the little gate clicked to than down went those friendly overalls on the floor.

"I swan to man, it's enough to crisp one's eyelashes to have sech pesterin' goin' on all the time. Why, in the name o' judgment, I can't be left to do what I darn please, is musical to me. Anyhow, I guess I'll do it, or I'll know why an' wherefore, as true's my name's Polly Mariner."

But Polly was troubled no more. On the contrary, aid and comfort came to her in the person of Isr'el Grubb, no later than the next morning, when he thrust his grizzled head and shrewd wrinkled face into the back-door early.

"Mornin', Miss Polly! Say, Jehiel wants to know if them overhauls o' his'n a'n't nigh about done?"

"Why, yes, they be. I set the last stitch into 'em last night."

"Well, Jehiel's wife she wants you to come over there a spell next week and fix up her boys: school's a-goin' to keep next week."

"Yes: I'll go any time after Tuesday night."

"I declare for't! you're real prompt. I do hate to see folks fiddlin' round's though they was so shif'less they didn't know nothin'. Say, I heerd down to the store you giv Miss Platt an all-fired dressin' when she come for to git you to go 'n' live with her."

"Well, now, that's a Taunton lie. I didn't do no sech thing. First she pestered me, 'n' then she sassed me; 'n' what I said back didn't no way square the bill, you'd better believe."

"I don't say but what I think you had the right on't, ef you did," pursued Isr'el, taking off his hat as if to find his rag of a handkerchief, and settling himself on the doorstep, where he resumed the hat after shaking and turning it round. "It allers seemed to me the foolishest thing a woman could do't hadn't got no folks, to go 'n' take 'em ón. Good land! *did* ever anybody see men-folks do sech a gawpin' thing? I guess it 'ud look pooty to see old Granther Styles, or me, took into somebody's house to do chores for nothin'. I don't know as men-folks ginerally knows more'n wimmen 'bout house an' sich; but they do know enough to work jest as long as bones an' sinners [he meant sinews] 'll hang together, 'n' then go to the town-haouse 'thout makin' no fuss."

"I guess there's all kinds o' folks in the world, Isr'el, 'n' I'm glad I a'n't one on 'em, as Miss Purkis used ter say; 'nd I do s'pose there's some wimmen's jest as good as some men, an' some men jest as good-for-nothin' as some wimmen."

"Well, I guess there be. Naow, I calkerlate to dig your garden for ye next week; 'nd in case you want any thing o' me dredful bad any time, you can jest put a white handkercher, or suthin', in your keepin'-room winder, or a lamp, ef so be it's night-time, 'n' ef I or my folks sees it, we'll be raound pootty spry, I tell ye."

"Well, I don't know but what I will, though I guess I sha'n't get skeered."

"But ye might be sick. Folks is flesh an' blood, if they be dredful mighty. I'll tell Jehiel to come round for ye real early Wednesday."

Isr'el sauntered off; and on that next Wednesday began the public life and services of Polly Mariner, tailoress. It needs a personal acquaintance with the

lonely and hard lives of New-England farmers, and
more especially their wives, to fully comprehend how
Polly became at once a power in the land. She was a
woman of strong character and great courage. Had
she lived in these days, the very queens of the women's
rights' party would have been domineered over, out-
scolded, and out-dressed by her. She would not have
stopped short of masculine garments in the adoption of
masculine privileges; for she had that rarest of feminine gifts, — except one, — a logical mind; and, beginning at the end of a clew, would unwind it with
precision and skill to the very end, bitter or not, as it
might be. But, happily for this generation, she lived
in the last; and Fate, always intelligent and benign
under its severest aspect, even when we hesitate to call
it by its Christian name of Providence, compelled her
to a sphere where she did good less mingled with evil
than it might have been in the unrestrained possession
of pulpit, platform, and press. If Polly (forgive the
misquotation)

"To a village gave up what was meant for mankind,"

mankind and the village were both the better. She
circulated among the solitary farmhouses far and near,
like a racy newspaper, for one thing. She had a
faculty, frequent in old maids, of having genealogies at
her tongue's end. She knew who everybody's grandfather's first wife's second-cousin married, and where
all their children had settled. All the children's ages
in every house were referred to her as final authority,
if they chanced to have been left out of the family
record. She was infallible on pickles, sweetmeats,
' jell," curing hams, and corning beef. Nobody made

such soap, or such yeast. Hens that recalcitrated
from their yearly duties quaked before her, and began
to set under her " methods " as if nothing could please
them better. She even knew how to eradicate smut
from wheat, and cut potatoes for planting better than
half the farmers. And as for news, not a mouse
squeaked anywhere within her rounds but she could
and would tell the next cat of it. Judge what tireless
gossip flowed from her vivacious tongue, and tickled the
dull pool of many a household into ripples of laughter,
regret, or astonishment, full of mental healing for
those stagnant lives.

Then Polly had another gift, equally beneficent, if
more poignant. She had the power and the will to tell
truths, pleasant or unpleasant, in a manner that was as
convincing as caustic; for the strong common sense
that gave her insight its practical value weighted all
her shafts, and sent them deep into the mark. Nobody
seemed to be much offended, or, if they were, they
sulked a while and got over it; for Polly was as imper-
vious to sullen looks or sharp words as a duck to rain,
and she was too necessary to be lightly set aside.
Poor Mr. Evarts, the minister who was once, for his
sins, preaching as " candidate " in Taunton, dated his
disappointment there from the day a sewing-circle met
at Deacon Griswold's, and Polly " freed her mind."

" What do I think about him, Miss Gris'l'd? Well,
I think he's small pertaters, and few in a hill. I don't
hev no faith in a man't gits up in a pulpit, an' preaches
away about flowers, 'n' stars, 'n' love, 'n' crystal
springs, 'n' all that. A'n't we sinners, 'n' pretty bad
ones too, at that? And what on airth did he expect
to do when he set up to preach, ef 'twan't to make

folks better? I don't like to hear his posies no better'n I did to hear Parson Tinker allers thunderin'
damnation, and 'lection, an' decrees. What I like's to
have him preach so't the men-folks'll go home an' try
to behave better to their wives, an' their children, an'
their helps; and the wimmen'll stop frettin' and
whinin' and fault-findin, and sayin' mean, stingin'
things to each other when they get vexed. Fact is, I
want to get kinder licked smooth myself, 'nd git some
patience drummed into me. I don't want a snip like
that set up to hash verses, and reel 'em off, cos he's
paid to do sumthin', an' that's all he can do. Sup-
posin' you was took dredful sick, 'n' struck with death,
and, naterally enough, your folks sent for the minister
to come 'n' see ye: what kind o' use or comfort would
this little peepin' crittur be, a-talkin' about harps, 'n'
angels, 'n' sech? I tell ye, Miss Gris'l'd, a minister
had ought to be a man, and a smart un', and a good
un'. Ef the Lord's work's worth doin', it's worth
doin' well jest as much as your'n or mine is: thet's
what I think about it."

"Well, I don't know but what ye're in the right
on't, Polly. I don't think husband reelly sets by him
much."

"Husband" was duly regaled with Polly's speech,
after the feminine conclave had folded their work, and
gone home to bed.

"Darn it all!" said the deacon ("darn" is a harmless expletive, even for deacons), bringing his right
hand down on his knee with a forcible slap, "Polly
Mariner is a master-hand to speak in meetin' as ever I
see. Them is jest my idees about the young man,
though I shouldn't never ha' ben so free-spoken afore

folks: 'twon't do! Folks had oughter hev more caution, partikerly ef they're deacons. I guess I shall tell the brethren't I don't think brother Evarts is equivalent to our work. Ye see, he's kinder feeble; an' our congregation is dreadful scattered, 'n' winter's comin' on, 'n' so. Thet's all trew; an' it won't hurt his feelin's none, and'll fix it just right. But I swan I do b'lieve Polly'll git into a real fix some day, speakin' her mind.''

"Law, no, she won't!" said Mrs. Griswold, in the intervals of her vigorous setting the kitchen to rights at once. "There sot Miss Peters; 'nd she's Parson Tinker's fust-cousin, 'n' she jest larfed. Nobody gits mad with Polly: 'tain't no use. Why, I tried it once. Fact is, I was pipin' mad when she come out about your 'stillin' cider-brandy, 'n' sellin' it down to 'ie corner; and I give it to her, I tell ye! But she sot there with her press-board, as composed as a clam, a-waitin till I got through; 'n' then she sed, sez she, ' What's the use o' gettin' riled, Miss Gris'l'd? 'Tis *so*, a'n't it?' Well, I couldn't deny but what it was; 'n' then, come to think, I knew I better ha' held my tongue; 'n' Polly was a-lookin' at me with them eyes o' hern, jest like two gimlets, and she see I was coolin' off. ' I sha'n't never say nothin' to nobody else about it,' sez she, 'now I've told ye, nor I sha'n't to you, Miss Gris'l'd. I've cleared my conscience, 'n' thet's as far as consarns me: so I guess we'll kinder let it alone now.' So I did. She was pootty near right, 'n' I never got mad with her sence. Fact is, besides, we've got three boys; 'n' they get through their coats 'n' things most amazin' fast, and '' — with which disjoined conjunction Mrs. Griswold stopped, and took breath.

"Well, she is the beateree, no doubt on't," rejoined the deacon, picking up his boots, and going off to bed.

So Mr. Evarts was not called to Taunton Street, but wended his way meekly to Mount Holyoke Seminary, married a well-recommended young person on five days' acquaintance, and was forthwith shipped to the wilds of Southern Africa, there to learn, let us hope, though by deadly experience, what preaching the gospel is, and what it is good for.

Perhaps the only things that defied Polly's common sense and experience were the love-affairs, that even in hard-working, unromantic Taunton, would spring up "even as a flower." The little god was no less capricious when properly "clothed upon" with good homespun and flannel than in his classic costume of wings and bow. Alike in either garb, he snapped his pink and dimpled fingers at the crabbedness of reality and the warnings of sense. Blessed little apostle of unreason! What a world of solitude and tears we should have, if all the ineligibles were forsaken in their uselessness, and only the good, sweet, prudent, and well-dowered people got married! Here was poor Louisa Platt, daughter of the aforesaid "Aunt Sary," a tall, weedy, sallow girl, as became her mother's daughter, yet with great eyes, whose dark splendor blazed beneath clustering curls of equal darkness, and full red lips, capable of a sweetness as intense as their ordinary sullen droop. She had led, for all her eighteen years, such a life as the sensitive daughter of a woman like Mrs. Platt must lead. Constantly fretted at, found fault with, shut in, as it were, in her narrow round of duty, which no tenderness, no sympathy, overflowed, with a hungry heart and an active mind, no wonder

tnat the first hand that offered her food was grasped at
eagerly; no wonder, that, in her want and ignorance,
she glorified into a hero almost too sublime for a husband Alonzo Sprague, clerk in the country store at
the corner; a youth whose adorableness consisted
chiefly in a great deal of hair-oil used on his light
locks, an unlimited amount of simper, some fine language, weak good-temper, and tolerable manners.
But he loved "Lowisy," as Taunton pronunciation
hath it, as much as he could love any thing but himself.
Her unequal but unusual beauty, for beauty it was,
once lighted up by fun or feeling, excited his admiration; and her father's reputed "means" enhanced the
feeling to seriousness, that might otherwise have died
out like a thousand other of his temporary loves.   But
to such a connection neither Mr. nor Mrs. Platt would
give any countenance.

"Lowisy's a fool, and you can clear out o' my
premises, 'Lonzo Sprague!" was the short and sharp
dictum of the father; while aunt Sary overwhelmed
Louisa with a persistent flow of tears, reproaches,
taunts, sniffs, and a sort of mongrel ridicule that had
in it no glitter of humor, or spark of fun, but was
simply senseless chatter.   And in the middle of these
tirades entered Polly Mariner, shears and press-board
in hand, come to repair the "trouses" of a small
Platt; for time and necessity had long ago grown
grass over her quarrel with aunt Sary; and, beside,
the Platt boys wore out clothes particularly fast.

"Good-mornin', Miss Platt! good-mornin', Lowisy!"   But the girl burst into a flood of passionate
tears, welcome enough to her hot eyes and face, and
ran out of the room, making no reply.

"What kettle's upset now?" inquired Polly, making herself at home in a low chair, and turning her sharp nose and sharper eyes toward Mrs. Platt.

"Oh, dear!" (rocking violently) "Lowisy's jest the ongratefullest crittur in the univarse! Here's her father an' me been an' gone an' waited on her, and fetched her up, and done for her all her days; 'n' now jest as she's a-gettin' good for somethin', she ups and takes a shine to that ninkum of a 'Lonzo Sprague, 'n' wants to marry him, I hope! He's a poor, mean, shiftless feller as ever stepped. He ha'n't got the fust cent to call his own, an' he never will hev; 'nd that girl wants to leave a good home, and me so dredful miserable, to go'n try her fortin' with him! It's jest my luck!"

"Folks's luck is generally their makin'," dryly put in Polly.

"I wish't you'd give her a piece o' your mind, Polly: she don't seem to set by what I say to her the least mite, and you've allers had a faculty at talkin' folks over."

"Well, I don't know's I hev got any partikler great faculty," said the secretly-gratified Polly. "I generally tell folks the trewth: there's some'll take it in, an' some won't."

But before dinner she got a chance, not unaided by Mrs. Platt, to tell Lowisy the truth, or rather fling it at her, stone fashion.

"So, Lowisy, I hear tell you've been a-takin' up with 'Lonzo Sprague down to the corners?"

No answer.

"I should ha' thought you could ha' done better'n that! He's a real shiftless feller, jest like his father afore him, and his grandfather afore that. I've allers noticed that shiftlessness runs in families pretty much like scrofooly, 'nd I tell *you* there a'n't no harder row to hoe than a woman's got that's got a shif'less husband. She ha'n't, so to speak, got nobody. Fact is, I'd ruther have a real sperrity man, ef he was real ambitious, than one that didn't never fix up, nor provide, nor fly round real spry, at least."

"What sort of a husband was yours, Miss Polly?" interpolated Louisa, inspired by feminine instinct. But Polly was arrow-proof, and put this little shaft aside.

"That ha'n't nothin' to do with it. I've got eyes 'nd I've used 'em; an' I've seen consider'ble many folks, both married an' single, sence I was born, and I know what I'm tellin' ye. You'd better think twice on't: you hev to lie on a hard bed ef you make it; 'n' when you're once tied up to him, you can't noway get away, that's the worst on't: there you be, an' there you'll hev to be; an' you may kick the breechin' to bits, 'nd break the bridle; but 'twon't be no good, the lines'll hold ye."

This, as we have said, was forty years ago, before Connecticut made it even an easier matter to break the marriage-tie than to form it.

"I don't care a mite, there!" burst in Louisa. "If I want to marry a man that a'n't wicked, nobody's got any right to say I sha'n't, anyway!" ante-dating the later axiom of our New-England philosopher, that "the soul has inalienable rights, and the first of these is love," in a more lucid and practical form.

"Mighty Cesar!" ejaculated Polly, "ef you a'n't a highflyer, Lowisy Platt! Ha'n't lost your senses, hev ye?"

"Guess I've got what'll keep me alive," said the girl, her whole face settling down into a sullen resolution that seemed to make Polly Mariner's curls crisp with fresh vigor as she pierced her with the penetrative eyes beneath them.

"Well," said the astonished tailoress, drawing a long breath; and that was all she said. Here was one thing that surpassed her comprehension. Never in all the long years of her life had that organ popularly supposed to be the heart given within her one unreasonable flutter; no delicious folly had ever kissed her eyelids down, no fire of passion ever kindled its resistless blaze in her respectable bosom. She had but a spare gift of the gentler affections; and here, flung in her very face like a hen defending her brood, was an inexcusable foolishness that regarded nothing beyond the insatiable hunger of the moment. Here was a soul parched with mortal thirst, intent on slaking it from the first woodside puddle; and Polly had never been thirsty — how could she understand it? For once her spells had failed. Truth itself is powerless against love; and so Louisa Platt and her simpering lover made a flitting over the State line, happily not far off, the first moonlight night, and, being married in Massachusetts, came home to Taunton, and settled down to reality.

Whether in her future life, when the little frame-house swarmed with puny children, and Alonzo developed the hereditary talent he possessed, and she burned with the fever of frequent headaches, and writhed with the torture of a lame back, in her hard but inevitable labor, Lowisy ever wished in her secret heart that she had been wiser and calmer, or even at the last moment taken Polly's advice, I do not know and cannot tell;

but one thing I do know, that Polly lost no opportunity
to say, "I told you so," either in word or act, or by
significant words and sniffs that added fresh thorns to
poor Lowisy's burden, already rasping enough.

Partly the wise woman did this from the natural
instinct of . humanity, partly to vindicate her own
superior wisdom, and partly because, as the cynical
Frenchman said, "there is something pleasant in the
misfortunes of our best friends," — particularly when
we have told them so.

But, notwithstanding this one failure of method,
Polly's life went on with its wonted usefulness and
fearlessness, year after year, though, be it observed,
she never again meddled with a love-affair, observing
once, with a sniff of defiance and contempt, "Them
that meddles with fools gets a fool's-cap for their
pains," à propos of somebody else's folly quite as bad
as Lowisy's.

Yet as the years rolled on, and brought Polly Mariner to the goodly age of fifty, she met with one of
those signal discomfitures that now and then befall
both the best and the wisest, — oftener, perhaps, befall
women than men, by reason of that lack of poise, of
caution, of far-seeing, that is characteristic of the
feminine mind.   Strange enough it was that Polly,
who had so successfully engineered the affairs of other
people so long, should at last make a fatal and ludicrous blunder in her own ; but it was, after all, the
gradual result of a process like that which loosens and
disintegrates the base of a granite bowlder, and sends it
slipping with still accelerated impetus down the grassy
slope where it has reposed so long.   In fact, Polly was
an illustration of that great law, "the eternal fitness of

things," in the result of its infraction. In spite of her strength, her courage, her self-assertion, her rage for independence, she was, after all, a woman ; and she is not a woman, but an anomaly, if not a monster, who can wear out a long life of social solitude with no quiver of failing resolution, no sinking of heart. To be a woman without a home, without a family where she is at least dear and necessary, if not supreme, is to be a dweller in the desert, lost and famished ; if not in the bright days of youth and strength, yet at least when the feebler pulses and the more faithful heart demand help and consolation against the desolation of age and the hour of death. And slowly, as time laid one finger after another on her life ; as her eyes became dim, none the less that she brandished her new spectacles defiantly before everybody, as if they had been an ornament instead of a necessary aid ; as she began to find her active limbs stiffen with every winter's frost, and her quick ears lose their acuteness of hearing ; when it grew a weariness and a burden to go home to her own solitary house at night, unlock the door, kindle the fire, and sit down beside it, tired and depressed, with not even a cat to purr under her hand, — Polly began, no doubt, to feel what Rachel Green had said to her long before, that it is not good for man to be alone, nor woman either.

Now there lived on Taunton Hill, on a road running at right angles from the street, a certain elderly man, long time a widower, whose name was Timothy Bunce. He was not a favorite in the village, being somewhat simple in mind, but crabbed in manner : not that he really was cross-grained ; but he was weak, and knew it, and defended himself with such weapons as he had against his craftier and stronger brethren. But he had a good farm, and money in the bank, and every thing comfortable about him ; his cows were sleek, and his fowls abundant ; his crops always fair, if not remarkable. And to a stranger it seemed odd enough that no woman had stormed his castle, and taken possession of him and his long ago. But, beside Timothy Bunce's weakness and snappishness, there was one thing that separated him yet more widely from the Taunton people : he was an Episcopalian. He was not born or " raised " in Taunton, where everybody that could go anywhere went duly to the big white meeting-house, and took in pure Calvinism with unquestioning simplicity. He had gone from a neighboring village to the city early in life, and there fallen into what Taunton held to be the wrong religion and wrong politics. And when he had amassed some money, at the age of forty, he bought this farm on the hill, and took up his abode there, religion, politics, and all, clinging to his old ideas simply because he had not wish or will to change them.

He had always had a niece to keep house with him ; but, a few weeks before he fell into collision with Polly, the niece had died, and left him in a peculiarly helpless and friendless condition, which was fully discussed in and about Taunton, not only as to its present wants, but their prospective supply. But nobody seemed to suggest just the right thing : in fact, nobody thought of Polly as a person attainable to fill Mary Ann Bunce's place. She was altogether too important to the town. But in Polly's mind there was a certain stir of expectation, a balancing of probabilities, an appraisement, as it were, of what was and what might be, that prepared her to receive a call from Mr. Bunce with a proper degree of composure, and to show no signs of its unexpectedness.

It was late Sunday afternoon; and Polly sat by the open door of her clean kitchen, rocking placidly. All her belongings were as spotless and orderly as ever. She herself looked, in her Sunday gown of black silk, something softer than usual. Age had not changed her, except to a kindlier aspect; a little threading of silver in the black curls, less fire in the blacker eyes, less snap and crackle in her movements and her voice: yes, Polly was really mitigated; and when she said to Tim Bunce, "Set down, set down, Mr. Bunce, take this cheer," there was something almost like suavity in her tones.

Timothy sat down. He was a little man, and in bodily presence contemptible enough. His narrow face, wandering blue eyes, sleek and scanty light hair, the very crack in his voice, bespoke him a weak brother. And yet he considered himself able to control and direct any woman on earth, regarding them as inferior creatures, useful about a house, as others have done before him. But Polly's aspect, exceptionally subdued as it was when he encountered it alone, rather daunted him. He began to stroke his hair nervously, to roll his eyes about like a timid rabbit, to clear his throat, and fidget on his chair, — symptoms which Polly regarded with a critical eye, and judged favorable.

"Well'm, Miss Polly," at last he stammered, "pretty good weather for corn."

"Well, yes 'tis, dredful growthy kind o' weather for most any thing: garden sass seems to be partiker lerly favored this year."

"Doos, doos it? I should think so by the look o' yourn. Quite a hand with a garden you be, I guess."

"Well, I don't know. Some hes faculty, an' some hesn't."

"Mary Ann she was a masterpiece of a gardener. I don't reelly know how to git along without her."

"It was quite an affliction for ye. I should think': you'd miss her a heap."

"I do, reelly now: I miss her consider'ble. Seems as though I couldn't get along no longer 'thout somebody." Here Timothy happened to look sidewise, and caught those black eyes fixed upon him with unwinking sternness, and his own rolled fearfully: the ground seemed uncertain under his feet. He was scared; but he went on, "Fact is, I don't feel as though I could stan' much more on't. Mary Ann she'd lived to our house a spell along back afore Miss Bunce died, so't she staid right along 'n' did for me, 'nd I didn't feel so kinder lost without Miss Bunce as I should hev otherwise; but now I do, I tell ye. And I've heered a lot about how dredful smart you be, and knowin'; and I stepped over to see ef mebbe you'd take her place." (O Timothy, Timothy! your last proper noun was "Miss Bunce;" and Polly knew it, though you didn't.) "I'd fix up the haouse 'nd I'd" —

Polly never let a driven nail go unclinched. Some vague instinct of femininity made her drop her eyes, but she spoke. "I d'clare for't! Mr. Bunce, you *hev* took me clean by surprise. I hadn't never thought changin' my condition" —

"Oh!" gasped Timothy, turning red and blue: but she did not hear or see him.

"But seein' you're so kind, and your lonesomeness,

'nd all, I don't know but what I'd as lives merry you as the next one.''

'' O-h!'' gasped Timothy again; '' oh, dear! I—I—I didn't, o-h!''

'' Why, suthin' ails ye, don't there? 'Pears as ef you was overcome : 'tis kind of a tryin' time. Won't ye hev some peppermint?''

Timothy sat with both hands on his knees, convulsed with rage and terror. Perhaps she would marry him then and there, in spite of him, and carry him home in triumph; and his dry tongue refused more words.

''Now, do hev some, or smell to the camphire. Time you had a wife to look after ye. I understand fits real well.''

'' O—h!'' shrieked Timothy, rising to his tottering feet in fresh fury that loosed his speech. '' I didn't! I don't! I a'n't a-goin' to. I didn't say nothin' about marryin'. I won't, I don't want to.''

Polly was purple herself now : her eyes snapped like sparks, her nose went up higher yet in the air, her chin quivered, the very curls on her head seemed to bristle. She was a spectacle of terror to Timothy, who literally shook in his shoes.

'' Well, I should think! You pitiful little rat, 't can't hardly squeak in your own barn, a-comin' round me, a respectable woman, to make me your music! Fust a-askin' of me plain as a pikestaff to marry ye, 'nd then a-backin' out on't right off! You're the meanest critter the Lord ever made, 'nd I guess you *was* made out o' the bits 'nd ends that was left. I wouldn't pick ye out o' the dirt with the tongs!''

'' I didn't, I didn't; oh! I didn't. I never thought on't. I don't want to.''

"Now go to lyin', will ye?" ejaculated Polly, calm with excess of anger, like a buzz-saw, and equally dangerous. "Hain't I got ears? 'nd didn't I hear ye ask me to take Miss Bunce's place jest as plain as the nose on your little sneakin' face, that's most all nose?"

"Oh, I didn't!" reiterated the abject and thoroughly terrified Timothy. "I didn't! I never! I said Mary Ann."

"Well, keep on a-lyin', do! I might ha' know'd there wan't no good in ye, — nothin' but a 'Piscopalian anyhow! Don't know enough to say your own prayers. What the Lord above made 'Piscopalians and muskeeters for I *don't* know, 'xcept to keep up an everlastin' buzz: they hain't nyther on 'em got souls thet's worth savin', nor bodies enough to hold 'em if they hed. Come!" Polly advanced in wrath. "Clear out o' my house! Quit, afore I ketch ye by the back o' your neck, 'nd drop ye out o' the window. Clear, I say!"

A whole troop could not have alarmed the luckless Timothy more. Snatching up his hat from the floor, he fled, ejaculating as he went, in broken accents, —

"O Lord! Oh, my! Good Lord, deliver us from all — Oh, darn this gate! Thunder — oh," far into the distance, finding, poor fellow, nowhere in the Litany, which involuntarily sprung to his lips, a petition for deliverance from furies or old maids.

Polly sank into her chair, breathless. For a while the excitement of rage supported her, then came the bitter after-taste of mortification and disappointment. As she sat in her door, the melancholy range of bare hills that lay before her sent unawares a chill into her heart. Polly was not ordinarily sensitive to Nature:

but Nature, like air and love, acts upon us without our
consciousness or connivance; and the sad peace of
those rolling summits, the plaintive quiet that settled
round closing day, all the solitary depths of the summer sky, untroubled with one spark as yet, seemed to
close about the exasperated and lonely woman like the
walls of a cloister, and sink deeper into her soul the
conviction that for her there was no centre, no home.
It may do for men to live their own lives, and die alone,
with the courage or the stoicism that is their birthright,
but not for women. The strongest, the best, the most
audaciously independent of us, will be conscious, as
age assaults us, of our weakness and helplessness, —
bitterly conscious if we are solitary.

Polly's mood of regret and bitterness was new to
her, and exquisitely painful; but at last she roused herself from it, growling, as she went about her work for
the night, —

"Well, he *was* a fool, that's a fact, 'nd I was consider'ble of one myself; but I skeered him mightily,
anyhow."

Neither of the parties cared to tell the tale of their
mutual discomfiture. But Timothy sold his farm, and
removed to the wilds of Vermont, haunted by the fear
of Polly Mariner; and people noticed, as years passed,
that Polly grew less and less aggressive, even more
friendly. She spared and pinched and saved, till
there was enough laid up in the Folland Bank to give
her rest in her last days; but rest she could not take.
Action was the breath of her existence; and, happily
for her, a sharp and brief fever ended her long and
busy life: a decline would have tortured her both in
her own incapacity and that of any available help.

But for a few days of delirium and unconsciousness
there was resource enough in neighborly kindness ; and
Rachel Green, herself lingering on the verge of her
days, but sweeter and gentler than ever, came and
staid to superintend the nursing she was unable to do :
while "Aunt Hanner Bliss," the only professional
nurse for miles about, was sent for, and installed as the
doctor's aid, and at times substitute, since a country
doctor must needs be "here and there and everywhere."

At last, worn with the cruel violence of fever, Polly
woke from her delirium weaker than a child, but clear-
headed as ever : her eyes fell first on Rachel Green's
calm face, where the very peace of heaven seemed
almost dawning.

"Well, Miss Green, I'm a dredful sick woman, I
guess."

'Thee has had a severe fever, Polly, and it is not
over yet '

There was something ominous in the sad tenderness
of the old lady's voice, that struck Polly : a strange
look passed over her countenance as this shock of an
untried and awful experience stared her inevitably in
the face ; and her voice was even feebler and more
quivering when she spoke again.

"Struck with death I be, a'n't I?"

"Thee is almost home, Polly," softly replied
Rachel.

"Home?" said she vaguely ! "oh, dear !" and then,
rousing herself, "I hain't never had a home. Miss
Green, do you rek'lect what you sed to me quite a
number of years ago? Well, I'd ha' done better ef I'd
ha' done your way. 'Tain't more'n honest to tell ye

I've hankered after a home 'n' folks o' my own many a time since; but I wouldn't tell on't: 'nd now I'm a-dyin', so to speak, by myself — or I should, ef 'twa'n't for you.''

"Anyhow," said Aunt Hanner, with the skill and experience of one of those Spanish nurses who thrust their elbows into the stomachs of the dying to shorten their agonies, — "anyhow, ef you hain't got nobody to cry for you, you hain't got nobody to cry for, 'nd you've hed your way.''

"Folks's way is worse'n the want on't," whispered Polly. They were her last words. The death-mist passed, and settled upon her sunken features, as Rachel Green stooped over her, saying low and clear, —

"'As one whom his mother comforteth, so will I comfort you,' saith the Lord of hosts.''

Two tears, the first and last that mortal ever saw her shed, stole gently out of Polly's closed eyelids: she smiled — and died.

UNCLE JOSH.

JOSH CRANE was a Yankee born and bred, a farmer on Plainfield Hill, and a specimen. If some strange phrases were grafted on his New-England vernacular, it was because, for fifteen years of his youth, he had followed the sea; and the sea, to return the compliment, thereafter followed him.

His father, old Josh Crane, kept the Sanbury grist-mill, and was a drunken, shiftless old creature, who ended his days in a tumble-down red house a mile below Plainfield Centre, being " took with the tremens," as black Peter said when he came for the doctor, — all too late; for the " tremens " had indeed taken him off.

Mrs. Crane, our Josh's mother, was one of those calm, meek, patient creatures, by some inscrutable mystery always linked to such men; " martyrs by the pang without the palm," of whom a noble army shall yet rise out of New England's desolate valleys and melancholy hills to take their honor from the Master's hand. For years this woman lived alone with her child in the shattered red house, spinning, knitting, washing, sewing, scrubbing, to earn bread and water, sometimes charity-fed, but never failing at morning and night, with one red and knotted hand upon her boy's white hair, and the other on her worn Bible, to pray, with an intensity that boy never forgot, for his well-being for ever and ever: for herself she never prayed aloud.

Then came the country's pestilence, consumption; and after long struggles, relapses, rallies, — all received in the same calm patience, — Hetty Crane died in a summer's night, her little boy asleep beside her, and a whippoorwill on the apple-tree by the door sounding on her flickering sense the last minor note of life.

When Josh woke up, and knew his mother was dead, he did not behave in the least like good little boys in books, but dressed himself without a tear or a sob, and ran for the nearest neighbor.

"Sakes alive!" said "Miss" Ranney. "I never did see sech a cretur as that are boy in all my days! He never said nothin' to me when he came to our folks's, only jest, 'Miss Ranney, I guess you'd better come cross lots to see mother: she don't seem to be alive." — "Dew tell!" sez I. An' so I slipt on my Shaker bunnet jist as quick's I could; but he was off, spry's a cricket, an' when I got there he was a-settin' the room to rights. He'd spunked up a fire, and hung on the kittle: so I sed nothin', but stept along inter the bedroom, and turned down the kiver, and gin a little screech, I was so beat; for, sure enough, Hetty Crane was dead an' cold. Josh he heerd me, for he was clos't onto me; and he never spoke, but he come up to the bed, and he put his head down, and laid his cheek right along hers (and 'twan't no redder'n her'n), an' staid so 'bout a minnit; then he cleared out, and I never see him no more all day. But Miss Good'in she come in; and she said he'd stopped there, an' sent her over.

"Well, we laid out Hetty, and fixed up the house

and put up a curtain to her winder. And Miss Good'in
she 'n' I calkerlated to set up all night; and we was
jest puttin' a mess of tea to draw, so's to keep lively,
when in come Josh, drippin' wet; for the dews was
dreadful heavy them August nights. And he said
nothin' more'n jest to answer when he was spoke to.
And Miss Good'in was a real feelin' woman : she
guessed he'd better be let alone. So he drink't a cup
of tea, and then he started off into the bedroom ; and
when she went in there, 'long towards midnight, there
he was, fast asleep on the bed beside of the corpse, as
straight as a pin, only holdin' on to one of its hands.
Miss Good'in come back cryin' ; and I thought I
should 'a' boo-hooed right out. But I kinder strangled
it down, and we set to work to figger out what was
a-goin' to be done with the poor little chap. That
house of their'n that old Josh had bought of Mr.
Ranney hadn't never been paid for, only the interest-
money whenever Miss Crane could scrape it up, so't
that would go right back into husband's hands ; an'
they hadn't got no cow, nor no pig ; and we agreed the
s'lectmen would hev' to take him, and bind him out.

"I allers mistrusted that he'd waked up, and heerd
what we said ; for next morning, when we went to call
him, he was gone, and his shirts an' go-to-meetin s
too ; and he never come back to the funeral, nor a
good spell after.

"I know, after Hetty was buried, and we'd resolved
to sell what things she had to get her a head-stone, —
for Mr. Ranney wouldn't never put in for the rest of his
interest money, — I took home her old Bible, and kep'
it for Josh ; and the next time I see him was five and
twenty years after, when he come back from sea-farin',

an' settled down to farmin' on't. And he sot by that
Bible a dredful sight, I expect: for he gin our Sall the
brightest red-an'-yeller bandanner you ever see; she
used to keep it to take to meetin'."

"Miss" Ranney was certainly right in her "guess."
Josh had heard in that miserable midnight the discussion of his future, and, having a well-founded dread
of the selectmen's tender-mercies, had given a last
caress to his dead mother, and run away to Boston,
where he shipped for a whaling-voyage; was cast
away on the Newfoundland shore after ten years of
sea-life; and being at that time a stout youth of
twenty, sick of his seamanship, he had hired himself to
work in a stone-yard; and, by the time he was thirty-
five, had laid up enough money to return a thrifty
bachelor, and, buying a little farm on Plainfield Hill,
settle down to his ideal of life, and become the amusement of part of the village, and the oracle of the rest.

We boys adored Uncle Josh; for he was always
ready to rig our boats, spin us yarns a week long, and
fill our pockets with apples red and russet as his own
honest face. With the belles of the village Uncle
Josh had no such favor. He would wear a pigtail, in
spite of scoff and remonstrance; he would smoke a
cutty-pipe; and he did swear like a sailor, from mere
habit and forgetfulness, for no man not professedly
religious had a diviner instinct of reverence and worship than he. But it was as instinctive in him to swear
as it was to breathe; and some of our boldly specula-
tive and law-despising youngsters held that it was no
harm in him, any more than "gosh" and "thunder"
were in us, for really he meant no more.

However, Uncle Josh did not quite reciprocate the

contempt of the sex. Before long he began to make
Sunday-night visitations at Deacon Stone's, to "brush
his hat o' mornings," to step spry, and wear a stiff
collar and stock, instead of the open tie he had kept,
with the pigtail, long after jacket and tarpaulin had
been dismissed the service : so the village directly discovered that Josh Crane was courting the school-mis-
tress, "Miss Eunice," who boarded at Deacon Stone's.
What Miss Eunice's surname might be, I never knew ;
nor did it much matter. She was the most kindly,
timid, and lovable creature that ever tried to reduce a
district school into manners and arithmetic. She lives
in my memory still, — a tall, slight figure, with tender
brown eyes and a sad face, its broad, lovely forehead
shaded with silky light hair, and her dress always dim-
tinted, — faded perhaps, — but scrupulously neat and
stable.

Everybody knew why Miss Eunice looked so meekly
sad, and why she was still "Miss" Eunice : she had
been "disapp'inted." She had loved a man better
than he loved her, and therein, copying the sweet
angels, made a fatal mistake, broke her girl's heart,
and went to keeping school for a living.

All the young people pitied and patronized her ; all
the old women agreed that she was "a real clever little
fool ;" and men regarded her with a species of wonder
and curiosity, first for having a breakable heart, and
next for putting that member to fatal harm for one
of their kind. But boys ranked Miss Eunice even
above Uncle Josh ; for there lives in boys a certain
kind of chivalry, before the world has sneered it out of
them, that regards a sad or injured woman as a creature claiming all their care and protection. And it was

with a thrill of virtuous indignation that we heard
of Josh Crane's intentions toward Miss Eunice; nor
were we very pitiful of our old friend, when Mrs.
Stone announced to old Mrs. Ranney (who was deaf
as a post, and therefore very useful, passively, in
spreading news confided to her, as this was in the
church-porch), that "Miss Eunice wa'n't a-goin' to
hev' Josh Crane, 'cause he wa'n't a professor; but
she didn't want nobody to tell on't:" so everybody
did.

It was, beside, true. Miss Eunice was a sincerely
religious woman; and though Josh Crane's simple, fervent love-making had stirred a thrill within her she
had thought quite impossible, still she did not think it
was right to marry an irreligious man, and she told
him so with a meek firmness that quite broke down
poor Uncle Josh, and he went back to his farming with
profounder respect than ever for Miss Eunice, and a
miserable opinion of himself.

But he was a person without guile of any sort. He
would have cut off his pigtail, sold his tobacco-keg,
tried not to swear, for her sake; but he could not pre-
tend to be pious, and he did not.

A year or two afterward, however, when both had
quite got past the shyness of meeting, and set aside, if
not forgotten, the past, there was a revival of religion
in Plainfield; no great excitement, but a quiet spring-
ing-up of "good seed" sown in past generations, it
may be; and among the softened hearts and moist eyes
were those of Uncle Josh. His mother's prayers
had slept in the leaves of his mother's Bible, and now
they awoke to be answered.

It was strangely touching, even to old Parson Pitcher,

long used to such interviews with the oddest of all people under excitement, — rugged New-Englanders, — to see the simple pathos that vivified Uncle Josh's story of his experience ; and when, in the midst of a sentence about his dead mother, and her petitions for his safety, with tears dripping down both cheeks, he burst into a hallelujah metre tune, adapting the words, —

"Though seed lie buried long in dust," &c.,

and adding to the diversity of rhythm the discordance of his sea-cracked voice, it was a doubtful matter to Parson Pitcher whether he should laugh or cry ; and he was forced to compromise with a hysterical snort, just as Josh brought out the last word of the verse on a powerful fugue, —

"Cro-o-o-o-op!"

So earnest and honest was he, that, for a whole week after he had been examined and approved by the church committee as a probationer, he never once thought of Miss Eunice ; when suddenly, as he was reading his Bible, and came across the honorable mention of that name by the apostle, he recollected, with a sort of shamefaced delight, that now, perhaps, she would have him. So, with no further ceremony than reducing his gusty flax-colored hair to order by means of a pocket-comb, and washing his hands at the pump, away he strode to the schoolhouse, where it was Miss Eunice's custom to linger after school till her fire was burnt low enough to "rake up."

Josh looked in at the window as he "brought to" (in his own phrase) "alongside the school'us," and there sat the lady of his love knitting a blue stocking, with an empty chair most propitiously placed beside her in front of the fireplace. Josh's heart rose up mightily; but he knocked as little a knock as his great knuckles could effect, was bidden in, and sat himself down on the chair in a paroxysm of bashfulness, nowise helped by Miss Eunice's dropped eyes and persistent knitting. So he sat full fifteen minutes, every row and then clearing his throat in a vain attempt to introduce the point, till at length, desperate enough, he made a dash into the middle of things, and bubbled over with, "Miss Eunice, I've got religion! I'm sot out for to be a real pious man. Can't you feel to hev' me now?"

What Miss Eunice's little trembling lips answered, I cannot say: but I know it was satisfactory to Josh; for his first reverent impulse, after he gathered up her low words, was to clasp his hands, and say, "Amen," as if somebody had asked a blessing. Perhaps he felt he had received one in Miss Eunice.

When spring came they were married, and were happy, Yankee fashion, without comment or demonstration, but very happy. Uncle Josh united with the church, and was no disgrace to his profession save and except in one thing, — he would swear. Vainly did deacons, brethren, and pastor assail him with exhortation, remonstrance, and advice; vainly did his meek wife look at him with pleading eyes; vainly did he himself repent and strive and watch: "the stump of Dagon remained," and was not to be easily uprooted.

At length Parson Pitcher, being greatly scandalized at Josh's expletives, used unluckily in a somewhat excited meeting on church business (for in prayer-meetings he never answered any calls to rise, lest habit should get the better of him, and shock the very sinners he might exhort), — Parson Pitcher himself made a pastoral call at the farm, and found its master in the garden, hoeing corn manfully.

"Good-day, Mr. Crane!" said the old gentleman.

"Good-day, Parson Pitcher, good-day! d—— hot day, sir," answered the unconscious Josh.

"Not so hot as hell for swearers," sternly responded the parson, who, being of a family renowned in New England for noway mincing matters, sometimes verged upon profanity himself, though unawares. Josh threw down his hoe in despair.

"O Lord!" said he. "There it goes again, I swear! the d—— dogs take it! If I don't keep a-goin'! O Parson Pitcher! what shall I dew? It swears of itself. I am clean beat tryin' to head it off. Con—— no! I mean confuse it all! I'm such an old hand at the wheel, sir!"

Luckily for Josh, the parson's risibles were hardly better in hand than his own profanity; and it took him now a long time to pick up his cane, which he had dropped in the currant-bushes, while Joe stood among the corn-hills wiping the sweat off his brow, in an abject state of penitence and humility; and, as the parson emerged like a full moon from the leafy currants, he felt more charitably toward Josh than he had done before. "It is a very bad thing, Mr. Crane," said he mildly, — "not merely for yourself; but it scandalizes the church-members, and I think you should take severe measures to break up the habit."

"What upon arth shall I do, sir?" piteously asked Josh: it's the d—dest plague! Oh! I swan to man I've done it agin!"

And here, with a long howl, Josh threw himself down in the weeds, and kicked out like a half-broken colt, wishing in his soul the earth would hide him, and trying to feel as bad as he ought to; for his honest conscience sturdily refused to convict him in this matter, faithful as it was in much less-sounding sins.

I grieve to say that Parson Pitcher got behind an apple-tree, and there — cried perhaps; for he was wiping his eyes, and shaking all over, when he walked off; and Josh, getting up considerably in a state of dust, if not ashes and sackcloth, looked sheepishly about for his reprover, but he was gone.

Parson Pitcher convened the deacons and a few of the uneasy brethren that night in his study, and expounded to them the duty of charity for people who would sleep in meeting, had to drink bitters for their stomachs' sake, never came to missionary meetings for fear of the contribution-box, or swore without knowing it; and as Deacon Stone did now and then snore under the pulpit, and brother Eldridge had a "rheumatiz" that nothing but chokeberry-rum would cure, and that is very apt to affect the head, and brother Peters had so firm a conviction that money is the root of all evil, that he kept his from spreading, they all agreed to have patience with brother Crane's tongue-ill; and Parson Pitcher smiled as he shut the door behind them, thinking of that first stone that no elder nor ruler could throw.

Nevertheless, he paid another visit to Josh the next week, and found him in a hopeful state.

"I've hit on't now, Parson Pitcher!" said he, without waiting for a more usual salutation. "Miss Eunice she helped me: she's a master cretur for inven-

tions. I s–sugar! There, that's it. When I'm
a-goin' to speak quick, I catch up somethin' else that's
got the same letter on the bows, and I tell *yew*, it goes,
'r else it's somethin'. — Hollo! I see them d–dipper
sheep is in my corn. Git aout! git aout! you d–dan-
delions! *Git* aout!'' Here he scrambled away after
the stray sheep, just in time for the parson, who had
quieted his face and walked in to see Mrs. Crane, when
Josh came back dripping, and exclaiming, '' Pepper-
grass! them is the d–drowndedest sheep I ever see.''

This new spell of '' Miss Eunice's,'' as Josh always
called his wife, worked well while it was new. But the
unruly tongue relapsed; and meek Mrs. Crane had
grown to look upon it — as she would upon a wooden
leg, had that been Josh's infirmity — with pity and
regret, the purest result of a charity which '' endureth
and hopeth all things,'' eminently her ruling trait.

Every thing else went on prosperously. The farm
paid well, and Josh laid up money, but never for himself. They had no children, a sore disappointment to
both their kindly hearts; but all the poor and orphan
little ones in the town seemed to have a special claim
on their care and help. Nobody ever went away
hungry from Josh's door, or unconsoled from Miss
Eunice's '' keeping-room.'' Everybody loved them
both, and in time people forgot that Josh swore; but he
never did: a keen pain discomforted him whenever he
saw a child look up astonished at his oath. He had
grown so far toward '' the full ear,'' that he understood what an offence his habit was; and it pained him
very much that it could not be overcome, even in so
long a trial. But soon other things drew on to change
the current of Josh's penitent thoughts.

He had been married about ten years when Miss
Eunice began to show signs of failing health.   She
was, after the Yankee custom, somewhat older than
her husband, and of too delicate a make to endure the
hard life Connecticut farmers' wives must or do lead.
Josh was as fond of her as he could be ; but he did not
know how to demonstrate it.   All sorts of comforts she
had, as far as food and fire and clothing went, but no
recreation.   No public amusements ever visited Plainfield, a sparse and quiet village far off the track of any
railroad.   The farmers could not spend time to drive
round the country with their wives, or to go visiting,
except now and then on Sunday nights to a neighbor's ;
sometimes to a paring or husking bee, the very essence
of which was work.   Once a year a donation-party at
the minister's, and a rare attendance upon the sewing-
circle, distasteful to Josh, who must get and eat his
supper alone in that case, — these were all the amusements Miss Eunice knew.   Books she had none, except
her Bible, "Boston's Fourfold State," a dictionary,
and an arithmetic, — relics of her school ; and, if ever
she wished for more, she repressed the wish, because
these ought to be enough.   She did not know, or dared
not be conscious, that humanity needs something for
its lesser and trivial life ; that "by all these things
men live," as well as by the word and by bread.

So she drudged on uncomplainingly, and after ten
years of patience and labor, took to her bed, and was
pronounced by the Plainfield doctor to have successively
"a spine in the back," a "rising of the lungs," and a
"gittaral complaint of the lights."   (Was it catarrhal?)
Duly was she blistered, plastered, and fomented, dosed
with Brandreth's pills, mullein-root in cider, tansy,

burdock, bitter-sweet, catnip, and boneset teas, sow-bugs tickled into a ball, and swallowed alive, dried rattlesnakes' flesh, and the powder of a red squirrel, shut into a red-hot oven living, baked till powderable, and then put through that process in a mortar, and administered fasting.

Dearly beloved, I am not inprovising. All these, and sundry other and filthier medicaments which I refrain from mentioning, did once, perhaps do still, abound in the inlands of this Yankeedom, and slay their thousands yearly, as with the jaw-bone of an ass.

Of course Miss Eunice pined and languished, not merely from the "simples" that she swallowed, but because the very fang that had set itself in the breast of Josh's gentle mother gnawed and rioted in hers. At length some idea of this kind occurred to Uncle Josh's mind. He tackled up Boker, the old horse, and set out for Sanbury, where there lived a doctor of some eminence, and returned in triumph, with Dr. Sawyer following in his own gig.

Miss Eunice was carefully examined by the physician, a pompous but kindly man, who saw at once there was no hope and no help for his fluttered and panting patient.

When the millennium comes, let us hope it will bring physicians of sufficient fortitude to forbear dosing in hopeless cases : it is vain to look for such in the present condition of things. And Dr. Sawyer was no better than his kind : he hemmed, hawed, screwed up one eye, felt Miss Eunice's pulse again, and uttered oracularly, —

"I think a portion of some sudorific febrifuge would probably allay Mrs. Crane's hectic."

"Well, I expect it would," confidently asserted
Josh. "Can I get it to the store, doctor?"

"No, sir: it should be compounded in the family,
Mr. Crane."

"Dew tell!" responded Josh, rather crestfallen,
but brightening up as the doctor went on to describe,
in all the polysyllables he could muster, the desirable
fluid. At the end Josh burst out joyfully with, —

"I sw–swan! 'tain't nothin' but lemonade with
gumarabac in't."

Dr. Sawyer gave him a look of contempt, and took
his leave, Josh laboring under the profound and happy
conviction that nothing ailed Miss Eunice, if lemonade
was all that she needed; while the doctor called, on his
way home, to see Parson Pitcher, and to him confided
the mournful fact that Miss Eunice was getting ready
for heaven fast, could scarcely linger another week by
any mortal help. Parson Pitcher grieved truly; for he
loved and respected Eunice, and held her as the sweetest and brightest example of unobtrusive religion in all
his church: moreover, he knew how Josh would feel;
and he dreaded the task of conveying to him this painful intelligence, resolving, nevertheless, to visit them
next day with that intent, as it was now too near night
to make it convenient.

But a more merciful and able shepherd than he preceded him, and spared Josh the lingering agony of an
expectation that could do him no good. Miss Eunice
had a restless night after Dr. Sawyer's visit; for, with
the preternatural keenness of her disease, she read the
truth in his eye and tone. Though she had long
looked on to this end, and was ready to enter into rest,
the nearness of that untried awe agitated her, and for-

bade her sleep; but faith, unfailing in bitter need, calmed her at length, and with peace wri'ten upon her face she slept till dawn. A sudden pang awoke her, and her start roused Josh. He lifted her on the pillow, where the red morning light showed her gasping and gray with death: he turned all cold.

"Good-by, Josh!" said her tender voice, fainting as it spoke, and, with one upward rapturous look of the soft brown eyes they closed forever, and her head fell back on Josh's shoulder, dead.

There the neighbor who "did chores" for her of late found the two when she came in. Josh had changed since his mother died; for the moment Mrs. Casey lifted his wife from his arm, and laid her patient, peaceful face back on its pillow, Josh flung himself down beside her, and cried aloud with the passion and carelessness of a child. Nobody could rouse him, nobody could move him, till Parson Pitcher came in, and, taking his hand, raised and led him into the keeping-room. There Josh brushed off the mist before his drenched eyes with the back of his rough hand, and looked straight at Parson Pitcher.

"O Lord! she's dead," said he, as if he alone of all the world knew it.

"Yes, my son, she is dead," solemnly replied the parson. "It is the will of God, and you must con-sent."

"I can't, I can't! I a'n't a-goin' to," sobbed Josh. "'Ta'n't no use talkin' — if I'd only 'xpected some-thin': it's that —— doctor! O Lord! I've swore, and Miss Eunice is dead! Oh gracious goody! what be I a-goin' to do? Oh, dear, oh, dear! O *Miss* Eunice!"

Parson Pitcher could not even smile: the poor

fellow's grief was too deep. What could he think of
to console him, but that deepest comfort to the bereaved, — her better state? "My dear friend, be comforted. Eunice is with the blessed in heaven."

"I know it. I know it. She allers was nigh about
fit to get there without dyin'. O Lordy! she's gone
to heaven, and I ha'n't!"

No, there was no consoling Uncle Josh: that touch
of nature showed it. He was alone, and refused to be
comforted: so Parson Pitcher made a fervent prayer
for the living, that unawares merged into a thanksgiving for the dead, and went his way, sorrowfully con-
victed that his holy office had in it no supernatural
power or aid, that some things are too deep and too
mighty for man.

Josh's grief raved itself into worn-out dejection,
still too poignant to bear the gentlest touch: his groans
and cries were heart-breaking at the funeral, and it
seemed as if he would really die with agony while the
despairing wretchedness of the funeral hymn, the wailing cadences of "China," poured round the dusty and
cobwebbed meeting-house to which they carried his
wife in her coffin, one sultry August Sunday, to utter
prayers and hymns above her who now needed no
prayer, and heard the hymns of heaven.

After this, Josh retired to his own house, and,
according to Mrs. Casey's story, neither slept nor ate;
but this was somewhat apocryphal: and, three days
after the funeral, Parson Pitcher, betaking himself to
the Crane farm, found Uncle Josh whittling out a set
of clothes-pegs on his door-step, but looking very
downcast and miserable.

"Good-morning, Mr. Crane!" said the good divine

"Mornin', Parson Pitcher! Hev' a cheer?"

The parson sat down on the bench of the stoop, and wistfully surveyed Josh, wondering how best to introduce the subject of his loss; but the refractory widower gave no sign, and at length the parson spoke.

"I hope you begin to be resigned to the will of Providence, my dear Mr. Crane?"

"No, I don't, a speck!" honestly retorted Josh. Parson Pitcher was shocked.

"I hoped to find you in a better frame," said he.

"I can't help it!" exclaimed Josh, flinging down a finished peg emphatically. "I ain't resigned. I want Miss Eunice. I ain't willin' to have her dead: I can't and I ain't; and that's the hull on't! And I'd a —— sight ruther— Oh, goody! I've swore agin. Lord-a-massy! 'n' she ain't here to look at me when I do, and I'm goin' straight *to* the d——! Oh, land, there it goes! Oh, dear soul! can't a feller help himself nohow?"

And, with that, Josh burst into a passion of tears, and fled past Parson Pitcher into the barn, from whence he emerged no more till the minister's steps were heard crunching on the gravel-path toward the gate; when Josh, persistent as Galileo, thrust his head out of the barn-window, and repeated in a louder and more strenuous key, "I ain't willin', Parson Pitcher!" leaving the parson in a dubious state of mind, on which he ruminated for some weeks; finally concluding to leave Josh alone with his Bible till time should blunt the keen edge of his pain, and reduce him to reason. And he noticed with great satisfaction that Josh came regularly to church and conference-meetings, and at length resumed his work with a due amount of composure.

There was in the village of Plainfield a certain Miss Ranney, daughter of the aforesaid Mrs. Ranney, the greatest vixen in those parts, and of course an old maid. Her temper and tongue had kept off suitors in her youth, and had in nowise softened since. Her name was Sarah, familiarized into Sally; and as she grew up to middle age, that pleasant, kindly title being sadly out of keeping with her nature, everybody called her Sall Ran, and the third generation scarce knew she had another name.

Any uproar in the village always began with Sall Ran; and woe be to the unlucky boy who pilfered an apple under the overhanging trees of Mrs. Ranney's orchard by the road, or tilted the well-sweep of her stony-curbed well to get a drink. Sall was down upon the offender like a hail-storm; and cuffs and shrieks mingled in wild chorus with her shrill scolding, to the awe and consternation of every child within half a mile.

Judge, then, of Parson Pitcher's amazement, when, little more than a year after Miss Eunice's death, Josh was ushered into his study one evening, and, after stroking a new stove-pipe hat for a long time, at length said he had "come to speak about bein' published." The parson drew a long breath, partly for the mutability of man, partly of pure wonder.

"Who are you going to marry, Mr. Crane?" said he, after a pause. Another man might have softened the style of his wife to be: not Josh.

"Sall Ran," said he undauntedly. Parson Pitcher arose from his chair, and, with both hands in his pockets, advanced upon Josh like horse and foot together. But he stood his ground.

"What in the name of common sense and decency do you mean by marrying that woman, Joshu-way Crane?" thundered the parson.

"Well, ef you'll set down, Parson Pitcher, I'll tell ye the rights on't. You see, I'm dreadful pestered with this here swearin' way I've got. I kinder thought it would wear off, if Miss Eunice kep' a-lookin at me; but she's died." Here Josh interpolated a great blubbering sob. "And I'm gettin' so d—— bad! There! you see, parson, I doo swear dreadful; and I ain't no more resigned to her dyin' then I used ter be, and I can't stan' it. So I set to figgerin' on it out, and I guess I've lived too easy, hain't had enough 'flictions and trials. So I concluded I hed oughter put myself to the wind'ard of some squalls, so's to learn navigation; and I couldn't tell how, till suddenly I brought to mind Sall Ran, who is the D—— and all. Oh, dear, I've nigh about swore agin'! And I concluded she'd be the nearest to a cat-o-nine-tails I could get to tewtor me. And then I reklected what old Cap'n Thomas used to say when I was a boy aboard of his whaler: 'Boys,' sez he, 'you're allers sot to hev' your own way, and you've got ter hev mine: so's it's pooty clear that I shall flog you to rope-yarns, or else you'll hev to make b'lieve my way's your'n, which'll suit all round.' So you see, Parson Pitcher, I w'an't a-goin' to put myself in a way to quarrel with the Lord's will agin; and I don't expect you to hev' no such trouble with me twice, as you've hed sence Miss Eunice up an' died. I swan I'll give up reasonable next time, seein' it's Sall."

Hardly could Parson Pitcher stand this singular screed of doctrine, or the shrewd and self-satisfied yet

honest expression of face with which Josh clinched
his argument. Professing himself in great haste to
study, he promised to publish as well as to marry Josh,
and, when his odd parishioner was out of hearing,
indulged himself with a long fit of laughter, almost
inextinguishable, over Josh's patent Christianizer.

Great was the astonishment of the whole congregation on Sunday, when Josh's intentions were given out
from the pulpit, and strangely mixed and hesitating
the congratulations he received after his marriage,
which took place in the following week. Parson Pitcher
took a curious interest in the success of Josh's project,
and had to acknowledge its beneficial effects, rather
against his will.

Sall Ran was the best of housekeepers, as scolds are
apt to be; or is it in reverse that the rule began? She
kept the farmhouse Quakerly clean, and every garment
of her husband's scrupulously mended and refreshed.
But, if the smallest profanity escaped Uncle Josh's
lips, he did indeed "hear thunder;" and, with the
ascetic devotion of a Guyonist, he endured every objur-
gatory torrent to the end, though his soft and kindly
heart would now and then cringe and quiver in the
process.

It was all for his good, he often said; and, by the
time Sall Ran had been in Miss Eunice's place for an
equal term of years, Uncle Josh had become so mild-
spoken, so kind, so meek, that surely his dead wife
must have rejoiced over it in heaven, even as his brethren did on earth.

And now came the crowning honor of his life. Uncle
Josh was made a deacon. Sall celebrated the event
by a new black silk frock; and asked Parson Pitcher

home to tea after the church-meeting, and to such a
tea as is the great glory of a New-England housekeeper. Pies, preserves, cake, biscuit, bread, short-
cake, cheese, honey, fruit, and cream, were pressed
and pressed again upon the unlucky parson, till he was
quite in the condition of Charles Lamb and the omni-
bus, and gladly saw the signal of retreat from the
table; he withdrawing himself to the bench on the
stoop, to breathe the odorous June air, and talk over
matters and things with Deacon Josh, while "Miss
Crane cleared off."

Long and piously the two worthies talked; and at
length came a brief pause, broken by Josh.

"Well, Parson Pitcher, that 'are calkerlation of
mine about Sall did come out nigh onter right, didn't
it?"

"Yes indeed, my good friend," returned the parson.
"The trial she has been to you has been really blessed,
and shows most strikingly the use of discipline in this
life."

"Yes," said Josh. "If Miss Eunice had lived, I
don't know but what I should 'a' ben a swearin' man
to this day; but Sall she's rated it out o' me. And
I'm gettin' real resigned too."

The meek complacency of the confession still gleamed
in Uncle Josh's eyes as he went in to prayers; but
Sall Ran looked redder than the crimson peonies on
her posy-bed.

Parson Pitcher made an excellent prayer, particularly descanting on the use of trials; and when he
came to an end, and arose to say good-night, Mrs.
Crane had vanished: so he had to go home without
taking leave of her. Strange to say, during the follow-

ing year a rumor crept through the village that "Miss Deacon Crane" had not been heard to scold once for months; that she even held her tongue under provocation; this last fact being immediately put to the test by a few evil-minded and investigating boys, who proceeded to pull her fennel-bushes through the pickets, and nip the yellow heads; receiving for their audacious thieving no more than a mild request not to "do that," which actually shamed them into apologizing.

With this confirmation, even Parson Pitcher began to be credulous of report, and sent directly for Deacon Crane to visit him.

"How's your wife, deacon?" said the parson, as soon as Josh was fairly seated in the study.

"Well, Parson Pitcher, she's most onsartainly changed. I don't believe she's got riled mor'n once, or gin it to me once, for six months."

"Very singular," said Parson Pitcher. "I am glad for both of you. But what seems to have wrought upon her?"

"Well," said Uncle Josh, with a queer glitter in his eye, "I expect she must 'a' ben to the winder that night you 'n' I sot a-talkin' on the stoop about 'flictions and her; for next day I stumbled, and spilt a lot o' new milk onto the kitchen-floor. That allers riled her: so I began to say, 'Oh, dear, I'm sorry, Sall!' when she ups right away, and sez, sez she, 'You hain't no need to be skeered, Josh Crane: you've done with 'flictions in this world. I sha'n't never scold you no more. I ain't a-goin' to be made a pack-horse to carry my husband to heaven.' And she never said no more to me, nor I to her; but she's ben nigh about as pretty-behaved as Miss Eunice ever since; and I hope

I sha'n't take to swearin'. I guess I sha'n't; but I do feel kinder crawly about bein' resigned."

However, Uncle Josh's troubles were over. Sall Ran dropped her name for " Aunt Sally," and finally joined the church, and was as good in her strenuous way as her husband in his meekness; for there are " diversities of gifts." And when the Plainfield bell, one autumn day, tolled a long series of eighty strokes, and Deacon Crane was gathered to his rest in the daisy-sprinkled burying-yard beside Miss Eunice, the young minister who succeeded Parson Pitcher had almost as hard a task to console Aunt Sally as his predecessor had to instil resignation, on a like occasion, into Uncle Josh.

POLL JENNINGS'S HAIR.

It is sometimes a relief to have a story without a
heroine, and this distinction alone can I claim for
mine. Nothing heroic or wonderful casts its halo about
little Poll Jennings, the seventh daughter of Abe Jennings, the south-side fisherman. Not even one of those
miraculous poor cottages that are always so exquisitely
clean, and have white curtains and climbing roses
through all depths of poverty and suffering, held my
little girl in its romantic shelter. Abe's house, lying
between three of those low sand-hills that back the
shore on our New-England coast, like waves of land
that simulate the sea, was not in the least attractive or
picturesque. At first a mere cabin of drift-wood, the
increasing wants and numbers of his family had, as it
were, built themselves out in odd attachments — square,
or oblong, or triangular — as wood came to hand, or
necessity demanded, till the whole dwelling bore the
aspect externally of a great rabbit-hutch or poultry-
house, such as boys build, on a smaller scale, out of old
boards from ruined barns, palings of fence, and refuse
from carpenters' shops. Though no constructive magazine furnished inside or outside of the fisherman's
home, it was all fashioned from the waifs of a great
destroyer, — all drift-wood from the sea, that raved
and thundered half a mile off, as if yet clamorous for

its prey. Still, uncouth and rude as was its shaping, a poet might have found it more suggestive than any model cottage in the land, — if a poet be not merely the rhymer of sentiment and beauty, but he whose creative soul, from one slight thread of association, spins a wide web of fancies, and tracks the idea through all its windings, till imagination becomes reality, and the real and the ideal are one. However, no poet ever entered there to talk or think all this nonsense ; and the old walls, where teak, that an Indian forest missed, stood side by side with oak from English uplands, and pine from the Æolian woods of Maine ; the windows, that had been driven ashore, void of their crystal panes, from some full-freighted steamer, gone down too deep for any more wistful eyes to watch receding shore or hurrying storm-rack through the sashes ; doors, that had swung to in the last lurch of the vessel, and made the state-rooms they guarded tombs of the dead, — all these spoke nothing to the practical brain of old Abe Jennings, nor softened to any pathos the high spirits of his six rosy daughters, who laughed and romped and worked, as regardless of any outside suffering as if they were the world, and their sand-hills comprised all life and destiny. But Poll, the last and least of the seven, was one of those exceptional creatures that come as some new and strange variety of a flower does, as unlike all its congeners in tint and habit as if it were the growth of an alien soil and climate. Ruth and Mary and Martha, Nancy, Jane, and Adeline, were all straight and strong, with thick, dark hair, varying only from the tar-black of Ruth's coarse curls to the shining deep-brown of Adeline's braids. Roses of the deepest dye bloomed

on their faces. Except Ruth, they were never sad or
moody : they had their sweethearts and their frolics,
and were altogether common-sense, ordinary, wholesome girls as one could find. Polly could lay claim to
none of these charms or virtues : she was slight and
pale, with great hazel eyes, that oftenest looked vague
and dreamy ; her very lips were colorless ; and her
skin, roughened and red, offered neither bloom nor
purity to attract the eye : but her hair was truly mag-
nificent. Of the deepest red, — undeniably red, as is the
glossy coat of a bright bay horse, — it fell to her feet in
shining waves, so soft, so fine, yet so heavy, that it
seemed as if the splendid growth had absorbed all the
beauty and strength that should otherwise have been
hers in face and form. But with this peculiar coloring
came also the temperament of which it is the index, —
sensitive, passionate, shy as a quail, yet proud as only
a woman can be. If Poll Jennings had been taught and
trained to the height of her capacities, or even had the
means of self-training, her latent genius would have
dawned on her sphere in one shape or another ; and
perhaps an actress, perhaps an author, some star of
art, some wonder of vocalization, might have delighted
or astonished the world. But, happily for Poll, another
and a better fate than these awaited her, though its
vestibule was only a hut, and its locality the sand-hills
of the Atlantic shore. Yet this special beauty of the
child's, her resplendent hair, was made her peculiar
torment. To her sisters and father it was red, and only
red ; and all the jokes that people will waste on that
tint — artistic, historic, exquisite as it may be — were
.avished on Polly's head, till hot tears filled her eyes,
and burning color suffused her face at the least allusion

to it. Moreover, her physical capacity was far inferior
to that of her sisters ; her slight hands and arms could
not row a boat through the rolling seas outside the bar ;
she could not toil at the wash-tub, or help draw a seine ;
and when a young farmer from inland came down "to
salt," or a sturdy fisher from another bay hauled up
his boat inside the little harbor of Squamkeag Light,
and trudged over to have a talk with old Abe, it was
never Poll who waded out into the mud with bare,
white legs and flying hair, to dig clams for supper ;
or who, with a leather palm, in true sailor-fashion,
mended sails by the fireside, singing 'longshore songs
at her work.   Poll's place was never there : she shrank
away to gather berries, or hunt for gulls' eggs, or
crouched motionless in a darker corner, her great,
luminous eyes fixed on some panelled fragment of the
wall that hungry seas had thrown ashore, painting to
herself the storm and the wreck till she neither heard
nor saw the rough love-making that went on beside her.
So it happened that Mary and Martha, the twins,
married two young farmers up the country, and led
the unpastoral lives that farming women in New
England must lead, — lives of drudgery and care.
Nancy went off with a young fisherman over to Fire
Island. Ruth, the oldest, had lost her lover, years
gone by, in a whale-ship that sailed away, and was
never heard of more ; while Jane was just about to
be married to hers, mate on a New-Haven schooner, —
"Mdse. to Barbadoes," as the shipping-list said ; and
Adeline laughed and coquetted between half a dozen
of the roughest sort.

There were enough at home to do the work ; and
Ruth's set sobriety, Jane's boisterous healthiness

Adeline's perpetual giggle, none of them chimed with Poll's dreamy nature. A weary sense of her own incapacity oppressed her all the time. She could not work as they did; and, worst of all, the continual feeling that she was ugly, "red-headed," "white-faced," "eyes as big as a robin's," brooded over her solitary thoughts, and made her more sad, more lonely, from day to day. Yet though no refinement of speech ever turned plain "Poll" into Pauline, and no suave ministrations of higher civilization toned her wild grace into elegance, or wove her beautiful locks into the crown they should have been, she had her own consolations; for Nature is no foster-mother, and she took this sobbing child into her own heart. Polly's highest pleasure was to steal out from the cabin, and wander away to the shore: there, laid at length among the rank grass whose leaves waved and glittered in the wind, she watched the curling waves of beryl sweep in, to leap and break in thunder, while the spray-bells were tossed far and sparkling from their crests on the beaten sands, and the crepitation of those brilliant bubbles, crushed beneath the wave, scarce finished its fairy peal of artillery ere another and a heavier surf swelled, and curled, and broke above it; while milk-white gulls darted and screamed overhead, or a lonely fish-hawk hovered with dire intent over the shoal of fish that dimpled and darkened the water with a wandering wave of life; and far beyond, through the purple haze that brooded on the horizon, white-sailed ships glided into sight, and, stately as dreams, vanished again whence they seemed to come. Here, while the fresh breeze swept her cheek with its keen odor of the seas, and the warm sands beneath quickened her lan-

guid pulses, Poll lay hour after hour, and dreamed, —
not such dreams as girls have whose life is led among
luxury and society, but pure visions of far-off countries
beyond the ocean, whose birds and flowers and trees
were all of earth's brightest, and all quickened with
the acute life of the sea itself to poignant beauty.
Here, in this paradise, no mocking mirth, no harsh
word, no cold or storm, intruded; and in its castles a
new life dawned for the fisherman's girl, that held her
in its trance safe from the harshness of her own, and
lapped her in its soft sweetness from all that was hard
and bitter in reality.   So all the summer days passed
away, lying on the shore, or wandering on the sand-hills
that rolled back to sand-plains or boggy stretches of
inland; plains that had their own treasures of great
open-eyed violets, azure as the sky above, or white as
its clouds, — milky strawberry-blooms and clusters of
their scarlet fragrant fruits, crowding flowers of pink
and purple, trails of starry blackberry-vines, and
swamps that beguiled her wandering feet through fragrant thickets of bayberry, tangled with catbrier and
sweetbrier, to great blueberry-bushes, hanging thick
with misty blue spheres, aromatic and sweet with a
sweetness no tropic suns can give; while beside them
bloomed the splendid wild lily, set thick as a pagoda
with bells; and at its foot the rare orange orchis showed
its concentred sunshine, and regal cardinal-flowers
flamed through the thin grass with spikes of velvet fire.
Not a flower blossomed, or a fruit ripened, for miles
about, that Poll did not know: it was she who hung the
shelf above the chimney with bundles of spearmint,
peppermint, boneset, marsh-rosemary, pennyroyal,
mountain-mint, tansy, catnip, sweet-fern, sweet-cicely,

prince's-piny, sassafras-root, winter-green, and birch-bark, part the gatherings of her own rambles at home, part a tribute from her sisters up the country, who brought Poll only "yarbs" instead of the squashes for Ruth, the apples that filled Jane's apron, and the hickory-nuts Adeline cracked in her great white teeth. So things went on till Poll was seventeen, and our story begins; when Jane's lover came home and they were married, and Adeline betook herself to see Nancy, leaving only the eldest and youngest of the seven sisters at home for the winter that set in early and bitter. The last day of November was a wild north-easter: rain, that the fierce wind drove aslant against the hut windows, froze as fast as it fell, and while Ruth sat by the stove, and sewed, drawing once in a while one of those deep sighs that are the echoes of a great sorrow gone past, Poll pressed her face against the blurred window-pane to see the storm she dared not be out in; and, while she looked and dreamed, the outer door burst open, and in came her father, dripping as if he had been drowned, followed by a stout young fellow as pale as a sheet, carrying his right arm in a sling.

"I veow!" said old Abe, shaking himself like a great water-dog, ef this a'n't about the most weathersome weather I ever see. I ha'n't ben only jest outside the bar, an' my jib's as stiff as a tin pan, and the old fo'sail took an' cracked fore an' aft afore I could get her head on so's to run in. Ef I hadn't a had Sam Bent here along, I dono but what I should ha' ben swamped, whether or no. He and me both done our darnedest, and then I'll be drowned ef he didn't fall foul of a board't was all glib ice, jest as we was a-landin': up flew his heels, and he kinder lay to on his right arm, so't I expect it's broke. I slung it up with my old comforter till he could get under hatches here, 'n' now you gals must take keer on him till I make sail over to Punkintown, and get that are nateral bone-setter to come along and splice him.''

Sam Bent was no stranger to the girls ; but, though Poll had often seen him before, she had never exchanged half a dozen words with him. But ceremonies are spared at Southside : so Poll took the scissors which Ruth handed her, and proceeded to cut the sleeve of Sam Bent's coat and jacket, while her sister set a spare bedroom to rights, and brewed some herb-tea, lest the youth might be ordered a sweat. Poll's fingers were slight and careful, and she did her office tenderly, — even Sam felt it through the pain of his doubly-broken arm ; and when at length Abe returned from his walk to Punkintown, a settlement some four miles inland, he found Sam, released from his heavy pea-jacket and coat, wrapped in Poll's shawl, with his feet to the fire, about as comfortable as he could have been under the disadvantages of the occasion. The ''nateral bone-setter'' worked his usual wonders on the occasion, and, having duly splintered and bandaged the young man, took his knife out of his pocket, and began to snap the blade out and in as a preliminary to conversation, while he tilted his chair back against the wall, and cleared his throat with a vigorous '' ahem.''

'' Well, sir, well, sir,'' began Dr. Higgs, ''that job is done, sir. You will have rather of a procrastinating season with such a fracter as that is ; but patience is a virtoo, sir. Yes, sir, and so is patients too, we doctors think. He, he, he ! Ho, ho, ho ! Well, I am pleased to see you reciprocate my little joke : raythei hard to be ludiciously inclined, sir, under the proximity of corporal anguish. Ahem: shows you have good grit into you. I expect you'll become evanescent very rapid, if you don't catch a cold, nor over-eat, nor over-do the prudential, noway. Do you reside in these parts, sir?"

"I live over to Mystic when I'm to home," modestly replied Sam, overcome with this torrent of words, but, fortunately for him, not knowing the difference between evanescent and convalescent.

"Well, I can't recommend to you a removal to your natyve spere immediately, sir. No, sir, I should rayther advise you, in order to abrogate your confinement as much as possible, to remain where you be. If any febrifugal disorders was to set in, it would concatenate the fracter, sir. Very serious, very serious! You will want considerble nussin', I think proberble; and, if you can indooce this here old gentleman to inhabitate you for a spell, why, I should counsel you to become stationary for the present."

"I guess I a'n't a-goin' for to turn Sam Bent out o' my cabin, ef 'twa'n't no bigger'n a yawl-boat's locker," growled old Abe. "He's his father's son, 'n' that's enough, if he was the miserblest hoss-shoe crab 't ever left his back behind him. Poll here can nuss him. She a'n't good for much but pokin' round, 'n' it's too consarned cold to do that this kind o' clymit."

"Well, sir, well, sir, I'll call over agin to-morrer, ef the weather is convenable. I am a-comin' into this region to see a poor indignant female who is laid up with a neuralogy of the marrer-bones, so't mebbe I shall be rather delayed in gettin' around; but I'm sure

certain to be on hand, Providence permitting, before
noon — by night whether or no.   Good-day, good-
day!''   Wherewith the verbose doctor departed ; and
Sam Bent, suddenly looking up, caught a little flicker
of fun just fading out of Poll's great eyes, and laughed
outright.

"He bears up hard onto big words, don't he?'' said
Sam, whose genuine nature detected the pretension he
did not understand.   "He's a kind of a nateral dictionary, I guess.''

Poll's eyes danced, and Sam fixed a long look on
her.   He didn't know why, no more did she ; but, being
both uncivilized enough to feel and think without asking why or how, they were not concerned about the
matter.   And, when Sam Bent was safely convoyed to
bed in the queer little five-angled room allotted to him,
he fell asleep, and dreamed he was drawing a seine on
the north shore, and a great sting-ray stood up on its
tail, and turned into Dr. Higgs ; while Poll only listened to the storm outside, and fancied that she heard
minute-guns and shrieks of terror through the wild
wind, and at length slept too heavily to dream.   But
for all this a great guest was drawing near to the fisherman's hut, though in silence and secrecy, — a guest
that pagans hailed with wine and roses, wreaths of
myrtle, and dances of joy, but we, sadder and wiser,
welcome oftenest with trembling and wonder.   Poll
knew neither.   She never even stopped to wonder why
she cared no more to search the beach for its treasures,
or pore over the odd pictures in their Bible.   Nor did
Sam Bent ever suspect why he liked to have his
bandages renewed daily, his black hair smoothed for
him, and his black ribbon knotted so carefully under

the coarse white collar that set off the muscular throat
and handsome head above it. Sam would not have
cared if his broken arm was not set for six months,
he liked so well his self-elected office of teacher to
Poll, who was learning to read at his knee like a child,
and listening to his discourses of other lands (as she
considered Maine and Georgia) with as much eagerness as if he had been Hakluyt himself, instead of
foremast hand to a coasting-schooner. Under the
pressure of her new duties, Poll grew into new devel-
opments. She became far more handy about the house ;
she spoke oftener of her own accord ; she moved more
rapidly, and never a hole in her apron or her frock lay
an hour unmended now ; and, taking patient lessons
of Ruth, she learned to mend Sam's stockings so
nicely, that he, at least, considered it an ornament
to have had a hole in the most conspicuous quarter
possible.

But at last Sam got well, and could not evade the
fact that he had been doing nothing for two months
but receiving care and a home ; and he began to wonder
to himself what he could ever do to escape from this
heavy weight of obligation. Now it never was supposed in old times that the aforesaid little deity meddled with lesser things than flowers and jewels ; but
great is civilization ! In its faintest influence comes
a subtlety unknown to dear primeval days ; and at this
juncture love — if love it was — dropped a timely rheumatism on Uncle Abe's old back ; and, the day after
Sam Bent left off his sling, the poor old fisherman came
home groaning and hobbling, and, I regret to say,
swearing after his own fishy fashion.

"Darn it !" growled he, as he let himself down

into an old rush-bottomed chair that stood by the fire.
"I'll be jiggered if I a'n't got to be in docks now!
I couldn't but jest h'ist her over the bar, 'n' make out
to git ashore. Flat-fish 'n' flounders! I ha'n't had
such a spell sénce ten year back; 'n' what's goin' to
become of the eyester bisness I should like ter tell?"

"You'd better take a sweat right away, father,"
said Ruth, taking down the sheaf of boneset for the
necessary brewage.

"Sweat! I calk'late I shall sweat enough with this
here screwin' in my bones, gal! Loddy Doddy! ef I
don't yell an' holler afore daybreak, I shall miss my
reckonin'; and all the eyesters in the bay'll be raked
up afore I'm stirrin' agin, for all't I know."

"No, they won't, Uncle Abe!" said Sam sturdily,
coming up to the fire as he spoke. "Ha'n't I had a
free passage here nigh on to two months, 'n' you
think I a'n't goin' for to work it out? I ken work
'The Mary Ann' fust-rate, and I know the lay of
the beds pretty near as well as anybody. I'm all right
now; and here I am, standin' on my feet, ready to do
the most a feller can, though I don't never expect I
can work out the kind o' care I've hed along back."
With which Sam cast a sheep's-eye at Poll's place,
and beheld — nobody; for she was behind him, looking hard out of the window at the new and interesting
prospect of an old seine and two wash-tubs — background a sand-hill. But Poll's eyes were too misty to
see; and her rough, red skin flushed to purple as she
heard her father go on : —

"Hold hard, Sam! You're your dad's son: there
a'n't a doubt on't. Old 'Paphro Bent never see a dis-
tress-signal h'isted, but what he lay to, an' sent aboard.

But you're a young feller, 'n' I a'n't a-goin' for to take your vittles 'n' put 'em into my jaws. You ken git a bunk aboard of any coaster, 'n' get your wages reg'lar: so you 'bout ship, and mind your own hellum. I can keep to my anchorage, I guess, for a spell; 'n' it's no use starving while them gals has got legs to go and dig clams. I shall weather it, boy; though I don't say but what you're a good feller to think on't.''

"Now look at here, Uncle Abe," said Sam vehemently, setting his feet as wide apart, and bracing his hands on his hips as firmly, as if he expected old Abe to make a rush at him, and try to upset him, " 'tain't no use hailin' this here schooner with that kind of talk. I a'n't a-goin' coastin'. I a'n't goin' away. I wish I may be drowñded off Hatteras, and come ashore at Point Judy, if I do! I'm a-goin' eysterin', an' deep-sea fishin' in 'The Mary Ann,' till that darned rheumatiz o' yours goes to Joppy, ef it lasts till day after never; 'n' ef you won't give me night's lodgin's and a meal of vittles here, why, I'll go over to Squamkeag Light 'n' get 'em out o' Ben Gould: so there's the hull on't!'' With which peroration Sam turned away, and spat energetically into the fire.

Old Abe held his peace a minute. It was hard for the sturdy man to own his dependence, to become useless; and Sam's strong youth and manhood mixed regret with his simple willingness of acceptance.

"Well," said he at last, "Lord knows I'd foller the sea till I dropped ef I hadn't no rheumatiz; but a rotten hulk a'n't no use outside. You ken take 'The Mary Ann,' Sam Bent. She's easy handled, and she's cute enough of herself to keep school to-morrer, 'n' I can tell you the lay of the eyester-beds tollerble well

But look here, young feller, ef I catch you a-takin' a meal of vittles, or a night's sleep, over to Ben Gould's, you'll hear thunder, 'n' ketch lightnin'.''

"Well, I won't," laughed Sam; and so the matter ended. And old Abe was put to bed with the dose of boneset, and rose no more for long weeks, — long enough to Ruth; for a sick man's attendant has no sinecure. But Poll never wearied of the lingering days, for a step tramping over the sand-hills, and a broad, brown face full of honest delight, waited to charm the day's ending, and in that anticipation nothing seemed dull or dreary. Nor did ever any man have gentler nursing than Poll lavished on her cross and unreasonable old father. One hears vast blame laid upon lovers for their seeming sweetness and excellence while yet love is new; but is not the blame unjust? For what can call out the latent lovelinesses of any character, if the one rose of life does not win them to the surface? Lost in that divine blooming, wrapped in that sacred spell, shall not the desert blossom, and the sands glitter with flowing springs? Still a desert; still the red sands: let us rather bless the transformer than sneer at the transformation. So the winter wore on; and if, in its routine, there was any bitterness, it was only when storms swept over the hut with fierce scream and heavy pinions, and Ruth shuddered over her dead lover, Poll over her living one. Meanwhile no storms wrecked Sam Bent. He raked oysters, and caught sea-bass, halibut, porgies, and various other finny creatures, in quantities unknown; discovered a new oyster-bed "inside," in one of his long voyages round Montauk; and made money at a rate that pleased nim even more than it did old Abe: while he thor

oughly enjoyed having a home to go to, and exulted
in his pupil's progress, who had got so far as to read
fluently the book of fairy-tales he bought for her in
New York by the first of April. But with April home
came Adeline; and, Adeline being one of those women
who are born coquettes, great was her delight at
finding a handsome young fellow like Sam Bent domes-
ticated in her house, and of course she immediately
began a vigorous flirtation with him. Now, Adeline
was a sort of woman Sam had seen before, understood,
and held in small account. With Poll he was respect-
ful, shy, timid, yet self-respectful; but he laughed,
jested, and romped with "Addy," spoke to her as if
she were another fisherman, helped her to dig clams,
and sculled her boat across the bay with as much ease
and carelessness as if she had been a boy. Poor Poll!
She did not know why she grew cross to Adeline, and
silent to Sam. Something told her that she ought not
to steal away to her old haunts, and neglect her home-
work, and let her father shift for himself as best he
could; yet Poll did all this, and the sea and sky comforted her no more. Neither was she particularly consoled by hearing from her sleepless pillow, one night,
Ruth remonstrating with Adeline on her manners to
Sam.

"I don't like to have you make so free with Sam
Bent, Addy," said poor prim Ruth, who had never
given so much as one kiss to Jonas Scranton before
he sailed away to be drowned, and probably regretted
it still. "'Tain't mannerly to be a-rompin' round so
with a young feller."

"O law!" laughed Addy; "jest as ef I was goin
to be stuck up with Sam Bent! I like to plague him

He's ben cooped up all winter with you an' Poll till he wants a livenin' up."

"Well, 'tain't a good thing for Poll to see you a-behavin' so, Addy. Maybe she might take to them ways, 'n' she a'n't a kind to take things so easy as you do, 'n' maybe folks would think hard of her ef she should foller your manners; for you never was nothin' but a kitten, sence you was knee-high to a hoptoad."

Adeline laughed harder than ever. "Well, I declare!" said she. "As ef our Poll would ever take to kitin' after a feller like Sam Bent! I guess he *would* feel crawly if she did, poor cretur! That red hair and pink-red face of her'n a'n't very takin'." With which she resumed her laughter as if the idea was delightfully absurd.

Ruth gave a little sigh, and knit more energetically than ever. She might as well have exhorted the sea-spray as Adeline. She never even moved her to petulance with her exhortations, which would have been some comfort. But Poll turned her face to her pillow, crushed and heart-sick; and slow, hot tears crept down her cheeks one after another, as she thought of her happy winter evenings, of Sam Bent's shy, kind looks, and, as climax, of her own horrid red hair, and rough skin, and saucer-eyes. Poor Poll!

But by May Uncle Abe's rheumatism began to be forgotten: his sturdy legs ached no more, his back straightened out, and his weather-beaten face recovered its old look of kindly shrewdness, and he was as fit as ever to handle "The Mary Ann." So Sam had been "down to York," and got a place as foremast hand on a brig bound for China, to sail the first of June, a good place, and good wages. Yet somehow Poll did

not receive the news joyfully; and she said nothing at
all to Sam Bent when he came to announce it.

Poll was not magnanimous; but who is — among
women? That is not their forte. A thousand other
virtues flourish with them; but this is the millennial
grace, and Poll owned it not. She was as weak, as
selfish, as jealous, as a humble and ugly woman is apt
to be when she is in love; and I shall not blame her,
though I know there are plenty who will. So, when
Ruth had said quietly, "I'm real glad, Sam, but we
shall kinder miss you;" and Adeline had giggled out,
"Well, that is first-rate, 'n' I guess you'll have to
get me something real pretty over to Chiny," — Sam
missed one voice that was, after all, the only one he
cared for; and, looking round, saw Poll's blue-check
gown flutter away over the top of a sand-hill, past the
window. "I declare for't," said Sam, "if I hain't
left a lot o' little fixin's down in 'The Mary Ann,' 't
I brought from York. I'll jest step down and fetch
'em."

I regret to say that Sam had left them on purpose,
having already learned the strategic lesson of lovers, in
order to provide some sure way of excuse to meet or
follow Poll, if she should happen to be out of the
house. Would he have followed her, had he known
that she ran away to avoid him? He might have been
a fool for his pains, like other men. But it happened
he had no provocation: so he betook himself to, or
toward, "The Mary Ann," but, as soon as the house
was hidden, changed his course, and followed after the
light track of Poll's steps till they were lost in the
thick beach-grass. Poor child! she had thrown herself down in the glittering blades, and buried her head

in her apron. Faster than the clear green waves, that
rolled relentless splendors on the failing shore below,
did the heavy surges of her first sorrow thunder and
sweep above her shrinking heart. Sam was going
away. That was first; and then came in the shame,
the self-contempt, the bitter grief, that had racked and
wasted her ever since she overheard Ruth and Addy
talking about her that unhappy night. What if he did
stay? He wouldn't care for her, handsome fellow!
How could he bear to look at such a homely thing as
she? And that dreadful hair! so red, and so much of
it! If Poll had ever read novels, she might have torn
it and scattered it with highly appropriate gestures.
But she had not: so she let her hair alone, and only
cried, and wished she was any body or any thing but
Poll Jennings. Even a little fiddler-crab in its hole
was enviable, since it never cared for Sam Bent, and
hadn't got red hair.

Between the thunder of the surf, and the checked
apron that covered her ears and tried to stifle her sobs,
Poll heard nothing; but, in the midst of her passive
anguish, suddenly a strong arm was passed round her;
and, stunned with surprise, she found herself lifted on
to Sam Bent's knee. Any woman who knew any thing
would have sprung to her feet and blazed with anger,
told seven lies in one breath, defied and scorned Sam,
and sent him to China a broken-hearted man, indifferent to sharks and cholera, to be rewarded, perhaps,
after ten years, with an elderly and acetous woman as
the meed of constancy. But Poll was a little fool: she
just laid her head against Sam's red shirt, and sobbed
harder than ever. Sam choked: he couldn't speak,
and yet he wanted to swear. Finally he sputtered out,

"Poll, what's to pay?" No answer, only a great big sob that seemed to shake the little creature in his arms all over, and made it incumbent on Sam to clasp her still tighter.

So he tried again : —

"Poll, don't! Hold up, dear! Don't keep a-cryin so!" Useless remonstrance; for, though the sobs ceased, bright drops of salt water that the sea disowned went hopping down that red flannel shirt in a deliberate way, as if they didn't care to, but rather thought it best.

"Polly," repeated Sam in a gentler tone.

"What?" said Poll faintly, lifting her head, and wiping her eyes with her apron.

"Don't do that! I see you through the winder, and I follered along; for you see, Poll, I'm a-going to Chiny, 'n' I wanted to — I — well — I dono. Poll, when I come back will you marry me?"

Poll's eyes opened wider and brighter than ever. She drew back, and looked into Sam's face: her cheek flushed as she met his steady gaze.

"Don't make fun of me!" said she piteously.

Sam's eyes blazed. "Make fun of you!" said he indignantly. "Why, Poll Jinnins! what are you thinkin' about? I should think you might believe a feller was honest when he said that."

"O Sam!" pleaded Poll, with moist eyes.

"*Will* you, Poll?"

"But — but — oh!" said she with half a sob. "Are you sure, Sam?"

"Sure of what?"

"Sure you like me," courageously ventured Poll.

"I don't know nothin' else I'm so sure on," said he dryly.

" But I've got such red hair, Sam ! "

Sam laughed outright. He could not help it. But those great hazel eyes, full of vague apprehension, and the trembling lips, sobered him.

" Well, Poll, I think your hair is the prettiest thing to you by a long sight. Sence I see it tumble down once, when you was a-bindin' up my arm, I ha'n't never see the sun risin' acrost the water but what I've thought on't : it's just like the wake the sun makes, — kinder crinkly, and yet slick and bright, and kinder draws your eyes to't. I wouldn't change your hair for nobody's 't ever I see."

With which Sam withdrew the comb from the massive knot, and its great bright coil slipped down over Poll's neck, and across his arm, and spread into a veil of length and splendor Athene might have coveted, had she " been there to see." Sam's big brown fist grasped the silken waves ; and, bringing them round before Poll's face, he caressed his capture as if it were real gold, and he a miser, threaded it through his fingers, held it in bright bows up to the sunshine, stroked its ripples over his unoccupied knee, till Poll, who had innocently laid one arm round his neck while she looked on, fairly smiled ; but a sigh followed instantly.

" But I am so humly, Sam ! " [Homely, she meant.]

" Well," said Sam, dropping the hair, and putting both arms round her, " what if you be ? And I don't say't I think you're like a pink-and-white figure-head to a liner. I a'n't one o' them that buys a boat for its paint. I never see a handsome gal I liked half so well, 'n' I guess I wouldn't 'a' had no better care out o' the prettiest cretur betwixt the reefs and the banks than I had last winter. Besides, Poll, to my mind your hair's a sight prettier'n most folks's hull faces ; 'n', if your eyes be ruther big, they're as bright as two starn-lanterns any day, 'n' as soft as a gull's be. I don't know what for you want to quarrel with your looks, so long's I don't.''

A more fastidious man would not have found fault with the look she gave Sam now, — so tender, so innocently glad, so trustful ; and, if Sam gave no audible reply, it was none the less fervently answered, and for the next hour Poll was happy. No more visions of over-sea now, no dream of tropic shores and unwithering blossoms : her tropic had come, and her fadeless flowers burst into glowing life. Her beautiful head safe on Sam's shoulder, and her face buried in his strong breast, except when he would lift it up to be kissed, she had no thought for the past or future : the only " now " of life held her fast ; and in its sweet embrace she lay basking till common life, in the shape of Adeline, came full upon the deaf lovers, and remarked sharply, —

" Well, if you hadn't ought to be ashamed, Sam. Bent, out here in the grass a-huggin' and kissin' our Poll ! ''

Sam rose up with a laugh, carrying Poll with him, circled still in his arm.

" She's my Poll now, Addy. I don't know who's a better right ! ''

" Good Jehoshaphat ! '' said old Abe, who had also come up behind Adeline.

At this singular expletive Addy herself laughed, though not a little piqued and provoked at Sam's defection from her, as she fancied it. " And all her red wig down her back ! '' exclaimed she, laying a rough grasp on the offending tresses.

"Hands off, Addy," threatened Sam smilingly. "That are's mine too, 'n' the biggest lady in the land might be proud on't, ef 'tis red."

Adeline sniffed.

"Well," said old Abe, regarding the pair with his hands in his trowsers-pockets, and his hat askew, as if they were some great natural curiosity, "this does beat all. Our Poll and Sam Bent! Well, I can't lay no course here-away. I ha'n't got my bearin's. — A'n't a-goin' to trade her off down to Chiny, be ye, Sam?" concluded he, chuckling at his own facetiousness.

"Money wouldn't buy her," said Sam, with a smile that consoled Poll for the family depreciation; and, still with his arm round her, the whole party drew to the hut to surprise Ruth.

She took it more quietly and kindly.

"Well, I won't say I haven't thought on't before," said she. "Poll's more of a girl latterly'n what she was. And looks a'n't of no account: they a'n't lastin'." Ruth sighed, wondering if Jonas would know the sad, dark face that looked at her from her cracked glass daily now, and went on, "I don't deny it's a misfortin' to have red hair; but then we didn't make it, 'n' can't mend it: so it's no use to be troubled."

"Her hair is splendid," growled Sam angrily, a little overdoing his praise to atone for the insult; and lifting the coil Poll was twisting, to his lips, he bestowed on it a hearty smack.

"Hain't you burnt you?" screeched Adeline; and Sam could scarce keep a straight face till he saw a tear cloud Poll's eyes.

"You want your ears boxed," said he to Adeline, between vexation and laughter.

"I guess it'll take more'n you to box 'em," was the retort, whereupon a slight scuffle ensued; but Ruth remarked to herself that Sam made no attempt to snatch the expected kiss from Adeline, and smiled as she noticed it; while Poll knotted up her hair, and wondered at herself for Sam's sake, and coiled the "red wig" tenderly, because he had praised and kissed it. Forgive her, sensible reader: I own she was a little fool.

Sam found his way to the sloop, and brought up the little package of gifts for the girls, — Adeline's red ribbon, and Ruth's silver thimble, entirely overtopped by the delicate collar and book of pictures for Poll. But this was natural enough; though Adeline took occasion afterward to remark that he must have felt pretty sure Poll would have him when he bought them, a remark utterly neutralized by Poll's *naïve* and humble "Why, of course he did."

The next morning Sam said good-by. He was going to Connecticut to see his grandmother, his only near relative living, and from there to join the brig. Poll cried bitterly but comfortably, if one may use so unsentimental a word; for she had a heart full of comfort, and just then it refused to face the possibility of loss, and bore up bravely against the need of separation.

Summer was come too, and its long days of wandering. The sea laughed again on the shore, and flung its flower-spray over the relentless rocks till they looked only strong, no longer cruel: the long grass waved in soft, southern winds; and the purple mists of the horizon were dotted with snowy sails, emerging and fleeing in incessant, silent change: and every day, that first

bright week of June, Poll strained her eager eyes to
see " The Flying Cioud ; " and every ship seemed to
her the ship she watched for, till at last came news that
she had been spoken far out at sea by a returning
vessel, and after that Poll watched no more. But not
now could she spend her whole time in the fresh fields
or on the shore : grave duties impended over her, and
Ruth would not let them be forgotten. Ruth herself
had been under a mother's care when Jonas left her,
and been trained to those duties in the sweet anticipation of their exercise in a home of her own ; and it was
with bitter memories that she set herself to teach Poll
how to keep house. Cooking and washing, ironing,
mending, cutting out new garments, and refitting old
ones, might have been a dull routine to Poll before ;
but now it was vividly pleasant. Her imagination, that
hitherto, aimless and void, had wandered far and wide
on fair but profitless journeys, now drew down its
wings for a narrower and more blessed sphere. Love
has its own miracles, whether human or divine ; and
they who have known what it is to do every daily duty,
whether trivial or important, as for one dearest object,
toward whom life tends in every leaf and bough, as
toward the light, can best understand what the apostle
meant in charging his Christian flock to do all things
as " unto the Lord." But Poll's idol was of the earth
as yet. She knew and aspired no higher ; though Sam
Bent's own earnest, rugged, every-day religion had
recommended itself to her admiration and reverence
long ago. So she did all these things as if Sam were
to be directly aided and comforted by them, and soon
surpassed her teacher in practice as far as she ex-
ceeded her in mental ability ; one's mind having, after

all, in spite of customary sneers to the contrary, an effect on something besides literary capacity. Before autumn Uncle Abe discovered that nobody on the shore made chowder like Poll's, or stewed such flavorous dishes from despised haddock and chip-dry halibut. Also a tiny bit of mould that the accretion of years of refuse had formed behind the house, much as it might have on a coral-reef, Poll had shorn of its rank weeds, dug, by means of an old fire-shovel, and planted with onions, beets, and potatoes; while in one corner bloomed and thrived a daily rosebush, Sam's parting token, brought from New York by Ben Gould the day after "The Flying Cloud" sailed. Those pink buds told Poll a great many tender stories as she watched their clean, bright petals unfold against the myrtle-green leaves; and, if care were a specific for rose-bushes, this one ought to have flourished even more than it did; and before autumn there grew about it, like a court about a queen, clusters of every blossom that was native to the soil, and Poll's "posy-bed" was brighter and fairer than many a parterre of exotics.

It is beyond the limits of fact to say, as we would be glad to, that this improvement of Poll's renewed her complexion, and re-dyed her hair: unfortunately, they remained as rough and red as ever; but she had grown so tidy and so self-respectful, her calico dress was always so clean and well-fitted, her rippling hair so smooth and bright, and carefully knotted, that a new attraction embellished her, and approved itself to the housewifely soul of Martha, who lived up in the country, not two miles from Mary, and had come down this hot September "to get recruited up," as she phrased it, after the labors of summer. She was so pleased with Poll, — whom she had held in the same estimation that the rest bestowed on her formerly, — that she asked her to go home with her for a visit; and Poll went.

But though the rich meadows and wet woods of Ewefield were beautiful enough, in their green breadth and October splendor, to bewitch Poll's unaccustomed eyes, she felt a strange languor assail her, and a sleepy sweetness in the air made it seem hard to breathe. She drooped and paled, and dragged her heavy feet from field to field in search of gay maple-leaves and new flowers, till she was fit only to sink on the doorstep when she got back, and could scarce hold up her head, it ached and throbbed so hard. Long before the end of her month's stay, she grew homesick for the queer old cabin and the poignant sea-breeze. Martha's gray farmhouse, neat and cool and spare as it was, looked chill and dreary in every square room and clean corner; the dairy smells of curd and cheese sickened her morbidly acute sense; the quiet of the inland pastures and hills stifled her like a shroud. She could not eat, or sleep, or work, and she did not know why, except that she was home-sick; and she heartily welcomed the day fixed for her to go home, and wondered at herself when the sea-wind failed to revive her, and her own little cot to rest her aching limbs. But a day or two of increasing weakness and sleeplessness revealed the secret of Poll's restless manner and flushed cheek. In the steaming meadows of Ewefield, its thick river-fogs, and deep black swamps, full of rotting vegetation, lurked the breath of malaria; and a violent fever had fas-tened upon Poll's unacclimated frame, and begun to

waste and burn and destroy like an invading army.
All Ruth's simples were tried in vain; and when the
redoubtable Dr. Higgs, the "nateral bone-setter,"
who was also the sole physician of Punkintown, was
summoned, he pronounced Poll to be "in a most
vicarious condition, — repugnant typhus, with a deter-
minacy to digestion of the brain." Perhaps his skill
was better than his language; for he had, at least,
sense enough to forbid either bleeding or blistering,
as old Abe alternately begged for one or the other,
simply because the only sickness he ever had was
allayed by both. But at last Poll became so delirious, and the danger to her brain so great, that every
bit of her splendid hair was shorn, and at last shaved
off, and the redundant tresses laid away in a drawer,
perhaps, as Ruth thought, to be all Sam should find
when he came back from China.

Days and weeks passed by. November became
December, and yet Poll wrestled with the death that
impended over her; for, though the fever was at
length mastered and abated, she was left in a state of
infantile weakness, and it required all Ruth's most
faithful care to keep her in life. Her mind, too,
seemed feeble as her body. She remembered nothing,
cared for nothing, but took her food and tonics, and
dozed away the days. But by the middle of January
she began to brighten, to say a few weak words,
though evidently Ruth and her father were her only
memoies. In her delirium she had raved about Sam
and her red hair, regretted it, wept over it, and
caressed it, by turns, till even Adeline felt painful
twinges of repentance for the pain she had given the
poor child in times past. But now she never men-

tioned Sam's name, nor alluded to her hair; and
though there was a letter carefully laid away in Ruth's
drawer, waiting to be asked for, it seemed as if Poll
had forgotten — but she only slept.

One warm day in February she sat up by her window, and her eye fell on the bare branches of the
little rose-tree. Something stirred in her brain, a
moment's painful struggle to catch the fleeting thought,
— one moment of that exquisitely painful wandering
and groping darkness that assails the weak will and the
faded memory, and Poll remembered. Ruth saw the
keen agony of look that pierced her vague eyes, and
died out almost as quickly, to renew its spark, the
flushing and paling cheek, the tremulous lips, till
those eyes brightened into certainty, and her cheek
burned with a blush and a smile at once, and she
spoke.

"Ruth," said she, "have you heard any thing from
Sam?"

"Yes," said Ruth quietly, stepping to her drawer
for the letter, which she handed to Poll. Perhaps even
you, refined and well-educated reader, may forgive its
spelling and grammar if I venture to transcribe it over
her shoulder.

AT SEA. August 17th

DEER POLL

This is to say I am alive And well and Hoap you enjoy the
saim blesing. we wayed Anker the first of June acording to
orders, and maid a Steddy run acrost the atlantick till we
stood off Sow-east for the cape. I now rite in hops of a Vesel
pasing bye I rite for to tell you agane How much I keep a
strate Course in my mind for the Port where you be Poll. my
deer I think of you evry Day and likewise when I keep Watch.
I seem somehow to sight the old Cabbin, and the beach-gras
a-shinin' all round you, where you lay when I ketched you

up. deer I am no grate fist at ritin, but I want for to hev you
know that I aint One of that sort o' Craft that shifts their
flaggs in knew Places. I be as trew to my bearin's as our
figger-head and I allays rekollects your Bewtiful hare when I
see the Risin Sun acrost the sea. So no more at Pressent from
your loving frend to Command   SAM BENT

Tears of pleasure filled Poll's eyes as she read ; but,
when she came to the last line, a sudden paleness
swept across her face. She put up her hand gropingly
to her head : it was smooth and soft as a mouse-skin.
"Ruth," said she eagerly, "where is it?"

Ruth had watched her, and answered, as if to a more
definite question, "We had to cut it off when you were
so sick, Poll : you wouldn't have got well without."

Poll lay back in her chair, faint and sick. She said
nothing at first ; but the slow, hot tears rolled down
her cheeks, and her wan face gathered a look of pain
that was sad to see. The thought that smote her so
bitterly was all of Sam : what would he say? Her
hair, that was "the prettiest thing about her," that he
thought of so far away, that he would want to see.
How she must look ! And with that came a strange
desire to see herself. She sat up, and asked Ruth to
get her some tea. A little stratagem only ; for, when
she left the room, Poll got up and tottered to the glass
that hung by the window. ' Poor Poll ! the spectacle
was not pleasant, — a thin white face, eyes bigger than
ever, and the small head in that ugly transition from
no hair, when any color of a coming crop seems only
slaty gray fom its extreme shortness. Poll turned
away : she was altogether humiliated. Surely she might
give up Sam now and forever, for the only attraction
she had possessed was gone, and she was actually re

pulsive besides. She was too weak to be passionately
disappointed ; but she laid herself on the bed like a
grieved and tired child, and cried herself to sleep.

A vainer or a more selfish woman might have fretted
and brooded over her trouble till the fever had returned with fatal consequences ; but Poll was too
absorbed in Sam and his future to give so much
thought to her own. She wept bitterly for days over
her loss — and his, but from the first accepted it as a
fact that Sam could not love her when he came back,
and tried earnestly to accustom herself to the belief.
And she succeeded very well till it occurred to her one
day that he would marry somebody else, perhaps Adeline, and then Poll found she had not sounded her
trouble before : she could no more face that thought
than she could the looking-glass, which she had never
looked into from that day when she first saw herself.
But the weeks did not stop to look at her, or to pity
Sam Bent.

Spring came stealing on with steady advance, and
Poll's naturally tenacious constitution revived in the
soft airs and breezes. Her best consolation was her
old out-of-door haunts ; and, though she was now habitually sad and silent, she did not mope or cry, though
Ruth wondered why she withdrew herself more and
more from her housekeeping duties, and even remon-
strated with her, to no effect except saddening her
more deeply, or bringing about a brief spasm of effort.

But Poll might have looked into the glass by the
middle of May with good effect. The long fever had
either renovated some torpid function of her skin, or
the long confinement to the house softened and soothed
its habitual inflammation ; for now it was smooth and

fair as a child's, and every breeze brought to it a light
bloom like a wild-rose petal. Her lips were reddened
with healthy crimson, and her broad white brow had
lost its burned and tanned look, for she had now to
keep on her sun-bonnet, missing the heavy covering
of her hair. Yet, to tell the truth, its loss was an
embellishment; for her head was covered with thick
soft rings and curls of the richest chestnut, glossy as
the new skin of that nut, and fine as floss. Nothing
prettier could have crowned her forehead, and shaded
so beautifully with her eyes of the same tint, — a shade
darker, but softened and deepened by suffering and
emotion. There was nobody to tell Poll all this.
Ruth was glad her red hair had gone; but she did
not say so for fear of hurting her feelings, and old Abe
did not understand any beauty but the type of sturdy
figures, red cheeks, and black eyes, — a type rather
forced on his admiration by repetition, till he preferred it from habit. Adeline had been gone since
March to see Nancy at Madison, and nobody ever
came to the hut whom Poll was willing to see now: so
she kept by herself, and waited with sad patience for
Sam's coming, that she might tell him what she
expected, and have it over with.

But one rarely does just what they mean to do beforehand; and "The Flying Cloud" was safe in New
York, without Poll's hearing of her arrival, for two
days; and Poll herself, sitting in her low chair, reading, was "taken all aback," as her father said, one
bright June morning, by the heavy "thud" of a box
set down on the sill of the door, and the quick jump of
a man over it.

"Why, Poll!" said Sam, after the first unresisted

kissing was over, holding her off to look at her, "I shouldn't ha' known you!"

"No, I guess not," said Poll, with quivering lips. "My hair is all gone, and — and Sam, I look so — I know" —

"Look so!" interrupted Sam: "I guess you do: Why, you've ben and got made over!"

"O Sam, don't!" said she. Somehow it was harder to bear than she had expected; and the tears would come as she went on, "I know I am as humly as a crab; but I sha'n't feel hard about you, Sam. I know you can't love me. I — I" — Here came a big sob.

"Jethunderation!" roared Sam, getting up his biggest expletive, — "you, humly? You're handsomer'n a picture this minnit. Why, Poll!"

"Sam!" said she indignantly, "don't! Do you think I don't know?"

"Yes, I do," said Sam. "Hold hard a bit!" With which little exhortation he put her down, and went to his chest. Out of its capacious interior he drew a great bundle done up in folds of canvas, wads of cotton, and wrappings of Chinese paper, which at last peeled off under his clumsy fingers, and displayed the prettiest little dressing-case of black lacker, studded with gold flowers and butterflies, its four drawers surmounted by an oval mirror in a frame of the same material. Sam triumphantly hoisted the whole of the affair on the top of the bureau, and, catching up Poll in his arms, held her up, and asked her to look. Oh, what a pretty vision was there! — a fair sweet face, with a deep glow on either cheek, its tender, panting mouth just parted over little snow-white teeth, its great brown eyes moist and bright with the tears they had but just shed, and a head wreathed with silky ringlets whose coils caught the light with a bronze lustre as lovely as rare. The blue-check dress and white ruffle identified her.

" Why ! " said Poll with a little start.

" You mean to say *that* a'n't hansum? " triumphantly asked Sam.

" I didn't know I looked like that " was the *naïve* answer.

" Don't you never look in the glass? " returned he.

"I haven't since I was sick, but once," said Poll, dropping her head.

"Here's a reef!" said Sam, light beginning to dawn on his mind. "Well, I am some took aback myself. I don't think a poor seafarin' man like me had oughter ask sech a three-decker to marry him. Poll, I b'lieve I must haul down my flag: I can't expect you to keer for me now."

Poll turned round, and looked at him : there was no mistaking the sparkle of that deep gray eye. Poll dropped her head on his shoulder. She could hear the light laughter he had repressed now.

" O Sam," said she, nestling still closer to his cheek, " I'm so glad ! "

The black lacker dressing-case, somewhat worn and tarnished, stands now in the " spare chamber " of a tiny gray house at the foot of a Squamkeag Lighthouse ; for Ben Gould was drowned, and Sam got his situation. In the upper drawer of the pretty luxury a mass of red hair, long and wavy, is coiled away, and tied up with an Indian ribbon that smells of sandalwood; but Poll Jennings's hair has grown again down to the hem of her dress, and its beautiful coil is as bright as ever, though no longer red. Sam offers to get a divorce now and then, on account of his "humliness;" but at the last advices his offer was not yet accepted—"on account of the children," Poll demurely says.

FREEDOM WHEELER'S CONTROVERSY WITH PROVIDENCE.

A STORY OF OLD NEW ENGLAND.

I.

AUNT HULDY and Aunt Hannah sat in the kitchen, — Aunt Huldah bolt upright in a straight-backed wooden chair, big silver-bowed spectacles astride her high nose, sewing carpet-rags with such energy that her eyes snapped, and her brown, wrinkled fingers flew back and forth like the spokes of a rapid wheel; Aunt Hannah in a low, creaky old rocker, knitting diligently but placidly, and rocking gently. You could almost hear her purr, and you wanted to stroke her; but Aunt Huldah! — an electric machine could not be less desirable to handle than she, or a chestnut-burr pricklier.

The back-log simmered and sputtered; the hickory-sticks in front shot up bright, soft flames; and through the two low, green-paned windows the pallid sun of February sent in a pleasant shining on to the clean kitchen-floor. Cooking-stoves were not made then, nor Merrimac calicoes. The two old women had stuff petticoats and homespun short-gowns, clean mob-caps over their decent gray hair, and big blue-check aprons: hair-dye, wigs, flowered chintz, and other fineries had not reached the lonely farms of Dorset in those days

" Spinsters " was not a mere name. The big wool
wheel stood in one corner of the kitchen, and a little
flax-wheel by the window. In summer both would be
moved to the great garret, where it was cool and out of
the way.

" Curus, ain't it? " said Aunt Huldah. "Freedom
never come home before, later'n nine-o'clock bell, and
he was mortal mighty then; kep' his tongue between
his teeth same way he did to breakfast this mornin'.
There's suthin' a-goin' on, Hanner, you may depend
on't."

" Mabbe he needs some wormwood-tea," said Aunt
Hannah, who, like Miss Hannah More, thought the only
two evils in the world were sin and bile, and charitably
preferred to lay things first to the physical disorder.

" I du b'lieve, Hanner, you think 'riginal sin is
nothin' but a bad stomick."

" Ef 'tain't 'riginal sin, it's actual transgression
pretty often, Huldy," returned the placid old lady with
a gentle cackle. The Assembly's Catechism had been
ground into them both, as any old-fashioned New-Eng-
lander will observe, and they quoted its forms of speech,
as Boston people do Emerson's Essays, by " an auto-
matic action of the unconscious nervous centres."

The door opened, and Freedom walked in, scraping
his boots upon the husk-mat, as a man will who has
lived all his days with two old maids, but nevertheless
spreading abroad in that clean kitchen an odor of the
barn that spoke of " chores," yet did not disturb the
accustomed nostrils of his aunts. He was a middle-
sized, rather " stocky " man, with a round head well
covered with tight-curling short hair, that revenged
itself for being cut too short to curl by standing on end

toward every point of the compass. You could not call him a common-looking man : something in his keen blue eye, abrupt nose, steady mouth, and square chin, always made a stranger look at him twice. Rugged sense, but more rugged obstinacy, shrewdness, keen perception, tempered somewhat by a certain kindliness that he himself felt to be his weak spot, — all these were to be read in Freedom Wheeler's well-bronzed face, sturdy figure, positive speech, and blunt manner.

He strode up to the fireplace, sat down in an arm-chair rudely shaped out of wood by his own hands, and plunged, after his fashion, at once into the middle of things.

"Aunt Huldy and Aunt Hanner, I'm a-goin' to git married." The domestic bombshell burst in silence. Aunt Hannah dropped a stitch, and couldn't see to pick it up for at least a minute. Aunt Huldah's scissors snipped at the rags with a vicious snap, as if they were responsible agents, and she would end their proceedings then and there: presently she said, "Well, I *am* beat!" To which rather doubtful utterance Freedom made no reply, and the scissors snipped harder yet.

Aunt Hannah recovered herself first. "Well, I'm real glad on't," purred she. It was her part to do the few amenities of the family.

"I dono whether I be or not, till I hear who 'tis," dryly answered Aunt Huldah, who was obviously near akin to Freedom.

"It's Lowly Mallory," said the short-spoken nephew, who by this time was whittling busily at a peg for his ox-yoke.

"Du tell!" said Aunt Hannah in her lingering, de-liberate tones, the words running into each other as she spoke. "She's jest's clever's the day is long. You've done a good thing, Freedom, 's sure's you live."

"He might ha' done wuss : that's a fact." And with this approval Freedom seemed satisfied ; for he brushed his chips into the fire, ran his fingers through his already upright hair, eyed his peg with the keen aspect of a critic in pegs, and went off to the barn. He knew instinctively that his aunts must have a chance to talk the matter over.

"This is the beateree!" exclaimed Aunt Huldah as the door shut after him. "Lowly Mallory, of all creturs! Freedom's as masterful as though he was the Lord above, by natur ; and ef he gets a leetle softly cretur like that, without no more grit'n a November chicken, he'll ride right over every thing, and she won't darst to peep nor mutter a mite. Good land!"

"Well, well," murmured Aunt Hannah, "she is a kind o' feeble piece, but she's real clever; an' I dono but what it's as good as he could do. Ef she was like to him, hard-headed, 'n sot in her way, I tell ye, Huldy, the fur'd fly mightily; and it's putty bad to have fight to home when there's a fam'ly to fetch up."

"Well, you be forecastin', I must say, Hanner ; but mabbe you're abaout right. Besides, I've observed that folks will marry to suit themselves, not other people. An' mabbe it's the best way, seein' it's their own loss or likin' more'n anybody else's."

"But, Huldy, 'pears as if you'd forgot one thing : I expect we'd better be a-movin' out into the old house, ef there's goin' to be more folks here."

"Well, I declare! I never thought on't. 'Tis best, I guess. I wonder ef Freedom's got the idee."

"I dono. But that hadn't oughter make no difference. There never was a house big enough for two
families; an', ef we go before we're obleeged to, it's a
sight better'n stayin' till we be."

"That's so, Hanner: you allers was a master-hand
for takin' things right end foremost. I'll sort out our
linen right off, 'nd set by our furnitoor into the back-
chamber. I guess the old house'll want a leetle
paintin' an' scrapin'. It's dreadful lucky Amasy
Flint's folks moved to Noppit last week: seems as
though there was a Providence about it."

"I shouldn't wonder ef Freedom had give 'em a
sort o' hint to go, Huldy."

"Well, you do beat all! I presume likely he did."

And Aunt Huldah picked up the rags at her feet,
piled them into a splint basket, hung the shears on a
steel chain by her side, and lifting her tall, gaunt figure
from the chair, betook herself up stairs. But Aunt
Hannah kept on knitting. She was the thinker, and
Huldah the doer, of the family. Now her thoughts ran
before her to the coming change, and she sighed; for
she knew her nephew thoroughly, and she pitied the
gentle, sweet nature that was to come in contact with
his.

Dear Aunt Hannah! She had never had any romance in her own life: she did not know any thing
about love, except as the placid and quite clear-eyed
affection she felt for Freedom, who was her only near
relation, and she saw little Lowly Mallory's future on
its hardest side. But she could not help it; and her
nature was one that never frets against a difficulty, any
more than the green turf beats against the rock to
whose edge it clings.

So the slow, sad New-England spring, with storm
and tempest, drifting snows and beating rains, worked
its reluctant way into May.   And when the lilacs
were full of purple and white plumes, delicate as cut
coral sprays, and luscious with satiating odor, and the
heavy-headed daffodils thrust golden locks upward from
the sward, Aunt Huldah and Aunt Hannah moved
their wool-wheel and their flax-wheel, the four stiff-
backed chairs, the settle and big red chest, the high
four-post bedstead, and the two rush-bottomed rockers
that had been Grandsir Wheeler's, back into the small
red house, for which these furnishings had been pur-
chased sixty years before, laid the rag-carpet, that
Aunt Huldah had sewed and dyed and woven, on the
" settin'-room floor, and, with a barrel of potatoes and
a keg of salt pork, went to housekeeping.

There was some home-made linen belonging to them,
and a few cups and dishes, also a feather-bed, and a
pair of blankets.   Freedom kept them supplied with
what necessaries they wanted, and, though he was
called "dreadful near" in the town, he was not an
unjust man.   His two aunts had taken him in charge,
an orphan at six, and been faithful and kind to him
all his days, and he could do no less than care for
them now.   Beside, they owned half the farm, and
though one was fifty-six, and the other fifty-eight, there
was much hard work left in them yet.   Aunt Huldah
was a skilful tailoress, in demand for miles about ; and
Aunt Hannah was the best sick-nurse in the county.
They would not suffer : and, truth to tell, they rather
enjoyed the independence of their own house ; for Freedom and Aunt Huldah were chips of the same block,
and only Aunt Hannah's constant, quiet restraint and

peace-making kept the family tolerably harmonious.
And in the farmhouse a new reign began, — the reign
of Queen Log.

Lowly Mallory was a fragile, slender, delicate girl,
with sweet gray eyes and plenty of brown hair ; pale
as a spring anemone, with just such faint pinkness in
her lips and on her high cheek-bones as tints that pen-
sile, egg-shaped bud, when its

> "Small flower layeth
> Its fairy gem beneath some giant tree"

on the first warm days of May. She had already the
line of care that marks New-England women across the
forehead, like a mark of Cain, — the signal of a life in
which work has murdered health and joy and freedom ;
for Lowly was the oldest of ten children, and her
mother was bed-ridden. Lovina was eighteen now,
and could take her place ; and Lowly loved Freedom
with the reticent, undemonstrative affection of her race
and land : moreover, she was glad of change, of rest.
Rest ! — much of that awaited her ! Freedom's first
step after the decorous wedding and home-coming was
to buy ten cows — he had two already — and two dozen
new milk-pans.

"I calkerlate we can sell a good lot of butter 'n'
cheese down to Dartford, Lowly," he said, on intro-
ducing her to the new dairy he had fitted up at one end
of the woodshed ; and, if the gentle creature's heart
sank within her at the prospect, she did not say so, and
Freedom never asked how she liked it. He was "masterful" indeed ; and having picked out Lowly from all
the other Dorset girls, because she was a still and hard-
working maiden, and would neither rebel against nor

criticise his edicts, he took it for granted things would
go on as he wished.

Poor little Lowly! Her simple, tender heart went
out to her husband like a vine feeling after a trellis;
and, even when she found it was only a bowlder that
chilled and repelled her slight ardors and timid caresses, she did still what the vine does, — flung herself
across and along the granite faces of the rock, and
turned her trembling blossoms sunward, where life and
light were free and sure.

Aunt Huldah and Aunt Hannah soon grew to be her
ministering angels; and if they differed from the gold-
haired, pink-enamelled, straight-nosed creations of Fra
Angelico, and would have figured ill, — in their short-
gowns and mob-caps, — bowing before an ideal Madonna, Lowly wanted no better tendance and providing
than they gave her, when in due season there appeared
in the farmhouse a red and roaring baby, evidently pat-
terned after his father, morally as well as physically;
the white down on his raw pink head twisting into tight
kinks, and his stubby fists set in as firm a grasp as
ever Freedom's big brown paws were.   Lowly was a
happy little woman: she had loved children always, and
here was one all her own.   Two weeks were dreamed
away in rest and rapture; then Freedom began to bustle and fret, and growl about the neglected dairy, and
the rusty pork, and the hens that wanted care.

"Don't ye s'pose she'll git 'raound next week, Aunt
Huldy?   Things is gittin' dredful behind-hand!"
Freedom had left the bedroom-door open on purpose.
Aunt Huldah got up, and shut it with a slam, while
he went on: "Them hens had oughter be set, 'n' I
never git time to be a half a day prowlin' araound after

'em: they've stole their nests, I expect, the hull tribe;
'nd Hepsy don't make butter to compare along-side o'
Lowly's; then there's that 'ere pork a-gittin' rusty, 'n'
Aunt Hanner, she's over to Mallory's, nussin' Loviny,
so's't I can't call on you; 'n' it doos seem's though
two weeks was a plenty for well folks to lie in bed."

Here Aunt Huldah exploded: "Freedom Wheeler,
you hain't got a mite o' compassion into ye! Lowly
ain't over 'n' above powerful, anyway: she'll break
clear down ef she ain't real keerful; mabbe I ain't"—

The shutting of the back-door stopped her tirade.
While she hunted in a table-drawer for her thimble,
Freedom had coolly walked off: he did not choose to
argue the subject. But next day Lowly got up, and
was dressed. There were two lines across the sad, low
forehead now, but she went about her work in silence.
There is a type of feminine character that can endure
to the edge of death, and endure silently, and that
character was eminently hers.

"Good little feller, so he was, as ever was; there,
there, there! should be cuddled up good 'n' warm, so
he should," Aunt Hannah purred to the small boy a
month after, seeing him for the first time, as she had
been taking care of Lovina Mallory through a low
fever, when he was born.

"What be ye a-goin' to call him, Freedom?"

"I calkerlate he'll be baptized Shearjashub. There's
allus ben a Shearjashub 'nd a Freedom amongst our
folks. I've heered Grandsir Wheeler tell on't more'n
forty times, how the' was them two names away back
as fur as there's gravestones to tell on't down to Litch-
field meetin'-house, 'nd back o' that in the old graveyard to Har'ford. I expect this here feller'll be called

Shearjashub, 'nd the next one Freedom: that's the way they've allus run."

"For the land's sakes!" sputtered Aunt Huldah. "I was in hopes you hadn't got that notion inter your head. Why can't ye call the child some kind o' pootty Scripter name, like David, or Samwell, or Eber, 'nd not set him a-goin' with a kite's tail like that tied on to him?"

"I guess what's ben good 'nough for our folks time out o' mind'll be good 'nough for him," stiffly answered Freedom. And Aunt Huldah, with inward rage, accepted the situation, and went out to the barn to help Lowly set some refractory hens, where she found the poor little woman, with suspiciously red eyes, counting eggs on a corner of the hay-mow.

"Hanner's come, Lowly," said she, "so she's got baby, 'nd I come out to give ye a lift about them hens. I've ben a-dealin' with Freedom about that there child's name; but you might jest as well talk to White Rock: I will say for't he's the sottest man I ever see. I b'lieve he'd set to to fight his own way out with the Lord above, if he hed to."

Lowly gave a little plaintive smile, but, after the manner of her sex, took her husband's part. "Well, you see, Aunt Huldy, it's kind o' nateral he should want to foller his folks's ways. I don't say but what I did want to call baby Eddard, for my little brother that died. I set great store by Eddy," — here Lowly's checked apron wiped a certain mist from her patient eyes, — "and 'twould ha' been my mind to call him for Eddy; but Freedom don't feel to, and you know Scripter says wives must be subject to husbands."

"Hm!" sniffed Aunt Huldah, who was lost to the

strong-minded party of her sex by being born before
its creation, — "Scripter has a good deal to answer
for!" with which enigmatical and shocking remark,
she turned, and pounced upon the nearest hen. Poor
old hen! She evidently represented a suffering and
abject sex to Aunt Huldah, and exasperated her accordingly. Do I not know? Have not I, weakly and
meekly protesting against their ways and works, also
been hustled and bustled by the Rights Women? —
even as this squawking, crawking, yellow biddy was
fluffed and cuffed and shaken up by Aunt Huldah, and
plunged at last, in spite of nips and pecks and screaks,
into the depths of a barrel, the head wedged on above
her, and the unwilling matron condemmed to solitary
confinement, with hard labor, on thirteen eggs!

So Freedom had his way, of course; and Lowly
went on, with the addition of a big naughty baby to
take care of, waking before light to get her "chores"
out of the way, prepare breakfast, skim cream, strain
new milk and set it, scald pans, churn, work and put
down butter, feed pigs and hens, bake, wash, iron,
scrub, mend, make, nurse baby, fetch wood from the
shed, and water from the well, — a delicate, bending,
youthful figure, with hands already knotted, and shoulders bowed by hard work; her sole variety of a week-
day being when one kind of pie gave place to another,
or when the long winter evenings, with dim light of
tallow candles, made her spinning shorter, and her
sewing longer.

For Sundays were scarce a rest: breakfast was as
early, milk as abundant, on that day as on any other
and then there was a five-mile ride to meeting, for
which ample lunch must be prepared, since they

staid at noon; there was baby to dress, and her own
Sunday clothes to put on, in which stiff and unaccustomed finery she sat four mortal hours, with but the
brief interval of nooning, on a hard and comfortless
seat, and then home again to get the real dinner of
the day, to feed her pigs and hens, to get the clamorous baby quiet: this was hardly rest. And summer
— that brings to overstrained nerves and exhausted
muscles the healing of sun, sweet winds, fresh air,
and the literal "balm of a thousand flowers" — only
heralded to her the advent of six strong hungry men
at haying, shearing, and reaping time, with extra
meals, increased washing, and, of course, double
fatigue. Yet this is the life that was once the doom
of all New-England farmers' wives; the life that sent
them to early graves, to mad-houses, to suicide; the
life that is so beautiful in the poet's numbers, so terrible in its stony, bloomless, oppressive reality. It
would have been hard to tell if Lowly was glad or
sorry, when, on a soft day in June, Aunt Hannah,
this time at home, was hurriedly called from the red
house to officiate as doctor and nurse both at the arrival of another baby. This time, Freedom growled and
scowled by himself in the kitchen, instead of conde-
scending to look at and approve the child; for it was
a girl.

Aunt Hannah chuckled in her sleeve. Freedom had
intimated quite frankly that this child was to be
called after himself, nothing doubting but that another
boy was at hand; and great was his silent rage at the
disappointment.

"Imperdent, ain't it?" queried Aunt Huldah, who
sat by the kitchen-fire stirring a mess of Indian-meal

porridge. "To think it darst to be a girl when ye was
so sot on its turnin' out a boy! Seems as though Providence got the upper hand on ye, Freedom, arter all!"

But Freedom never gave retort to Aunt Huldah. He
had been brought up in certain superstitions, quite
obsolete now, about respecting his elders; and, though
the spirit was wanting sometimes, the letter of the law
had observance. He could rage at Aunt Huldah privately, but before her he held his tongue. It was his
wife who suffered as the sinner should for disturbing
his plans in this manner. He snubbed her, he despised
the baby, and forthwith bought two more cows, with
the grim remark, "Ef I've got to fetch up a pack o'
girls, I guess I'd better scratch around 'n' make a
leetle more money."

But, if the new baby was an eyesore to Freedom,
she was a delight to Lowly. All the more because
her father ignored and seemed to dislike her, the afflu-
ent mother-heart flowed out upon her. She was a coo-
ing, clinging, lovely little creature; and when, worn
out with her day's work, Lowly had at last coaxed her
cross, teething boy to sleep, and she sat down in the
old creaky rocker to nurse and tend her baby, the
purest joy that earth knows stole over her like
the tranquil breath of heaven. The touch of tiny fingers on her breast; the warm shining head against her
heart; the vague baby-smile and wandering eyes that
neither the wistfulness of doubt, the darkness of grief,
nor the fire of passion, clouded as yet; the inarticulate
murmurs of satisfaction; the pressure of the little helpless form upon her lap; the silent, ardent tenderness
that awoke and burned in her own heart for this precious creature, — all made for the weary woman a daily

oasis of peace and beauty that perhaps saved her
brain from that common insanity we call nervousness,
and her body from utter exhaustion; for happiness is
a medicine of God's own sending: no quack has ever
pretended to dispense its potent and beneficent cordial;
and the true, honest physician, he whose very profession is the nearest approach to that of the Saviour and
Healer of men, knows well that one drop of the only
elixir he cannot bring outweighs all he can. Shearjashub grew up to the height of three years, and the baby
toddled about, and chattered like a merry chipping-
bird, when, one Fast Day morning, Lowly staid at
home from meeting with a sinking heart, and Aunt
Hannah was sent for again. Freedom went off to
hear the usual sermon, on a pretence of taking Shearjashub out of the way; he being irrepressible except by
his father, whom alone he feared. Mother and aunts
the youngster manfully defied and scorned; but the
very sound of his father's steps reduced him to silence.
Shingles were not out of fashion then as a means of
discipline; and the hot tingle of the application dwelt
vividly in the boy's mind ever since he had been
"tuned mightily," as his father phrased it, for dis-
obedience and obstinacy; Aunt Huldah's comment at
the first punishment being, "Hemlock all three on
'em, — man an' boy an' shingle: it's tough to tell
which'll beat."

Little Love staid at home with old Hepsy, and prattled all day long in the kitchen. Lowly could not
spare the sweet voice from her hearing, and she had
need of all its comfort: for, when Freedom came home
from Dorset Centre, a great girl-baby lay by Lowly in
the bed; and if its welcome from the mother had been

bitter tears, whose traces still shone on her wan face,
from the father came far bitterer words, — curses in all
but the wording ; for Freedom was a " professor," and
profanity was a sin.   Mint and anise and cumin he
tithed scrupulously ; but mercy and judgment fled from
him, and hid their shamefaced heads.   Aunt Huldah
and Aunt Hannah made their tansy-pudding that day,
after the custom of their forefathers, and ate it with
unflinching countenances ; but Lowly fasted in her
secret soul ; and since her husband grimly remarked,
" 'Tain't nothin' to me what ye call her : gals ain't
worth namin' anyhow ! " the new baby was baptized
Marah, and behaved herself neither with the uproarious
misconduct of Shearjashub, nor the gentle sweetness of
Love, but, quite in defiance of her name, was the mer-
riest, maddest little grig that could be, afraid of nothing and nobody, but as submissive to Lovey as a lamb
could be, and full of fight when Shearjashub intruded
himself on her domains.   For this baby was a sturdy,
rosy girl of three, before the fourth appeared.   Lowly
by this time had fallen into a listless carelessness
toward her husband, that was simply the want of all
spring in a long down-trodden heart.   Lovey alone
could stir her to tears or smiles.   Marah tired and
tormented her with her restless and overflowing vitality,
though she loved her dearly ; and her boy was big
enough now to cling a little to " mother," and reward
her for her faithful patience and care : but Lovey was
the darling of her secret heart ; and, being now five
years old, the little maid waited on mother like a
cherub on a saint, ran of errands, wound yarn, and did
many a slight task in the kitchen that saved Lowly's
bent and weary fingers.

It was with an impotent rage beyond speech that Freedom took the birth of another daughter, — a frail, tiny creature, trembling and weak as a new-born lamb in a snow-drift, but for that very reason rousing afresh in Lowly's breast the eternal floods of mother-love, the only love that never fails among all earthly passions, the only patience that is never weary, the sole true and abiding trust for the helpless creatures who come into life as waifs from the great misty ocean to find a shelter or a grave. Lowly was not only a mother according to the flesh, — for there are those whose maternity goes no further, and there are childless women who have the motherliness that could suffice for a countless brood, — but she had, too, the real heart: she clung to her weakling with a fervor and assertion that disgusted Freedom, and astounded Aunt Huldah, who, like the old Scotch woman, sniffed at the idea of children in heaven : " No, no ! a hantle o' weans there ! an' me that could never abide bairns onywhere ! I'll no believe it."

"It doos beat all, Hanner, to see her take to that skinny, miser'ble little crittur ! The others was kind o' likely, all on 'em ; but this is the dreadfulest weakly, peeked thing I ever see. I should think she'd be sick on't."

"I expect mothers — anyway them that's real motherly, Huldy — thinks the most of them that needs it the most. I've seen women with children quite a spell now, bein' out nussin' 'round, an' I allers notice that the sickly ones gets the most lovin' an' cuddlin'. I s'pose it's the same kind o' feelin' the Lord hez for sinners : they want him a sight more'n the righteous do."

" Why, Hanner Wheeler, what be you a-thinkin
of ! Where's your Catechis' ? Ain't all men by nater
under the wrath an' cuss o' God 'cause they be fallen
sinners? And here you be a-makin' out he likes 'em
better'n good folks.''

" Well, Huldy, I warn't a-thinkin' of Catechism : I
was a-thinkin' about what it sez in the Bible.''

Here the new baby cried ; and Aunt Huldah, confounded but unconvinced, gave a loud sniff, and carried
off Shearjashub and Marah to the red house, where
their fights and roars and general insubordination soon
restored her faith in the Catechism.

Lowly got up very slowly from little Phœbe's birth ;
and Freedom grumbled loud and long over the expense
of keeping Hepsy a month in the kitchen. But his wife
did not care now : a dumb and sudden endurance possessed her. She prayed night and morning, with a certain monomaniac persistence, that she and Lovey and
the baby might die ; but she did her work just as faithfully and silently as ever, and stole away at night to lie
down on the little cot-bed in the back-chamber by
Lovey and Marah, her hot cheek against the cool, soft
face of her darling, and the little hand hid deep in her
bosom, for an hour of rest and sad peace.

Freedom, meanwhile, worked all day on the farm,
and carried Shearjashub, whose oppressive name had
lapsed into Bub, into wood and field with him ; taught
him to drive the oxen, to hunt hens' nests in the barn
on the highest mow, to climb trees, in short to risk his
neck however he could " to make a man of him ; '' and
the boy learned, among other manly ways, a sublime
contempt for " gals,'' and a use of all the forcible
words permitted to masculine tongues. But Shear-

jashub's sceptre was about to tremble. Little Phœbe
had lingered in this world through a year of fluttering
life, when another baby was announced ; but this time it
was a boy ! — small even to Phœbe's first size, pallid,
lifeless almost, but still a boy.

"By Jinks !" exclaimed Freedom, his hard face
glowing with pleasure. "I told ye so, Aunt Huldy !
There's bound to be a Freedom Wheeler in this house,
whether or no."

"Hm !" said Aunt Huldah.   "You call to mind old
Hepsy Tinker, don't ye ? — she that was a-goin' to Har'-
ford a Tuesday, Providence permittin', an' Wednesday
whether or no.   Mabbe ye'll live to wish ye hadn't fit
with the Lord's will the way ye hev."

"I've got a boy, anyhow," was the grim exultant
answer.   "And he'll be Freedom Wheeler afore night ;
for I'm a-goin' to fetch the parson right off."

Strenuously did Parson Pitcher object to private
baptism : but he was an old man now ; and Freedom
threatened that he would go to Hartford and fetch the
Episcopal .minister, if Parson Pitcher refused, and the
old doctor knew he was quite sure to keep to his word :
so, with a groan at the stiff-necked brother, he got out
his cloak and hat, and rode home with victorious Freedom to the farmhouse.   Here the punch-bowl was
made ready on a stand in the parlor, and a fire kindled
on the hearth, for it was a chilly April day ; and from
the open door into Lowly's bedroom the wailing day-
old baby was brought, and given into its father's arms,
a mere scrid and atom of humanity, but a boy.

The rite was over, the long prayer said, and Freedom
strode into the chamber to lay his namesake beside its
mother ; but, as he stooped, the child quivered suddenly

all over, gasped, opened its half-shut eyes glazed with
a fatal film, and then closed the pallid, violet-shadowed
lids forever.

The next entry in the family Bible was, —

"Freedom.   Born April 11 ; died same day."

" Well, he hain't got nobody but the Lord to querrel
with this bout!" snapped Aunt Huldah.   " He's had
his way, 'nd now see what come on't!"

Lowly got up again, after the fashion of her kind,
without a murmur.   She felt her baby's death, she
mourned her loss, she was sorry for Freedom.   She
had loved him once dearly ; and, if she had known it,
Freedom loved her as much as he could·any thing but
himself : but it was not his way to show affection, even
to his boy ; as much of it as ever came to the surface
was a rough caress offered now and then to Lowly, — a
usage that had died out, and died with no mourning on
either side.   But as there is a brief sweet season often-
times in our bitter climate, that comes upon the sour
and angry November weather like a respite of execu-
tion, a few soft, misty, pensively sweet days, when the
sun is red and warm in the heavens, the dead leaves
give out their tender and melancholy odor, and the
lingering birds twitter in the pine-boughs as if they
remembered spring, so there came to Lowly a late and
last gleam of tranquil pleasure.

Aunt Huldah brought it about, for her tongue never
failed her for fear.   She caught Freedom by himself
one day, looking like an ill-used bull-dog, all alone in
the barn, setting some new rake-teeth.

" I've hed it on my mind quite a spell, Freedom,"
began the valorous old woman, " to tell ye, that, ef ye
"xpect Lowly is ever a-goin' to hev a rousin' hearty

child ag'in, you'll hev to cosset her up some. She ain't like our folks."

"That's pretty trew, Aunt Huldy," was the bitter interruption.

"She ain't a nether millstone, thet's a fact," answered Aunt Huldah with vigor; "nor she ain't bend leather, by a good sight: she's one o' the weakly, meekly sort; 'nd you can't make a whistle out o' a pig's tail, I've heerd father say, 'nd you no need to try: no more can ye make a stubbid, gritty cretur out o' Lowly. She's good as gold: but she's one o' them that hankers arter pleasantness, an' lovin', an' sich; they're vittles an' drink to her, I tell ye. You an' I can live on pork an' cabbage, and sass each other continooal, without turnin' a hair; but Lowly won't stan' it; 'nd ef ye expect this next baby to git along, I tell ye it's got to be easy goin' with her. You want to keep your fight with the Lord up, I s'pose: you're sot on hevin' another Freedom Wheeler?"

"I be," was the curt response. But though Aunt Huldah turned her back upon him without further encouragement, and marched through the ranks of "garden-sass" back to the house, her apron over her head, and her nose high in air, like one who snuffeth the battle from afar, her pungent words fell not to the ground. 'reedom perceived the truth of what she said, and his uneasy conscience goaded him considerably as to past opportunities; but he was an honest man, and, when he saw a thing was to be done, he did it. Next day he brought Lowly a new rocking-chair from the Centre. he modified his manners daily. He helped her lift the heavy milk-pails, he kept her wood-pile by the shed-door well heaped, and was even known to swing the great dinner-pot off the crane, if it was full and weighty.

"For the land sakes!" exclaimed Aunt Hannan, "what's a-comin' to Freedom? He does act halfway decent, Huldah."

Aunt Huldah shook her cap-ruffle up and down, and looked sagacious as an ancient owl. "That's me! I gin it to him, I tell ye, Hanner! Lowly wants cossetin', 'nd handlin' tender-like, or we'll be havin' more dyin' babies 'round. I up an' told him so Wednesday mornin' out in the barn, 's true's I'm alive."

"I'm glad on't! I'm real glad on't!" exclaimed Aunt Hannah. "You done right, Huldy. But, massy to me! how darst ye?"

"Ho!" sniffed Aunt Huldah. "Ef you think I'm afeard o' Freedom, you're clean mistook. I've spanked him too often, 'n' I wish to goodness I'd ha' spanked him a heap more: he'd ha' ben a heap the better for't. You reklect I had the tunin' of him, Hanner? You was allus a-nussin' mother: Freedom come to us jest as she got bedrid. Land! what a besom he was! His folks never tuned him, nor never took him to do, a mite. I hed it all to do, 'nd my mind misgives me now I didn't half do it. 'Jest as the twig is bent the tree's inclined,' ye know it says in the Speller."

"But, Huldy, 'tain't so easy bending a white-oak staddle; 'specially ef it's got a six-years' growth."

"Well, I got the hang of him, anyhow; 'nd he'll hear to me most allus, whether he performs accordin', or not."

"Mabbe it's too late, though, now, Huldy."

"Law, don't ye croak, Hanner. The little cretur'l hev a pleasant spell anyhow, for a while."

And so she did. Lowly's ready heart responded to sunshine as a rain-drenched bird will, preening its feathers, shaking its weary wings, welcoming the warm gladness with faint chirps and tiny brightening eyes, and then — taking flight.

A long and peaceful winter passed away, and in early May another boy was born : alas, it was another waxen, delicate creature. The old parson was brought in haste to baptize it. The pallid mother grew more white all through the ceremony, but nobody noticed her. She took the child in her arms with a wan smile, and tried to call it by name : "Free," was all she said. Her arms closed about it with a quick shudder and stringent grasp ; her lips parted wide. Lowly and her baby were both "free," for its last breath fluttered upward with its mother's ; and in the family Bible there was another record : —

"Lowly Wheeler. Died May 3."

"Freedom Wheeler. Born May 3, died same day."

"Well," said Aunt Huldah, as they came back to the ghastly quiet of the shut and silent house, after laying Lowly and her boy under the ragged turf of Dorset graveyard, "I guess Freedom'll give up his wrastle with Providence now, sence the Lord's took wife, 'nd baby, 'nd all."

"I don't feel sure of that," answered Aunt Hannah, for once sarcastic.

II.

Aunt Huldah and Aunt Hannah took Love and Phœbe over to the red house to live with them ; for they found a little note in Lowly's Bible requesting

them to take charge of these two, and their father did
not object. Phœbe was a baby still, hopelessly feeble : she could not stand alone, though she was more
than two years old ; and Love was devoted to her.
Bub and Marah could "fend for themselves ; " and
the old woman, who came as usual in Lowly's frequent
absences from the kitchen, had promised to stay all
summer. But, before the summer was over, Phœbe
faded away like a tiny snow-wreath in the sun, and
made a third little grave at her mother's feet; and
Lovey grieved for her so bitterly, that Aunt Hannah
insisted she should stay with them still, and made her
father promise she should be their little girl always ;
certain forebodings of their own as to the future,
prompting them to secure her a peaceful home while
they lived.

As for Freedom, if he mourned Lowly, it was with
no soft or sentimental grief, but with a certain resent-
ful aching in his heart, and a defiant aspect of soul
toward the divine will that had overset his intentions
and desires, — a feeling that deepened into savage
determination ; for this man was made of no yielding
stuff. Obstinacy stood him in stead of patience, an
active instead of a passive trait ; and in less than six
months after Lowly's death he was "published," according to the custom of those days ; the first intima-
tion his aunts or his children had of the impending
crisis being this announcement from the pulpit by
Parson Pitcher, that "Freedom Wheeler of this town,
and Melinda Bassett of Hartland, intend marriage."

Aunt Huldah looked at Aunt Hannah from under
her poke-bonnet with the look of an enraged hen ; her
?ap-frill trembled with indignation : and Lovey shrank

up closer to Aunt Hannah than before ; for she saw two
tears rise to her kind old eyes as they met Huldah's,
and she loved Aunt Hannah with all her gentle little
soul. As for Freedom, he sat bolt upright, and perfectly unmoved.

"Set his face as a flint!" raged Aunt Huldah as
soon as she got out of church, and went to take her
"noon-spell" in the graveyard, where the basket of
doughnuts, cheese, pie, cake, and early apples, was
usually unpacked on the stone wall on pleasant Sundays, and the aunts sitting on a tombstone, and the
children on the grass, ate their lunch. To-day Lovey
and Marah were left on the stone to eat their fill. Bub
had gone to the spring for water, and Freedom nobody
knew where ; while the aunts withdrew to "talk it
over."

"Yis," repeated Aunt Huldah, "set his face like a
flint. I tell ye he hain't got no more feelin' than a
cherub on a tombstone, Hanner! She ain't cold in her
grave afore he's off to Hartland, buyin' calves. Calves !
I guess likely, comin' home jest as plausible as a pass-
nip : 'I sha'n't make no butter this year : so I bought a
lot o' calves to raise.' Ho! heifer-calves every one on
'em, mind ye. Ef we hadn't ha' ben a pair o' fools, we
should ha' mistrusted suthin'. Ef that gal's Abigail
Bassett's darter, things'll fly, I tell ye." And here
Aunt Huldah blew a long breath out, as if her steam
was at high pressure, and could not help opening a
valve for relief ; and wise Aunt Hannah seized the
chance to speak.

"Well, Huldy, I declare I'm beat myself ; but we
can't help it. I must say I looked forrard to the time
when he would do it ; but I didn't reelly expect it jest

yet. We've got Lovey anyway; and, if Melindy ain'
a pootty capable woman, she'll hev her hands full with
Bub and Marah.''

"Thet's a fact,'' returned Aunt Huldah, whose in-
most soul rejoiced at the prospect of Bub's contuma-
ciousness under new rule; for he was not a small boy
any more, and shingles were in vain, though he still
made a certain outward show of obedience. Marah,
too, was well calculated to be a thorn in the flesh of
any meek step-mother, with her high spirits, untamed
temper, and utter wilfulness; and Aunt Huldah, whose
soul was sore, — not because of Freedom's marriage,
for she recognized its necessity, but because of its
indecent haste, which not only seemed an insult to
gentle Lowly, whom Aunt Huldah had loved dearly, but
a matter of talk to all the town where the Wheelers had
been respected for many a long year, — Aunt Huldah
rejoiced in that exasperated soul of hers at a prospect
of torment to the woman who stepped into Lowly's
place quite unconscious of any evil design or desire on
the part of her new relatives.

But it was no meek step-mother whom Freedom
brought home from a very informal wedding, in his
old wagon, some three weeks after. Melinda Bassett
was quite capable of holding her own, even with Aunt
Huldah, — a strapping, buxom, rosy-faced girl, with
abundant rough dark hair, and a pair of bright, quick,
dark eyes, an arm of might in the dairy, and a power
of work and management that would have furnished
forth at least five feeble pieces like Lowly. Freedom
soon found he had inaugurated Queen Stork. Bub
was set to rights as to his clothes, and "pitched into,''
as he sulkily expressed it, in a way that gave him a

new and unwilling respect for the other sex; and
Marah entered at once into an alliance, offensive and
defensive, with the new " mammy ; " for Melinda was
pleasant and cheerful when things went right, and generally meant they should go right. She was fond of
children, too, when they were " pretty behaved ; " and
Marah was bright enough to find out, with the rapid
perception of a keen-witted child, that it was much
better for her to *be* pretty behaved than otherwise.

But Freedom — it was new times to him to have
his orders unheeded, and his ways derided. He had
been lord and master in his house a long time ; but
here was a capable, plucky, courageous, and cheery
creature, who made no bones of turning him out of her
dominions when he interfered, or ordering her own
ways without his help at all.

" Land of Goshen ! " said Melinda to the wondering
Aunt Hannah, "do you s'pose I'm goin' to hev a
man tewin' round in my way all the time, jest cos he's
my husband? I guess not. I know how to 'tend to
my business, and I expect to 'tend right up to it :
moreover I expect he'll tend to his'n. When I get
a-holt of his plough, or fodder his team, or do his choppin', 'll be time enough for him to tell me how to work
butter, 'n' scald pans. I ain't nobody's fool, I tell ye,
Aunt Hanner."

" I'm glad on't, I'm dredful glad on't ! " growled
Aunt Huldah, when she heard of this manifesto.

" That's the talk : she'll straighten him out, I'll bet
ye ! Ef poor Lowly'd had that spunk she might ha'
been livin' to-day. But I guess she's better off," suddenly wound up Aunt Huldah, remembering her Catechism, no doubt, as she walked off muttering, " Are at

their death made perfect in holiness, and do immediately pass into glory," — an assurance that has upheld many a tried and weary soul more conversant
with the language of the Assembly of Divines than
that of their Lord and Head; for in those old days
this formula of the faith was ground into every infant
memory, though the tender gospel words were comparatively unknown.

So the first year of the new reign passed on; and in
the next February Freedom was mastered by a more
stringent power than Melinda, for he fell ill of old-
fashioned typhus-fever, a malign evil that lights down
here and there in lonely New-England farmhouses,
utterly regardless of time or place; and in a week this
strong man was helpless, muttering delirious speech,
struggling for life with the fire that filled his veins and
consumed his flesh.   Aunt Hannah came to his aid,
and the scarce neighbors did what they could for him.
Brother-farmers snored away the night in a chair beside
his bed, and said that they had "sot up with Freedom
Wheeler last night," — ministrations worse than useless, but yet repeated as a sort of needful observance.
And at the end of the first week Aunt Hannah was
called away to the "up-chamber" room, where Melinda slept now, and a big boy was introduced into the
Wheeler family; while Moll Thunder, an old woman
skilled in "yarbs," as most of her race are, — for she
was a half-breed Indian, — was sent for from Wingfield, and took command of the fever-patient, who
raged and raved at his will, dosed with all manner of
teas, choked with lukewarm porridge, smothered in
blankets, bled twice a week, and kept as hot, as feeble,
and as dirty, as the old practice of medicine required.

till disease became a mere question of "the survival of the fittest." Our grandfathers and grandmothers are vaunted to this day as a healthy, hard-working race, because the weakly share of each generation was neatly eliminated according to law.

But, if Freedom was helpless and wandering, Melinda was not. A week was all she spared to the rites and rights of the occasion ; and when she first appeared in the kitchen, defying and horrifying Aunt Huldah, there ensued a brief and spicy conversation between the three women concerning this new baby, who lay sucking his fist in the old wooden cradle, looking round, hard, and red as a Baldwin apple, and quite unconscious what a firebrand he was about to be.

"It's real bad, ain't it?" purred Aunt Hannah, "to think Freedom shouldn't know nothin' about the baby? He'd be jest as tickled!"

"I don' know what for," snapped Melinda. "I should think there was young uns enough round now to suit him."

"But they wasn't boys," answered Aunt Hannah. "Freedom is sot on havin' a boy to be called for him. There's allus ben a Freedom Wheeler amongst our folks, as well as a· Shearjashub, and I never see him more pestered by a little thing than when them two babies died, both on 'em bein' baptized Freedom ; and he's had a real controversy with Providence, Parson Pitcher sez, his mind's so sot on this business."

"Well, this little feller isn't a-goin' to be called Freedom, now, I tell ye," uttered Melinda, with a look of positiveness that chilled Aunt Hannah to the heart. "He's jest as much my baby's he is his pa's, and a good sight more, I b'lieve. Sha'n't I hev all the trouble on him? an' jest as quick as he's big enough tu help, instead o' hinder, won't he be snaked off inter the lots to work? I've seen men-folks afore; and I tell ye, Aunt Hanner, you give 'em an inch, 'n' they take a harf a yard certain.''

"Well, Melindy," interfered Aunt Huldah, for once in her life essaying to make peace, "Freedom's dreadful sick now: reelly he's dangerous." [This is New-England vernacular for in danger.] "What ef he should up 'n' die? Wouldn't ye feel kind o' took aback to think on't?"

"Things is right 'n' wrong jest the same ef everybody dies: everybody doos, sooner or later. I don't see what odds that makes, Aunt Huldy. I ain't a-goin' to make no fuss about it. Fust Sunday in March is sacrament day, and childern is allers presented for baptism then. I'll jest fix it right; and, ef his pa gits well, why, there 'tis, 'nd he'll hev to git used to't; and, ef he don't, it ain't no matter, he won't never know. I guess I've got folks as well as you, and names too. There's old Grandsir Bassett: he sot a sight by me, 'nd he was ninety years old 'n' up'ards when he died. Why, he fit the British out to Ticonderogy long o' Ethan Allen! He was a dredful spry man, and had a kind o' pootty name too, smart-soundin'; and I'm a-goin' to call the boy for him. Freedom! Land o' Goshen! 'tain't a half a name anyhow; sounds like Fourth o' July oh-rations, 'nd Hail Columby, 'nd fire-crackers, 'nd root-beer, 'nd Yankee Doodle thrown in! Now Grandsir Bassett's name was Tyagustus. That sounds well, I tell ye!—kinder mighty an pompous, 's though it come out o' them columns o' long proper names to the end of the Speller.''

Here Melinda got out of breath ; and dismayed Aunt
Huldah followed Aunt Hannah, who had stolen off to
Freedom's room with a certain instinct of protecting
him, as a hen who sees the circling wings of a hawk
in the high blue heaven runs to brood her chicks.

Moll Thunder was smoking a clay pipe up the wide
chimney ; and Freedom lay on the bed with half-shut
eyes, drawn and red visage, parched lips, and restless,
tossing head, murmuring wild words, — here and there
calls for Lowly, a tender word for Love (whom he
scarce ever noticed in health), or a muttered profanity
at some balky horse or stupid ox-team.

"Kinder pootty sick," grunted Moll Thunder, nodding to the visitants. "Plenty much tea-drink drown
him ole debbil fever clear out 'fore long. He, he, he!
Moll knows : squaw-vine, pep'mint, cohosh, fever-wort ;
pootty good steep." And from a pitcher of steaming
herbs, rank of taste and evil of smell, she proceeded
to dose her patient, a heroic remedy that might have
killed or cured, but that now Aunt Hannah was no
more needed up stairs, and could resume her place by
Freedom. And Moll was sent home to Wingfield with
a piece of pork, a bag of meal, and a jug of cider-
brandy, — a professional fee she much preferred to
money.

But even Aunt Hannah could not arrest the fever : it
had its sixty days of fight and fire. While yet it raged
in Freedom's gaunt frame with unrelenting fierceness,
Melinda carried out her programme, and had her baby
baptized Tyagustus Bassett. Parson Pitcher came now
and then to visit the sick man ; but, even when recovery
had proceeded so far that the reverend divine thought
fit to exhort and catechise his weak brother in reference

to his religious experience, the old gentleman shook his head, and took numerous pinches of snuff at the result.

"There seems to be a root of bitterness, — a root of bitterness remaining, Huldy. His speritooal frame is cold and hard. There is a want of tenderness, — a want of tenderness."

"He didn't never have no great," dryly remarked Aunt Huldah.

"Grace has considerable of a struggle, no doubt, with the nateral man; it is so with all of us: but after such a dispensation, an amazing dispensation, — brought into the jaws of death, — Huldy, where death got hold of him, and destruction made him afraid, in the words of Scripter, I should expect, I did expect, to find him in a tender frame. But he seems to kick against the pricks, — to kick against the pricks."

"Well, Parson Pitcher, folks don't allus do jest as ye calc'late to have 'em here below; and grace doos have a pootty hard clinch on't with Freedom, I'm free to confess. He's dredful sot, dredful; and I don't mind tellin' ye, seein' we're on the subject, that he's ben kinder thwarted in suthin' whilst he was sick, an' he hain't but jest found it out, and it doos rile him peskily: he dono how on airth to put up with't."

"Indeed, indeed! Well, Huldy, the heart knoweth its own bitterness. I guess I will pray with the family now, and set my face homeward without dealing with Freedom further to-day."

"I guess I would," frankly replied Aunt Huldah. "A little hullsome lettin' alone's good for grown folks as 'tis for children; and after a spell he'll kinder simmer down: as Hanner sez, when ye can't fix a thing your way, you've got to swaller it some other way; but it doos choke ye awful sometimes."

There is no doubt that "Tyagustus" did choke Freedom, when he found that sonorous name tacked irremediably on to the great hearty boy he had hoped for so long, but never seen till it was six weeks' old, and solemnly christened after Grandsir Bassett. A crosser and a more disagreeable man than this convalescent never made a house miserable. The aunts went delicately, in bitterness of soul, after Agag's fashion; Bub fled from before the paternal countenance, and almost lived in the barn; Marah had been for two months tyrannizing over Lovey at the Red House, as happy and as saucy as a bobolink on a fence-post; while Melinda, quite undaunted by the humors of her lord and master, went about her work with her usual zeal and energy, scolding Bub, working the hired man up to his extremest capacity, scrubbing, chattering, and cheery, now and then stopping to feed and hug the great good-tempered baby, or fetching some savory mess to Freedom, whose growls and groans disturbed her no more than the scrawks and croaks of the gossiping old hens about the doorstep.

By June he was about again, and things had found their level. If this were not a substantially true story, I should like to branch off here from the beaten track, and reform my hero, — make the gnarly oak into a fluent and facile willow-tree, and create a millennial peace and harmony in the old farmhouse, just to make things pleasant for dear Aunt Hannah and gentle little Lovey: but facts are stubborn things; and, if circumstances and the grace of God modify character, they do not change it. Peter and Paul were Paul and Peter still, though the end and aim of life were changed for them after conversion.

So Freedom Wheeler returned to his active life unchastened, indeed rather exasperated, by his illness. The nervous irritation and general unhinging of mind and body that follow a severe fever, added, of course, to his disgust and rebellion against the state of things about him. His heart's desire had been refused him over and over; but it grew up again like a pruned shrub, the stronger and sturdier for every close cutting; and, grinding his teeth against fate, — he dared not say against God, — he went his bitter way.

Melinda never feared him, but he was a terror to the children; and, had there been any keen observer at hand, it would have been painful to see how "father" was a dreadful word, instead of a synonyme for loving protection and wise guidance. Aunt Hannah was shocked when Marah refused to say the Lord's Prayer one night. "Me won't! Me don't want Father in heaven: fathers is awful cross. Me won't say it, aunty."

"Now, you jest clap down 'nd say, 'Now I lay me' quick as a wink!'" interposed Aunt Huldah. "Hanner, don't ye let that child talk so to ye. *I'd* tune her, afore I would, I tell ye."

But, in the secrecy of her own apartment, Aunt Huldah explained, "You see, Hanner, I've took the measure of that young un's foot. She's pa all over, — no more like Lowly'n chalk is like cheese. Ef you'd ha' battled it out with her, she'd ha' got the better of ye, 'nd more'n likely gone home an' told the hull story; and then Freedom would nigh about ha' slartered her; 'nd I don't want the leetle cretur's sperit broke. Fact is, I feel jes' so myself. He is so all-fired ugly, seems as though I should bust sometimes.

Moreover, 'nd above all, 't ain't never best to let childern git the better of ye.   They don't never go back
on their tracks ef they do.   I put in my finger that
time so's't she shouldn't querrel with you, 'nd she
said t'other thing jest like a cosset lamb : she was
sort o' surprised into't, ye see."

"I presume likely, I presume likely, Huldy.   She's
a masterful piece, Mara is.   I'm afeard she'll taste
trouble afore she dies.   Sech as she has to have a lot
of discipline to fetch 'em into the kingdom."

"Don't seem to be no use to Freedom, 'flictions
don't, Hanner.   Sometimes, I declare for't, I have my
doubts ef he ever got religion, anyhow."

"Why, Huldy Wheeler!" Aunt Hannah's eyes
glowed with mild wrath, — "'nd he's ben a professor
nigh on to thirty year.   How can ye talk so?   I'm
clean overcome."

"Well, I can't help it.   There's some things stand
to reason, ef they be speritooal things ; 'nd one on 'em
is, that, ef a man's born again, he's a new cretur.
You're paowerful on Bible-texts ; so I won't sling no
Catechism at ye this time : but there's suthin', somewhere 'long in some o' the 'Pistles, about ' love, joy,
peace, gentleness, goodness, meekness,' 'nd so on, for
quite a spell ; and, if that cap fits Freedom, why, I'm
free to say I don't see it."

"Well, Huldy, we must make allowances : ye see,
he's dreadful disapp'inted."

"That's so.   You'd better believe *he* don't say the
Lord's Prayer no more'n Marah ; or, ef he doos, it
goes, ' My will be done :' he hain't learnt how to spell
it t'other way."   Aunt Hannah sighed.   She was getting old now ; and Freedom was as dear to her as an

only child, wayward and wilful though it be, to a loving
mother; but she rested her heart on its lifelong comfort, — a merciful presence that was her daily strength,
— and hoped for the best, for some future time, even
if she did not live to see it, when this stubborn heart of
her boy's should become flesh, and his soul accept a
divine Master, with strong and submissive faith.

Poor Aunt Hannah!   She had shed countless tears,
and uttered countless prayers, to this end, but as yet
in vain.   Next year only brought fresh exasperation
to Freedom in the birth of a daughter, as cross, noisy,
and disagreeable as she was unwelcome.   He flung out
of the house, and went to ploughing the ten-acre lot,
though the frost was only out of the surface : he broke
his share, goaded his oxen till even those patient
beasts rebelled, and at last left the plough in the furrow, and took a last year's colt out to train.   Melinda
escaped a great deal through that poor colt; for what
he dared not pour on her offending head in the way
of reviling, he safely hurled at the wild creature he
found so restive in harness; and many a kick and
blow taught the brute how superior a being man is —
particularly when he is out of temper.

"Keep that brat out o' my sight, Aunt Hanner,"
was his first greeting to the child.   "Don't fetch it
'round here : it's nothin' but a noosance."

Aunt Hannah retreated in dismay; but she dared
not tell Melinda, whose passion for fine-sounding
names was mightily gratified at the opportunity to
select a girl's appellation.   Before she issued from her
sick-room she made up her mind to call this child
Chimera Una Vilda.

Dear reader, give me no credit for imagination here.

These are actual names, registered on church records and tombstones, with sundry others of the like sort, such as Secretia, Luelle, Lorilla Allaroila, Lue, Plumy, Antha, Loruhama, Lophelia, Bethursda, and a host more. But it mattered little to Freedom: the child might have any name, or no name, as far as he cared. It was a naughty baby, and rent the air with cries of temper in a manner that was truly hereditary.

"I never see such a piece in all my days!" sighed Aunt Hannah, whose belief in total depravity became an active principle under this dispensation. "I declare for't, Huldy, you can hear her scream way over here."

"Well, I b'lieve you, Hanner: the winders is wide open, and we ain't but jest acrost the road. I guess you could hear her a good mile. An' she keeps it up the hull endurin' time. Makes me think o' them cherubims the Rev'lations tells about, that continooally do cry : only she ain't cryin' for praise."

"I expect she'd cry for suthin' besides crossness ef she knew how her pa feels about her. It's awful, Huldy, it is awful, to see him look at the child once in a while."

"She knows it in her bones, I tell ye. Talk about 'riginal sin! I guess she won't want no sin more 'riginal than what's come down pootty straight from him. She's jest another of 'em, now I tell ye."

But Melinda was equal to the situation, whether she picked up the last maple-twig Marah brought in from driving the cows, or pulled the stiff wooden busk from her maternal bosom, or "ketched off her shoe," or even descended upon that chubby form with her own hard hand, and pungently "reversed the magnetic cur-

rents," as they say in Boston. Those currents were
reversed so often, it might have been matter of doubt
which way they originally ran after a year or two.
But the old Adam was strong; and when Chimera —
no chimera to them, but a dreadful reality — was sent
over to stay a while at the red house, the aunts were at
their wits' ends, and Lovey both tired and tormented.

This time, for Chimera's visit to the aunts was
occasioned by the immediate prospect of another baby,
Aunt Hannah was not able to take care of Melindy.
The dear old woman was getting old: a "shockanum
palsy," as Aunt Huldah called a slight paralytic stroke,
had given her warning; her head shook perpetually,
and her hands trembled. She could still do a little
work about the house; but her whole failing body was
weary with the perpetual motion, and she knew life
was near its end for her. So they sent to Dorset
Centre for the village nurse, — a fat, good-natured creature; and one morning, early, a boy — a rosy, sturdy,
big boy — appeared on the stage.

Now Freedom exulted: he strode over to the red
house to tell the news. "Fact, Aunt Hannah! I've
got him now, — a real stunner too. You won't see no
tricks played now, I tell ye! By jingo! I'm goin' off
for Parson Pitcher quicker'n lightnin'. I'll bet ye
Melindy won't git ahead o' me this time. That leetle
feller'll be Freedom Wheeler in two hours' time, sure's
ye live."

"Providence permitting," put in Aunt Hannah
softly, as if to avert the omen of this loud and pre-
sumptuous rejoicing. But, soft as the prayer was,
Freedom heard it, and, as he opened the door, turned
on his heel, and answered, "Whether or no, this
time."

Aunt Hannah lay back in her chair, utterly shocked.
This was rank blasphemy in her ears : she did not
remember the illustrative story Aunt Huldah told Freedom, on a time long past, about a certain old woman's
intention to go to Hartford, or she might, perhaps, have
been less horrified.   Still it was bad enough ; for, if
the words were lightly spoken, the spirit within the man
accorded fully with his tone, and never was keener
triumph rampant in any conqueror's heart than in this
rough, self-willed farmer's as he drove his horse, full
tilt, down the long hills, and up the sharp ascents, that
lay between him and the parsonage.   But Parson
Pitcher had been called up higher than Freedom
Wheeler's.   That very morning he had fallen asleep in
his bed, weak and wasted with a long influenza ; and,
being almost ninety years old, the sleep of weakness
had slipped quietly into the deeper calm of death.

He had for a year past been obliged to have a colleague : so Freedom hunted the young man up at his
boarding-place, and took him instead, — a little aggrieved, indeed, for long custom made Parson Pitcher
seem the only valid authority for religious observances
of this kind ; and, years after he ceased to preach, the
little children were always brought to him for baptism.

"But I s'pose one on 'em's reelly as good as t'other
ror this puppus," hilariously remarked Freedom to the
old lady who lodged the colleague, receiving a grim
stare of disapproval for his answer, as he deserved.
However, there was one advantage in having Mr.
Brooks instead of the parson.   Freedom was but
slightly acquainted with the new-comer : so he poured
out all his troubles, his losses, and his present rejoicing,
ill the way home, with a frankness and fluency strange

enough ; for New-Englanders as a race are reticent both of their affairs and their feelings, and Freedom Wheeler was more so by nature than by race. This exultation seemed to have fused his whole character for the time into glowing, outpouring fervor : a deep and ardent excitement fired his eye, and loosed his tongue ; and Mr. Brooks, who had a tinge of the meta-physical and inquisitive about him, was mightily inter-ested in the man ; and being, as he phrased it, a " student of character," — which is, being interpreted, an impertinent soul who makes puppets of his fellows to see how their wires work, and discover the thoughts of their hearts for his own theories and speculations, — he gently drew out this intoxicated man, " drunken, but not with wine," as he was, with judicious sugges-tions and inquiries, till he knew him to the core ; a knowledge of use to neither party, and to the young clergyman only another apple off the tree from which Eve plucked sin and misery, and a sour one at that.

Once more the old china punch-bowl that had been a relic in the Wheeler family beyond their record, and would have crazed a china-fancier with the lust of the eye, was filled from the spring, and set on the claw-footed round table in the parlor, the door left open into Melinda's room so she could see all the ceremony, the aunts and nurse assembled in solemn array (all the children being sent over to Lovey's care at the red house) ; and with due propriety the new baby, squirming and kicking with great vigor in his father's arms, was baptized Freedom Wheeler.

Why is it that " the curse of a granted prayer " comes sometimes immediately ? Why do we pant and thirst, and find the draught poisonous ? or, after long exile, come home, only to find home gone? Alas! these are the conditions of humanity, the questions we all ask, the thwarting and despair we all endure, and also the mystery and incompleteness which tell us in hourly admonition that this life is a fragment and a beginning, and that its ends are not peace and rapture, but discipline and education. Freedom Wheeler was no apt pupil, but his sharpest lesson came to-day.

Full of exultation over fate, Melinda, and the aunts, chuckling to himself with savage satisfaction at the conscious feeling that it was no use for anybody— even the indefinite influence he dared not call God — to try to get the better of him, he strode across the room to give his boy back to Melinda, stumbled over a little stool that intruded from below the sofa, fell full-length on the floor, with the child under him; and when he rose to his feet, dazed with the jar of the fall, it was but just in time to see those baby eyelids quiver once, and close forever. The child was dead.

Melinda rose up in the bed with a dreadful face: shriek on shriek burst from her lips. The women crowded about Freedom, and took the limp little body from his arms. He leaned against the door-way like a man in a dream. The torrents of reproach and agony that burst from Melinda's lips seemed not to enter his ears: " Now, you ve done it! you've killed him! you have! you have! " But why repeat the wild and bitter words of a mother bereft of her child in the first hours of its fresh, strong life? Melinda was not a cruel or ungenerous woman naturally ; but now she was weak and nervous, and the shock was too much for her brain.

In this sudden stress Mr. Brooks forgot his metaphysics, and fell back on the old formulas, which, after

all, do seem to wear better than metaphysics in any real
woe or want. He drew near to Freedom, and put his
hand on the wretched man's shoulder. "My brother,"
said he gently, "this evil is from the hand of the
Lord : bear it like a Christian."

"He ain't no Christian!" shouted Melinda, with
accents of concentrated bitterness. "Christians ain't
that sort, growlin' and scoldin', and fightin' with the
Lord that made him, cos he couldn't hev his own way,
and uplifted sky-high when he got it : 'nd now look to
where 'tis ! The hypocrite's hope is cut off, cut off !
Oh, my baby, my baby, my baby!" Here she fell
into piteous wailing and fainting ; and Mr. Brooks led
the passive, stricken man away ; while Aunt Huldah
despatched Reuben Stark for the doctor, and Aunt
Hannah and the nurse tried to calm and restore
Melinda.

But it was idle to try to draw Freedom from his
silent gloom. He would neither speak nor hear, apparently ; and Mr. Brooks, seeing Reuben hitching the
horse to the wagon, took his hat to leave. Aunt
Huldah followed him to the door for politeness.

"Send for me when you are ready for the funeral,
Miss Huldah," said he in taking leave. "I feel deeply
for you all, especially for brother Wheeler. The Lord
seems to have a controversy with him indeed."

"That's so," curtly replied Aunt Huldah ; "an' I
don't see but what he's kep' up his end on't pootty
well. But I guess he's got to let go. This makes
three on 'em ; and it's an old sayin', ' three times an'
out.' "

A suddenly subdued smile curled the corners of Mr.
Brooks's mouth for a second. Poor man, he had a

keen sense of the ludicrous, and was minister in a country parish.

"Good-day," nodded Aunt Huldah, quite unaware that she had said any thing peculiar; and then she returned to Freedom. But he had gone out of the kitchen; nor did any one know where he was, till the horn called to supper, when he came in, swallowed a cup of tea, and went speechless to bed, not even asking about Melinda, whom the doctor found in the first stage of fever, and pronounced "dangerous."

But Melinda was strong, and could bear a great deal yet. She was comparatively a young woman; and, after a month's severe illness, she began to improve daily, and in another month was like her old self again, — perhaps a trifle less cheery, but still busy, vivacious, and unsparing of herself or others. But Freedom was a changed man. The scornful and bitter words Melinda had uttered in her frantic passion burnt deep into his soul, though he gave no sign even of hearing them.

Kingsley speaks of "the still, deep-hearted Northern, whose pride breaks slowly and silently, but breaks once for all; who tells to God what he never will tell to man, and, having told it, is a new creature from that day forth forever;" and something after this fashion was Freedom Wheeler shaped. He had been brought up in the strictest Calvinism, had his "experience" in due form, and then united with the church. But Parson Pitcher never preached to anybody but unconverted sinners: hell-fire drove him on to save from the consequences of sin. Its conditions, people who were once converted must look out for themselves. And Freedom's strong will, sullen temper, and undisciplined character, grew up like the thorns in the parable, and choked the struggling blades of grain that never reached an ear. Melinda's accusations were the first sermon that ever awoke his consciousness. He had always prided himself on his honesty, and here he saw that he had been an utter hypocrite.

With all his faults, he had a simple faith in the truths of the Bible, and a conscientious respect for ordinances; and now there fell upon him a deep conviction of heinous sin, a gloom, a despair, that amounted almost to insanity. But he asked no counsel, he implored no divine aid: with the peculiar sophistry of religious melancholy, he considered that his prayers would be an abomination to the Lord. So he kept silence, poring more and more over his Bible, appropriating its dreadful texts all to himself, and turning his eyes away from every gracious and tender promise, as one unworthy to read them.

He worked more faithfully than ever, — worked from day's first dawn into the edge of darkness, as if the suffering of a worn-out body had a certain counter-irritation for the tortured mind. There are many rods of stone wall on that old farm to-day, laid up of such great stones, made so wide and strong and close, that the passer-by looks at it with wonder, little knowing that the dreadful struggles of a wandering and thwarted soul mark the layers of massive granite, and record the exhaustion of flesh mastered by strong and strenuous spirit.

When Melinda was herself again, it was yet some time before she noticed the change in Freedom. There was a certain simple selfishness about her that made her own grief hide every other, and impelled her to try with all her might to forget her trouble, to get rid of the sharp memory that irked her soul like a rankling thorn. She hid all her baby-clothes away in the garret; she sent the cradle out to the shed-loft, and never opened her lips about that lost boy, whose name Aunt Huldah had recorded in the same record with the two who had preceded him, and whose little body lay under the mulleins and golden-rods, beside the others, at Lowly's feet.

But, as time wore on, Melinda began to see that some change had passed over her husband. She had quite forgotten her own mad words, spoken in the first delirium of her anguish, and followed by the severe fever that had almost swept away life as well as memory. No remorse, therefore, softened her heart; but it was not needed. Though Melinda was an incisive, stirring, resolute woman, with her warm temper she had also a warm heart: she could not live in the house with a dog or a cat without feeling a certain kindly affection for the creature. Her step-children never suffered at her hands, but shared in all the care she gave her own, and loved her as well as shy, careless children of a healthy sort love anybody. She loved her husband truly. Her quick, stormy words meant no more than the scolding of a wren: in her heart she held Freedom dear and honored, only he did not know it.

But she began now, in her anxiety about his sad and gloomy ways, to soften her manner toward him daily. She remembered the things he liked to eat, and prepared them for the table; she made him a set of new shirts, and set the stitches in them with scrupulous neatness; she kept the house in trim and pleasant order, and sat up at night to mend his working-clothes, so that they were always whole, — homely services and demonstra

tions, no doubt, but having as much fitness to place
and person as the scenic passion of a novel in high life,
or a moral drama where the repentant wife throws herself into a stern husband's arms, and, with flying tresses
and flowing tears, vows never to vex or misunderstand
his noble soul again.

Freedom's conscious controversy with his Maker still
went on within him, and raged between doubt and
despair; but he was human, and the gentle ray of
affection that stole from Melinda's "little candle" did
its work in his "naughty world." He felt a certain
comfort pervading home when he came in at night sad
and weary : the children's faces were clean, the hearth
washed, the fire bright; warmth and peace brooded
over the old kitchen, crackled softly from the back-log,
purred in the cat, sang from the kettle-nose ; Melinda's
shining hair was smooth, her look quiet and wistful ;
the table was neatly spread, — little things, surely ; but
life is made up of them, and hope and happiness and
success.

The dark cloud in this man's soul began to lift im-
perceptibly ; and he was called out of himself presently to stand by Aunt Hannah's bed and see her die.
A second shock of paralysis suddenly prostrated her,
and she was laid on the pillows speechless and senseless. Twenty-four hours of anxiety and tears passed,
and then she seemed to revive : she stirred her hand,
her face relaxed, her eyes opened ; but the exhaustion
was great, and she was unable to speak. Conscious
and patient, she endured through a few days more, and
then the final message came. Another paralysis, a
longer silence, and those grouped about her bed in the
old red house, thinking every moment to see the shadow

of death fall over those beloved features, beheld with surprise the soft brown eyes open, and fix upon Freedom such a look of longing, tender, piteous affection as might have broken the heart of a stone ; a long, long gaze, a very passion of love, pity, and yearning, and then those eyes turned heavenward, grew glorious with light and peace, and closed slowly, — closed forever.

Freedom went out and wept bitterly : he had denied his Lord too ; and it was a look that smote him to the heart, as that divine glance did Peter. But no man knew or saw it. Hidden in the barn, a dim and fragrant oratory that has seen more than one struggle of soul in the past and unknown records of New England, Freedom " gave up," and gave up finally.

He was no longer a young man, and he was not the stuff that saints are made of ; but he had a stern honesty, an inward uprightness, that held him to his new resolve like hooks of steel. If his temper softened a little, his obstinacy yielded here and there, his manner gave out now and then some scanty spark of affection and consideration, these were the outward signs of a mighty change within ; for an old and weather-beaten tree does not bloom in its spring resurrection with the flowers and promise of a young and vigorous growth : it is much if the gnarled boughs put out their scanty share of verdure, if there is a blossom on a few branches, and shelter enough for a small bird's nest from sun or rain. Lovey, grown by this time a tall and helpful girl, with her mother's delicate sweetness in face and figure, was first perhaps to feel this vital change in her father. Aunt Hannah's death was a woful loss to her tender, clinging nature ; and she

turned to him with the instinct of a child, and found a
shy and silent sympathy from him that was strangely
dear and sweet, and bound them together as never before. Aunt Huldah, too, noticed it. "Dear me!"
said she to herself, as she sat alone by the fire, knitting
red stockings for Chimera, who had begun to mend her
ways a little under the steady birch-and-shingle discipline, — "dear me, I'm real afraid Freedom ain't long
for this world. He is kinder mellerin', like a stone-
apple in June: it's onnateral. I expect he's struck
with death, Hanner, don't you? Oh, my land, what a
old fool I be! Hanner's gone, 'nd here I be a-talkin'
to her jest as though" — Aunt Huldah wiped her
dimmed eyes with a red silk handkerchief, and rubbed
her misty glasses before she went on, still leaving the
sentence unfinished. "Mabbe it's a triumph o' grace.
I s'pose grace can get the better o' Freedom: seems
kinder doubtful, I must confess; but I don't see nothin'
else that could fetch him, and he is a-growin' soft, sure
as ye live."

But Melinda, less sensitive or perceptive, perceived
only that her efforts had "kinder sorter slicked him
down," as she said.

It was reserved for the birth of another child to demonstrate how Freedom had laid down his arms, and
gone over to the king at last. Yes, two years after
Aunt Hannah's death, another fine and hearty boy
entered the family, but not this time with such acclaim
and welcome as the last. Melinda, weak and happy,
grew gentler than ever before, between present bliss
and future fear: and Freedom, hiding his face in his
hard brown hands, thanked God with shame and trembling for this undeserved mercy; and even while he

shuddered, naturally enough, at the possibilities the past recalled, he could say humbly and fervently, "Thy will be done."

Nobody spoke of sending for the minister now, nor was even a name for baby suggested till two months after, when Melinda said to Freedom one night, when the children were all in bed, and they sat alone by the fire, waiting for the last brand to fall in two before it could be raked up, "Next Sunday but one is sacrament Sunday, Freedom. It's good weather now: hadn't the little feller better be presented fur baptism?"

"I guess so," answered he.

"What do ye calkerlate to call him?" asked Melinda shyly, after a pause.

"Thet's for you to say, Melinda: I wish ye to do jest as ye're a mind to," he said gently, with a stifled sigh.

"That's easy settled then," she replied, a pretty smile about her red lips, and laying her hand on her husband's knee: "I don't want to call him nothin' more nor less than Freedom."

He put his hand on hers for a moment, looked the other way, and then got up and went out silently.

So one bright June day baby was taken to the meeting-house, and received his name, and was duly recorded in the family Bible, but with no ominous monosyllable added to his birth-date; and Aunt Huldah, as she went out of church, said to Mr. Brooks, by no means inaudibly, "I guess Freedom's gin up his controversy finally. He did keep up his end on't quite a spell; but he's gin up for good now, I expect."

"Yes," answered the young parson, with a smile of mingled feeling and reverence. "The Lord was in the still small voice."

MRS. FLINT'S MARRIED EXPERIENCE.

"WELL, Mindwell, I have counselled a good deal
about it. I was happy as the day is long with your
father. I don't say but what I cleaved to this world
consider'ble more than was good for my growth in
grace. He was about the best. But it pleased the
Lord to remove him, and it was quite a spell before
I could reely submit: the nateral man rebelled, now I
tell you! You can't never tell what it is to lose a
companion till you exper'ence it."

A faint color, vanishing as rapidly as it came, almost
as if ashamed that it bore witness to the emotion within
her, rose to Mindwell Pratt's face as her mother spoke.
She was a typical New-England woman, — pale, serious,
with delicate features, grave dark eyes, a tall, slight,
undeveloped figure, graceful from mere unconsciousness, awkward and angular otherwise. You could
compare her to nothing but some delicate and slender
tree of the forest that waves its fragile but hardy
branches fresh and green in spring-time, and abides
undaunted the worst blast of winter, rooted in the fis-
sures of the rock, fed by the bitterest showers, the
melting snows, the furious hail that bends but never
breaks it; perfect in its place, fitted utterly to its sur-
roundings. Her mother, the Widow Gold, was externally like her; but deep in Mindwell's heart lay a

strength of character, and acuteness of judgment, the elder woman did not possess, and a reticence that forbade her to express sympathy, even with her mother's sorrow, further than by that reluctant blush; for sympathy implied an expression of her love for her husband, — a hidden treasure she could not profane by speech, which found its only demonstration in deeds, and was the chief spring of her active and devoted life as wife and mother.

Mrs. Gold had been a happy woman, as she said, while her husband lived, and had not yet ceased to reproach herself for mourning him so bitterly. The religion of New England at that time was of a stern type : it demanded a spiritual asceticism of its followers, and virtually forbade them to enjoy the blessings of this life by keeping them in horrid and continual dread of "the pains of hell forever," as their Catechism expresses it. It was their purpose to work out their own salvation with fear and trembling under the curse of the law. The gospel was a profound and awful mystery, to be longed for afar off, no more daily bread than the show-bread of the Temple.

They lived and worked, and suffered and died, with few exceptions, in an awful sense of flying time, brief probation, an angry God, a certain hell, but a very uncertain heaven. No wonder that they were austere and hard : the wonder was that even natural temperament and mental organization should ever resist this outside pressure, and give play to humor, or fancy, or passion of any sort. Yet in this faithless faith lay elements of wonderful strength. The compelling force of duty made men nobly honest, rigidly upright, just, as far as their narrow views allowed, and true to the outward relations of this life, however they violated their inner principle and meaning. Speculation, defalcation, divorce, were crimes they called by other names than these, and abhorred. Can we say as much for ourselves? However we may sneer at Puritanism, it had its strong virtues; and its outgrowth was honesty. decency, and respect for law. A share of such virtues would be worth much to us now.

Mrs. Gold was "a professor," and it behooved her to submit to the will of God when her husband died. He had been a strong, generous, warm-hearted man; and, though undemonstrative as his race, his wife had been loved and cherished as the very blossom of his life. She was a sweet, fair girl when Ethan Gold married her, clinging and dependent by nature, though education had made her a hard worker; but her fragile beauty and soft temper had attracted the strength and fervor of the man, and their short life together had been exceptionally happy. Then fever struck him down in his full prime; and their only child, a girl of six, could but just remember all her life that she once had a father whose very memory was sacred. Fifteen years of mourning, at first deeply, then steadily, at last habitually, and rather as a form than a feeling, passed away.

Ethan had left his wife with "means;" so that poverty did not vex her. And now Mindwell was a grown woman, and married to Samuel Pratt, a well-to-do young farmer of Colebrook, a hearty, jovial young fellow, whose fun and animal spirits would bubble over in spite of reproving eyes and tongues, and who came into Mindwell's restrained and reserved life like a burst of sunshine. Are the wild blossoms grateful to the

sun that draws them with powerful attraction from the
cold sod,

> " Where they together,
> All the cold weather,
> Keep house alone "?

Perhaps their odor and color are for him who brings
them to light and delight of life.   Mindwell's great
fear was that she made an idol of her husband, yet
he certainly had not an idea that she did.

If the good soul had stopped to analyze the relation
between them, his consciousness would have been
found, when formulated, to be, that his wife bore with
him as saints do with rather amusing sinners ; while he
worshipped her as even the most humorous of sinners
do sometimes secretly worship saints.   But what the
wife did not acknowledge, or the husband perceive,
became in a few years painfully perceptible to the
mother's feminine and maternal instinct.   Mindwell
treated her with all possible respect and kindness, but
she was no longer her first object.   There is a strange
hunger in the average female heart to be the one and
only love of some other heart, which lies at the root of
fearful tragedies and long agonies of unspoken pain, —
a God-given instinct, no doubt, to make the monopoly
of marriage dear and desirable, but, like all other instincts, fatal if it be not fulfilled or followed.   Utterly
wanting in men, who grasp the pluralities of passion
as well as of office, this instinct niches itself deepest in
the gentlest of women, and was the ruling yet unrecognized motive in the Widow Gold's character.   If Mindwell had not had children, perhaps her mother would
have been more necessary to her, and more dear ; but
two babies had followed on her marriage within three

years, and her mother-love was a true passion. This
the grandmother perceived with a tender jealousy fast
growing acute. She loved the little girls, as grandmothers do, with unreasoning and lavish fondness. If
there had been a maiden aunt in the family, — that
unconsidered maid-of-all-work, whose love is felt to be
intrusive, while yet the demands on it are insatiable, —
the Widow Gold would have had at least one sympathetic breast to appeal to; but as it was she became
more and more uneasy and unhappy, and began to
make herself wretched with all the commonplaces she
could think of, — about her "room being better than
her company," "love runs down, not up," and the
like, — till she was really pining, when just at this
moment an admirer came upon the scene, and made
known the reason of his appearance in a business-like
way.

"Deacon Flint's in the keepin'-room, mother, wish-
ful to see you," said Mindwell one day, about five
years after her marriage. Deacon Flint was an old
acquaintance, known to Mrs. Gold ever since she was
a girl in Bassett. When she married, and moved to
Denslow, the acquaintance had been partly dropped,
though only nine miles lay between them; but she had
then her family cares, and Ethan Gold and Amasa
Flint were as unlikely to be friends as a Newfoundland
dog and a weasel. Since she had come to Colebrook
to live with her daughter, she was a little farther still
from her Bassett friends, and therefore it was a long
time since she had seen the deacon. Meanwhile he
had lost his wife, a silent and sickly woman, who crept
about and worried through her daily duties for years,
spent and fainting when the last supper-dish was

washed, and aching at early dawn when she had to get
up to milk. She did not complain : her duty lay there,
in her home, and she did it as long as she could — then
she died. This is a common record among our barren
hills, which count by thousands their unknown and
unsung martyrs. It was a year after her death when
Deacon Flint made his first visit to Widow Gold. He
was tired of paying Aunt Polly Morse seventy-five
cents a week to do housework, though she spun and
wove, and made and mended, as faithfully as his wife
had done, confiding only to one trusty ear her opinion
of her employer.

"He's a professor, ye know, Isr'el, and I make no
doubt but what he's a good man ; but he is dreadful
near. Seems as if he reelly begrutched me my vittles
sometimes ; and there ain't a grain o' salt in that house
spilt without his findin' of it out. Now, I don't calc'late
to spill no salt, nor nothin' else, to waste it ; but, land's
sakes ! I can't see like a fly, so's to scare up every
mite of sugar that's left onto the edges of the paper he
fetches it hum in. I wish to gracious he'd get somebody else. I'd ruther do chores for Mirandy Huff
than for the deacon."

Old Israel's wrinkled face, puckered mouth, and
deep-set eyes, twitched with a furtive laugh. He was
the village fool, yet shrewder than any man who stopped
to jest with him, and a fool only in the satiric sense
of jester ; for though he had nothing of his own but a
tiny brown house and pig-pen, and made his living,
such as it was, by doing odd jobs, and peddling yeast
from the distilleries at Simsbury, he was the most independent man in Bassett, being regardless of public
opinion, and not at all afra'd of Parson Roberts.

"Well, Aunt Polly," he answered, "you stay by a spell: the deacon won't want ye too long. He's got a sharp eye, now I tell ye, and he's forehanded as fury Fust you know, Miss Flint'll *come* home, and you'll *go* home."

"Miss Flint!" screamed Aunt Polly. "Why, Isr'el Tucker, you give me such a turn! Poor cretur, she's safe under the mulleins this year back. I guess I shall go when she comes, but 'twon't be till the day o' judgment."

"Then the day o' judgment's near by, Aunt Polly; and I reckon it is for one poor cretur. But you don't somehow seem to take it in. I tell ye the deacon's gone a-courtin'."

"Courtin'! Isr'*el!* you be a-foolin' of me now, certain sure."

"Not a mite on't. I see him a-'ilin' up his old harness yesterday, and a-rubbin' down the mare, and I mistrusted he was up to suthin. And Squire Battle he met him a'most to Colebrook this mornin': I heerd him say so. I put this 'n' that together, and drawed my own influences; and I figgered out that he's gone to Colebrook to see if Widder Gold won't hev him. A wife's a lot cheaper than hired help, and this one's got means."

"For mercy's sakes! You don't suppose Sarepty Gold would look at him, do ye?"

"I never see the woman yet that wouldn't look at a man when he axed her to," was the dry answer. But Aunt Polly was too stunned with her new ideas to retort. She went on, as if the sneer at her sex had not reached her ear, —

"Why, she ha'n't no need to marry him: she's

got a good home to Sam Pratt's. And there's that farm here that Hi Smith runs on shares, and money in Har'ford bank, they do say. She won't have him: don't ye tell me so."

" Women are mortal queer," replied old Israel.

" If they wa'n't, there wouldn't no men get married," snapped Aunt Polly, who was a contented old maid, and never suspected she was " queer " herself.

" That's so, Aunt Polly. Mabbe it's what Parson Roberts calls a dispensation, and I guess it is. I say for't, a woman must be extry queer to marry Amasy Flint, ef she's even got a chance at Bassett poor-house."

Yet Israel was right in his prophecy. At that very moment Deacon Flint was sitting bolt-upright in a high-backed chair in Sam Pratt's keeping-room, discoursing with the Widow Gold.

Two people more opposite in aspect could hardly be found. Mrs. Gold was not yet fifty, and retained much of her soft loveliness. Her cheek was still round and fair, her pale brown hair but slightly lined with gray, and the mild light of her eyes shone tenderly yet; though her figure was a little bent, and her hands knotted with work.

She looked fair and young in comparison with the grizzled, stern, hard-favored man before her. A far-off Scotch ancestry had bequeathed to him the high check-bones and deep-set eyes that gave him so severe an aspect; and to these an aquiline nose, a cruel, pinched mouth, a low forehead, and a sallow, wrinkled skin, added no charms. But the charm of old association brought him a welcome here. Bassett was the home of Mrs. Gold's childhood, and she had a great many questions to ask. Her face gath

ered color and light as she recalled old affections and
sympathies ; and the deacon took a certain satisfaction
in looking at her. But this was a mere ripple above
his serious intention. He meant business, and could
not waste time : so, as soon as there came a little lull
in Mrs. Gold's fluent reminiscences, he curtly began, —

"I came over to-day on an arrand, Miss Gold, — I
may say quite a ser'ous arrand. I lost my companion,
I suppose ye know, a year ago come September the
10th. She was a good woman, Miss Flint was, savin'
and reasonable as ever was."

"I always heard her well spoke of," modestly rejoined the widow.

"Yes, her children praise her in the gates, — or they
would hev, if she'd had any. I feel her loss. And
Scripter says, 'It is not good for man to be alone.'
Scripter is right. You are a woman that's seen affliction too, Miss Gold : you've passed under the rod.
Well, folks must be resigned : professors like you and
me have got to set example. We can't fault the Lord
when he takes our companions away, and say, ' Why do
ye so?' as though 'twas a man done it. We've got
this treasure in earthen vessels. Well, to come to the
p'int, I come over to-day to see ef you wa'n't willin'
to consider the subject of uniting yourself to me in the
bonds of marriage."

"Oh!" said the astonished widow.

"I don't want to hurry ye none," he went on :
"take time on't. I should like to get my answer right
off ; but I can make allowance for bein' onexpected.
I'll come agin next week — say this day week. I
hope you'll make it a subject of prayer, and I expect
you'll get light on your duty by that time. I've got

a good house and a good farm, and I'll do well by ye.
And, moreover and besides, you know Mr. Pratt's
folks are pressed some for room. I expect. I guess
they won't stand in the way of your goin' to Bassett.
Good-day, good-day."

And the widow received a calm up-and-down hand-
shake, with which decorous caress the deacon — for
we cannot call him the lover — departed, leaving Mrs.
Gold in a state of pleased amazement, partly because
she was a woman and a widow, partly because it was
Deacon Flint who had asked her to marry him ; for
the deacon was a pillar in Bassett church, owned a
large farm and a goodly square house, and was a
power in the State, having twice been sent to the General Assembly. She could not but be gratified by the
preference, and as she pondered on the matter it grew
more feasible. Her girl was hers no longer, but a
wife and mother herself ; and she who had been all in
all to Mindwell was now little more than "grandma"
in the house, — a sort of suffered and necessary burden
on Samuel's hands. But here a home of her own was
offered her, a place of dignity among other women, —
a place where she could ask her children to come to
her, and give rather than receive.

There is nothing so attractive to a woman who is no
longer young as the idea of a home. The shadow of
age and its infirmities affrights her ; loneliness is a
terror in the future ; and the prospect of drifting about
here and there, a dependent, poor, proud, unwelcome,
when flesh and heart fail, and the ability to labor is
gone, makes any permanent shelter a blessed prospect, and draws many a woman into a far more dreadful fate than the work-house mercies or the colder char
ity of relatives.

This terror was strong in Mrs Gold's feeble heart. She was one of the thousands of women who cannot trust what they do not see, and she misjudged her daughter cruelly. Mindwell felt that to-day, as her mother avowed to her Deacon Flint's offer and her own perplexities. When Mrs. Gold asserted that her daughter could never understand what it was to lose a husband, Mindwell felt a sure but unspoken conviction that the terror of such a bereavement, which confronted her whenever her heart leaped up to meet Samuel, was experience enough for her to interpret thereby the longings of a real bereavement; but she only colored faintly, and answered, —

"Well, mother, I don't see my way clear to offer you any advice. You must use your own judgment. You know Samuel and me think every thing of having you here; and the children just begin to know grandma by heart. But I don't want to be self-seeking: if it's for your best good, why, we sha'n't neither of us say a word. I don't skerce know how to speak about it, it's so strange like and sudden. I can't say no more than this: if you're going to be happier and better off with Deacon Flint than with your own folks, we haven't no right to hinder you, and we won't."

Mindwell turned away with trembling lips, silent, because strong emotion choked her. If she had fallen on her mother's neck and wept, and begged her to stay, with repeated kisses and warm embrace, Mrs. Gold never would have become Mrs. Flint; but she could not appreciate Mindwell's feeling. She took her conscientious self-control and candor for indifference, and her elderly lover loomed through this mist in grander proportions than ever. She resolved then and there that it was her duty to accept him.

Mindwell had gone down stairs to find her husband, who sat by the fire, fitting a rake-tail more firmly into a hay-rake. He had been caught in a distant field by a heavy shower, and was steaming now close to the fireplace, where a heap of chips was lighted to boil the kettle for tea. Mindwell stole up to him, and laid one hand on his handsome head. He looked up, astonished at the slight caress, and saw his wife's eyes were full of tears.

"What's the matter, darling?" he said in his cheery voice. It was like a kiss to her to have him say "darling," for sweet words were rare among their class; and this was the only one he ever used, kept sacredly, too, for Mindwell.

"O Sam!" she answered, with a quiver in her delicate voice, "don't you think, Deacon Flint wants to marry mother!"

"Thunder an' guns! You don't mean it, wife? Haw, haw, haw! It's as good as a general trainin'. Of all things! What does she say to't?"

"Well, I'm 'most afraid she favors him a little. He's given her a week's time to consider of it; but, someway, I can't bear to have it thought of."

"Don't pester your head about it, Miss Pratt: you can't make nor meddle in such things. But I'm free to own that I never was more beat in all my days. Why, Amasy Flint is town-talk for nearness an' meanness. He pretends to be as pious as a basket o' chips, but I hain't no vital faith in that kind o' pious. I b'lieve in my soul he's a darned old hypocrite."

"O Sam, Sam! you hadn't ought to judge folks."

"I suppose I hadn't, reelly; but you know what Scripter says somewhere or 'nother, that some folks's sins are open, an' go to judgment beforehand, and I guess his'n do. I should hate to have mother take up with him.''

" What can we do, Sam?''

" Nothin', strenoously. I don't know what 'tis about women-folks in such matters: they won't bear no more meddlin' with than a pa'tridge's nest; you'll spile the brood if you put in a finger. I'd say jest as much as I could about her bein' always welcome here. I'll do my part of that set piece o' music; and that's all we can do. If she's set on havin' him, she will; and you nor me can't stop it, Miss Pratt.'' With which sound advice, Sam rose from the milking-stool with his reconstructed rake, took down a coarse comb from the clock-case, ran it through his hair by way of toilet, and sat down to supper at the table with the three other hay-makers. Mindwell and her mother were going out to tea, so they did not sup with the men.

After they came home, Sam expressed himself in a succinct but forcible manner to Mrs. Gold on the subject of her marriage, and Mindwell attempted a faint remonstrance again; but her morbid fear of selfishness shut the heart-throbs she longed to express to her mother back into their habitual silence. She and Sam both, trying to do their best, actually helped, rather than hindered, this unpropitious marriage.

Mrs. Gold, in her heart, longed to stay with her children, but feared and disliked so heartily to be a burden on their hands, that she was unjust to herself and them too. A little less self-inspection, and a little more simple honesty of speech, would have settled this matter in favor of Mindwell and Colebrook: as it was,

Deacon Flint carried the day. On the Friday following he arrived for his answer ; his gray hair tied in a
long cue, his Sunday coat of blue, and brass buttons,
his tight drab pantaloons, ruffled shirt, and low boots,
all indicating a ceremonial occasion.

"Gosh," said old Israel Tucker, jogging along in
his yeast-cart, as he met the gray mare in clean harness, whipped up by the deacon in this fine raiment, the
old wagon itself being for once washed and greased, —
"gosh ! it's easy tellin' what he's after. I should think
them mulleins an' hardhacks in the buryin'-ground
would kinder rustle round. I don't know, though ;
mabbe Miss Flint's realized by now that she's better
off under them beauties of natur' than she ever was in
Amasy Flint's house. Good land ! what fools women-
folks be ! They don't never know when they're well
off. She's had an easy time along back ; but she's
seen the last on't, she's seen the last on't. — Get up,
Jewpiter."

Nothing daunted by any mystic or magnetic sense of
this vaticination by the highway, Deacon Flint whipped
up his bony steed still more, and to such good purpose
that he arrived in Colebrook before the widow had
taken down the last pinned-up curl on her forehead, or
decided which of her two worked collars she would put
on, and whether it would be incongruous to wear a
brooch of blue enamel with a white centre, on which
was depicted (in a fine brown tint produced by grinding up in oil a lock of the deceased Ethan Gold's hair)
a weeping-willow bending over a tomb, with an urn,
and a date on the urn. This did seem a little personal
on such an occasion : so she pinned on a blue bow instead, and went down to receive the expecting deacon.

"I hope I see you well, ma'am," said Mr. Flint.

"Comfortably well, I'm obleeged to you," was the prim answer.

But the deacon was not to be daunted at this crisis: he plunged valiantly into the middle of things at once. "I suppose you've took into consideration the matter in hand, Miss Gold?"

The widow creased her handkerchief between her finger and thumb, and seemed to be critical about the hemming of it; but she pretty soon said softly, "Yes, I can't say but what I have thought on't a good deal. I've counselled some with the children too."

"Well, I hope you're fit and prepared to acknowledge the leadin's of Providence to this end, and air about ready to be my companion through the valley of this world up to them fields beyond the swellin' flood stands dressed in livin' green. Amen."

The deacon forgot he was not in a prayer-meeting, and so dropped into the hymn-book, as Mr. Wegg did into secular poetry.

"H'm, well there's a good deal to be thought of for and ag'inst it too," remarked Mrs. Gold, unwilling to give too easy an assent, and so cheapen herself in the eyes of her acute adorer. But, when her thoughts were sternly sifted down, they appeared to be slight matters; and the deacon soon carried his point. He wasted no time in this transaction. Having "shook hands on it," as he expressed himself, he proceeded at once to arrange the programme.

"Well, Sarepty, we're both along in years, and to our time o' life delays is dangerous. I think we'd better get married pretty quick. I'm keepin' that great lazy Polly Morse, and payin' out cash right along; and you no need to fix up any, you've got good clothes enough: besides, what's clothes to worms of the dust sech as we be? The Catechism says ' Man's chief end is to glorify God and enjoy him forever;' and if that's so, — and I expect 'tis so, — why, 'tain't nothin' to be concerned about what our poor dyin' bodies is clothed in."

Mrs. Gold did not agree with him at all. She liked her clothes, as women ought to; but his preternatural piety awed her, and she said meekly enough, " Well, I don't need no great of gowns. I sha'n't buy but one, I don't believe."

A faint color stole to her cheek as she said it, for she meant a wedding-dress; and Deacon Flint was acute enough to perceive it, and to understand that this was a point he could not carry.

" One gown ain't neither here nor there, Sarepty; but I aim to fix it on your mind, that, as I said afore, delays is dangerous. I purpose, with the divine bless-in', to be married this day two weeks. I suppose you're agreeable?" The widow was too surprised to deny this soft impeachment; and he went on, " Ye see, there's papers to be drawed up: you've got inde-pendent means, and so have I, and it's jest as well to settle things fust as last. Did Ethan Gold leave you a life-int'rest in your thirds, or out an' out?"

The widow's lip trembled: her dead husband had been careful of her, more careful than she knew, till now.

" He didn't will me no thirds at all: he left me use an' privilege, for my nateral life, of every thing that was his'n, and all to go to Mindwell when I'm gone."

" Do tell! He was forehanded, I declare for't!"

exclaimed the deacon, both pleased and displeased; for, if his wife's income was to be greater than he supposed, in case of her death before his there would be no increase to his actual possessions.

"Well, I always calc'lated you had your thirds, an' prob'ly, knowin' Ethan was free-handed, you had 'em out an' out. This makes some difference about what papers I'll have to have drawed up. Now, I guess the best way is to have a agreement like this: I agree not to expect to hev an' to hold none of your property, an' you don't none of mine; but I to have the use of your'n, and you to have your livin' out o' mine. You see, you don't have no more'n your livin' out of your'n now: that's all we any of us get in this here world. 'Hevin' food an' raiment, let us therewith be content,' as Scripter says. You agree to this, don't ye?"

Bewildered with the plausible phrases ballasted by a text, unaware that even the Devil can quote Scripture to serve his turn, Mrs. Gold did not see that she was putting herself entirely into the hands of this man, and meekly agreed to his arrangement. If this story were not absolutely true, I should scarce dare to invent such a character as Deacon Flint. But he was once a living man, and hesitating to condemn him utterly, being now defenceless among the dead, we can but hope for him and his like that there are purifying fires beyond this life, where he may be melted and refined into the image of Him who made him a man, and gave him a long life here to develop manhood. Not till after he was gone did Mrs. Gold begin to think that he had left her to explain his arrangements to Mindwell and Sam, and instinctively she shrank from doing so. Like many another weak woman, she hated words, particularly hard words. Her life had flowed on in a gentle routine, so peacefully that she had known but one sorrow, and that was so great, that, with the propensity we all have to balance accounts with Providence, she thought her trouble had been all she could bear. But there was yet reserved for her that sharp attrition of life which is so different from the calm and awful force of sorrow, — so much more exasperating, so much more educating. Some instinct warned her to avoid remonstrance by concealing from her children the contract she was about to make, and she felt, too, the uncertainty of a woman unaccustomed to business, about her own clear understanding of the situation. So she satisfied herself with telling Mindwell of the near approach of her marriage.

"O mother, so soon!" was all Mindwell said, though her eyes and lips spoke far more eloquently.

"Well, now the thing's settled, I don't know but what it may as well be over with. We ain't young folks, Mindwell. 'Tain't as if we had quite a spell to live."

Tears stood in her eyes as she said it. A certain misgiving stole over her: just then it seemed a good thing that she could not live long.

Mindwell forced back the sob that choked her. A woman of single heart, she did not consider a second marriage sacred. For herself, she would rather have taken her children to the town-farm, cold as corporative charity is, than married another man than Samuel, even if he had been dead thirty years ; and she bitterly resented this default of respect to her father's memory. But her filial duty came to the rescue.

"Dear mother, I can't bear to think of it. What shall I do? What will the children say? I did hope you would take time to consider."

" It ain't real dutiful in you to take me to do, Mind-well: I'm full old to be lessoned, seems to me. As for you and the children, I don't feel no great distress : love runs down, not up, folks say ; and I don't believe you'll any of ye pine a long spell."

This weak and petulant outburst dismayed Mindwell, who had never seen her mother otherwise than gentle and pleasant; but, with the tact of a great heart, she said nothing, only put her arms about the elder woman's neck, and kissed her over and over. At this, Mrs. Gold began to cry ; and, in soothing her distress, Mind-well forgot to ask any further questions, but set herself to divert both their minds from this brief and bitter outburst by inquiring what preparation her mother meant to make in the fortnight.

" I don't look to no great preparation," sighed the widow. " I have always had good clothes enough, and there's a piece of linen I wove before we come here that'll do for all I want. I suppose I had ought to have a new gown to be married in. When I was married to Ethan, I had a white dimity gown and a blue levantine petticoat; and if he didn't fetch me a big bunch of sand-violets — they was blossoming then — for to match my eyes and my skirt, he said. But that's past and gone, as the hymn-book says. I do want to have one good gown, Mindwell ; and, now I'm a little along in years, I guess I'll have a dark one. T'other night, when we was up to Squire Barnes's to tea, Miss Barnes was telling about a piece of plum-colored paduasoy Mr. Battle bought in Har'ford for 'Lecty's weddin'-gown, and she wouldn't hev it. She said 'twasn't lively enough, and so she's set her mind on a blue levantine. But I should think the plum-color vould become me real well."

So the plum-colored silk was bought; and arrayed in
its simple folds, with a new worked collar and a white
satin bow, the Widow Gold was dressed for her second
wedding.

Did she think, as she looked into her oval mirror
that morning, what a different vision was this quiet,
elderly, sober woman, in decent but not festal garments, from the smiling, blushing, blue-eyed creature
in her spotless dimity gown opening over a blue petticoat, and clasped at the throat with a bunch of still
bluer violets? What does a woman think who is married the second time? A man is satisfied that now his
house will be kept once more, his clothes mended, his
whims humored, his table spread to his taste, and
his children looked after. If it is needful, he can
marry six wives one after the other. They are a domestic necessity: the Lord himself says it is not good
for *man* to be alone. But it is quite another thing for
the woman. Such a relation is not a movable feast to
her: it is once for all; and, if circumstance or pique
betray her into this faithlessness, what does she think
of herself when it becomes inevitable?

The Widow Gold did not tell. She was paler when
she turned from the glass than when she looked into
it: and she trembled as she went down stairs to sign
the papers before Parson Roberts should arrive.

The best parlor was opened to-day. The high-
backed chairs with old brocade cushions, that had belonged to Sam Pratt's grandmother, were ranged along
the wall like a row of stiff ghosts ; the corner-cupboards
were set open to display the old china and glass that
filled them ; there was a " bow-pot " of great red
peonies, abundant and riotous with color and fatness,

set under the chimney in the well-whited fireplace; and
a few late roses glowed in a blue china jar on the high
mantelpiece.   On a square table with a leaf lay a legal
paper that Sam was reading, with his hands supporting
his head as if it was hard to understand the document.

The deacon, in his Sunday garments, was looking at
him askance; and Mindwell, with the little girls Ede
and Sylvia clinging to her gown, was staring out of
the window, down the road, — staring, but not seeing;
for the splendid summer day that lavished its bloom
and verdure and odor on these gaunt New-England
hills, and hid their rude poverty with its royal mantle,
was all a dim blur to the heart-wrung woman.

"Mother," said Sam Pratt, raising his head, "do
you know what's the sum and substance of these here
papers? and do you agree to't?"

The widow glanced aside at Deacon Flint, and caught
his "married eye," early as it was to use that ocular
weapon.

"Why, yes, Samwell: I don't know but what I
do," she said slowly and rather timidly.

"Well," said Sam, rising, and pushing the paper
away, "if you do, why, then you're going right into't,
and it's right, I s'pose; but, by Jinks! I think it's the
d—"

Mindwell's touch on his arm arrested the sentence.
'There's Parson Roberts, Samwell. You jest help
him out of the gig, will you? He's quite lame, I see."

Sam Pratt went, with the half-finished sentence on
his lips. He was glad his wife had stopped him, on
many accounts; but he did long to give Deacon Flint
his own opinion of that preliminary contract.

He indulged himself for this deprivation, after the

stiff and somewhat melancholy wedding was over, and
the staid couple had departed for Bassett in the deacon's
wagon, by freeing his mind to his wife.

"Miss Pratt, I was some riled to hev you stop me
when I was a-goin' to tell the deacon what I thought
about that there contrack; but I don't never stay riled
with you, marm, as you'd ought to know by this time."
And Sam emphasized this statement with a hearty kiss.
"Besides, I will own on second thoughts I was glad
you did stop me; for it's no use pinchin' your fingers
in a pair o' nippers. But I do say now and here, it
was the darndest piece o' swindlin' I ever see, — done
under a cover of law an' gospel, you may say; for the
deacon had stuck in a bit of Scripter so's to salt it like.
He's got the best of the bargain, I tell ye, a long sight.
I'm real glad your father went and fixed that prop'ty
so she has the use on't only; for she wouldn't have two
cents in two years' time, if she'd had it to do with what
she's a mind to."

"I am glad he did," said Mindwell. "I have felt
as though mother would be better suited if she did have
it to do what she liked to with; but if this was to
happen, why, it's as good she is provided for. She
can't want for nothing now."

"I guess she'll want for more'n money, and mabbe
for that too. The paper says she's to have her livin'.
Now, that's a wide word. Folks can live on bread and
water, I expect; and he can't be holden for no more
than he's a mind to give."

"O Sam, you don't think Deacon Flint would
grudge her a good living? Why, if he is near, as folks
tell he is, he's a professor of religion."

"I'd a durned sight ruther he was a practiser on't,

Miss Pratt. Religion's about the best thing there is, and makin' believe it is about the wust. I b'lieve in Amasy Flint's religion jest so far forth as I hear him talk, an' not a inch farther. I know he'll pinch an' shave an' spare to the outside of a cheese-rind; and I haven't no great reason to think he'll do better by Mother Gold than he does by himself." Mindwell turned away, full of foreboding; and Sam, following her, put his arm about her, and drew her back to the settle.

"Don't worry, dear. She's made her bed, and she's got to lie on't. But, after all, it's the Lord who lets folks do that way, so's to show 'em, I expect, that beds ain't always meant to sleep on, but sometimes to wake folks up. We're kind of apt to lie long an' get lazy on feathers. I expect that's what's the matter with me. I'll get my husks by and by, I guess."

Mindwell looked up at him, with all her heart in her eyes; but she said nothing, and he gave a shy laugh. Their deep love for each other was "a fountain shut up;" and so far no angel had rolled away the stone, and given it visible life. It was still voiceless and sleeping.

Before her wedding-day was over, Mrs. Flint's new life began; for Polly Morse had been sent off the night before, being the end of an even week, lest she might charge ninepence for an extra day. So her successor without wages had to lay aside her plum-colored silk, put on a calimanco petticoat and short-gown, and proceed to get supper; while Polly, leaning over the half-door of the old red house which she shared with the village tailoress, exchanged pungent remarks with old Israel on the topic of the day in Bassett.

"No, they didn't make no weddin', Isr'el. There wa'n't nobody asked, nor no loaf-cake made for her: he wouldn't hear to't, noway. I'd have staid and fixed up for her to-day; but he was bound I shouldn't. As for me, I'm most amazin' glad to get hum, now I tell ye. I'd a sight ruther be in Simsbury prison for a spell, if it wa'n't for the name on't."

"Say, Polly, do you call to mind what I said three weeks back about Miss Flint comin' home? Oh! ye do, do ye? Well, I ain't nobody's fool, be I? I guess I can see through a millstone, providin' the hole's big enough, as well as the next man. I'm what ye may call mighty observin', now. I can figger consider'ble well on folks, ef I can't on 'rithmetic; and I know'd jest as well, when I see him rigged up in his sabba'-day go-to-meetin's, and his nose p'inted for Colebrook, what he was up to, as though I heerd him a-askin' her to hev him."

"Well, I never did think Sarepty Gold would demean herself to have him. She's got means and a real good home; and Mindwell sets a sight by her, and so does Sam Pratt: but here she's ben an' gone an' done it. I wouldn't ha' thought it, not if th' angel Gabriel had have told me on't."

"Guess he's in better business than goin' round with Bassett gossip, anyhow. But what was you so took back by? Lordy! I should think you was old enough to git over bein' surprised at women-folks: them and the weather is two things I don't never calc'late on. You can't no more tell what a woman'll do, 'specially about marryin', than you can tell which way in the road a pig'll go, onless you work it back'ard, same as some folks tell they drive a pig; and then 'tain't reel reli-

able : they may go right ahead when you don't a mite
expect it.''

"That is one thing about men, I allow, Isr'el : you
can always tell which way they'll go for sartain ; and
that is after their own advantage, an' nobody else's,
now an' forever.''

"Amen ! They'd be all fools, like me, if they
didn't,'' assented the old man, with a dry chuckle, as
he drove off his empty cart. Yet, for all his sneers and
sniffs, neither Polly nor the new Mrs. Flint had a truer
friend than Israel. Rough as he was, satiric as a chestnut burr that shows all its prickles in open defiance,
conscious of a sweet white heart within, his words only
were bitter : his nature was generous, kindly, and perceptive. He had become the peripatetic satirist and
philosopher that he was out of this very nature,

"Dowered with a scorn of scorn, a love of love,"

and free with the freedom of independent poverty to
express pungently what he felt poignantly, being in his
own kind and measure the "salt of the earth" to
Bassett.

But, in spite of comment and pity, the thing was a
fixed fact. Mrs. Flint's married life had begun under
new auspices, and it was not a path of roses upon
which she had entered. Her housekeeping had always
been frugal, with the thrift that is or was characteristic
of her race ; but it had been abundant for the wants of
her family. The viands she provided were those of
the place and period, simple and primitive enough ; but
the great brick oven was well filled with light bread of
wheat and rye both ; pies of whatever material was in
season, whose flaky crust and well-filled interiors testi-

fied to her knowledge of the art; deep dishes of baked beans; jars of winter pears; pans of golden-sweet apples; and cards of yellow gingerbread, with rows of snowy and puffy biscuit. Ede and Sylvia knew very well where to find crisp cookies and fat nut-cakes; and pie was reiterated three times a day on Sam Pratt's table.

It was a part of her "pride of life" that she was a good housekeeper; and Mindwell had given her the widest liberty. But now the tide had changed. She soon found that Deacon Flint's parsimony extended into every detail. Her pies were first assailed.

"Sarepty, don't make them pies o 'your'n so all-fired rich. They ain't good for the stomach: besides, they use up all the drippin's, and you had ought to make soap next month. Pie is good, and I think it's savin' of meat. But it pompers up the flesh, too good livin' does; and we hev got to give an account, ye know. I don't mean to have no wicked waste laid to my account."

So she left out half the shortening from her crust, and felt ashamed to see the tough substance this economy produced. Next came the sugar question.

"We buy too much sweetenin', Sarepty. There's a keg of tree-molasses down cellar. I expect it's worked some; but you jest take an' bile it up, an' stir consider'ble saleratus into't, an' it'll do. I want to get along jest as reasonable as we can. Wilful waste makes woful want, ye know."

Yet in his own way the deacon was greedy enough. He had the insatiable appetite that belongs to people of his figure far more often than to the stout.

"He's a real racer," said Uncle Israel, reverting to

his own experience in pigs, — "slab-sided an' lank.
I bet you could count his ribs this minnit ; and that's
the kind you can feed till the day after never, and they
won't do ye no credit. I never see a man could punish
vittles the way he can ; but there ain't no more fat to
him than there is to a hen's forehead."

Mrs. Flint was not "hungry nor hankering," as she
expressed it, but a reasonable eater of plain food ; but
the deacon's mode of procedure was peculiar.

"Say, Sarepty, don't bile but a small piece o' pork
with that cabbage to-day. I've got a pain to my head,
an' I don't feel no appetite ; an' cold pork gets eat up
for supper when there ain't no need on't."

Obeying instructions, the small piece of fat pork
would be cooked, and, once at the table, transferred
bodily to the deacon's plate. "Seems as though my
appetite had reelly come back. I guess 'twas a hungry headache." And the tired woman had to make
her dinner from cabbage and potatoes seasoned with
the salt and greasy water in which they had been
cooked.

There were no amusements for her out of the house.
The younger people had their berrying frolics, sleigh-
rides, kitchen-dances, nuttings, and the like ; and their
elders, their huskings, apple-bees, and sewing-societies :
but against all these the deacon set his hard face.

"It's jest as good to do your own extry chores yourself as to ask folks to come an' help. That costs
more'n it comes to. You've got to feed 'em, and like
enough keep a big fire up in the spare room. I'd ruther
be diligent in business, as Scripter says, than depend
on neighbors."

The sewing society, too, was denied to poor Mrs

Flint, because they had to have tea got for them
Prayer-meetings he could not deny her; for they cost
nothing, and officially he attended them.   Meeting on
Sunday was another outlet, when she could see friendly
faces, receive kind greetings, and read in many eyes a
sympathy and pity that at once pleased and exasperated her.

Another woman in her place might have had spirit
or guile enough to have resisted the pressure under
which she only quailed and submitted.   She was one
of those feeble souls to whom a hard word is like a
blow, and who will bear any thing and every thing
rather than be found fault with, and who necessarily
become drudges and slaves to those with whom they
live, and are despised and ill-treated simply because
they are incapable of resentment.   There are some
persons who stand in this position not so much from
want of strength as from abounding and eager affection for those whom they serve; and their suffering,
when they discover how vain has been their labor and
self-sacrifice, is known only to Him who was

> "At once denied, betrayed, and fled
> By those who shared his daily bread."

But Mrs. Flint had no affection for her husband: she
married him because it seemed a good thing to do, and
obeyed him because he was her husband, as was the
custom in those days.   So she toiled on dumbly from
day to day, half fed, overworked, desperately lonely,
but still uncomplaining; for her constitution was naturally strong, and nerves were unrecognized then.

Her only comfort was the rare visits of her children.
Mindwell found it hard to leave home; but, suspicious

of her mother's comfort, she made every effort to see
her as often as possible, and always to carry her some
little present, — a dozen fresh eggs, which the poor
woman boiled privately, and ate between her scanty
meals, a few peaches, or a little loaf of cake, — small
gifts, merely to demonstrate her feeling. She did not
know what good purpose they served, for Mrs. Flint
did not tell her daughter what she endured. She
remembered too well how Mindwell had begged her to
delay and consider her marriage; and she would not
own to her now that she had made any mistake: for
Mrs. Flint had as much human nature in her composi-
tion as the rest of us; and who does like to hear even
their dearest friend say, " I told you so " ?

Matters went on in this way for five years, every
day being a little more weary and dreary than the pre-
ceding. The plum-colored paduasoy still did duty as
the Sunday gown, for none of her own money ever
passed into Mrs. Flint's hands. By this time she
understood fully what her ante-nuptial contract meant.
She had her living, and no more. People could live
without finery, even without warmth. A stuff gown of
coarse linsey-woolsey for winter wear replaced the soft
merinoes she had always bought for that purpose; and
homespun linen check was serviceable in summer,
though it kept her busy at flax-wheel and loom many
an hour. She had outlived the early forbearances of
her married life, and learned to ask, to beg, to persist
in entreating, for what she absolutely needed; for only
in this way could she get her " living." Her only vivid
pleasure was in occasional visits from Ede and Sylvia,
— lovely little creatures in whom their mother's beauty
of character and their father's cheery, genial nature

seemed to combine, and with so much of Mindwell's
delicate loveliness, her sweet, dark eyes contrasted with
the fair hair of their father's family, that to grand-
motherly eyes they seemed perfectly beautiful. For
them the poor woman schemed and toiled, and grew
secretive. She hid a comb of honey sometimes, when
the deacon's back was turned, and kept it for Sylvia,
who loved honey like a real bee-bird ; she stored up red
pearmains in the parlor-closet for Ede ; and when Sam
Pratt went into Hartford with a load of wool, and
brought the children as far as Bassett to stay at Deacon Flint's over night, the poor woman would make for
them gingerbread such as they remembered, and savory
cookies that they loved, though she encountered hard
looks, and hard words too, for wasting her husband's
substance on another man's children.

Ede, who had a ready memory and a fluent tongue,
was the first to report to Mindwell these comments of
" Grandsir Flint," as they were taught to call him.

" O mother," she exclaimed, " I do think grandsir
is real mean ! "

" Edy, Edy, you mustn't talk so about your elders
and betters."

" I can't help it," chattered on the irrepressible
child. " What did he want to come into the kitchen
for when granny was giving us supper, and scold
because she made cookies for us ? Granny 'most cried ;
and he kept tellin' how he'd said before she shouldn't
do it, and he wouldn't have it."

" Don't talk about it, Edy," said her mother, full
of grief and indignation.

" Mother, it's true. I heard him too," interposed
Sylvia, who thought Ede's word was doubted ; for the

voluble and outspoken child was a little apt to embel-
lish her reports.

"Well, Sylvy dear, it isn't best to talk about a good
many things that are true."

But, for all that, Mindwell did discuss the matter
with Sam before she slept, in that "grand committee
of two" which is the strength and comfort of a happy
marriage.

"What ever can we do about it, Sam?" she said,
with tears in her voice. "I can't bear to keep the
children to home, — mother sets by 'em like her life ;
but, if they're going to make trouble between her
and Deacon Flint, don't you think I had ought to prevent their going there?"

"Well, it does seem hard on mother every way ; but
I guess I can fix it. You know we had a heap of
wheat off that east lot last year, and I've sent it to
mill to be ground up for us. I guess I'll take and
send a barrel on't over to mother for a present. The
deacon won't mistrust nothing ; nor he can't say nothing about her usin' on't for the children."

"That's the very thing," said Mindwell. And so
it was, for that small trouble ; yet that was only a drop
in the bucket. After a few years of real privation,
and a worse hunger of spirit, Mrs. Flint's health
began to fail. She grew nervous and irritable, and
the deacon browbeat her more than ever. Her temper had long since failed under the hourly exasperation of her husband's companionship, and she had
become as cross, as peevish, and as exasperating
herself as a feeble nature can become under such a
pressure.

"I never see nobody so changed as Miss Flint is,"

confided Aunt Polly to old Israel. "I've always heerd tell that 'flictions was sent for folks's good; but her'n don't seem to work that way a mite."

"Well, Polly, I expect there's a reel vital differ'nce in 'flictions, jest as there is in folks. She picked her'n up, as you may say, when she married him. 'Twan't reelly the Lord's sendin'. She no need to ha' married him, if she hadn't ben a min' to."

"I sorter thought the Lord sent every thing't happened to folks."

"Well, in a manner mabbe he doos. But don't ye rek'lect what David said, — how't he'd ruther fall inter the hands of the Lord than inter men's? I expect we're to blame for wilful sins, ain't we? And I guess we fetch 'flictions on ourselves sometimes."

"I don't see how you make them idees jibe with 'lection and fore-ordination," rejoined Aunt Polly, who was a zealous theologian, and believed the Saybrook Platform and the Assembly's Catechism to be merely a skilful abridgment and condensation of Scripture.

"I don't know as I'm called to, Polly. I don't believe the Lord's ways is jest like a primer, for everybody to larn right off. I shouldn't have no great respect for a ruler an' governor, as the Confession sez, that wa'n't no bigger'n I was. Land! ef I was to set sail on them seas o' divinity, I should be snooped up in the fust gale, an' drownded right off. I b'lieve He is good, and doos right, anyhow. Ef I can't see the way on't, why, it's 'cause my spiritooal eyes ain't big enough. I can't see into some littler things than him, and I don't hold to takin' up the sea in a pint cup: 'twon't carry it, nohow." With

which aphorism old Israel travelled off with his bar-
row, leaving Polly amazed and shocked, but perhaps
a little wiser after all.

Just about this time a cousin of Deacon Flint's died
"over in York State," as he said, and left him guardian of her only daughter, a girl of eighteen. A couple
of thousand dollars was all the property that the Widow
Eldridge had to give her child; for they had both
worked hard for their living after the husband and
father left them, and this money was the price of the
farm, which had been sold at his death. It was something to get so much cash into his own hands; and the
deacon accordingly wrote at once to Mabel, and offered
her a home in his house, intimating, that, the interest of
her money not being enough to board and clothe her,
he would, out of family affection, supply these necessities for that inadequate sum, if she was willing to help
a little about the house. Mabel was friendless enough
to grasp eagerly this hope of a home; and very soon
the stage stopped at Deacon Flint's door, and a new
inmate entered his house.

Mabel Eldridge was a capable, spirited, handsome
girl, and, before she had been a week in the Flint
family, understood her position, and resolved only to
endure it till something better could be found. In
her heart she pitied Aunt Flint, as she called her, as
much as she detested the deacon; and her fresh girlish
heart fairly ached with compassion and indignation
over the poor woman. But she was a great comfort and help while she staid; though she made that
stay as short as possible, and utterly refused to give
up her savings-bank book to the deacon, who was
unable legally to claim it, since her mother left no will,

having only asked him, in a letter written just before
her death, to act as Mabel's guardian. Her three
months' sojourn in the house made her thoroughly
aware of Deacon Flint's character and his wife's sufferings. She could not blame Mrs. Flint that she
snapped back at the deacon's snarls, or complained
long and bitterly of her wants and distresses.

"You don't know nothing what it is, Mabel," she
said one day, sobbing bitterly. "I'm put upon so
hard! I want for clothes, and for vittles, and for some
time to rest, so's't I don't know but what 'twill clean
kill me: and, if 'twa'n't for the childern, I'd wish to
die; but I do cleave to them amazingly."

Indignant tears filled Mab's eyes. "I don't know
how you bear it, aunty," she said, putting her arms
about the old lady's neck. "Can't you get away from
him anyhow?"

"I could, but I suppose I hadn't ought to. There's
a house on my farm that ain't goin' to be in use come
next April. Hiram Smith — him that's rented it along
back — wants some repairin' done on't, and Mr. Flint
won't hear to't: so Hi he's been and gone and bought
a piece of ground acrost the road, an' put up a buildin'
for himself. He's got a long lease of the land; but
he don't want the house no more, and he won't pay
for't. I s'pose I might move over there for a spell,
and have some peace. There's enough old furnitoor
there that was father's. But then, agin, I do suppose I
haven't no right to leave my husband."

"Haven't you got any right to save your life?"
indignantly asked Mabel.

"It ha'n't come to that, not quite," said Mrs. Flint
sadly.

But before April she began to think it was a matter
of life and death to stay any longer with the man.
Mabel had left her some months before, and gone
into the family of Sam Pratt's mother, in Colebrook,
promising her aunt, that, if ever the time came when
she needed her in another home, she would come and
take care of her.

Toward the middle of February Mrs. Flint was
seized with congestion of the lungs, and was very ill
indeed. A fear of public opinion made Deacon Flint
send for the doctor; but nothing could induce him to
let a nurse enter the house, or even to send for Mindwell Pratt. He was able to do for his wife, he said,
and nobody could interfere.

It was the depth of winter; and the communication
between Bassett and Colebrook was not frequent in
the best weather, neither place being dependent on the
other for supplies; and now the roads were blocked
with heavy drifts, and the inhabitants of both places
had hibernated, as New-Englanders must in winter. It
was a matter of congratulation with Deacon Flint that
he had no out-door work to do just now, and so was
spared the expense of a woman to care for his wife.
He could do it, too, more economically than a nurse.
It did not matter to him that the gruel was lumpy, or
burned, or served without flavoring. Sick folks, particularly with serious sickness, ought not to pamper the
flesh: their souls were the things to be considered.
He did not want to have Sarepta die, for she had an
income that helped him much; but he did not want
her to be a "bill of expense," as he phrased it. So
while he read the Bible to her twice a day, and prayed
to. or rather at, her by the hour, he fed her on sloppy

gruel and hard bread, sage-tea, and cold toast without butter, and just kept life flickering within her
till she could get about and help herself, unknown to
him, to draughts of fresh milk, and now and then a
raw egg.

But she did not get well: she was feeble, and
wasted a long time. The village doctor, knowing
what Deacon Flint was, and filled with pity for his
wife, called often, carefully stating that his visits were
those of a friend, but urging, also, that Mrs. Flint
should have a generous diet, and a glass of wine daily,
to restore her strength. The deacon heard him through
in silence, and when he left began to growl.

"Well, fools a'n't all dead yet. Wine! I guess
not. A good drink o' thoroughwort-tea's wuth all the
wine in creation. 'Wine's a mocker, an' strong drink
is ragin'.' Dr. Grant don't read his Bible as he'd
ought to."

"There ain't nothin' in the Bible aginst beef-tea, I
guess," feebly piped his wife. "I do feel as though
that would fetch me up. Can't you get a piece o'
meat down to the slaughter, deacon?"

"I don't see no need on't, Sarepty: you're doin'
reasonable well. Meat is reel costly; an' pomperin'
the flesh is sinful. I'll git another cod-fish next time I
go to the store: that's nourishin'. I don't hold to
Grant's idees entire. Besides, 'twa'n't nothin' what
he said: he come as a friend."

The poor woman burst into tears. Indignation gave
her momentary strength: she did not hear the shed-
door open behind her; but she rose in her chair like a
spectre, and looked at him with burning eyes.

"Amasy Flint, I b'lieve you'd a sight rather I'd die

than live. I hain't had decent vittles since I was took sick, nor no care whatever. You're a loud pray-er an' reader; but, if 'twa'n't for the name of it, I b'lieve you'd kill me with the axe instead of starvation. I've a good mind to send for Squire Battle, and swear the peace against ye."

Deacon Flint at this moment saw a shocked face behind his wife's chair: it was Polly Morse. His acuteness came to the rescue. "She's a leetle out," he said, nodding to the unexpected guest. "Come right along, Polly."

This was too much for the weak woman to bear. She fell back, and fainted. Her indignation had overborne her weakness for a moment, but exhausted it also. And, when she awoke to life, Polly was rubbing her, and crying over her; but her husband had gone. Those tears of sympathy were more than she could endure silently. She put her arms round Polly's neck, and, sobbing like a child, poured out the long list of her sorrows into that faithful ear.

"Bless your dear soul!" said Polly, wiping her eyes, "you can't tell me nothing new about him. Didn't I summer an' winter him, so to speak, afore you come here? Don't I know what killed the fust woman? 'Twa'n't no fever, ef they did call it so. 'Twas livin' with him — want o' food, an' fire, an' lovin'-kindness. Don't tell me. I pitied ye afore ye was married, an' I hain't stopped yit."

But Polly's words were not words only. From that day on, many a cup of broth, vial of currant-wine, or bit of hot stewed chicken, found its way surreptitiously to Mrs. Flint; and her strength of mind and body returned fast, with this sympathy for one, and

food for the other. She made up her mind at last
that she would leave her husband, at least for a time,
and in her own house endeavor to find the peace and
rest necessary to her entire recovery. If she could
have seen Mindwell and Sam, and taken counsel with
them, her course might have been different; but the
roads were now well-nigh impassable from deep mud,
and she could not get to Colebrook, and in sheer des-
peration she resolved to leave her present home as
soon as Hiram Smith moved from the farmhouse.
Fortunately for her, the deacon had to attend town-
meeting, three miles off, on the first Monday in April;
and, with Polly and Israel to help her, Mrs. Flint was
established in the other house before he returned, and
found her flown. His wrath was great but still. He
said and did nothing, never went near her, and, for
very shame's sake, did not speak of her — for what
could he say?

Perhaps in that solitary house, whose silence was
like balm to her weary and fevered soul, she might
have starved but for the mercy of her neighbors.
Polly Morse had a tongue of swiftness, and it never
wagged faster than in Mrs. Flint's behalf. Dr. Grant
sent half a barrel of flour to that destitute dwelling,
and Israel, a bushel of apples. Polly, out of her poverty, shared her kit of pork with the poor woman; and
Hiram Smith brought in a barrel of potatoes and a bag
of meal, which he duly charged against her account
with the farm. But there were many who dared not
help her; for the deacon held notes and mortgages on
many a house and of many a man in Bassett who could
not afford to offend him. And old Parson Roberts was
just then shut up with an attack of low fever: so he

knew nothing about the matter. However, the deacon was not long to be left nursing his wrath. Food and fire are not enough for life sometimes. The old house was leaky, damp, comfortless; and in a few weeks Mrs. Flint was taken again with disease of the lungs, and Polly Morse found her in her bed, unable to speak loud, her fire gone out, and the rain dripping down in the corner of her bedroom. Polly had come to tell her that Israel was going to Colebrook to buy a pig, and would take any message. She did not tell her, but, stepping to the door, called to him across the yard to tell Sam Pratt he must come over to Bassett directly. This done, she hunted about for something to make a fire, and then looked for the tea; but there was none. Nothing like food remained but a half-loaf of bread and some cold potatoes: so she had to break the bread up in some hot water, and feed the exhausted woman slowly, while she chafed her icy feet, and covered her closely with her own shawl. The next day Sam and Mindwell came over, shocked and indignant, their wagon loaded with provisions; and the old house was soon filled with odors of beef-broth, milk-porridge, fragrant tea and toast, and the sharp crackle of a great fire in two rooms; while, best of all, tender hands fed and soothed the poor woman, and soft filial kisses comforted her starved soul.

Mindwell could not stay, — there was a little baby at home, — but Sam would be left behind while old Israel drove her back to Colebrook, and fetched Mabel Eldridge to take her place.

Mab burst into a passion of tears when she entered the kitchen.

"I knew it!" she sobbed: "I knew that old wretch

would kill her!" And it was long before Sam could calm her anger and grief, and bring her in to the invalid.

In the course of two or three weeks, however, Mab's faithful nursing, and Sam's care and providing, brought back life and some strength to the perishing woman. And meanwhile Polly's tongue had wagged well: it flew all over Bassett that Deacon Flint's wife had left him, and almost died of cold and hunger.

To-day such a rumor would have had some direct effect on its object; but then to find fault with authorities was little less than a sin, and for a wife to leave her husband, a fearful scandal. In spite of the facts and all their witnesses, the sentiment of Bassett went with the deacon. Conjugal subjection was the fashion, or rather the principle and custom, of the day, and was to be upheld in spite of facts. However, Parson Roberts by this time had heard of the matter, and called Deacon Flint to account, thinking it to be his duty.

"This is the hull sum and substance on't, parson," explained the deacon: "Miss Flint is a miser'ble hystericky female, a dreadful weak vessel, and noways inclined to foller Scripter in the marriage-relation. I've gin her the same livin' I had myself. I hain't denied her food an' raiment wherewith she had ought to be content, as the 'Postle Poll says. But she is real pernickity, and given to the lusts of the flesh about her eatin'; and I feel it to be my dooty to be a faithful stooard of my substance, and not pomper up our poor perishin' bodies, while there is forty million more or less o' heathen creturs lyin' in wickedness in foreign parts. Ye know, parson, I hain't never stented my contributions to them things: I've ben constant to means of grace allus, and I may say a pillar — mabbe a small and creaky one, but still a pillar — in the temple sech as 'tis. I don't know as I had ought to be disturbed by this strife of tongues."

Parson Roberts was a little confounded. He himself loved a bit of good eating, — a cantle of chicken-pie, a tender roast pig, a young chicken broiled on hickory coals, or a succulent shad from the Connecticut, washed down with sparkling cider or foaming flip, — and the consciousness of this mild weakness gave undue exaltation to Deacon Flint's boasted asceticism. The parson was too honestly humble to see that Deacon Flint loved money with a greed far surpassing that of any epicure; that his own fault was but a failing, while the other was a passion. Besides, he considered that Mrs. Flint had made light of the sacred ordinance of marriage, and set an awful example to the wives of the parish: so he went away from this interview convinced that the deacon was a stern saint, and his wife a weak sinner.

Next day, however, the deacon himself was surprised by another visit. Pale and worn, clinging tight to Sam Pratt's arm, and followed by Mabel carrying a cushion, his wife entered the kitchen, where he sat devouring salt pork and potatoes with the zest of a dog who gnaws his bone unmolested.

"I come back, Amasy, to see if we couldn't agree to get along together agin," she said weakly and meekly. "I hear there's ben consider'ble talk about my leavin' on ye, and I don't want to cast no reflections. I was tired all out, an' I wanted to rest a spell. Sam an' Mab has nursed me up, so't I could get along now, I guess."

The man turned his cold green-gray eyes on her slowly. "I don't know what you want to come back for now," he said.

"Why, I want for to do my duty so far as I can."

"You had oughter have considered that afore you went off," was the dogged answer.

Tears ran down the poor woman's face: she could not speak. Mabel's beautiful eyes blazed with wrath: she made a step forward; but Sam Pratt gently put her back, and said, —

"Look here, Deacon Flint. Mother left you because she hadn't food, nor care, nor nothing she needed, nyther when she was sick, nor when she was gettin' better. She thought a spell o' rest would do her good. She knowed by that smart contrack you got out of her that you owed her a livin' anyhow; and you hain't done a thing to'rds it sence she went to her own house. Now, I don't call that conduct honest, by no means, much less Christian."

"Jedge not, Samwell Pratt. Scripter, no less'n statoot law, commands a wife to be subjeck to her husband. Sarepty had what I had. I done what I jedged best for her; and, instead of submittin' to her head, she up and went off to live by herself, and lef' me to git along as I could. I wa'n't noway bound by no law nor no contrack to supply her with means, so long as she went away from her dooties, and made me an astonishment an' a hissin' in Israel, so to speak."

"Stop right there!" broke in Mabel, furious. "I've heard say the Devil could f'tch Scripter to further his own purposes, and I b'lieve it. Didn't you have no duties to your wife? Don't the Bible say you've got to love and cherish her? Don't tell me! I lived here

long enough to see you starve and browbeat and torment her. I know your mean, hateful, crabbed ways ;
and I don't know how she lived with you so long. She
ought to have run away years ago ; and, if folks do hiss
at you, it's more'n time they did. Christian ! — *you* a
Christian ! You're a dyed-in-the-wool hypocrite. If
you're pious, I hope I shall be a reprobate."

"I ha'n't no doubt but what you will be, young
woman," answered the deacon with cold fury.
" You'd ought to be put under the pump this minnit,
for a common scold. Get out of my house, right
off ! ' "

And with this he advanced upon her. But Sam
Pratt, lifting the old lady in his arms, carried her away,
and gently shoved Mabel, glowing with rage, before
them till they reached the wagon. Then he himself
went back, and tried to make terms with the deacon.
At last, moved by the worldly wisdom of Sam's argument, that it would put him in a bad light before people if he refused to do any thing for his wife, he did
agree to let her have half of his share of the produce
from her farm, if Sam and Mindwell would provide for
her other wants. And, making the best of a bad bargain, the poor woman retired to the old house, which
Sam had repaired, so that most of it was habitable ;
and Mabel, who had agreed to teach the district school
the next year, took up her abode with her.

Now the deacon had a clear field, and appeared in
the arena of Bassett in the character of an injured and
forsaken husband. His prayers at meeting were longer
and more eloquent than ever ; and the church, sympathizing with his sorrows, — the male members especially deprecating Mrs. Flint's example, lest it should

some time be followed by their own wives, — unanimously agreed to withdraw their fellowship from Mrs.
Flint, — a proceeding in kind, if not in degree, like the
anathema of the papacy. The poor old woman quivered under the blow, imparted to her by Parson Roberts, awful in the dignity of his office and a new wig.
But the parson was human ; and the meek grief of the
woman, set off by Mab's blazing indignation, worked
upon his honest soul, and caused him to doubt a little
the church's wisdom. Mab had followed him across
the door-yard to the gate in order to "free her mind."

"I want to know what you wanted that poor woman
to do, Parson Roberts. She was dyin' by inches for
want of vittles fit to eat, and the care most folks would
give a sick ox. Do you think, now, honest, she'd
ought to have staid with that old wretch?"

"Speak not evil of dignities, young woman. Amasy
Flint is a deacon of Bassett church. It does not
become you so to revile him."

This glittering generality did not daunt Mab a
moment.

"I don't care if he was deacon in the New Jerusa-
lem, or minister either. If he was the angel Gabriel,
and acted the way he did act, I shouldn't have no faith
in his piety, nor no patience with his prayers."

Parson Roberts glared at her over his spectacles with
pious horror. "What, what, what!" he sternly cried.
"Who be you that set in judgment on your elders
and betters?"

"I'm one that's seen him where you haven't, anyway, nor your church-members. I've lived to his
house, and I know him like a book."

Was it possible, the parson thought, that brother

Flint might have been in fault, — just a little? But he was faithful to his dogmas and his education.

"Do not excuse the woman's sin. She has left her lawful husband, threatened to swear the peace against a Christian man whom she was bound by human and divine law to obey, and caused a scandal and a disturbance in the fold of Christ. Is this a light matter, you daughter of Belial?"

Mab laughed, — laughed in the parson's face, in full front of his majestic wig, his awful spectacles, his gold-headed cane uplifted in the heat of argument. He could not see that she was a little hysterical. He grew red with ungodly rage, but Mab did not care a pin.

"You ain't a fool, Parson Roberts," she said undauntedly. "You've got eyes in your head; and you'd know, if you'd use 'em, that Aunt Flint is a weak sister anyway. She wouldn't turn no sooner'n the least worm that ever was; but *they* will turn, if you tread right on 'em. And, whatever you say, you know, jest as well as I do, that Amasy Flint drove her into leavin' him, and drove her with a whip of scorpions, as the Bible tells about."

"Woman, do you mean to say I lie?" thundered the parson.

"Well, yes — if you don't tell the truth," returned Mab, completely at bay now. An audible chuckle betrayed some listener; and the parson, turning round, beheld old Israel silently unloading a wheelbarrow-load of potatoes at the corner of the fence, and wondered in his soul how long the man had been there, but considered it the better part of valor to leave the scene, now that it had ceased to be a *tête-à-tête:* so he waved his hand at Mab with a gloomy scowl, and went his way.

"Land o' liberty!" ejaculated the old man, drawing the back of his hand across his mouth to smother a laugh. "Didn't you give him jesse! I swan you're the gal for a free fight, now. He's heerd the fac's in the case, if he never did afore. Of all things! What be you a-cryin' for now, eh?" For Mab, a real woman, had flung her apron over her face, and was sobbing violently. Uncle Israel gently tried to pull the check screen away; but she held on to it.

"Let me cry," she said. "I ain't sorry: I'm mad, and I've got to cry it out."

"Well," said Israel, returning to his potatoes, and slowly shaking his head, "women-folks air the beat-eree. I don't know nothing about 'em, and I'm five an' sixty year old come Friday. Lordy! there ain't no riddles nor Chinee puzzle-rings to compare with 'em. I've hed a wife, an' lost a wife, praise the Lord! but I never was sure o' her even. I wouldn't no more try it agin than I'd slip down into a bee-tree; for there's full as much stings as honey to 'em, and, take an ever-idge, I guess there's more."

Whether or not the parson's silent ideas coincided with those Israel expressed is not for the ignorant chronicler to say; but it is certain that his candid and generous soul was so far moved by Mab's tirade, however he denied and defied it during its delivery, that the next day he resolved to call in a council of his neighboring brethren to discuss the matter, and indorse or reprobate the action of his own church.

So he wrote to the Rev. Ami Dobbins of Dorset, and the Rev. Samuel Jehoram Hill of Bassington, better known as Father Hill; and, in compliance with his request, they repaired to Bassett, and investigated the matter. Being advised of the pastor, who had had his experiences, they went to Mrs. Flint's during school-hours; and Mabel had no chance to pour out her soul before them. They encountered only a pale, depressed, weak woman, who was frightened out of what little heart was left her by past trials, when these two august personages came into her presence, and with severe countenances began their catechism of her life with Deacon Flint. As in the case of many another woman, her terror, her humiliation, and a lingering desire to shield her husband from his own misdeeds, all conspired against her. Her testimony was tearful, confused, and contradictory; though through it all she did feebly insist on her own sufferings, and depicted them in honest colors. From her they went to the deacon, whom they found resigned, pious, and loftily superior to common things; then he was a man, and a deacon! Is it to be wondered at that their letter to the church at Bassett was in the deacon's favor? They did indeed own that Mrs. Flint had "peculiar trials," but went on to say, —

"Nevertheless, she cannot be fully justified, but has departed from meekness and a Christian spirit . . . particularly in indulging angry and passionate expressions, tending to provoke and irritate her husband; and, however unjustifiable his conduct may be, that doth not exculpate her. We think that it would be proper and suitable for her to make suitable reflections, acknowledge she hath given her brethren and sisters of the church occasion of stumbling and to be dissatisfied; and, upon her manifesting a becoming spirit of meekness and love, we think they ought to restore her · but if she should refuse to make such reflections, they can-not consistently receive her."

And with a few added remarks on the perplexity of the case, and advising the church to call the ecclesias-tical council, the Rev. Ami Dobbins and Father Hill retired for the present.

But Bassett was not content. Weeks passed, and no act of confession or contrition came from this poor old offender. To tell the truth, Mabel stood behind her now, afire with honest rage at the way she had been put upon.

"You sha'n't do it, aunty!" she said, with all her native vehemence.

"You confess! I like that! It is that old hypo-crite's place to confess. He drove you out, now when you get down to it; and he hain't asked you to come back, that I've heard tell. I'd let him and the church, and Bassett too, go to thunder, if they're a mind to. If you make 'suitable reflections,' they'll reflect on old Flint and Bassett church-members. Dear me! I know one thing: I'd rather be an old maid ten times over than married to that man."

A faint smile crept over the old woman's pale face. From her high pillows she had a good outlook, and more than once she had seen an interview by the little gate that did not augur long maidenhood for Mab.

"Well, Mabel, if that's your say, why, it behooves you to be real cautious, though I don't know as Sam Pratt's brother could be anyways other than good."

Mab blushed like a Provence rose, but said nothing, vet day after day kept hardening her aunt's heart as well as she knew how; and Parson Roberts, receiving no "reflections" from the offender, and having great faith in Father Hill's power of persuasion, invited him to come again by himself, and hold a conversation with sister Flint on the subject of her trials and her contumacy.

Father Hill was a quaint, gentle, sweet-natured old man, steeped, however, in the prejudices of his time and his faith. He, too, went to the house mailed with his fixed assurance of ecclesiastical dignity and marital supremacy. Sympathy, pity, comprehension of her side of the case, would have disarmed Mrs. Flint completely; she would have sobbed, confessed, laid her hand on her mouth, and her mouth in the dust, and been ready to own herself the chief of sinners : but to be placed in the wrong from the first, reproved, admonished, and treated as an impenitent and hardened culprit, made it easier for her weak nature to accept the situation than to defy or to deny it. Nothing Father Hill could say moved her, but her dull and feeble obstinacy stirred his tender heart to its depths : he felt a despair of human means and a yearning tenderness that could find no outlet but in prayer. He fell on his knees before the chair in which he had been sitting, and lifted his earnest face to heaven.

" O dear Lord and Master," he said, speaking even as a man unto his friend, " thou hast borne our griefs, and carried our sorrows. Thou knowest by heart every pain and woe that we feel. A stranger cannot intermeddle, but, O thou Hope of Israel, why shouldst thou be as a stranger that passeth by, and a wayfaring man that tarrieth but a night, in this dwelling of thy handmaid? Dear Lord, it is not in man that walketh to direct his own steps, how much less the steps of others ! Come thou in the might of thy great gentle

ness and thine all-knowing sympathy and love, and
show this child of thine the right way, saying, 'Walk
ye in it.' Thou knowest every sorrow she has passed
through, every bitter draught she has drunk, every sin
she has been led into: yea, when she said there was
no comforter, thine eye pitied and thine arm waited
to save her, though the eye of flesh saw it not. Come
now, and place beneath her weary heart and failing
flesh the everlasting arms of thy overflowing love and
care; give her peace and rest; give her an understanding heart; above all, with thy love and pity redeem
her, as thou didst the elder Israel, and bring her with
tender leading and divine affection, not only into 'thy
fold on earth, but to the general assembly and church
of the first-born in heaven. And to thee shall be
praise and love and glory forever. Amen.''

When he arose, his old face fair with the shining of
the mount from whence he came down, the poor
woman, who had dropped her head on her hand, lifted
it, and tried to thank him; but streaming tears choked
her, and behind the door into the shed a stifled sob
betrayed some hidden auditor.

''Farewell!'' said Father Hill, and with a look of
heavenly benignity went out from the house. His deep
and earnest piety had got the better of his dogmas;
and, so strange is human nature, he was a little
ashamed of it. But on his departing steps the shed-
door opened, and Mab came in, her face all washed
with tears.

''*That* man's got religion,'' she said decisively.
''I never heerd a mortal creature pray like that:
seemed as though he see right into glory, and talked
face to face with the Lord. If that's bein' pious, I
wish I was as pious as fury myself.''

"He's a good man," sobbed Mrs. Flint; "one of the Lord's an'inted, I make no doubt. And, Mabel, I don't know but what I have did wrong. I ain't noways heavenly-minded like him: mabbe I had ought to have put up with every thing."

"No, you hadn't: that ain't so. But if it's goin' to make you easier, aunty, to 'make reflections,' as old Parson Roberts says, why, make 'em: only don't tell no lies to the church because you've got into a heavenly mood all to once. Folks that ain't just to themselves don't never get justice elsewheres, now I tell you."

Father Hill, despairing of having impressed Mrs. Flint, had cast the matter into his Master's hands, and from his study in Bassington sent a letter to Parson Roberts, running thus: —

"REV'D AND DEAR BROTHER, — I have had Opportunity with Mrs. Flint, and find that she conceived her leaving the Deacon was a real duty at that time; that her Recovery under Providence turned upon it; that she did not then foresee the Consequences that such a step would issue in her final Separation. . . . She stands ready to reflect upon herself as far as she can be convinced she ought to do so, but thinks the fault is not on her Side as things now are.

"I feel unable to direct or advise further. The cause of Religion, the cause of the Christian Church, you are very sensible, is of more Consequence than the Honor or Pease of any individual. If such a settlement can be made as may secure Religion from suffering, it must be an object to be desired. . . . Sensible of the Embarrassments you and the church labor under, and desirous to contribute my mite, I use this Freedom.

"This from your affectionate Brother,

"SAMUEL J. HILL.

To REV'D MR. ROBERTS.

"To be communicated if you think expedient."

But, while the ministers were in this strait about their obstinate parishioner, the Lord had answered Father Hill, unknown to himself, while he was yet speaking. Moved, and indeed melted, by the love and sympathy that prayer showed, Mrs. Flint, no longer hindered by Mabel, prepared herself to write "proper reflections" to the church; but in doing so was also perpetually prompted by Mabel not to traitorously deny her own cause, or slip aside from the truth in a voluntary humility; and in due time the following confession was laid before that august body : —

"I, the subscriber, Sarepta Flint, a member of the church of Christ in Bassett, sensible that the Church are dissatisfied with me on account of the Separation that has taken place between Deacon Flint and myself, and that they are Apprehensive that I have not been innocent as to measures which have led to this unhappy Event, whereby Religion is wounded and the Pease of the Church disturbed, take this opportunity to publickly acknowledge myself a poor, imperfect Creture, and to own that under my Weak state of Body and weakness of mind, with which I was attended at one Time or another, I no doubt manifested on certain Occasions an unsuitable Temper of mind, said and Did things which under other Circumstances I should not have said or done. I am far from justifying myself in all my conduct. Particular I would reflect on myself for that Expresion in regard to swearing the Pease against Deacon Flint. . . . I ask the Forgivness of God and this church, and of all others who are aggrieved, and request the prayers of my Christian Brethren and Sisters that I henceforth conduct as a true and faithful Disciple of Christ, and adorn the Solem Vocation by which I am called.

"SAREPTA FLINT.

"P.S. — I stand ready also to return to my Husband as soon as a suitable Door opens for that Purpose."

Perhaps something in the self-respecting yet honest humility of this document touched the heart of Bassett

church; or perhaps only their self-love and pride of
place was soothed by it. Be that as it may, the confession was accepted; and Parson Roberts, with a valor
and persistence that did him honor, insisted that
Deacon Flint should go with him to inform his wife
of her release from interdict, and also to open that
"Door" of reconciliation to which she had so patheti-
cally alluded. The parson's wig was fresh buckled, the
deacon's cue new wound and tied, and their sabbath-day
garments prim and speckless, as the next morning they
opened the door of the old house where Sarepta Flint
had taken refuge from her oppressor. A scene they
little expected met their eyes. On the low bed, covered
with its rough blue homespun spread, lay an evidently
dying figure. A more "Solem Vocation" than life
had called Deacon Flint's wife, and she was about to
obey. Mindwell and Sam Pratt upheld her as she
gasped for breath, and the two children clung together
sobbing at her feet; while Mabel, with Joe Pratt's arm
about her, and her face streaming with tears she did
not feel, stood by the bedside gazing at her friend.
Her face blazed as the deacon and Parson Roberts
entered; but, roused by the click of the latch, Mrs.
Flint opened her eyes, and looked at the youthful pair
with a gentle smile. They had been the one bright
outlook of her latter life, and to them she gave her
last smile; for, as her eyes turned toward her husband,
a cold terror filled them, the lids fell, her head drooped
on Mindwell's shoulder, and with one long, shuddering
sigh she escaped forever. The forgiveness of the
church and the condescension of her husband came too
late : she was already safe where the wicked cease
'rom troubling, and the Consoler dries all mortal tears

Deacon Flint stood like a stone. Did remorse trouble him? Was regret busy at his heart? Or did he feel a bitter and deep chagrin at the loss of so much income?

Mabel's tears ceased: she withdrew from Joe's arm, and went round to where Deacon Flint stood. "Are you proper pleased now?" she said in a low voice of concentred contempt and rage. "You've got her turned out of church, and into heaven. You won't never see her again, — no, never! not to all eternity. But you've killed her as good as if you took an axe to her. You can take that hum to sleep on."

"Hush!" said Parson Roberts, with all the dignity a little man could give to his voice and manner. "When the Lord giveth quietness, who, then, can make trouble?"

But even as he spoke, Joe Pratt — his face full of black wrath — set his hand to the deacon's collar, and walked him summarily into the road. Mabel had spoken truth: never again did he see his wife's face, not even in the fair peace of death. Whether ever, in that far world of souls, they met again, is perhaps doubtful: let us pray not. Mrs. Flint's married experience was over in this world a hundred years ago, and in the next "they neither marry nor are given in marriage."